BY MARTIN COPELAND

FICTION

LA Love Stories
Manhunt in France
A Star Falls in Cannes

PHOTOPLAYS

River of Doubt
Right Proud: the Buffalo Soldiers
Counterforce

THE BOYS FROM DOGTOWN

Martin Copeland

RAINBOW BRIDGE

In memory of Walter and Margaret Copeland,
who loved watching their sons play baseball.

And the Boys from Dogtown

Table of Contents

BOOK 1

FINDING WAYS TO LOSE

1. BELLEVILLE

The Dogtown Boys were going to have a reunion at the park where the Arkansas Travelers played, our minor league baseball team, in a club suite where we could watch the game and reminisce while chowing down on burgers and hot dogs and cheesy quesadillas, popcorn and roasted peanuts, plus beer and wine—principally beer. Spencer quipped, "I guarantee their pot guts haven't come from pot. Another habit-forming substance has created their avoirdupois."

Spencer still talked like that. He himself had stayed trim, mainly by working in the fields but also by eschewing the latter habit-forming substance in favor of the former. He swore he indulged less these days, partly from age and partly because "Arkansas' finest have me on the radar."

The Dogtown Boys had kept in touch individually over the years but never reunited since our memorable last game, and in between working the phones and making arrangements with our sponsor to organize the reunion, I remembered what it was like way back when. Games and scores but mostly people came back large as life, like figures in a big screen film.

The 1960s were a special time, but really that wild and crazy summer in the heart of the decade didn't start to make sense to me until years later, on a day when my life changed.

#

I was back in Belleville, a town in the northeastern corner of the Arkansas Delta that had never been lucky for me, pitching my container wares to a bunch of local small business folk and farmers who were doing well financially, but getting them to part with some of their finances gave new meaning to the word "hardscrabble."

"Friends," I said, "I know your town. It's not near as big as Memphis" —I could have said "nearly," but in those days I still felt superior to the people I later would realize had the same solid grit as the tough earth they plowed and could be counted on. Rockhard country folk like my Dad, I would spiel a few minutes later after they'd heard enough to figure I spoke the same lowfalutin' language

And, I hoped, give me a few orders. Hell, one would do, as I was at the stage of desperation where you won't admit it to yourself, but the time when you'd be obliged to was drawing near.

"Or West Memphis or Forrest City or Jonesboro or, uh…"

"Paragould," piped up Lester, one of the farmers, in coveralls and smoking a pipe, his drawl so long and leisurely I knew he had money to spare, hopefully to me today.

"Right you are, neighbor, but size don't matter when it comes to people and quality of life. Shoot, your Legion baseball team goes to the State playoffs pretty much every year. Now, how do you explain that? Small town boys going belly to belly with the hotshot big city teams like Little Rock and Fayetteville and whipping them. I mean whipping them, bad."

They nodded and smiled, every one. Had them on the hook and now just needed a bite.

My friend Rick, the hardware and feed store owner who had organized my sales presentation, beamed from a discreet corner and relaxed a little. It was going good and he was figuring the buyers would hang around later and he'd make a bundle himself. Most everybody listening had arrived in a pickup with a huge flatbed, and the couple of local merchants present worked a hoot and a holler away.

"I'll tell you why. 'Cause they've got inner strength. Gut strength. You don't have to look like Paul Bunyan to be strong. What's inside is what counts. Grit.

"Take a look at this container, neighbors. You might call it a box, but it's so much more than that."

I opened the flaps and held it up.

"Now what do you see? Look hard now, real hard. Something's there you just don't see just anywhere."

They did look, but didn't utter a peep, just looked puzzled.

"Jim?"

He was the local drugstore owner and we'd just met, but calling folks by their first names is one of the secrets of salesmanship—or so I'd always believed.

"Well, uh... "

"Tom."

"Tom...it just looks like a box to me...four sides and all."

The others nodded. Lester smiled, nodded and puffed.

"You are exactly right, Jim. From the outside you see plain old inexpensive cardboard. But inside, there's fiber. Inner strength.

"This container will take anything and everything you've got to store and not buckle a lick. The word collapse isn't in its vocabulary. You know those thunderheads that build up on August afternoons? I've been in a couple right here in Belleville."

Maybe I wasn't built as strong as my merchandise, because my insides roiled at the memory of one of those storms, but I didn't let them see the old wound, or how much it still hurt.

"Gullywashers, some of 'em. You leave an ordinary cardboard box out in that rain, total destruction. This little container—oh, I'm not saying it's waterproof. But you'll be amazed at what solid construction and reinforced materials can do.

"Neighbors, I hope you hear what I'm saying. We're talking exceptional."

Pause.

"Now, there is one drawback to this superb piece of handiwork. If by chance you have a tendency to run around, all your little lady has to do is order the jumbo version of this here container. Once she's got you in, you'll have a hell of a time getting out." I didn't know where this came from, unless Freud had slipped in a reverse identification.

In any event the joke went over like the leadest balloon ever constructed, and the awkward silence went on till Lester mercifully and thankfully had smoked out his pipe.

WHAP! WHAP! he tapped the remaining tobacco in a wooden trash barrel and now, with pipe empty, he felt liberty to speak.

"Exceptional prices, too?"

"Friend Lester, you get what you pay for."

"Tom, I got me a barnful of tow sacks. Feed, tools, my old duds—those sacks been doing the job for 40 years and never let me down. Don't break, neither."

"Tow sacks! Neighbors, let me tell you a little story. You all know how every spring we've got one eye cocked for those big twisters that come rolling in off the flatlands. The good Lord in his wisdom put the Ozarks in the West and up Missouri way and here he laid down the farmland you all make your living from—one way or another.

"But flat means tornadoes. I've seen 'em down north of Little Rock, and God bless, far enough away I can still stand in front of you right now."

"God bless," one of the businessmen chimed in—a gas station attendant like my Dad before he passed. I had slipped this into our small talk earlier. Lester added, "They're God's wrath, Tom. Nothing to do when they hit but pray."

"Amen." I paused for effect, but I was really into my pitch now and they felt the sincerity that always came hard for me in sales in those days but sometimes came through for real.

"One of them hit over in Texas last year. My heart went out to those folks when I heard about the trail of devastation that big ole twister caused. No one died, God be praised, but for 20 square miles, where there'd been homes and cars and trees, nothing. Nothing. Like the biggest bulldozer they ever made just came through and leveled all creation." Another pause for effect. "Except for one brick wall. That still stood. It was that solid."

"Musta mixed in some concrete," the drugstore owner added.

"Now I'm no scientist and I don't know how they measured, but they said that twister was one of the most powerful ever recorded."

"Number 2 or 3," Rick helped. "I read about that one. Hell of a thing, that twister."

"Friends, it was so strong, that tornado blew a straw right

through that brick wall. A straw!"

Rick: "I read that too! He's right, fellas. They said it was like neutron bombardment."

"What in the blazes is that?" someone piped up, but I wasn't going to get into details.

"But I tell you what, 'cause I've made some tests and I believe what I say."

This time it was me: WHAP! WHAP! on the reinforced fiber of my box sample. "There's no twister on this green earth that can blow a straw through this box."

My audience was impressed and truth be told, so was I. As Henry Cross used to say, when you're down you got to grow some claws to fight your way back up. There was a long pause and I waited for an order. Finally Lester said: "Tom, I like you, son. I like any man who says what he believes and believes in what he says. You have my word, soon as I run out of them tow sacks, I'm gonna come calling."

He relit his pipe. I helped him hammer the nail in my coffin and said, "You got a barnful, you say?"

#

Rick ended up selling a lot of feed and some tools. I sold a lot of good will. "They're country folk," Rick consoled. "Takes them time to chew things over. Give them a while and we'll see."

"Already saw it," I grumbled,

"Hey good buddy, it's not like you to be hangdog." He thought a moment. He'd known me for a long time. "You still in touch with the ex?"

"When I can track her down. You know, back when we were together we weren't together. Gone today, gone tomorrow, that's her in a nutshell."

"Hey, I hear Dogtown's got a leash law now."

"They don't make 'em short enough for her kind of breed." I was surprised I could be so harsh about my ex but maybe I'd crossed a threshold. Rick just shook his head.

I told him, "Thanks a bunch for setting this up."

He patted me on the back and I could see he was thinking of something comforting to say. "Listen, like the lady said, tomorrow's another day."

Rick had opened up his home for me the night before and Marlene fixed up the couch as comfortable as she could.

"How is Dogtown?" Rick had asked.

"You know, I still miss it," Marlene said. We'd finished her homecooked dinner and were sitting around reminiscing while the 3 kids bustled around like dervishes and the TV kept us current on a Cardinals-Cincinnati game.

"That Rose," Rick commented, "the way he runs out everything at full speed, you'd think he has a burr up his butt."

Marlene reprimanded him: "Rick, the kids." He snorted. "You really think they're listening?" The kids had noticed there was a visitor in the house, but it had taken them a while. Like most all country kids, they'd played outside till dark had truly settled in and then brought their nonstop motion inside. Their parents had another one on the way and I could see the strain on their faces even as we laughed and talked over old times.

#

I didn't want to eat at the local restaurant called the Catfish Hole and maybe have to abide watching the locals I'd just struck out with laughing and talking about everything under the sun except my wares. If they felt a tad bit guilty they might invite me over to their table but even though I knew this might be good business for the future, my heart wasn't in it tonight. My heart wasn't in any of the sales jobs I'd taken the last three years after my divorce, one reason I wasn't getting much of anywhere. I didn't know where my heart was. I knew I'd left a part of it here in Belleville years ago, but the past was past.

I went to the local Dairy Queen and bought a cup of their vanilla ice cream, my alltime favorite. I didn't want to hang out there too long with the town teenagers who'd escaped home and parents for a while to canoodle and make out, but night was falling and though it was futile battling the heat and humidity of an Arkansas evening, even a couple of degrees would make a difference in the long drive home.

Locusts were humming and fireflies floating around in the gloaming. It was good to see them. As a kid I had caught lightning bugs in a bottle or cupped them in my hands and loved to watch them light up and off, but they'd gotten more scarce as the years went by and I'd half forgotten the thrill of watching them. Tonight in the soft breeze of early evening I realized some of the thrill remained.

I finished the ice cream and was just about to hit the road when a bright, broad ray of reflected light hit the car and all around me. I turned to look. It wasn't God or one of his angels or a streak of lightning, but the tier of stadium lights above Belleville Field.

I had almost forgotten where the ballpark was, or that there might be a game tonight. I could get a hot dog and slop it good with yellow mustard, swig a coke or Dr. Pepper and watch some of the game before leaving. I could hear the jingle music piped out from the concession stand, still the same familiar melodies.

I got in my truck and drove the short way to the field's parking lot. I hadn't yet unloaded the samples from my truck, and I didn't do it now. Hell, I thought, if somebody steals them tonight it'll prove there's still a market.

I walked toward the concession stand and got my dog and coke. As I ate I looked around at the place where a lot of memories lived.

Not much had changed. The parking lot had been enlarged and the grandstands too, and a new scoreboard about twice the size of the old one had been installed, with a different font for the number of runs, but even from a distance as I passed along the outfield fence, I could see the same man whose job it was the post the score each half-inning hunkered down on the parapet.

He was an old codger now, but clad in the same brown overalls I had seen him wear. I hoped they were the same brand

and not the same pair.

A new concession stand had been built, and it was already dispensing snow cones, glazed cupcakes and corn or hot dogs. Like before, a lot of parents and players and spectators came directly to the park from work or field without passing by the house.

Quite a few still forsook the hard wood benches in the stands and set up folding chairs on the sidelines, as my parents used to do. My father had appreciated this because he could smoke cigars without fear of asphyxiating anyone, a precaution he never took at home.

Some were already settled in as I passed, and I noticed that one man was discreetly dipping into his six-pack, snuggled (and smuggled) in a large brown sack ostensibly full of picnic chips and sandwiches—very much as my father also used to do.

I made a mental note to myself, if I stayed in the business, to see about branching into the kind of very practical foam rubber container he was using.

In the pressbox, such as it was, above the stands the announcer was rattling off the names of team sponsors who were organizing and paying for a barbecue after the upcoming 4th of July doubleheader.

I remembered how annoying the blatantly biased announcer had been in our own day and was very pleased to hear a woman's voice, enthusiastic and, it seemed to me, quite young. Unfortunately the man seated in the pressbox and very visible, making notes as she talked, was the same Chet Williams whose bylines I had unhappily read. He was no doubt the same unregenerate gung-ho booster who made no pretense of objectivity in his reporting on the games for the Belleville Times. Regretfully he had not yet been put out to pasture, and why not? In his reports all was right with the world when the home team won, and when they didn't, it was just a bump on the road to the next victory.

That kind of optimism made the start of days in Belleville, if you were a sports lover, a good reason to get on with your work and life, knowing that that night you could head out to the game and put whatever troubles behind for a few hours. And like I'd told my skeptical audience that afternoon, the Belleville team had a tradition of winning. Troubles got hid harder when you lost. The local players were starting to arrive, most of them in pickups even though none were older than 17.

One came walking by me, his girl friend hanging on to his shoulder so tightly I wondered if he'd really be able to convince her he needed that arm to field grounders.

"Who you playing?" I asked.

"Bentonville."

"They tough?"

"Reckon we'll find out." She dragged him away, no doubt thinking he'd wasted enough time on this old dude past 30 asking inane questions.

They looked toward the parking lot and I followed their gaze. A bus had just rolled up and was disengaging members of the Bentonville Patriots team. They had clean, bright, colorful uniforms, and even when they took the field for warmups, I got the impression no dirt would stick. I was surprised to see this kind of expense and class for an ordinary league game, but I noticed their sponsor's logo on the side of the bus, "Wal-Mart, " a retail store that was more and more in the news and obviously devoting money to advertising and marketing.

The visitors' dugout was in front of me on the third base side of the field and I watched their pitcher warm up. He was young and still battling acne but had long arms and big wrists.

He was bringing some serious heat to his catcher, who I noticed had resorted to the old trick of putting a cloth rag inside his mitt to cushion the shock and pain.

Cletus had never done that, but then again Cletus used to admit, "I ain't the sharpest tool in the woodshed." I did ponder for a moment if I could still get around on a pitcher like him, but not long: probably not.

The national anthem was piped in over the loudspeaker. This version had been recorded by Aretha Franklin, and she gave it soul. Then the Belleville Pioneers took the field to their home crowd's raucous cheers and jingle music from the pressbox.

The stands were almost full. Up here the Tigers weren't religion, but they weren't far behind. I saw a State Police car drive to a stop beside the outfield fence and park. It wasn't there to keep the peace, I figured--that spot was ideal for watching the action. If any miscreant had chosen this moment to rob the local bank, he'd have no problem making a getaway.

In the visitors' dugout, the visitors stood and watched their leadoff hitter rifle through their bat rack and choose the one he hoped had a base hit in it. As he walked toward the plate and the waiting catcher, I roamed back into the past and saw myself.

2. FIRST PRACTICE

When our last baseball season began I was working in the main office of Frankenheimer Foods.

This day of our first practice in May was even more hectic than usual: white-coated plant employees moving in and out from office front door to entrance to plant proper, delivery men wheeling in boxes and bales of meat products and by-products, solicitous salesmen and questing customers.

I was having a hell of a time getting away because one of our county's biggest farmers, Mr. Fred Snookums, was considering making us his sole meat supplier and also processor for his beef and pork, and I wasn't about to rush him.

I was surprised that my boss, Charles "Big Chuck" Frankenheimer, had let me close the paperwork on the deal, but like I said this day had been non-stop hurly-burly and Big Chuck was on the phone in his office lambasting a competitor. I could hear his voice booming through the windows.

He had purposely made the glass thin, not quite enough for him to eavesdrop on what we were saying in the front office, but isinglass thick, so when he raised his voice in anger or shouted, we'd all come to attention right quick. Sometimes it even looked like the glass bowed under the blast of his verbal sound waves.

He was a master at dressing-downs and hurled reproofs, and that was one reason he wasn't coaching us this year and had turned over the reins to Henry Cross in a last desperate attempt to make us winners.

He'd cowed one too many players, and though he admitted his method hadn't worked, he made no apologies. He loved the word "cow" as both noun and verb. "Made for a man in my business," he said. "A dictionary is drawn from life, you know. Every word reflects a facet of life, or it wouldn't exist. Me, I cow people."

He made these remarks around the dinner table and sent his

daughter into a fit of mocking laughter and a riff about him turning people into bovines, but I rather thought he was right, even if he was the kind of person the dictionary didn't have enough adjectives to describe.

Mr. Snookums, as I would learn over and over again when dealing with local farmers who'd grown up with the seasons, liked to assess the lay of the land before taking an important step. Or most steps, for that matter. "Tom," he said, "I've et all the shitty Texas bacon I'm gonna."

"We use prime Grade-A stock, Mr. Snookums, homegrown right here in Arkansas. We believe in quality, from hoof to horn, that's one of our mottoes."

"What I wanted to hear. You reckon I've ordered enough of that sausage?"

"Let's put it this way. After today there's gonna be an awful lot of hogs running scared."

Mr. Snookums lit up and literally rubbed his hands with satisfaction, maybe thinking of a huge sausage and pot roast dinner, with cornbread and turnip greens and mashed potatoes and purple hull peas, lemon pie and jugs of iced tea like my country relatives often served on Sunday. "Home cookin'," he said, "if you've got the right fixins, can't beat it. Can't even try."

Big Chuck came charging out, a solid 300 pounds and counting. He liked to say that before drinking a great wine, you had to taste it, and he did the same for his meat products.

I told him once at dinner that winetasters would usually spit out the wine before swallowing, and he looked at me like I'd commit heresy if I suggested he do the same with a mouthful of pork chop. And second, in such a case the stake would be lit and waiting for me to be strapped onto. I shut up right quick and chowed down on my own pork chop.

Today Big Chuck was mad. "That sucker's undersellin' me and he's gonna pay. I'm gonna put belly on belly and get mean. He'll wish he never saw a ham hock."

Big Chuck meant Sam Carson, his local rival who "stuck in his craw like a rib bone," but he had others. At this time he was not yet worried about the meats grown and raised by Winthrop Rockefeller on Petit Jean Mountain.

He viewed him as a dilettante Yankee—"Hell, I heard he thought a heifer was a Broadway dancer!"—but a Rockefeller had deep pockets and I sometimes thought Big C was whistling in the wind.

"Tom treating you right, Fred?" As usual, he didn't wait for an answer, but said to me, "Let me know when he signs the contract. So I don't have to be nice to him any more!"

He boomed out a laugh, put his arm around Mr. Snookums and led him to the side for some serious talk about meat and politics. In general both agreed that the country was going to hell and only businessmen like them kept the ship upright. That was another reason for suspicion of Yankee Republicans like Rockefeller, who knew a thing or two about business and hence were more capable of ruining the country.

I glanced at the clock: 3:50. Time to jump into action. "George!"

George was engrossed in a conversation with Jackson, whose full name believe it or not was Jackson Jackson, which meant he never knew if Big Chuck was being friendly or ready to read the riot act when he bellowed "Jackson!"

He rarely left the slaughterhouse or doffed his lab coat, which always sported splotches of blood, recent and not-so, as if a modern abstract artist had just tossed red paint against a wall to see what would stick. With Jackson, it all did, or seemed to, and since he didn't cotton much to hygiene, head arms hands and face also bore the marks of his métier. "Comes with the job," he used to say—and say.

For that reason and the general themes of his conversation, such as it was when it occurred, we all thought Jackson had nothing on the ball and that an abstract painter's wall would make a better canvas for anything interesting in the way of red forms or otherwise, but what he was saying to George surprised me as I went behind my desk and doffed shirt and tie.

"Used to, I could butcher a hundred a day and not think nothin'. Now look—"

He held up his hands. They were jittery. George nodded sympathetically and said, "You shouldn't have adopted that piglet. It's always a mistake to make pets out of them."

"Yeah. He eats with us now. Tours the table waitin' for scraps. Damn thing'll eat anything."

"Well, he is a pig."

"I call him 'Porky.'"

"Inspired choice."

"George!" I repeated.

George saw me in my grungy T-shirt and how I was hopping around taking off my dress pants and pulling my shorts out of a drawer.

"Time!"

He nodded and hurried off to get his duds, but he had a last word for Jackson:

"Go on a water diet for a couple of days. You'll look at Porky from a whole different perspective."

George wanted to study English lit in college and even our high school teacher had been impressed when he said he'd already read the first volume of Proust.

"Unfortunately, in translation," he added.

George said from the look on Mr. Garfield's face, he wasn't sure he knew that it'd been written originally in French. George said he'd been much impressed when Mr. Garfield had gone off on a historical tangent one class about the doctrine of "laissez faire," and how he thought this attitude of letting things ride, as he interpreted it, was pernicious and one should take his destiny in hand, even in old age, and he cited Tennyson's Ulysses: "To strive, to seek, to find and not to yield."

"That's my credo now," George declared in a very serious tone—and for him to get serious always meant he was truly serious—and he was the only 17-year-old I knew who would use the word credo. "Call me Ulysses."

However, he said, though he, George, didn't know too many French words, he was quite sure that "laissez faire" wasn't pronounced "lazy fear," as Mr. Garfield did.

I started to slip on my shorts and was watching the clock

when the phone rang. I answered with the customary "Frankenheimer Meatpacking, Tom speaking."

It was hard balancing the phone and dressing. I was only halfway done when naturally, a well-dressed couple happened to walk through the door that very minute and spotted me. I could have sworn she raised her eyebrows approvingly but he frowned, all decorum and such.

Naturally too Franklin happened to come in from the back office. He was sure I'd been promoted because I was dating the boss' daughter and since we all knew said boss was a stickler for neatness and putting on a spick and span front for customers ("We're butchers but we can't show it," he would say), Franklin enjoyed the awkward spot I was in.

"Big Chuck's gonna ream you," he said, and smiled.

Naturally too it was Mrs. Morley on the line.

"Oh, how are you, Mrs. Morley?"

I knew if she was calling that she wasn't good but it had to be asked. Good business protocol. She went into a rant. I listened to what a literary guy like George once told me was a "wave of imprecations."

"Er, that particular no-good peckerwood is no longer with the company, Mrs. Morley." The way she strung together cuss words and less vulgar imprecations always astounded me, and sometimes I wished I could tape record her complaints.

At this point I only needed to interject sympathetically from time to time, and it allowed me to pull up my shorts and tuck in my T-shirt and get my shoes and glove out of a drawer.

"I'm sure it was just an unfortunate choice of words, Mrs. Morley."

This really set her off. Her complaint centered around a late delivery of steaks, and how this discombobulated her ritual TV dinner.

Big Chuck lumbered over with Mr. Snookums in tow. He could hear the tirade even though the phone was at my ear. I cupped it.

"Mrs. Morley," I said to him.

Big Chuck shook his head and said to Mr. Snookums, "That

woman can cuss the fleas off a dog."

Franklin had perked up, waiting for his boss to chew me out as only he could do for undressing on duty. He caught Big Chuck's eye and sort of nodded toward the couple, as if Big C needed any hint like that. Instead he growled at Franklin: "Get your tail over there. Tom's got more important business."

"Got to go to practice now, Mrs. Morley. I'll turn you over to my colleague Franklin, Mrs. Morley. We take this matter very seriously, so tell him what you've just told me."

For Franklin's benefit I said, "Don't hold anything back."

I handed the phone to said hapless colleague, who put the phone to his ear and visibly flinched as Mrs. Morley vented her displeasure. George was waiting. I gathered up all my gear and headed out.

The well-dressed couple looked surprised.

Mr. Snookums had a word for us:

"You boys try not to stink up the field this year."

Big Chuck added, "We're gonna win." And then in what he probably figured was hope over experience: "Big."

Just before we got out the door Franklin yelled:

"Hey!"

We turned back:

"Mrs. Morley says to give 'em hell."

We literally ran out to my car. Mr. Snookums was right, we stunk up the field last year, but the year before we stunk it up worse, so we were getting better and our hopes sprang eternal.

It was a warm May day, really pleasant in the late afternoon as the heat started to wane, but still lingered enough for us to sweat and keep our throwing arms from tightening up.

We tossed our gloves and bats and shoes inside and I zipped my used Chevy out of the plant parking lot.

"Big Chuck's not coming?"

"Not today. He said he wanted to give Coach Cross time to fire us up."

"That could take all summer, if not the rest of this decade."

George liked to play cynical, but he had reason to be. Most of us players had been selected after tryouts 2 years ago when

Big Chuck had pulled strings and gotten a new team formed, with him as sponsor and head coach. Technically that was against the rules, but not if you invested enough moolah in the league, as rumor said he did.

"Dammit, it's America," he would say. "This country runs on democracy and dollar bills, not in that particular order."

Big Chuck loved the military and he loved to win battles of any kind, especially against someone who'd insulted him. Little Rock had been insulting our fair city since long before his arrival on the stage, and he like all of us had grown up with the stigma of "Dogtown."

Legend has it that the city fathers of Little Rock had been so incensed at our city's refusal to incorporate with them—"We can be like Paris and have a Right Bank and Left Bank"--that they promptly rounded up every stray mutt, mongrel and puppy they could catch, carted them across the river and turned 'em loose. Big Chuck embraced the monicker.

"What kind of city defines itself by being north of another? I'll tell you what kind. An offshoot. Branch. Bastard child. We should have stuck with 'Argenta', now that was an original name." But since we couldn't, he proudly called us the Dogtown Packers and said, "We're gonna whup their asses so bad they'll beg for mercy," adding, "which they won't get."

For two years nothing had gone right. Big Chuck had had the first ten selections in the tryouts, and he'd chosen the best--a core of proven players from Little League and Pony League like Spencer and Billy Aycock and George who had grown up with Big Chuck as a coach. And when he was done with this core nucleus, he added a few other players who with time might develop into good or very good players--like me.

He was the only coach around who would bellow from the dugout when a player made an error. "C'MON HOSS!" was his favorite chide, and it came with the force of a 300-pound foghorn, resounding throughout field and stadium. The luckless player would have to trot off the field and toward the dugout for several seconds of full public humiliation, or else stand out at his position after a costly error, knowing that all eyes were on him.

This was hard for the player and the parents who had to listen while their sons were pilloried, but it was accepted because those teams won championships. "Everyone loves a winner, and I am," he crowed. "Ain't that right, Hoss?" The players burned with mortification but they were young.

At 15 and 16 though we hit puberty harder than a baseball and to make a long story short, didn't want to take Big Chuck's shit anymore. When he chewed out someone, that someone would now chew back.

And in practical baseball terms, though we'd come up together as the best around, we were younger than the players on all the other teams. They had strength and maturity on their side.

We lost. We never formed into a cohesive unit, more concerned about hormones and not taking shit than playing together. Big Chuck couldn't change his spots and he knew it, and now that we'd entered our final year, he made the momentous and unexpected decision to become Boss Cheerleader and turn over the day-to-day coaching to Henry Cross, who we all knew to be a firm but patient coach whose teams always played well, no matter what their talent or lack of it.

"Hell," George said, "he may even put you in the lineup."

Mostly I'd been a pinch hitter the last few years, because it turned out I could hit in the clutch when the game was on the line. Most players freeze up or completely choke at those moments, but for some reason I didn't and Big Chuck kept me on the bench until crunch time came. Then he'd yell at me to "grab a bat" and I'd head to home plate with adrenaline running to the max. Everybody knew I could field grounders with the best, but Big Chuck was set in his ways and mostly I just sat, watched the game and tried not to pose my derrière on a splinter.

Bubba Beasley kept me company, and we would often play golf together even on days when we had a night game. One day when it was very sunny and hot, over 100° Fahrenheit, with what seemed like 100% humidity, we played a round of 18 holes and even though no other stronghearted souls chose to tackle the course in those conditions and we could take mulligans whenever we hit a bad shot, our scores left something to be desired.

"You mean, everything to be desired," Bubba corrected.

"How about another round?" I challenged.

Bubba looked dubious, but then again, "Yeah, we can rest up on the bench tonight." By the time we finished this second round the temp had passed 106° and the wind was blowing somewhere on earth, but not on this golf course. We straggled home, took a shower and changed into our uniforms.

We'd just settled in to our habitual spots on the bench when Big Chuck announced our shortstop was sick and I'd be starting. It was a long game, made so by our opponents who slammed hits all over the field and rounded the bases one after another with only occasional interruptions to let us go to bat and make outs.

Bubba had a good long rest on the bench and afterward said he'd been impressed by my stamina.

I was too tired to say thank you.

#

We passed through Levy, where my Uncle Bob had his gas station and for so many years had employed my late father as mechanic and all-around station attendant, passing the hardware store, Huggins Lumberyard, barber shop and drugstore where I bought comic books if my father felt generous, which he often did with me.

Levy truly was its own little community. Uncle Bob was its unofficial co-mayor along with Mr. Huggins from the lumberyard. He was a gruff rough man who spoke as if a bushel of sawdust had permanently lodged in his throat, but his son Ronnie had such a melodious voice he'd formed a gospel quartet that sang every week on local TV.

Past Levy we crossed the railroad tracks and headed down Pike Avenue. We stopped at the local Dairy Queen for fortifications. I loved their vanilla ice cream and got a cone. "My protein booster," I said to no laughs whatsoever from my heartless teammates.

Bobby, George's younger brother, was waiting there for us, but George being a typical older brother despite his erudition, he could have cared less whether Bobby hopped in the back with us or hitched, even though he was a valuable utility player.

And he may not have noticed Randy was sipping a soda and waiting for our ride because his eyes were popping out of their sockets staring at Sally, Randy's sister. He'd always had a crush on her even if he knew it was pretty hopeless. Sally was so beautiful she could hold out for bigger fish, and over the winter she'd only gotten more sexy and basically just all-around traffic-stopping.

George went through the motions of keeping cool—"Hurry up bro, we're running late."

"When I'm ready," Bobby replied—-he was used to being the younger brother and took his sweet time gathering his gear.

I knew George's mind was spinning with comparisons of Sally to Dante's Beatrice, Romeo's Juliet and the great Cleopatra VII of Egypt. All that tied his tongue, so I helped him out:

"You're looking good, Sally."

"Why thank you, Tom." She didn't say it coquettishly. She could have talked about taxidermy and been coquettish. She was wearing jean shorts and a T-shirt that form-fit because with her form, anything would.

"Randy said you'd forgotten all about us."

"I said that? When?" Randy asked.

Randy had a rep for being so slow on the draw the gun stayed in the holster.

"No way," Sally assured me.

George said, sounding like Walt Disney's Goofy, "I'm glad to hear that."

As Bobby got in the car, he enjoyed hearing his older brother sounding goofy. "Like she cares if you're glad, idjit."

Sally added, sweetly and sincerely I thought even if she said it with an arch smile, "My heart belongs to the Dogtown boys."

Couldn't help it—had to let out a Rebel yell at this. George unraveled his tongue and said, not so much goofily as lustily: "Shit, what about the rest of you?"

I figured we'd better get out of there before George committed a real faux pas. He could astound with his eloquence in a lit class, but one on one with a force of nature like Sally, he was, as Bobby suggested, a doofus with a capital D. He even lost his literary cool and resorted to plain language as we headed out and sadly Sally was lost from view.

"How'd you ever get a sister that stacked?" he asked Randy. "Hey, God had to put my brains somewhere." For once George was speechless and I couldn't find any words either. It took a while down Pike Avenue for George to express verbally our astonishment.

"I never knew you to have wit before."

"Wit? Jeez, even when you talk English I can't understand you. I need Cliff Notes or something."

"More wit," George continued. "It really is a new season."

Spencer and Mickey were waiting for us at roadside and I stopped to pick them up.

Spencer hadn't finished off his cigarette and he said between puffs as he and Mickey got their gear and piled in: "Not throwing this one away, boys."

Last year he began rolling his own brand of cigarettes and we'd never seen anything like them, except in Westerns, and these, well--

"It smells like puke," Bobby said. "Your puke maybe," his brother offered. Mickey added, "Looks a little bit like it too. He rolled it himself."

"Like the Marlboro Man," Spencer added, "one hand. Leaves one free for other pleasures."

It did look roiled and wrinkled and we wondered where he'd got the tobacco, if that is what it was. The fumes filled my car and they certainly didn't smell like ordinary tobacco.

"How does it taste?" Randy asked. Spencer sighed seraphically.

"Like a woman's tongue." Randy's eyes boggled.

We passed by the railyards and saw Coach Cross just leaving, still wearing his Missouri Pacific overalls.

I stopped and asked, "Want a ride, Coach?"

He took one look at all of us jammed in the car and thought better of it. "It's safer walking." We waved goodbye and sped on. In the back seat Spencer took a last puff of his cigarette which he'd managed to conceal when we stopped.

"Was that Coach?"

I could see he looked pretty zonked out and wondered if he'd be able to practice. Spencer was far more worldly wise than the rest of us. He'd made trips to San Francisco and Los Angeles and other points west and at one or more of them, apparently, had made intimate acquaintance with women. Or studied the biology of tongues.

This struck me like a beanball as we turned off Pike Avenue and passed the church and my former elementary school. Like Macbeth trembling before Banquo's ghost, I felt a shiver each time I came this way, mortally afraid--as in, mortal sin--I'd see Sister Jerome blocking the street and pointing at me with a big Scarlet "A" T-shirt.

She had been our most severe, inflexible teacher, and besides instilling the fear of the Lord in our souls in between math and grammar lessons, she'd warned us repeatedly about the Devil and his wiles, the worst of which clearly seemed to be kissing.

Not your regular kissing. One day in an exchange I could never forget, she had inveighed seriously and soberly and gravely against the dangers of French kissing. One of our boldest, most mature classmates had questioned whether it should be classified as a mortal sin.

Sister Jerome had countered most fervently that it was, and would lead like a chain reaction to "further mortal sins from which only the forgiveness of the Lord could save you," adding, "you should not count on that."

I was shocked and fearful, but too embarrassed to ask a question that had been on my mind from the getgo: what was French kissing? Now I knew, had been practicing it and intended to do so again this very day, which meant that for the moment and foreseeable future, the Devil had won.

Luckily a a smoking rattletrap car pulled up on our left, effectively blocking the school as we passed and Sister Jerome if she was waiting and watching.

"It's Cletus," Bobby confirmed.

Even more than last year his vehicle, if it could be called that, looked held together by spit and baling wire.

He had pulled over in the reverse lane and as we turned onto the long straight roadway leading to the field, toward a dead end past residential houses--the city planners having had the foresight to build the park beyond houses with fragile glass windows--Cletus had the gall to yell: "Race you!"

I leaned my head out the window and yelled back:

"You're on!"

George yelled: "Now!"

We both burst ahead, his used Chevy pumping out a black cloud of smoke. I saw an elderly pedestrian wheeze and literally stagger as the fumes hit him. What a way to go, I thought, and wondered if Cletus could face a charge of manslaughter. Most likely not, and the fact I was pondering such showed how unworried I was about losing.

"Come on!" Bobby screamed at me, not realizing I was coasting and letting Cletus stay parallel.

His car belched, growled and choked but stayed close. Up ahead I saw a car turn onto our street turned raceway. Seeing Cletus coming straight ahead on a collision course, he wisely pulled over and off the road, waiting for us lunatics to pass. He didn't have to wait long. I saw the ballpark looming ahead. We were bumper to bumper as we approached the intersection where we'd have to turn to arrive at the park—if that is, we wanted to wait that long, and I didn't.

"Hang on!" I yelled.

There was an embankment lining the field that was created by the mud and dirt of so many days and nights when our ground crew, which for years consisted of one courageous person who didn't mind the heat and dirt and who for a time was none other than Coach Cross—he said he needed a little extra money—would just take any excess and lump it on a lengthwise pile.

With rain and time it eventually became a sort of manmade mound with grass growing on it, an artificial barrier, and sometimes I wondered if it would ever be compared to the state park in eastern Arkansas with its historic Toltec mounds. It had a ways to go before becoming archaeology-worthy, but it was high enough and few people in their right minds would use it as a short cut, but I wanted to beat Cletus.

I gunned the gas pedal and left the street, roared toward our very own Toltec mound and sent my car zooming up the rise and hurtling into air.

Oops. George and the others screamed because I'd forgotten about the recent rains and how afterward there was a ditch created by water and erosion that formed and only got deeper each storm.

We came down smack dab into it with a huge splash of mud and water that blasted my windshield. I didn't stop. My wheels spun in the mud but I slammed gears down and with our momentum and the shift to low was able to wrench us out of the ditch.

I was just able to screech the brakes and come to a stop on the sideline where I'd sent my teammates who'd arrived early scattering for their dear lives.

I poked my head out the window and yelled "Safe!" Mickey Crutchley said "Geez Louise," and that seemed to be about the collective sentiment.

Randy added, "I may be dumb but I ain't crazy. This boy's got a ballbearing for a brain."

My riders sort of fell out of the car like they'd seen a ghost, or expected to become one. "Get thee to a nunnery, said the Bard, meaning you," George said with a pointed look, but I knew he'd liked it. For all his bookworm side, he loved living dangerously.

Spencer was finishing off another of his cigarettes. "Are we here?" he asked to no one in particular. Larry Bain had been tying his shoes when I arrived like a banshee. Bubba Beasley was doing same, and it was this moment when Billy Aycock walked up. As usual he had the most expensive equipment bag anyone could find hanging on one shoulder, and on the other just about the curviest girl. Usually he kept both away from us, figuring we were worthy of neither.

And especially Larry. Billy smirked. "Well looky here, preacher boy's learned how to tie his shoes. Next thing you know, he'll get his first hardon."

He swaggered away. Furious, Larry leaped up to charge him and we knew what that meant. George and I helped Bubba hold him back, but it took a while before he calmed down enough just to stop flailing his arms and trying to punch us to get free.

It didn't help that Billy didn't even look back, just took a seat in the stands with his latest conquest. She didn't look concerned either, and that probably made Larry even madder. He didn't have a girl friend and maybe had never had one who he thought could get past inspection by his father.

"Larry!" Bubba said, over and over.

Finally when he was restrained enough we thought we could let him go. Bubba breathed freer but he still held on to Larry's arm while I said, "You know what Coach told you about fighting."

Larry was still seething: "That was last year."

I got back in my car and eased it off the field, drove over and parked beside Cletus' rebuilt jalopy.

Cletus had seen he was licked and taken his time pulling into the parking lot. His motor shut off with a series of death rattle sputters.

He got out with his spikes and catcher's gear in hand.

His baseball bat was his pride and joy because he'd carved it himself, out of some wood in his father's lumberyard. He said it came from Grade A top of the line ash and he'd even chosen and cut the tree himself.

It was wedged between the front seat and back door arm rest. Cletus reached over and pulled it out.

The back door promptly fell off, as it obviously had no other support. Cletus nonchalantly propped the door against the car and starting walking with me to the field.

Looking at the car, I just shook my head. "Thirty miles here and back to Junction City. How does that sorry-ass crate make it?"

"Lots of love and lots of grease."

I walked and he shuffled toward the field. That was how he walked, shuffling a little bit like a crab. That was one reason he played catcher—only occasional chases for a foul popup required him to leave his position and get up speed, and he never did it once in the years we played together without a loud grunt. When he got on base everybody knew it was best to hit a home run and not worry about overtaking him on the basepaths.

I saw Bill Bowers leaning against the fence, waiting for practice and already taking notes. He was a cub sports reporter for the Arkansas Democrat and we had become friends.

"Got a quote for me, Tom?"

"This year we're gonna kick butt and take no prisoners."

"Naw, something I can print." I ventured, "The Dogtown Packers seem determined this year to find their Manifest Destiny in a state championship."

"Naw, something our illiterate readers can understand."

"This year the Packers are primed like their beef."

"Fucking A!"

He wrote it down word for word.

"You won't get any credit as usual but I sure thank you. Buy you a Coke next time we play at Burns." The golf course at Burns Park was Dogtown's municipal pride and joy and work never stopped on its fairways and greens, and Bill penned many articles about things like its upgrade, or downgrade, from Tipton grass to Bermuda and the occasional floods when the river overflowed and pretty much drowned Hole #4, a very long Par 5.

"Like that really would make a difference in my score," Bill said, "two more feet of water. I play water on that hole anyway." It was the most difficult hole on the course, where if you went to the right just a little, the ball would inevitably roll down into the bayou flanking the river.

I'd met Bill on that hole when he was waiting with a friend for the foursome ahead of them to poke their heads up from the bayou where they'd been hunting their balls.

"Vainly," Bill chortled, and I was impressed that someone would use the word "vainly."

"Drop one and play on, pardner!" Bill shouted. My partner Bubba and I shook hands with him and his pardner, shot the bull and decided to play the rest of the way as a foursome.

I couldn't believe how well Bill slammed his drive, not because it went over 200 yards—it barely made that—but that it went that far at all, or anywhere.

Bill had overcome polio as a kid and one of his legs barely functioned. It could not straighten and flopped at a right angle as if it were permanently broken—which it was in a sense and always would be—and he hobbled rather than walked. But he never let it slow him down and I am not sure he considered himself handicapped. The one and only time I ever heard him refer to it with a note of bitterness was once when he'd sent his ball into said same bayou.

The grass was high in front of the water but it was still theoretically possible to find the ball if you were willing to rustle through it and the mud and search. You'd get your ball back and not lose a stroke, but you might step on a snake and lose your health in a big way.

For that reason anybody who dared to go searching had to arm self with an iron, preferably a wedge or 9-iron because they were short with club heads angled enough to chop off a snake's head—if you saw it in time and could get a hard backswing going. I never pressed my luck. The ball was lost and snakes were welcome to it.

This time though Bill was pissed as he wasn't shooting well and he'd had a spat with his editor who didn't appreciate Bill's sarcasm about the state's eminent football coach.

Bill loved sarcasm, which was never bitter but could be pretty biting, and I rather thought it was his way of coping.

He'd learned enough about frailty to know life was built on dust and once you realized that, how could you tolerate pretension in any form?

We liked to say in Arkansas that if you held an election between God and our coach, always spelled with a capital "C, " God wouldn't even make it close. For sure, if the Devil could play quarterback and beat Texas, we'd recruit him and no questions asked about past behavior. Bill said he'd just come from covering a boosters lunch where the Coach, besides gigging for money from the well-heeled big shots to improve sports facilities at the university— "probably need a new toe massage room," Bill quipped—he was trying to defuse a rumor that one of his assistant coaches had punched a player when he came off the field after a busted play.

Bill had spoken to a dozen spectators who'd witnessed the incident, but the Coach assured everyone it wasn't true and "Ladies and gentlemen, please, if you hear any kind of rumor like this, call me and let me know first. These Christian young men need you and me to look after them and I assure you I would never countenance anything that would demoralize them or reflect badly on our program. God bless them and keep them, that's our priority first and last. Football comes second."

Bill said, "Yeah, and you see me holding up any fingers? That's how many persons in that room put football second. Here's coach in his five hundred dollar suit and red tie and Rolex watch telling these turkeys, 'Call me personally. I'm always there to hear your concerns.' Shoot, they didn't even pass out any plates. They were all just eating out of his hand. By dessert time they'd forgot all about getting what they needed to call Coach Jesus —his phone number!" Bill told me, and it was the first time I heard it, that this was called a non-denial denial. In other words, Coach didn't say the incident hadn't happened. He just said it was a vicious rumor.

"In Vietnam they have a thing now called 'deniability.'" They love it on the news desk. Some general says, 'I had no knowledge of any napalm wiping out that village,' and technically that's true. But technically they're still dead.'"

"What's napalm?"

"You don't want to know." Anyway Bill's editor hadn't appreciated his mockery and bounced him back to covering down and out local teams like the Dogtown Packers. Some day he'd move back up, and up, but it wasn't going to be this summer.

So Bill didn't care much about moccasins or anything else at that moment and just plunged into mud and stagnant water looking for his errant 6-iron shot. He'd taken a pitching wedge with him and while he slashed the tall wet weedgrass to make a path he yelled, "Come on, sucker!" —meaning a snake--"Take a bite!"

And he flayed out his afflicted leg. "Go on, bite—see what poison tastes like!" Whop! Whop! against the weeds. "You ever see a snake all crooked up? He'll be bent in two like an L wrench."

He went on like that for another few minutes, like he didn't want to give up. He finally did, and hit a new ball he laid out on the fairway. But Bill never gave up on the things that counted.

After a while we saw Coach Cross walking across the field toward us. He always walked deliberately, never seemed rushed —and it was this kind of calm purposefulness we were looking for now that Big Chuck had handed over the reins, but truth was Coach Cross was afflicted with ulcers and we'd see him sometimes downing a medicinal drink to ease the pain. Maybe that's why he'd hesitated to take on our team. He didn't need to do this any more. But this year, this one time he'd said yes.

Maybe he felt sorry for us or maybe, as Bill Bowers said, he took pity on us and didn't want us to end our youth baseball careers as pathetic losers.

He noticed the tire marks where I'd crushed the grass, but he didn't say anything—maybe figured it was a last sign of what we'd have to put behind us. Anyway he motioned us to come over and gather around, so we all sat on the grass and listened to his pep talk.

"So here we are again. New season. Some new players. But

are we gonna be the same old team. Randy."

"Sir?"

"What do the other teams in our league think about us?"

Randy looked puzzled.

"Well sir, kinda hard to get in their heads."

Billy unhelpfully said, "Take your time dummy, we got all summer."

Randy glared at him.

Coach added, "I mean, do they fear us? Do they respect us?" This time Randy had the ready answer and didn't mince words, though he wouldn't have known how to mince anyway.

"No sir. They think we're horse shit."

"You bet they do. And you know what? They're right." Billy blurted out, "We've got a problem in the infield, Coach." Larry came back at him: "Who you got in mind, Aycock?"

"Look in a mirror, ugly." Larry made an angry move to get up and go after Billy but this time George and I were ready and we restrained him.

Coach Cross just shook his head at the spectacle.

"Boys—"

It was almost like he was ready to give up before he started. He turned his back on us and moved a step away. We didn't know what to think or do.

The silence grew more and more awkward. I looked up toward the stands and saw Sally Bright taking a seat beside Billy's latest girl friend.

George saw her too, nudged me and in a low voice asked, "Where's Mary Louise?"

I shrugged. She'd promised to come watch after I told her it was our first day.

"First day of what?" she'd asked.

It was a good couple of minutes before Coach Cross turned back and I thought he had a special sentiment in his voice, like he was remembering something from his past, but then as he went on it turned out he was thinking about us. "Boys, most of you started playing on this team two years ago, so this this is your last summer of baseball. Pretty soon you'll be going out into the world. It's not an easy place, especially in these times. Some of you can go off to college."

I noticed Spencer nodding but Randy just shrugged. Not him. Maybe a vocational school but what vocation?

"Some of you won't. But sooner or later you're going to meet life square, like the fastest pitcher you ever faced or worst doubleheader you ever played. It can beat you. Beat you bad. Worse than any loss we've ever suffered. And you all know, considering our record, that's gonna be something awful."

This got a little smile from us.

Randy looked almost misty-eyed. In a soft voice he said to no one in particular, or for the record…"That man puts the V in vocabulary," adding, "It's got a V, don't it ?"

"At times like those, when you're feeling whipped and got no way to turn and see no way out, you're gonna need folks who'll stand by you, no matter how much you've screwed up. It's called friendship. Camaraderie. Another word for teamwork. Brotherhood. 'Cause that's what this team should be, brothers working together."

I saw Larry look at Billy. When their eyes met Larry shook his head, meaning 'No way.'

"Win or lose. You play together and back each other up when times get tough, you'll learn brotherhood. In the long run that's more important than winning or losing." And then after a pregnant pause: "Just don't quote me on that." That got a chuckle.

Suddenly we heard a sound that reminded me of one of the pigs on my uncle's farm chowing down on a slab of bacon fat. Coach Cross looked for its source and we followed his look toward Bobby. He'd been riveted by Coach's speech because his eyes fixed in a stare like he'd been hypnotized. His only movement came from his jaws, where we noticed a big black glob rolling around in his mouth.

A charitable man would say he'd been smacking tobacco, but from the look of things no one could be sure.

Coach Cross didn't have to pose the question. Bobby understood.

"Chaw tobacco, Coach. Help me conc'ntrate."

The glop was so stuffed in his mouth some spilled out when he spoke.

George said: "Looks like a turd." His brother glared at him but even Bobby had to laugh when Coach chimed in: "So it does."

Bobby's laugh sent the glop spewing out of his mouth. Coach yelled: "Let's hit it!" We got up and with a big Rebel yell charged out onto the field.

It was good to be back out there in the warm spring afternoon sunshine and start working out the kinks of winter. Some of us had played football and basketball for our high school teams and the muscles used in those sports had to be tamped down in favor of the long lean ones needed for baseball.

The general practice under Coach Cross was to start with him hitting grounders to all of us on the infield while somebody—today it was Bubba—hit long flies to the outfielders.

Everybody took part because we didn't have many subs and sooner or later everyone was going to get to play. After we'd got warmed up it was time for our pitchers to take the mound and pitch batting practice. Each player got his cuts, and some did better than others, sometimes this depending on whether a pitcher could consistently fire hittable balls.

On this day Sammy was wild and it took forever to get a pitch to hit—you didn't want to just flail around or swing at a bad pitch—if you did, for sure Coach Cross would get on you. But he didn't do it like Big Chuck who would foghorn a scream that all the neighbors around could hear.

This was our first proof that a new sheriff was in town, someone who'd discipline but not humiliate. It was our first step toward better teamwork, and I said that to George.

"Yeah," he said, "but brothers? I've got enough trouble dealing with the coprophiliac," meaning Bobby, his natural real life brother. Early in the practice Bobby had to dive to catch a fly ball and he swallowed his chaw. George like an all too typical older brother didn't ask him if he'd hurt himself, just "How's it taste, bro?"

Bobby wouldn't give him the satisfaction of an answer, but his grimace said a lot.

Bobby made it through practice even though he didn't seem to have the proverbial bounce in his step, and he surely didn't look happy when Coach ended the practice by making us do 10 laps around the field.

This was new: Big Chuck never made us run, maybe because just watching us made him imagine himself running laps or even jogging and the thought was too much to bear for a 300-pound lover of good beef and pork spareribs.

But George said that night at dinner, in mid-mashed potatoes Bobby barfed "all the tobaccy" right onto his plate. George had never seen anything like it and neither had their parents, who there and then banned chewing tobacco from the house and Bobby at least until he reached the age of adulthood but preferably till the end of the universe.

Anyway Bobby didn't need any more persuasion, and he fell back on our standard Topps bubble gum. With that he got a baseball card, not indigestion.

After the practice Coach Cross called us over for some practical info.

"I'm not going to announce a starting lineup yet. I may move some of you around. We want a lot of movable parts, but we want stability too. It'll work out.

"Something new this year. First, we're going to practice every day but Sunday, rain or shine. Second, when the season starts we're not going to limit ourselves to the league. Mr. Frankenheimer's got games lined up for us at towns all across the state. He figures if we're ever going to play our best, we have to play the best."

Now this was news. We'd never gone on the road like that before.

"We got a bus?" Cletus asked.

"Nope. Going to have to car pool." And then Coach reflected that it was Cletus who'd asked the question: "Better check the oil, fellas. We don't want you stranded outside Toad Suck Ferry."

That got a laugh and everybody looked at Cletus. He had a mountain to climb with that jalopy of his, and even in first gear it might not make it. Coach Cross stared at us, for five minutes it seemed like. "I've got a question for you all." And after the most pregnant pause we'd all likely ever experienced, he said, "Do you want to win?"

We exchanged looks. Amazingly, no one had ever posed the question before.

"Why, yes sir," I answered for the team. George and Mickey nodded, and so did Spencer though as usual his thoughts seemed to be floating elsewhere.

"You're going to have to want to, real bad. This is your last chance. Don't forget that. See you tomorrow."

We broke up and headed our separate ways. I took a seat in the stands and took off my spikes and put on my sneakers.

Bill Bowers had listened in to Coach's parting shot.

"Well Henry, what's the prognosis?"

"We need pitching."

"So does everybody."

"Our starters are going to be fine. Relief pitching."

"You find one of those let me know, so you can help me find a needle I just lost in my neighbor's haystack."

"I've got an idea."

"Love to hear it."

Coach Cross shook his head. "Not yet."

"When the time's right, don't be a stranger." I moved away toward the parking lot but I could still overhear, even if they didn't think so. Bill's voice changed to a more serious register.

"Nice kids. I hate to think what some of 'em might be doing next year."

"Let's let them enjoy the summer."

Coach meant Vietnam. Uncle Sam had just sent me my notice to take a draft physical in July.

It seemed far away. My mind focused on baseball and Mary Louise, who still hadn't showed up. Generally she was always

42

late, and I'd got to the point where I'd set a rendezvous time 30 minutes in advance, but she'd figured out that ruse pretty quick.

I was getting more steamed with each step but then heard a screech of tires and saw her flashy red Mustang speeding at twice the limit toward me and the lot.

She braked so hard it left rubber on the asphalt.

I hurried over.

George yelled: "Come to mama!"

3. MARY LOUISE

Mary Louise revved the car like a locomotive as I got in.

"You got a ticket to ride, big boy?" The new Beatles song had just come out and it was playing on the radio.

"Where were you?"

"At a little cocktail bash, honey. Johnny Benson gave it."

"Who the hell is he?"

She tossed her hair. "One of Daddy's sales reps. He literally begged me to come."

"I'll bet."

"Don't be mad at me, honey. Look."

She had hung a brown, stuffed Esso station tigertail on the rearview mirror. Esso at that time was promoting their mascot "Tony the Tiger" and Uncle Bob had dozens of them as giveaways. I'd taken one thinking for no particular reason that she might like it.

"It reminds me of you."

She fingered the tigertail seductively, and I realized what she already had, that it it resembled nothing so much as a furry phallus.

My testiness gave way right quick.

#

Big Chuck had spoken of his wife and daughter from time to time the last two years but I'd never met them. They never came round to the games and since we'd been pitiful losers, he saw no occasion for a party at home.

His wife Marvela, he said, would never consent to sitting on a wooden bleacher seat, and he wasn't about to invest in a Louis XIV settee for the sideline. He said his daughter--whose name I never remembered being mentioned--only knew the kind of bats that came out at night and didn't much care to know more.

They both viewed his baseball activities as a kind of "big boy's hobby" to which they'd have to be indulgent, though sometimes he wondered if they didn't view it as an unhealthy fetish. So that was why I didn't meet Mary Louise until our senior year football game against the Wildcats.

I played safety on defense, and had time between plays to check out the opposing team's cheerleaders. She stood out, to say the least, and I figured I'd better do something to meet her before a long pass got completed over my head and our coach realized I wasn't paying attention. Anyway we didn't have a great team and the 'Cats were leading comfortably, so I seized the chance when one of their wide receivers caught a pass just inbounds on the sideline where the cheerleaders were dancing.

All I had to do was push him out of bounds but I wrapped him up and propelled him toward the cheerleaders before finishing the tackle. When I got up from the ground I found myself where I wanted to be, face to face with the blonde bombshell and her pom poms.

"Hey there. How you doing?" were my immortal words. She stared at me for a couple of seconds then waved her pompoms and responded: "Go, Wildcats!"

Transfixed, I didn't even realize that the wide receiver, royally PO'd by my excessive tackle, was shoving me in the back so I'd turn around and get punched. All I noticed was that some force was pushing me closer to her.

"My name's Tom."

"Congratulations."

Finally the wide receiver spun me around but his teammates grabbed him and order was restored. As I headed back to the field I turned back to look at her and let her know what she already knew, that I was smitten. She said, "Go, Wildcats" and swirled her pom poms.

George played cornerback and had a front row view of my unconventional courting ploy. He must have laughed a good five minutes before he divulged the name of my mystery blonde. "She was right there in your own backyard," adding,

"You are so far out of her league they won't even let you be a fan."

I'd only had a crush on a couple of girls to that point in my youth, as our boys high school principal regarded the opposite sex as a threat directly descended from Eve and the serpent, and Sister Jerome had effectively stifled a lot of pre-puberty longings. Thus I'd come very late to the game by Billy Aycock standards, but late didn't mean last and I promptly applied for a part-time job at Frankenheimer Foods.

Big Chuck sat me down for an interview—"Business ain't a game like baseball, son, remember that," he said solemnly. "Now then, what do you know about the beef and pork business?"

I thought long and hard. I realized that the job might depend on this answer and I need to marshal all I knew and articulate it well. After a long pause, I replied, "Well sir, I eat those meats each and every week."

"Some would ascribe that response to mental deficiencies, but I appreciate it." He asked me a few more questions that, based on my previous response, seemed designed to discern if I could read, write or understand spoken English. Here I did better and got hired, and one day when Mary Louise came by to pick up the week's meat supplies for the family, I made sure to be the person who hauled them out to her car--a Mustang convertible.

I made the mistake of saying, "Remember me from the football game? Tom?"

"No. Why should I?" I then started in with an explanation of how I'd met her when I went out of bounds etc. etc. and as any beautiful girl would who'd got stuck with a boring mooning suitor, cut me off:

"Have a good day, er..."

"Tom." As she sped away I convinced myself it was normal she might forget my name; after all, a good ten seconds had passed from the time I reminded her. I managed through assiduous work and not a little obsequiousness to get invited to Big Chuck's Easter barbecue, where I found myself among

Mary Louise and her high school teammates and assorted flotsam like me.

One guy buttonholed me and asked, "Remember me?"

"No, why should I?"

"I owe you a lickin' for hitting me out of bounds but I figure you'll get it from her. We call ourselves paper napkins, 'cause she throws us away so fast."

Spoken like a dumped boy friend, I thought.

"What she needs is a good cloth napkin, " I countered.

"Yeah, you and my mama's old dish rag."

Despite my higher brand of fabric Mary Louise hadn't said boo to me and maybe didn't realize I was there, but I stayed late and helped clean up the rib bones and other barbecue leavings, none of which saw her lifting a finger but it kept me in her orbit and little by little she noticed me circling around regularly like a mosquito. She was lying on a lounge chair soaking up the sun.

"Can you fix me a bourbon and branch, Tom?"

She wasn't old enough to drink, numerically speaking that is, but she was nothing if not worldly wise.

"Daddy says you might have a future, once you learn the 99.5% of the business you don't know."

"That's good to hear. Hey, have you ever been to the Juroy Drive-In?"

"We have a private space. With enhanced microphones."

"Oh." In my naiveté I took her to see Mary Poppins. I enjoyed it and the music came across great with the enhanced microphones, but had the distinct feeling that if we'd come in Mary Louise's car, we'd have been out of there at Chim Chim Cheree.

"So we are to believe that a banker can't be happy till he goes fly a kite? Give me a break. Clearly Daddy did not name me after her."

Still, I started to grow on her--"like a fungus," George said-- and we'd gotten to the heavy making-out stage that Sister Jerome would have excommunicated me for. I realize now I was intoxicated by her and what she represented, a rich girl

47

with a big house on the Hill dating a poor boy from Levy. As well as her looks.

#

As we passed the parking lot I motioned for her to stop. Larry was being helped to his feet by Bubba and Sammy while Billy Aycock preened to his curvy girl du jour, a not-natural blonde with the kind of figure often seen on the covers of motorcycle magazines.

"He all right?" I asked Billy.

"Dumb ass never learns. He'd fight the good Lord himself if he looked at him sideways."

"You take out our second baseman you'll be squaring off with me next time."

"Back off. I caught him flush on the jaw. He just won't be able to mouth off for a while."

"You boys will be boys," Mary Louise said, and Billy leaned in closer.

"Hey, when you going to wise up and give me a call?"

"Back off," I said. "You've got enough on your hands with Jayne Mansfield over there," Mary Louise said.

"Aw, she's cotton candy. You're a five-star dessert."

"Go soak it," I said, "you're walking funny."

This made Mary Louise laugh. She hit the gas pedal and we roared off. I could see Larry on his feet and shaking the cobwebs out of his head--a good sign. I relaxed.

Instead of heading home, we zipped down Pike Avenue and crossed over the Broadway Bridge into Little Rock.

"I've got something to show you. Out in the boondocks." She drove fast, way beyond the speed limit even here in town. When I first rode with her and hinted something about the speed limit as I gripped the door handle for safety and security, she said, "I don't believe in limits."

This seemed so clearly a personality trait (or else they were bedazzled) that when cops did stop her, more often than not they let her off with a warning.

Once they and she were out of sight, she simply sped up again. She'd warned me from the beginning: "No need to tell me to hit the gas, darling. I always do."

We sped the length of Broadway and when we reached the Interstate, Mary Louise turned and headed west toward Benton.

"We going to Vegas?"

"Why not? We could sin together. You know, today is our two-month anniversary. That's a new record for me. We should start thinking about our future." We passed cars and trucks like they were standing still. "Speaking of that..." and I chose my words carefully—"I don't think I'm cut out for the sausage trade. I'm thinking of looking for something else."

"Like what?

"Something where I can be more independent. I want more on my horizon than a bunch of ham hocks."

"Have you told Daddy?"

"Not yet."

"I'll talk to him. He likes men with ambition. And so do I." She took my hand. "Men who want to reach the next level." She turned off before reaching Benton and we cruised through the small downtown of Bryant, taking the direction toward Bauxite, a town central for decades to the country's need for aluminum.

We didn't make it that far, though. Mary Louise turned left some miles outside of Bryant and we headed down a country road.

"You're kidnapping me."

"You wish."

After a few miles she pulled over and parked at roadside in the middle of nowhere.

Pine forest stretched thick and deep on the left side of the road. On the right the trees topped a plateau and she pointed toward it and the red and white clay hill we'd have to climb to get up there.

"Ready to walk on the wild side?"

"This better be good."

"Baby, it will be."

49

She led the way, scrambling directly up the hill in her designer tennies. I followed. The evening would close in soon but plenty of daylight remained and anyway, "Going to have a full moon tonight" she assured me.

Whatever she had in store for me, it was exciting to think I'd have her alone and in the pine country, dependent on me--or vice versa. She would have to hug me close in the event we ran across a wild razorback, or angry rabbit or possum--any critter would suffice for me.

The loose rock and shale went sliding down as we clambered up the slope.

"Shoulda worn my cleats."

"Shoulda."

When we reached the top of the plateau we looked out on a large pond of rainwater in a shallow basin stretching from one end to the other. I thought with an inner tube or inflatable mattress you could while away some wonderful hours up here, watching the white clouds scud by in a sky much bluer than what we saw in the city and just dreaming the day away.

"Too shallow for swimming," Mary Louise said. "I've tested it."

"You came up here alone?"

"In another life, honey. Before I met you."

I flattered myself, it's no country for paper napkins and I was privileged she'd brought me here. Almost as if she was reading my thoughts, she said, "Picnic spot."

We'd reached the edge of the plateau and looked down on a flat bed of pine needles shaded by a tree, on a cliff overlooking an immense lake formed when a bauxite quarry had been dug out, emptied and finally abandoned. Over time, rainwater had created the lake and down below I could see a sand and dirt beach.

Mary Louise started down the slope toward it and in five minutes we reached the beach, looking out over the water.

"Our private swimming hole," Mary Louise said. "I'm so hot I'm about to burn up."

She quickly doffed her T-shirt and shorts.

50

I had enough sense left to say, "Roughly 100% of swimmers drown in these pits."

"Roughly? That leaves room for exceptions. Don't you think we're exceptional? Ready or not, here I go."

And just like that she was nude and in the water. I watched her for a moment.

"From here on, it's deep water, honey. You going to let me go it alone?" Nope. I ripped off my clothes as quickly as possible and stepped into the water.

"It's cold!"

"I'll warm you up."

The setting sun spread golden light on the cliffs all around us. A wind ruffled the pine trees and their scent spread all around, as if I needed any more intoxication. I took her in my arms and got warmed up rapidly. She stretched her arms wide to soak in the scenic beauty.

"What better place to plunge in?"

All the guys on the team talked a good game when it came to sex, but I'd noticed that when Billy Aycock regaled us with his escapades, nobody ever chimed in with theirs. Among them, me. I'd gone to a high school where if you danced too close to your date, the principal would come out, grab you and haul you off the dance floor to hug a pillar in full view of everyone. A modern version of the pillory, and it was effective in tamping down acts if not desires.

"Well, there's my Louisville Slugger."

And I'd believed she didn't know anything about baseball.

#

The next stage in my education involved finding protection, and that at the time in Arkansas was no easy feat. A few weeks after our swim the Supreme Court ruled for the right of birth control among married couples in the USA, but we weren't hitched—yet.

"Like we should get married for the right not to have babies? I don't think so," Mary Louise said, and she was right.

51

In the end her goofball admirer Johnny Benson got a couple of packages of condoms.

"You actually asked him to do that?"

"Why not? He'll do anything for me and you know, when salesmen go on the road...Can you believe it, he looked really disappointed when I said my boy friend would be so grateful. I think he thought they were for him and me."

"Silly him."

Bill Bowers came to me one day with a package of three "Razorback condoms." The state sports mascot had begun appearing on all sorts of ancillary products: coffee and soda cups, T-shirt, shirts and pants, caps, including a big plastic hat in the shape of a head and snout--all bright red. Now someone had added condoms to the list.

Bill said he figured I'd caught a tigress by the tail and if you ventured into the jungle, best go equipped. "If you watch the first Tarzan movie with Johnny Weissmuller, when he speaks to the natives in their language, he's really saying, 'Bwana needs rubbers.' He'd just met Jane, you see."

Such was the logic and thinking process of Bill Bowers. He said he'd got them from a coach "who must remain nameless," who refused to say if they'd been furnished to members of the university sports teams. He would only say, "They're for when a desirable situation becomes an undesirable situation."

They were standard condoms, except each one was tinged red at the tip. "That's carrying the state colors far," I said. Bill riposted, "American enterprise is what it is. Even in the throes of passion, you can be reminded of the Razorbacks." Unfortunately I had visions of how at football games whole stands would stand and call the Hogs, waving arms and yelling "Woooooooooo Pig, Soooieee!!!" Would Mary Louise go for that? I looked closer at the box and saw a testimony the manufacturers had added to their effectiveness: "They'll make your sow squeal with delight."

I decided I'd best keep these far away from Big Chuck, not because he'd erupt with anger at his daughter and me engaging in carnal practice--he rather thought it was about time, though he never came right out and said so--but that someone had taken sows to a lucrative ancillary market and they weren't his.

4. WHERE WE ARE AIN'T WHERE WE'RE AT

Big Chuck listened to the radio in his office at the plant because he liked music and it calmed his nerves.

He listened to his daughter because he was obliged to and, given her personality, was a little afraid not to, but when she harangued him about giving me a promotion, she said he hesitated.

She gave him an earful, but he protested:

"Hell honey, my middle name is favoritism, second to nepotism. That don't burn any skin off my butt. I'm just wondering if I promote him, how can he help me make money? Frankenheimer Foods isn't in the charity business."

At first he thought about a supervisor role, and gave me an in-depth look at all the company functions. I went over sales figures and sales personnel (finding out that Johnny Benson, who resembled Ichabod Crane and from all I heard was as boring as an unpainted fence post, nevertheless consistently racked up big sales), stock procurement contracts and state regulations.

He booked a place for me at the annual Arkansas Hereford Field Day and said I didn't have to inspect the stock, just make nice and pick the brains of his competitors there and if we came across a good idea, well "hell, no one can copyright an idea."

Then he gave me a tour of the slaughterhouse. I had avoided it and hitherto worked only in the front office, greeting and coddling customers.

I donned a lab coat and carried paper and a clipboard for notes. We weaved through lines of strung carcasses and cut meats of all sizes and varieties. Knives flashed like scimitars at flank and rump and I noticed one was a savage-looking middle-aged woman who seemed to enjoy slashing with a meat ax so hefty I thought it could have severed the head off a buffalo.

Big Chuck caught me glancing her way and said, "Lizzie Borden would've had gainful employment here."

As we strolled he'd occasionally pat a carcass or slab of meat, run his fingers along it to sample the texture.

"Tom, you're now part of what I call my meat Gestapo. Check for topnotch quality, nothing less. You see a thin shank or a rot gut, jump on it like a maggot."

"Yes sir."

"We've got a reputation. I aim to keep it."

"Yes sir."

"Hey, I know you've got big plans, college and all. But you want to keep a prime cut like Mary Louise, well, you better keep the larder full. The meat business may not be glamorous, but the bacon's already home. Know what I mean?"

"Not exactly."

He grabbed a handful of ground sausage off a pile of same. "Feel that."

I did and felt my nostrils arch back at the smell.

"Mushy, ain't it. Somebody fed this hog some real shit."

He disgustedly flung the sausage into a waste bin. I dutifully made a notation on my clipboard.

"I swear, some of these so-called farmers, we'd be better off puttin' them in the wallers and their pigs on the tractors."

We now found themselves in a corner of garbage bins piled high with the plant's offal.

"Geez," I said, "kind of rank around here."

"Rank? I don't smell anything."

I felt my eyes rolling back in their sockets with the effort to contain revulsion.

"Oh, you mean this stuff."

He grabbed a pile of entrails off the top of a bin and put his nose to them.

"Ain't nothing here but a few guts and gizzards." He held them under my nose. "See?"

I felt very queasy. The glop in Big Chuck's hand looked abominable and smelled worse, but he just boomed out a laugh.

"Listen son, here we got a saying, 'Offal don't mean awful.' Here, get a good whiff." He handed the stuff to me.

"In a coupla days you'll say this stuff smells sweeter'n roses."

He slapped me on the back and moved away roaring with laughter that reverberated throughout the plant.

I couldn't look at the odious mess in my hand and didn't need to. My intestines were heaving with distress and in short order I added my personal touch to the bin of non-awful offal.

After I assured Big Chuck that despite my commitment to him and Frankenheimer Foods and desire to move up in the business, "I don't have the stomach for this kind of work," he got the picture and came up with another idea.

He'd been puzzled over the past few years by all the longhairs who were making hit music and dominating the radio waves. He'd grown up with crooners and he still loved crooners and couldn't understand why they'd become a dying breed.

"Hell, you gotta wait all day to hear Perry Como's new song. It's what, #40 on the charts?"

Like almost all our parents he'd been baffled by the arrival of Elvis and the Beatles. My high school's fiery and feared principal, Father Tribou, believed in learning and put our noses to a grindstone engraved with literature, history and science, and we received a solid education.

He was a most rigid disciplinarian and had fabricated a broad wooden boat paddle, with three holes bored to cut down on wind resistance, to pound the butts of any student who crossed over his lines. Sometimes he would do it publicly, at a school assembly in the gym. It could be a fearsome spectacle.

He detested long hair and felt it equated with the decline of Arkansas, nay American civilization. Every boy had his hair cut as close to the pate as possible. Inevitably he disapproved of the moptop Beatles.

When the Fab Four first came to America every teenager in America, with the possible exception of those living under a very big rock or busy making out in a back seat, glued eyes to the Ed Sullivan show to watch them play.

I was struck by the music. I said to my mother, "These are good songs. Even Father Tribou might like them. If he's watching." So when we filed into his classroom the next day we couldn't wait to discuss the phenomenon we'd witnessed.

But he'd pre-empted us. Considering that any such discussion would waste valuable time from young lives and his as well, he'd simply written on the blackboard, "What did I think of the Beatles? One word: blech."

Which we thought was a synonym for barfing.

Bottom line however: he had watched the show. Big Chuck had too, and he realized "There's a market out there, Tom. A big one. All that caterwauling takes energy, and we know that means fuel. Good red meat."

By fortuitous serendipity the Rolling Stones had just released "I Can't Get No Satisfaction."

"That's talkin' like us," Chuck said. "Listen, I don't care if we do live in the land of the Razorback. Lots of folks in this state get their satisfaction from sex—one way or another—but they don't get good beef and pork."

He chomped on his cigar. Looked me straight in the eye.

"Find me a song we can put on a radio ad. Something they can hum and make 'em think Frankenheimer Foods. Art that leads to digestion. Hell, if them Beatles and Hermits and whatdya call 'em, Kinks can do it, we can."

I wasn't so sure about that, but Big Chuck was my boss and my girl friend's father and I set to work. I had a budget and carte that wasn't quite blanche but left me a lot of leverage considering Arkansas prices. I tracked down a country singer who had a good local reputation after striking out in my efforts to get in touch with Johnny Cash. He'd been arrested recently for trespassing ("For picking flowers! Now that's Mississippi po-lice for you," Big Chuck railed) and rumors made the rounds about drug problems.

Country Joe Slade was playing in a big cinder block building just outside the limits of our dry county where you could buy liquor and so served as a night club, with square dancing and Country Joe's music in between rounds.

At night I wouldn't have been allowed in as I wasn't 21 and didn't look anywhere near it, but Country Joe graciously allowed me an interview.

He chain-smoked and chained beer as well, coughing frequently.

"How much dinero we talking about?"

I don't have a figure yet, but Mr. Frankenheimer can be generous if he finds a song he likes."

"You got lyrics?"

"Working on them," I lied. "We're kind of waiting on the performer."

"Well son, you came to the right man. I've played clubs all over this state and got an audition in Nashville coming up. Played backup in Memphis too, Sun Records, Johnny Cash's stompin' grounds. You know he's on drugs, don't ya? They're lookin' for new blood."

Country Joe's blood didn't look a day over 55 or clean as a whistle either, but he believed in himself even at that late date in his earthly journey and insisted on playing two songs he'd composed.

The first was a mournful ballad about a man who went squirrel hunting after breaking up with his girl, and the second a lively number about a pickup truck called Old Joe.

"Named after me," he explained, though I'd guessed.

He didn't manage to stop coughing even during the singing and explained the beer was to wash down the "frog in my throat."

He was opening up a new pack when I said I'd get back in touch, which I never did because inspiration began coming from unusual quarters.

That night I ate at one of what Mary Louise called her "grunt work dinners," which happened once a month around the time she was due to receive her considerable monthly allowance. "Time to butter up those who bread the butter," she would announce, dragging me along.

We had just finished a gigantic platter of spare ribs, sausage and beef brisket. As the maid gathered up the dinner plates Big

Chuck gave a thunderous belch of appreciation

Mary Louise's mother Marvella, who I doubt had ever belched in her life, reproved him gently.

"Really, Charles."

Big Chuck pinched her affectionately on the leg. "Aw mama, I make my meat to taste like that."

Mary Louise said, "Ellie Mae outdid herself."

Her mother countered, "Don't forget your poor mother, dearie. I spent an hour in that ghastly hot kitchen myself."

"I'm sure she'd have been lost without you, mother."

Big Chuck bellowed a laugh, struck a match for his cigar in a blaze of flame, eased back in his chair. His dining room was furnished in a kind of tacky opulence, expensive furniture and settings alternating with memorabilia of the sausage and bacon trade.

Big Chuck turned to me.

"Son, you probably think I'm a happy man. And you're right, I'm living high on my hogs. But inside I got some big old hookworms. One of 'em's called the Dogtown Packers."

"If we can get a real esprit de corps going, we're gonna win some games this year."

Big Chuck grunted. "While you're workin' on that esprit de corps, find us a relief pitcher."

Marvella said, "I don't understand this game, Tom. Balls, bats, TKO's."

"Jesus," Mary Louise jeered.

"So let's talk about the other thing gnawing at me. My little girl."

"Not again. Chuck, that's their business."

"Aw Marvella, it only took me two months to hogtie you. He's been dilly-dallying too long."

Mary Louise toyed with her necklace, cast her eyes down and waited for my reply with an air of demure calculation.

Hadn't expected this. By my calculation, we'd been dating about 2 and one half months. "Uh..." I answered brilliantly.

Marvella rescued me. "You'll let us know when the time is right, won't you Tom?"

"Oh yes m'am, most definitely." Big Chuck "harrumphed," chomped his cigar, shook his head.

"Me, I'd make the time right. I remember when I first started Frankenheimer Foods--"

"Oh oh, here it comes. 'How the little tadpole grew up to be a big frog.' Next time, Daddy. We've got to catch a movie."

She hopped up and grabbed me by the hand, led me out of my chair. I was happy to go.

Big Chuck glowered as we headed out.

"Maybe I've been too generous with my silver spoons." Then, just before the door closed, a sally meant for me. "When you come up for air, boy, find me a song!"

Mary Louise had snitched a bottle of bourbon from the family stash and I'd brought a six-pack of Coca Colas, so we went to the pine tree copse overlooking the quarry pit. We'd planned on some swimming but I said:

"Tonight it's down to business."

"What the hell are you talking about?"

I pulled out my transistor radio and turned it to the hits station.

"I'm looking for inspiration."

"If you came here for that I'm with the wrong cowboy."

I laid down a tarp and blanket and mixed the drinks in paper cups. We quickly chugged a cocktail.

"I just need a tune."

"I know one. Mine. I'm going to make you whistle it."

The way she said it was so seductive my thoughts quickly left the aforementioned business and only vaguely remember some of the songs piped over the transistor that evening. Wooly Bully, Mr. Tambourine Man, Help Me, Rhonda. True Love Ways which we'd danced to at our prom was still going strong and played a couple of times. I think.

And then as the night got late, the song that had set Big Chuck and me on a mission blared out.

"Don't tell me you can't get no satisfaction," Mary Louise said.

The next day when my head had cleared some from her and

the bourbon, I thought, why not indeed tell the story of the little piglet who became Boss Hawg. I'd call it "The Ballad of Big Chuck."

Some lyrics came easily:
He came from the hills of Arkansaw
Best durn butcher you ever saw
Pork and beef and poultry too
Big Chuck chops the meat for you.

And the refrain:
Big Chuck's got the meats for you,
Sausage and ham and bacon too.

Others came harder. Big Chuck wanted a line about his effort to make meat affordable, and this didn't come to me till I walked in to my Uncle Bob's service station to buy a couple of quarts of oil.

He was behind his big oak desk waxing on about the issues of the day, mostly political. I never saw him do any manual labor, or any labor for that matter. He was too modest to say it, but others did, calling him the unofficial co-mayor of Levy, our little village in the city.

It was at a crossroads where one branch led outside the city to Burns Park, the largest municipal park in the United States, another straight north to the Camp Robinson military base from which President Eisenhower had ordered troops to enforce school integration at Little Rock's Central High School in 1957, the first real battle in the civil rights war; another branch south to the Arkansas River and into Little Rock over the Broadway or Main Street bridges; and a third branch up to Park Hill, a spiffy neighborhood like most hills in a city do attract, passing Uncle Bob's home where my beloved Aunt Bess reigned with intelligence, love and blissful, benign neglect of her husband's politics.

Just across the street ran the tracks of the Missouri Pacific railroad, and trains would pass day and far into the night, lulling many a youngster to sleep with mournful whistles.

My father had worked in Uncle Bob's garage along with Joe Wright, who was called in those days a "colored man" from the

61

"colored community." Besides being, along with my father, one of the nicest men who ever lived, a most skilled mechanic and utterly reliable, good-tempered worker, he negotiated without misstep the complicated racial relations of that tumultuous epoch.

He was calm and utterly patient, though his patience was tested the first day he took me out on a rural road to teach me how to drive. After a couple of hours of terrible gear grinding with the stick shift he said very politely, "Well, next time we'll see how you do with an automatic."

At this time he would always refer to white men he knew well and called friends with a respectful preface, as for example his employer, my uncle, "Mr. Bob."

This did not prevent him from noticing clearly when white people did something patently illogical or not sensible, and he would not hesitate to point it out--but with such a good-humored chuckle that no one ever took offense. He was the principal reason--though my father and even Uncle Bob never once publicly indulged in racist diatribes--that the colored community always felt welcome at the service station for something more than their greenbacks, and for this reason alone Levy formed a little island of tolerance and harmony in the city.

When my father died Joe was the only colored man in the church, and my mother hugged him as if he'd been my father's brother, which given all their years working together in the garage, winter and summer, amid the grease and oil and muffler pipes, they had been.

#

Joe Wright was understandably amused by my mission to craft a radio ad for Big Chuck Frankenheimer, and chuckled. "Well, sometimes it takes a ham to sell ham." And he kept on chuckling as he went off to repair a flat.

Right then and there I found another mini-verse:
Saw those prices way up there,

Said "Whoa brother, that ain't fair."

Hurrying to write them up, I ripped out an ad page from one of the motorcycle magazines lying around for customers to read while they waited. I spared the front cover which had an incredibly voluptuous blonde draped over a Harley.

Uncle Bob asked me what I was writing. I explained.

"What you need is the dadblamed Huggins Quartet."

"They sing gospel."

"You don't think that dadblamed Frankenheimer believes he's God?"

Before I knew it my Uncle Bob had pulled strings and set up a meeting with the quartet. It helped that his unofficial Levy co-mayor, owner of the Huggins Lumberyard, was the father of the quartet's founder and lead singer Ronnie.

Ronnie I knew from the quartet's evening show every Sunday where their melodious harmonies based faith in classic gospel songs. Where his father was the roughest of 2-by-4s, Ronnie looked as if he'd been cut, sawed, sanded and planed and then varnished into the smoothest of smooth surfaces where no lint or dirt could ever cling.

"They'll be here tomorrow, " my Uncle Bob said.

"Who?"

"The Quartet."

"Where?"

"Here, my office. That table right there."

It was right next to the rack holding Esso 30 and 40-weight motor oil quart cans.

The table was clean enough, though I removed the motorcycle magazines before their arrival. As they took their seats I offered helpfully, "There's a discount today, 30 per cent off all brands of oil."

I nodded toward the oil rack, as if they needed any help spotting it. I launched immediately into my pitch, figuring they'd reject everything immediately and might as well get it over with.

Uncle Bob observed from behind his desk and discreetly shushed the customers who came in from time to time—all impressed by the sight of the Huggins Quartet in the flesh.

I showed them my lyrics and suggested timidly that on each refrain of "Big Chuck," the four could go solo so listeners could relish the four "wonderful voices" (in fact I'd rewritten the lyrics to cater to them).

"True sharing," I said, as evangelistically as I could.

"We always share," Ronnie said crisply.

They were all dressed in white shirts and black bow ties, and Ronnie's was by far the most expensive. I felt stupid in my jeans and St. Louis Cardinals T-shirt.

They listened politely but I could tell weren't really hearing, even when I dropped the carrot of how much money they'd be making.

"We make a lot of money," Ronnie said even more crisply.

Divine providence arrived in the person of Ronnie's father Harold. Whenever a point had to be made, he would invariably make it right off the bat, and he and my Uncle Bob were not only the local Brahmins, but close friends. "Sounds good, right boys?"

"It's not gospel," Ronnie said.

"Boys, in these times, and damnation I'm sorry to have to say it, you've got to sell the Lord. Shouldn't be that way but it is. The future's comin' and woe's a-comin' to all those who sit by the roadside waiting for salvation. I help sponsor your show and I'm proud to do it, but old Frankenheimer's money could help you expand to an hour."

Ronnie said, "We sing for Jesus. I wouldn't feel right comfortable singing for uh, products of the flesh."

My Uncle Bob jumped in: "Loaves and fishes. Wine and water. Manna from heaven. Jesus fed his flock, and don't you think they didn't appreciate it. Dadblame it, time's a-wastin', Harold."

Mr. Huggins chimed, "The Lord's callin' you, boys, and I don't mean Bob here. This is no time to be self-righteous."

The deal got done, right then and there, and Uncle Bob sold a few quarts of oil in the bargain.

The Quartet quickly recorded their version and it began

running on local radio. Against all my expectations, it became a household item. Each of the singers added their individual voices to the lyrics and one could be forgiven for thinking this was gospel and the Lord was endorsing Frankenheimer Foods.

Big Chuck had insisted on adding a slogan. "Something folks can remember," he said." It's like GE's bullshit slogan, 'Progress is our most important product.' Yeah, right, like they're gonna start calling theirselves 'General Progress.' When my first girl friend dumped me she said 'Our relationship isn't progressing.' Yeah, like I should have turned on a couple more lights. How's that for progressing, honey?"

I racked what passed for my brain and somehow a phrase popped into it: "Where we are ain't where we're at." And I even found a line to rhyme: "Big Chuck's bacon has less fat."

Big Chuck loved it even though I said I didn't know what it meant. "Plus it's bad grammar."

"This is Arkansas. We don't believe in grammar. They'll understand what they want to understand. Whether it's life or politics or selling pork, a good slogan carries you far."

Sure enough, the line became part of Arkansas lingo in a matter of days. When Coach Cross sat us down one day after a game we'd won but where we'd made some errors and played sloppy, he said: "Where we are ain't where we're at."

I looked around at everybody and to a man they looked like they understood exactly what he was saying.

5. THE LINEUP

Coach Cross finally settled on the starting lineup after whipping us into shape with four weeks of daily practices, and that included Sundays. Larry said his father, a Baptist preacher, wasn't so happy about this at first but came around when Coach explained it was "expiation for sins of the past."

We'd understood that as a metaphor, or in George's flowery explanation, "a gauntlet run by the knights before the big joust," but it's possible that Larry's father saw it literally. Anyway he dropped his objection and Larry happily joined us.

FIRST BASE

Billy was our first baseman and he was textbook tall, 6 foot 3 and most of it muscle. Infielders want a first baseman who makes a large target for your throws that have to be done often as not on the run, someone who can reach out and grab it when it's high or wide.

He wasn't the best fielder for ground balls hit in the dirt toward him, but he was competent. Ideally the first baseman should resemble the giant octopus in Jules Verne's 20,000 Leagues Under the Sea that wrapped up Nemo's sub and took it down, but no octopus had shown up at tryouts so Billy had to do. Larry said anyway if he had that many arms he'd be playing with himself full time, and this once we had to hold Billy back from charging him.

Big as he was, he had a lot of home run power, and Coach put him in the #4 cleanup position. You want a good power hitter there because if your first three hitters get on base, the cleanup man can literally clean the bases with a home run and just like that, you have four on the scoreboard.

He was prone to strike out a lot, like many power hitters, but when he made contact the ball was sure to go far and hard and opposing teams had to respect him and worry about him coming up to bat. This element of nerves and distraction can make a big difference in a game and when Billy was focused on playing, he anchored the batting lineup.

Of course, he had a lot of distractions, and to hear him tell it, almost too many to count. He used to say, "You know that expression 'She threw herself at me'? That really happened to yours truly, and not just once."

He resembled the Marlboro Man and liked to pronounce his last name "Aycock" to emphasize both syllables. "I am a cock, boys."

This drove some of his high school teachers nuts, but "That's how it's pronounced, sir," he'd chuckle.

He didn't have to work to be a wise ass, and generally everything he did or said infuriated Larry Bain, who didn't need much provocation by any means from any source. Every other day Billy'd have a story about his latest exploits. "I'm a pussy hound and proud of it. Some day I'll give you a lesson, Bain."

In those days in our dry county of Pulaski you'd have to cross over the county line to buy liquor and Billy was big for his age and always let his beard grow before a booze run. He said he preferred bourbon mixed with coke. He'd drive out into the woods after dark "with a pretty lady" and mix drinks and "make out till the cows came home."

It was a wonder he hadn't knocked up a dozen girls, but then again, none of us ever made it a point to verify his conquests. For sure, he always brought along someone he liked to call a knockout to our games, and invariably ask her to sit on the sideline near first base. There he could look over and see his admirer and if a foul popup came that way, we suspected he'd make the catch look tougher than it was.

"Showboat, that's what he is," Larry seethed. "One day I'd like to see him trip and fall right in the babe's lap." He grinned at the thought. "They'll laugh his pussy hound ass right out of the ballpark."

SECOND BASE

Coach decided to keep Larry at second base even though it

was the position next to Billy and sometimes on a ball hit to his left he had to decide in a split second whether to try and field it himself or let Billy do it, which meant our pitcher would have to run over and cover first base for the throw before the runner arrived, and this was never easy. It was better if Billy could stay on first and let Larry field the ball and make the short flip to first. This meant communication.

Coach said to Larry, "You'll have to make a quick decision on the run. Just yell 'I got it,'" adding, "not 'Go to hell' or something like that."

This got a smile out of both Larry and Billy, which amounted to a triumph of diplomacy in their three-year long feud.

Coach told me that even though that side of our infield crackled with tinderbox tension and if Larry made the wrong decision he was sure to hear about it from Billy, Larry could scoot right and left better than any of us.

Plus he never hesitated to get his uniform dirty by diving in the dirt.

Plus he never flinched when a runner came sliding into second trying to upend him and prevent a double play.

Au contraire. Coach said, "Larry's got a reputation and if a runner's thinking about that it can slow him down. Baseball's a game of inches and this team needs every inch we can get."

Coach was thinking of a game last year when human tank Harvey Harris came barreling into second and knocked Larry on his rear. He dropped the ball and we lost the out.

Larry seethed in the dugout afterward, railing that Harvey had laughed "like he'd just swallowed some strawberry shitcake." It took all we could do to calm him down.

Later in the game another runner came roaring in to second with the same intention as Harvey but this time Larry got off the throw and by some coincidence—not—it happened to hit the runner squarely in the forehead.

While we all gathered around—the runner got up and walked off the field after a few minutes of ministrations, but more crosseyed than before--Larry protested, "Sorry man, I was so shook up from last time, just lost control I guess. You know, in Little League they used to call me scatter-arm."

We shoved him away from the scene of the crime before he set a new Guinness record for hypocrisy. That was what Coach meant. Larry had sent a message.

Big Chuck had put his arm around Larry and said, "Bull in a china shop. Things get broke. Don't mess with a bull, that's the lesson here."

Coach Cross didn't quite agree with that interpretation of events because he took me and Larry aside and said, "We're not here to hurt somebody. This is a game, a sport." But then he thought a little more and said, "That doesn't mean you let a baserunner step all over you."

In fact, since Larry's "errant" throw, we'd noticed a new respect on the part of baserunners.

"When you tag 'em, tag 'em with uh, authority," Coach concluded.

We knew what he meant. If a runner for example tries to steal second base, either I or Larry had to catch the throw from the catcher and tag the runner with the ball before his foot or hand reached the base.

"Nothing says you got to be gentle," was how Larry interpreted Coach's words.

"Well, it doesn't mean you should slip some brass knuckles inside your glove," I cautioned.

"Why not?" he said, and I wasn't sure he was kidding.

Like Coach said, he had a reputation.

SHORTSTOP

Coach Cross had seen me play in Little League and also how I'd sat on the bench the last two years. He said he knew I could pinch hit.

After our second practice where again I'd played various positions, he asked me and Bubba to stay after. He put me out at shortstop and stationed Bubba at first base.

"You've still got time to play 9 holes before sunset," he said. We looked at each other.

"Ready to do what it takes, coach," I said.

He proceeded to hit grounder after grounder my way—straight at me, to the left, to the right, some soft, some as hard as he could hit.

If I missed and the ball got past me, I'd have to go after it. He just stood there waiting for me to retrieve it. Then we'd start over again. Once I'd chased down about a dozen balls, I got extra motivation to catch anything that came my way. There was no lack of adrenaline.

If I bobbled the ball or otherwise didn't hustle to get the ball over to first, he'd yell "Safe!" And three in a row meant "you're running laps."

I didn't want that. I was already winded enough after a long day at work, intense practice and my adventure with Mary Louise the night before.

Shortstop is a tough position because even if the second baseman has as much ground to cover, the throw to first isn't nearly as far. On some balls to his right the shortstop has to roam almost into the outfield, glove the ball and fire a bullet way across the diamond before the speeding runner arrives at first base.

It takes fielding skill and a very strong arm.

I didn't have the strongest arm but I fielded very well and most of all could anticipate where the ball would go when it came off the bat. I studied hitters and knew their tendencies.

Coach kept hitting and hitting and I kept fielding and fielding. If it hadn't gotten dark I believe he would have continued all night.

In fact, he kept on even after I couldn't see the ball myself until it was right on me. He stopped only because he couldn't see well enough to hit the ball.

He said, "Same drill tomorrow, okay?" turned his back and headed home without as much as a "That's all she wrote."

Bubba said, "Guess what? You're the shortstop, buddy."

And so it went practice after practice. At first I didn't quite understand why he singled me out, and didn't believe it when he said "We can't have a captain who just takes the lineup card to the ump."

I believe he wanted an anchor in the infield, a wall. Maybe I wouldn't or couldn't be, but he was damn determined it wouldn't be for lack of trying.

Mary Louise didn't take it at all well that I'd be late for our trysts.

"Does Mr. Cross"--and she pronounced his name with distaste--"realize the position he's put me in? 'Where's your boy friend, Mary?' 'Oh he's busy catching worm burners.' Why don't you dig a ditch while you're at it.'"

I didn't think she knew what a worm burner was, but maybe she'd learned it from her father.

Big Chuck just smiled, put his arm around my shoulder and said, "Party's over, hoss."

THIRD BASE

Randy manned the hot corner at third base like he'd done since we played Little League together. It's called that because even though it's the same ninety feet from home plate as first base, because most batters are righthanded, many more hardhit line drives scream toward third, giving very little time to react.

Best not to think too much about what might be coming your way, and here Randy had both genetics and experience to call on. His last name was Bright and whenever he gave his name to a stranger he'd add, "And I ain't." He didn't like to study or read or write and for awhile it was a mystery to me how he ever learned anything in school.

"Who said I ever did? At one time or another, I flunked every course I had except Phys Ed."

"You passed, didn't you?"

"Yeah, age pass."

"What's that?"

He explained that his wit's end teachers had resorted for a while to adding cupcake questions to their tests. They thought that even Randy could answer these, and ergo they could justify passing him on to the next class the following year.

"Like what cupcake questions?"

"Like, 'Where do we live?' I said, 'Right here,' but the correct answer was 'the state of Arkansas.' So then they added some fill in the blanks. I got one right-- 'My name is blank'--but the others were tough.

"I can imagine."

"So then they asked me 'Randy, when's your birthday?' I said next week, end of June. 'Perfect! You've succeeded in getting a year older. Congratulations, son.'"

"You've got to be kidding."

"Age pass. It's a good system. Sure worked for me."

Once during a Little League game we needed to get the last out and the other team had bases loaded and their big power hitter at bat. He swung and hit a line drive so hard Randy didn't even have time to get his glove up and the ball slammed into his skull, then ricocheted--to me at shortstop where I caught it for the last out, the ball having never touched the ground.

Randy was staggering but didn't go down. His cap though landed way out in left field.

"Call a doctor!" I yelled.

"Shoot, I'm all right," still staggering. He already had a big knot on his head. I came up to him and even though in those days we didn't know about concussion protocol or any other protocols for that matter, I said, "Count to ten."

"Aw, give me something easier." He was kidding I hoped, and anyway except for the knot he seemed none the worse for wear. For years afterward he would say, "Weren't for that ball I'da been a rocket scientist. It knocked out all my smarts."

Sally Bright had run out from the stands to see about her brother and had tears in her eyes from worry, which only made her more attractive. She had just turned 16 and "full flower of youth" didn't do her justice.

I noticed that coaches and players and random spectators, who hadn't seem too worried previously, suddenly surrounded us, all no doubt having developed sincere concerns about Randy's health and heartfelt desires to comfort his panicked sister.

Randy literally got pushed out of the circle and quite rightly said, "She ain't the one got plunked."

He used to say that when they went to a department store, the saleswomen scrammed so they wouldn't have to stand next to her and suffer by comparison, and the salesmen stumbled all over themselves to "help her with her shopping choices."

He said one guy once was so blinded by the light he didn't notice he'd followed her to the lingerie department.

"What can you show me in your range of pantyhose?" she asked him sweetly.

"He got redder than Rudolph the Reindeer," Randy said, "Santa Claus shoulda signed him up."

Whenever I thought of Randy's rise through our state's scholastic system, I remembered why we used to say "Thank God for Mississippi"--the only state that spent less on education than us, or had the least satisfying results.

On the other hand, Randy got his high school diploma and made his way through life and work quite satisfactorily. He explained this simply: "Each year I kept gettin' older."

LEFT FIELD

Big Chuck had moved Mickey Crutchley from third base to left field even though he'd played third base since Little League. Coach Cross kept him there.

Mickey did fine in left field which calls for some speed and quick reactions, both of which he had, because most wellhit balls go to left and also Mickey had a strong arm from all his years as a pitcher.

As a hitter, he was respectable but every now and then you'd hear after a strikeout, "afraid of the ball." Always matter of factly, never really angrily. Mickey batted lower down in the order, just ahead of Spencer if he was pitching and Cletus if he wasn't. In baseball the batting order equates with pecking. If you're hitting well, you don't hit seventh or eighth or ninth.

This was a comedown from Mickey's Little League days when he was a feared power hitter in the #4 cleanup position. He was one of the stars in the league.

He was tall, an early bloomer, and was talked about in awed

tones befitting a hitter who could mash a baseball.

Something happened along the way. For one thing, he wasn't bigger than everybody else.

For the other, no one could really say and never did. Mickey could still hit, and when he connected he had good power, but he struck out a lot and could never hit the best pitchers. Coach would work with him and push him hard to "make more contact," figuring this was the key to getting him back to the stud Mickey of former years.

But to do that, you have to stand in at the plate and be willing to eye the ball no matter how fast it's coming toward you.

And if the element of fear enters in, the concentration veers from hitting to not being hit. You start to "bail out" of the batter's box, lurching backwards. This can be painfully obvious, for all to see, or more subtle as with Mickey, only appearing when the hardest throwing pitchers took the mound.

Another way of describing certain kinds of players is to say, "He doesn't want to get his uniform dirty," meaning self-preservation comes before winning, and other pejorative things besides.

And it's true that Mickey always managed to look neat and well-groomed, even in the infernal summer heat. I admired his tote bag, which was leather and must have cost a few pennies.

When we went once to a barbecue at his parents' place in Sherwood, which was then becoming one of the city's chic places to be, I remember the burgers and dogs he was grilling never seemed to drip too much fat and grease--an incredible phenomenon. As soon as you finished a plate, he or his folks were there to grab it before any crumbs hit the pool deck.

Inside, the family had ornate furniture of various designs, all very expensive and all very polished. When many years later I toured the Chateau at Versailles and saw the elaborate Louis XIV chairs in various salons, all pristine and preserved, I thought of Mickey Crutchley and felt sure the Sun King was spinning in his *tombeau* at the very idea of such comparison.

When I marveled to Mickey that the fabulous mahogany

chairs looked as good as if they'd never been sat on, he said they hadn't.

"If you sit on them, they deteriorate," he said aptly."My mother couldn't stand that." So guests and family would eat at the formica table in the den or at poolside, on some plastic or formica chairs.

In sight of the museum pieces, however. Don't touch, but you can look, as it were.

I noted that at the barbecue, I could never find the mustard.

I don't know if Mickey ever heard the rumors or cared if he did, but I do know that in later life he withstood a lot of hardballs thrown his way and over time got back some way to the star he had been in Little League.

CENTER FIELD

George was my best friend on the team and we had grown up together not far from Levy. We would walk together to the drugstore for ice cream or sundaes in the days before Dairy Queen infringed on the market and became the hangout place simply because it was outside and you could amble around freely, depending if your "luck be a lady tonight," George would sing, and by then some of us had cars.

George had speed, absolutely necessary for a center fielder who had the most ground to cover, and could chase down a fly ball with the best of them. He was great at getting a jump on the ball, anticipating as soon as it left the bat where it was going and how deep. He could charge in and make a diving catch on a blooper before it hit the ground or go back to the fence, leap high and virtually climb the wall to glove a ball.

Once he actually went over the wall. It was in Morrilton and the town hadn't yet got Rockefeller money, so their fence was just head high. George went up with glove high, caught the ball and his momentum carried him right over.

The umpire had run out to center and when George immediately leaped up, brandishing the ball snugly in glove, he yelled "Out!" so loud I thought people in the next county heard it.

The batter was one angry dude. His homer had become just another out. He took his batting helmet and hurled it out of the field and into the dirt flat that served as parking lot.

"That's team equipment, Johnny!" his coach yelled, and after Johnny had kicked a whole pile of dirt on his way back to the dugout, the coach grabbed him by the shoulder and let him have it.

We heard scattered phrases like "sportsmanship" and "equipment" but Johnny was giving back as good as he got, and we were glad to get two more quick outs and finish the game.

Worse for Johnny, the Coach came over with the rest of the players to shake hands after the game, like we always did, and everybody told George in one way or another that it was the damnedest catch they'd ever seen.

All except Johnny, who now was kicking the chainlink fence down the sideline.

George wanted to go over and say something but didn't dare. "He could be like the woman in the James Bond movie," he said, "you know, got a poisoned spike in the toe of her shoe."

What made him feel bad though was when everybody was leaving, George saw the Coach peel out in his truck, leaving a stunned Johnny in his dust, yelling "Hey! Hey!"

"So that's when I figured the coach was his Dad and royally pissed. I mean, I felt bad. What if Johnny never got taken back in the family nest 'cause he didn't respect the equipment? Shoot, maybe I created a homeless bum. Kilroy misses a home run but finds the street."

George batted second behind me and we worked well together. When I got on base he could expertly bunt me over or we'd work a hit and run where as soon as the pitch was delivered, I'd take off running. George was outstanding at making contact with the ball and hitting it somewhere in those situations, especially "where they ain't"--so if the second baseman had vacated his position when I'd started running to cover second base, he could poke the ball right into the vacated space. Then we would both be on base, representing two runs and big trouble for our opponents.

"We play so good between the white lines, let's live there, okay?" he joked to me once, but maybe after all he wasn't joking.

RIGHT FIELD

Anybody who plays right field has to have a strong arm if only to cut off a runner who tries to go from first base to third on a single.

You have to rush in, glove the ball and fire diagonally across the infield to third. If you can throw out the runner it's a huge lift to the defense, whereas if it's too late, the hitter arrives at third and then the big trouble can begin.

In a lot of situations like that, if we had less than 2 outs and the game was tied or close, Coach Cross preferred to tempt the odds and intentionally walk the next batter to set up force outs at every base and home plate, so you only had to step on a base for the force out without tagging the runner, or even set up a double play.

Once Coach did it when we had no outs and it worked out great.

The batter lined to Randy's left at third base, he fired to Cletus who stepped on home plate for the force out, then fired to first to beat the runner. Two outs, just like that. If the ball had been grounded to Randy's right, he could have stepped on third base and fired to Cletus who'd then tag out the oncoming runner, again two quick outs. But that was the best of circumstances.

Most of the time when the bases are loaded with nobody out nothing much good can happen for the defense, and this strategy backfires big time. That is why a good right fielder with a strong arm can change a game for his team.

Once my friend Don and I took the train up to St. Louis to watch the St. Louis Cardinals play the Pittsburgh Pirates and their great right fielder Roberto Clemente. I'll never forget how Clemente caught a fly ball just in front of the outfield wall. His back was almost touching it, meaning he was as far away from home plate as he could be.

There was a runner on third who tagged up and when the ball was caught, raced home at full speed. He like everyone else in the park figured there was no way Clemente could throw him out, as far away as he was.

Wrong. Clemente's amazing throw that seemed faster than a speeding bullet arrived so quickly, the runner actually had time to see it arrive and head back to third base.

When he got there, he looked at his third base coach who was just shaking his head in amazement. What could he say? The throw was out of this world.

Sammy was no Clemente but he had an arm good enough he doubled as one of our starting pitchers. We could always count on him to stay consistent.

A left-handed power hitter, he strolled through life on one register, which didn't mean lackadaisical. The term loosey-goosey was invented for someone like him.

This served him well in the various duck and deer blinds where he spent hours waiting for his luckless prey to come into his hunter's sight. More than once he'd spent the day out in the woods or bottoms before a game, or as he would say in one of the few clever lines we ever heard him speak, "game before the game."

His rifle always hung at the ready on his pickup's rear window, and we made fun of him for being a redneck cliché.

He just chortled, as usual. His hunting boots and vest were piled on the seat so he could never take a passenger, unless the latter didn't mind posing his feet on a pile of ammo sufficient to fight a small war.

He invited me to come along once or twice on one of his hunting trips but between working and one thing or another...anyway I might have been a drag.

He did furnish me more than once with squirrels, all skinned and properly cleaned for the freezer, and it pleased my father greatly to add them to the stock. We spent more than one winter evening feasting on them, though my father remarked as we spit out shotgun pellets that maybe Sammy needed to be told you only needed to kill an animal once.

In the suspense and tension of a close baseball game, Sammy seemed calm as the day is long. One day he told us how he'd spotted a deer and started stalking it. He came to a slough and had no choice but to cross it it if he wanted to corner the deer.

It was deeper than he supposed but he had his thigh-high rubber boots on and anyway, "What's a little water? So I step in and start crossing and the water's getting higher and who should come floatin' along but two big old moccasins."

Mickey, who I could never picture dipping his polyester pants in a muddy slough, piped up: "Holy shit, did you shoot 'em?"

"No time. I said to myself hell, you got a right to this slough just like them and they got to accept it. Just stood there with a fuck-you attitude."

"Laws of access to public property, you had a point. You'd have gone to your grave knowing you were in the right and had the law on your side."

"They did this big circle around me, both of 'em two or three times like this little ballet. Hell I don't know, maybe just checking me out."

"Or consulting the law."

"Then they just went on swimming downstream. I got my ass outta there fast as it could go and bagged that deer."

"That's just it," Billy opined, "they saw your ass and said no way we're biting into that."

We all laughed and Sammy chortled. But we all knew if you had to jump into a slough full of moccasins or go to war or count on someone in a big game, you'd want Sammy by your side.

CATCHER

Cletus wasn't short but he wasn't tall either. Mostly he was stubby and he didn't so much walk as shuffle.

Junction City is 29.8 Miles away and he took advantage of a loophole in league rules that allowed anyone eligible to play who lived within 30 miles.

I asked him once why he made the effort and sacrifice to

play for us when Junction City had a team a stone's throw away from where he lived and he just said cryptically, "I got my reasons." Once I met his father I understood one, but that came later.

No buses went to Junction City--"Why would you waste a bus on us?"--so Cletus drove and each trip was an exercise in suspense and sometimes crisis management as to whether his car would make it.

I told him we'd talked about taking up a collection for a new one--"Trade it in for a bag of peanuts and Dr. Pepper and go from there"--but he rejected it out of hand.

"'56 Chevies are a classic and they're only gonna get more valuable. One of these years I'm gonna sell this sucker for a fortune and you boys are gonna regret dumpin' on it like you do."

"Yeah," I said, "but not all '56 Chevies are created equal. You ought to ask the parts store to fix you up a bed. This junk heap is going to end its days as a terrarium."

Cletus was used to these jibes and they rolled off him like water off a mallard's back.

He could squat behind the plate for hours and without getting tired and even though it's possible he never read a book straight through in his life--"Hey, smart guy," he said once to George, "answer me this: why should I?" and George said, "To give a proper answer would take a book, and like he just said, he wouldn't read it, so what's the point?"--he studied hitters and for a catcher, besides having a strong arm to throw out would-be base stealers, that is desirable trait #1.

A catcher has got to work with the pitcher to decide what kind of pitch to throw, for example fastball or curve or slider, and when, and where--inside or outside the plate, high or low. It's a strategy duel that goes on throughout the game, and Cletus was very good at keeping hitters guessing and off balance and never able to "sit on a pitch," e. g. ignore other pitches and wait for a fastball, which because you're expecting it, becomes easier to hit.

Coach Cross knew Cletus had been our catcher for a while

but he decided to sit him down with me and get his "philosophy about the tools of ignorance."

Cletus looked dumbfounded, so Coach explained.

"The great Bill Dickey, greatest catcher of all time and from right here in Arkansas, called your face mask and knee pads and chest protector tools of ignorance because you have to be stupid to play a position where you need protection like that. Which is ironic because the catcher's got to be the smartest man on the field."

"Yessir. I always say catching is 150% mental."

"Right...so, tell me how you call a game."

"Well sir, that's a long story."

"We're not going anywhere. You going anywhere, Tom?"

"No sir." I'd just been elected captain by my teammates and Coach wanted me to sit in on 1-on-1's like this.

"In my own words?"

"Tell it like it is, in your own words."

"Well sir, let's say this sumbitch comes up and he's a good fastball hitter. I know it 'cause I've seen him before or else he hit one good his first time up. I'm gonna call for a curve till he proves to me he can hit it."

"Right."

"Now if he hits it as good as he did the fastball, I got to start gettin' in his head. You know, talkin' a lot of BS about him and their team or the price of tea in China--anything to get his mind off hittn' that little round baseball. If that don't work I might complain to the ump he's standin' too close to the plate, even if he's not. That really ticks 'em off and see, then he's thinkin' about me."

"And what do you do if he gives back as good or better? Some guys in this league like Harvey Harris can't be intimidated."

"Yeah," I said, "Harvey can't think."

"Well, sometimes it happens that a pitch gets away from Spencer or another one of our guys. It comes in real tight like it's fixin' to rearrange their collarbone."

"Coincidence, right?"

"Yessir. And then that sumbitch don't act so cocky. I call it a 'purpose pitch.' I want to get 'em so confused they don't know whether they're comin' or goin'. You know, like politicians."

"If they hit like politicians, I'll be satisfied. All right, now tell me. Who on this roster could we mould into a relief pitcher?"

Cletus drew a blank and so did I.

"Bobby?"

"They'll eat him for lunch. And still have an appetite."

Coach looked at me. "They'll stampede to the plate."

"All right. Well, at least we've got a catcher." Looking at Cletus.

"Shoot Coach, ain't nobody else on this team ignorant enough."

THE BENCH

Bubba Beasley was just good enough to fill in at every position except catcher but not good enough to start at any of them, a textbook definition of "utility player."

He liked that term--"Utility means useful, and I am. Makes up for all the splinters that get stuck in my butt" warming the bench.

We played a lot of golf our first two years when I wasn't starting and we didn't much care if the round in the heat of summer wore us down because all we had to do during the games was man the first base side coaching box, where your job is to watch a base hit and tell the charging runner whether or not he should continue toward second base.

And if the runner holds at first, your job is to monitor how far he leads off the base before each pitch, and alert him to get back to the base if the pitcher tries a pickoff throw.

If your Coach, coaching in the third base coaching box, gives a sign to steal, you try to ensure that the runner has understood the signal. A task easier said than done, as you don't want to give anything away to the opposing first baseman.

Bubba got into Big Chuck's doghouse more than once when

he got too slow on the uptake, shouting "Back!" too late and watching our runner get picked off right before his eyes--and earning Big Chuck's wrath shouted out for everyone in the stadium to hear.

Big Chuck asked me once, "Is he a zombie or just act like one?"

In retrospect, based on his later career, I think Bubba's mind simply had a tendency to wander elsewhere, to other kinds of fields--not girls, who seemed at that time to paralyze him quicker than jivaro juice. He told me years afterward how much he'd learned from being a utility player."You can sit there game after game just watching and then suddenly there you are on the field with the game on the line, and you've got to keep your cool and play good. It's like the stock market, see. Everything's rolling along fine and then boom, panic. You didn't think it would happen but it is and you're deep in the shit and you'd damn well better make the right decision or lose big time.

"Yeah, utility player. Real useful, I can tell you that."

#

Bobby I think always suspected that he made our team because of his brother George, and he may have been right. But he was a good player, and fast. It was just that he could not compete in any athletic department with his older sibling. He could play well and Coach tried to get him playing time as often as possible.

If we had a big lead, he was sure to substitute for someone in the outfield and even occasionally infield, at third base for Randy. If it was a close game he rarely played, and here we had the problem many teams do where if you do not groom your players to play when the stakes are high, they can't habituate themselves to intense competition.

So instead of relaxing, they start thinking about all the bad things that can happen. That happened with Bobby, and it didn't help that his brother didn't cut him any slack. But that was the way it was.

I kind of thought that was the way he was as well, and one time he confirmed it.

"I don't mind living in the shade. Cooler, you know." He meant temperature-wise. Bobby would never be cool and never wanted to be.

He was a sub, and as George paraphrased one day from some poem, "They also serve who sit and wait."

HITTING

The game of baseball revolves around the duel between hitter and pitcher, and the majority of times the pitcher wins. Any batting average over .300 is considered excellent, and to reach .400...well, it has not been done in major league baseball since the great Ted Williams did it in 1941, and one wonders if it will ever be done again.

We had several good hitters on the Packers, and Coach hoped that by practicing us day after day and asking the pitchers to "not take it easy on them," he could make us even better. He gave us a speech about hitting and he repeated it more than once, so I remember it almost down to the last syllable.

No one who hasn't played the game of baseball, he said, can ever imagine what it's like to stand 60 feet, 6 inches from home plate and try to hit a small round baseball coming toward you at a speed that routinely approaches 100 miles an hour.

You notice it when you walk to the plate. Who's waiting? The catcher and umpire. These gentlemen are safeguarded by big styrofoam chest protectors and solid metal masks to prevent their teeth from being knocked out.

"You still feel it pretty good, Coach," Cletus interrupted, "and it ain't as soft as your girl friend's lipstick."

You however, the batter, do not have the benefit of this gear. After too many decades of indifference, organized baseball finally required hitters to wear plastic batting helmets to protect their heads. But as any luckless hitter who's been struck on one of these helmets can tell you, they can prevent a concussion but not a significant shakeup of your brains. You will still feel the shock.

A couple of years before, Gerry and the Pacemakers had had a hit version of "You'll Never Walk Alone," and everyone was humming it.

Coach said a bit grimly, in baseball this "never" doesn't apply. You've got to walk alone up to that plate. Once there, the first challenge is simply this: stand there without flinching or bailing out, i.e. stepping back from the plate as the ball arrives. If the ball goes astray--and it frequently does, because the pitcher is only human or in the case of Cletus' "purpose pitch," somewhat inhuman if the purpose is to actually "bean" the batter if he's not quick and agile enough to jump out of the way--the hitter becomes the hit, and there goes the comfort of a healthy elbow or rib or leg, and alas, higher portions of the anatomy.

No getting around it, to hit a baseball you've first got to get over the fear factor of a projectile blazing at you that can cause serious bodily harm.

If you can't deal with it, you can't play. If you can stand in and face said projectile, now comes the task of hitting it, but more than that--hitting it "where they ain't.'"

This is about one thousand times easier said than done.

There are times when hitters get in such a groove they can hit even the best pitchers, and those pitchers who aren't get lit up like a firecracker, no matter what they throw--times where they start to think they could sprinkle the ball with invisibility powder and they'd still hit it.

No one can explain why those games happen, or why they don't. We played doubleheaders where we might win the first game in a laugher, 15-1, then in the second game squeeze through by a score of 2-1. Maybe the second pitcher was just better, or maybe we had used up all our hits in the laugher.

In hitting, the humiliation factor figures strongly. You're mano à mano against the pitcher and everyone can see your success or failure in full view.

Once you strike out, you must take the long walk back to the dugout while behind you the opposing infielders throw the ball around the infield and sometimes, people in the stands mock and ridicule you. Thankfully there's the dugout where you can take temporary refuge. Nothing else for it but to swallow your pride, accept your failure and hope to do better next time.

Though once Larry found a way to salve his ego somewhat. A side-armed pitcher from Conway had made him look silly and struck him out four times in a row. "He can't hit that boy to save his life," Coach said. Four times Larry had to shuffle back to the dugout, knowing that each time he'd reinforced the spectators' belief that he was a pathetic excuse for a baseball player. Larry couldn't fistfight them because even he had to admit that the evidence was right before their eyes. The ballpark in Conway happened to be right next to some woods and as soon as we made the last out--yep, another Larry strikeout--he took his bat and just marched into the woods and started banging it against trees, brush, rocks, anything that stood in his way.

"Good thing he doesn't have an axe," Coach said.

Billy chuckled, "Paul Bunyan he ain't."

As I rolled out of the parking lot, in the rear view mirror I spotted him heading out of the woods toward his car, carrying a splintered stick that used to be his bat.

He still looked pissed as all get out, and I speeded up so as to leave the road free--I felt sorry for any stray dog, possum or armadillo that might cross in his path, and later we heard he had in fact seen a deer and tried to run it down. The deer bounded off the road and Larry actually swerved off the route and chased it toward the woods and didn't stop till he'd run into a tree. Happily the deer escaped scotfree. Larry dented the hell out of his front fender but he said later, "I felt better. Next time I'll get that sumbitch". I hoped he meant the pitcher who'd whiffed him, not the deer.

PITCHING

The pitcher must throw toward the strike zone, a space measured in height from the top the batter's shoulders to his knees, and in width by the home plate.

Anything within this zone can be hit and hit well by the batter, but a pitch which hits the edges of the zone, and with sufficient force or movement on the ball, obviously poses more difficulty for the batter, so the goal of a good pitcher is to hit these spots.

A pitcher who for example can consistently hit the knee-high outside corner of the plate with a hard fastball will succeed most of the time. However, this also is about one thousand times easier said than done.

Coach said over and over, "Pitching is 90% of the game," and nobody disagreed.

Randy would take this in and look like he was thinking hard, and since this was an unusual sight to see, I asked him what he was thinking about, if indeed he was thinking.

"What's the other 10%?"

"Ask Coach." So one day after Coach had repeated the mantra, Randy piped up with his question and Coach said, "Well I think you all know without me having to tell you."

We nodded, all except Randy, but I wasn't sure any more than anybody, and Randy looked lost.

Coach saw that we looked clueless, and with a look of exasperation, he gave us the answer. "Pitching!"

With which he turned on his heel and left us to, as they say, ponder.

"That don't make no sense at all," Randy said. "It's not like we go out there and play with ourselves. Except Aycock."

While the mystery hung in the air unresolved, Coach named Spencer our #1 starter. He didn't have the best fastball or curveball or slider, but he could throw them all and spot them where he wanted--excellent control--and each one had an outstandingly effective and rare feature, which was that each one confounded the laws of physics.

That is, neither Spencer nor our catcher Cletus nor perhaps the gods in heaven could predict precisely what the ball would do.

"I call it, Spencer's Uncertainty Principle," he said.

A fastball is normally straight and hard, but Spencer's might tail off suddenly as it arrived at the plate, so if the batter had timed his swing perfectly to connect with the meat of the bat, just like that the ball hit the end and a line drive to center turned into a weak grounder tapped toward second base.

Spencer's curve did curve all right, but sometimes it unaccountably dipped, and even his slider wiggled a little.

In short, Spencer's repertoire could create as much fog and confusion as he seemed to move through in life.

For second and third starters we had Sammy Hobbs and Mickey Crutchley. Sammy had good stuff, an outstanding curveball and was very reliable--we could count on him to give us six solid innings minimum. He rarely got pummeled and he usually kept us in the game. That was big.

Mickey was the weakest of our pitchers because he could not overpower hitters. He aimed to hit the corners of the plate and if he didn't, if he was off, he could get hit and sometimes hit big.

Mickey tried experimenting with a knuckleball, and if he'd succeeded he'd have been formidable, possibly one of the best pitchers around. But few pitchers can master it, and he said ruefully, "I'm too straight."

He was making an excuse, because personality doesn't count when it comes to a knuckleball, just a certain talent from the gods and few people are able to consistently wrap their knuckles around the ball and send it floating toward home plate with adequate speed.

If you've thrown it right, the ball doesn't spin at all, but remains stationary and something about this and wind resistance causes it to dip and swerve in a completely arbitrary fashion.

Spencer said he was working on a treatise to explain the knuckleball, but between life and our games and his smoking habits, he never got around to finishing it.

The switch hitter Mickey Mantle once struck out four times against a righthanded knuckleball pitcher, and became so frustrated he batted righthanded in his last at-bat. To no effect, as he went down swinging again.

The only knuckleballer we ever faced pitched one year for Sheridan, and we all looked pretty futile, but Mickey Crutchley flailed away so badly, hitting nothing but air, that the local reporter took a picture and splayed it across the front page of their sports section with a caption, "CLUELESS AND HELPLESS."

Mickey was incensed."I'm not clueless. Can you imagine what this could do to my future career? I'm going to sue these people for defamation."

He was already angling to be a lawyer, and even took steps to contact a local attorney in Sheridan, but finally he got convinced that the game was a public affair and by playing he became a public figure, plus his lawsuit would only draw unwelcome attention, etc. All good legal and common sensical arguments that he explained to us in cumbersome detail.

"I learned a lot from the experience," he said. "Discovery, that's the legal term, and we never got that far but I discovered some things."

"Some day," I said, "maybe you'll thank those knuckleballs."

"Yeah."

#

We had never had and didn't have now, a good relief pitcher. In fact none of the teams in our league had a good one. Belleville, the defending state champions, had a deep and solid pitching staff and could use their best pitcher, Jim Bunch, in relief. It gave them an immense advantage and Coach wanted the same, a relief pitcher who could come in and put out fires.

But where could we find one?

6. MOSES SAVES

Coach Cross explained: "Boys, for many years in the major leagues there was no such thing as a relief pitcher. That's why Cy Young won over 500 games in his career and no one has come close since. In the early days you stayed in till your arm fell off.

"Then somebody somewhere had a bright idea. It's the ninth inning, we've got a lead, we've got to hang on but our pitcher's running out of gas and they've got him figured out. Why not bring in somebody else? He's going to throw one inning if he does the job and so has no need to pace himself. He can pitch his guts out, give it everything he's got and then some."

Coach cited as a textbook example Ryne Duren, the New York Yankee reliever. He would never make a starting pitcher because he couldn't keep up the pace beyond three innings. But he had just enough control over an inning or two to dominate batters, because he had the fastest fastball in the game.

What's more, he had a very effective warmup tactic. He'd be throwing bullets to the catcher and suddenly one would fly way up and over and not stop till it hit the screen in front of the stands. About as wild a pitch as you could ever imagine.

"He did that to scare batters," Coach said. "He's throwing 100 miles an hour and when you step up to that plate you're maybe thinking, what if one of those hits me? Coach will be happy 'cause I get a free trip to first base--IF I can get up off the ground. Yeah, if you're shaking in your cleats you're not going to hit a ball very far, IF you hit it. I've seen some batters face Duren and just make three quick swings, three strikes and they're out. Back in the dugout where it's safe.

"We need somebody like that."

We all thought that unless Arkansas' answer to Ryne Duren was hiding under a rock, Coach was just whistling in the wind.

But then one day he turned over a rock and changed us and Dogtown for the good.

I was busy dealing with the next installment of Mrs. Morley's complaint. Even if she had vented a sackful of frustration and cussing about the "red-necked peckerwood" delivery boy to Franklin, she felt it necessary to repeat everything to me. The peckerwood's offense had been to leave her meat delivery on her doorstep instead of waiting for her to answer the doorbell.

"I'm always home and available for appointments except when I do my toilette." She pronounced it like that, "twalette," to emphasize she was not referring to a simple bodily function.

"Making myself presentable and prepared for whatever the Lord wills the day to bring. DO you understand?"

The way the question was posed meant there could be only one answer, and I assured her I did.

I did not dare ask a logical followup, which was how much time did Mrs. Morley spend on her toilette, or why she couldn't hear the doorbell from inside her bathroom.

Apparently Franklin had posed questions, and now he came in for a roasting as well, for being insufficiently attentive to an elderly lady's necessities in the matter of preparation for a day's events. "I'll wager he's snot-nosed. Is he snot-nosed, Tom? Just a young whippersnapper who did not get properly weaned. Do not let me deal with him any more till he's lost his training wheels."

Mrs. Morley had jumbled so many metaphors I didn't quite know how to respond, but Coach Cross came in and I was saved by the bell.

"I have to go, Mrs. Morley, a really really important meeting with Coach and Mr. Frankenheimer."

"My health will not permit me to come watch one of your games Tom, but this town does not need another year of jackasses. That's what my circle of friends tell me, you all have resembled nothing more than jackasses. I have tried to get this message across many times to Frankenheimer."

"We're taking steps to change things, Mrs. Morley. That's what this meeting is all about."

"Big steps. Don't tip-toe."

"Yes m'am."

"You call me back now, hear?"

#

I went into Big Chuck's office. Coach had taken a seat across the desk our sponsor was already pounding on.

"Dammit Henry, we got to do something. Light a fire under them! I haven't seen such a lifeless bunch since…last year. And the season hasn't even started! Old Joe Flynn at the quarry works has a winning team every year. Every August he holds a picnic on the Arkansas River. Watermelons, a barrel of cokes, square dancing, the works. And me, I'm sitting home with a goddamn BLT."

"I need a relief pitcher."

"Put Tom in there."

"You want a son-in-law with a bum elbow?"

"Come to think of it, no. He'll need a strong arm to sign Mary Louise's charge accounts."

Big Chuck's intercom blinked.

"Yeah?"

The secretary announced "Mr. Carson is here, sir."

"Caved in, huh? Wants to smoke the peace pipe. Well, keep his butt waiting."

Coach Cross had gotten up and moved over to the window, staring outside. I got a sense he had something on his mind and it wasn't the price of ham. That he wanted to choose his words carefully because of what he had to say next.

"I saw a kid the other day with the best fastball for his age I've ever seen."

"Well suit him up."

"He lives on Division Street."

I saw Big Chuck clamp down hard on his cigar, weighing the import of this fact. Division was a street in a neighborhood that was in the "colored community."

"I sounded out Bob Habiner about him. He said as Legion commissioner he couldn't say yes and he couldn't say no.

92

Speaking for himself and what he was taught to believe, he said he'd say no."

"Others will too."

"It has to happen sometime."

"But do we have to be first?"

Coach Cross shrugged. Big Chuck didn't hesitate long and I and a lot of other folks eventually appreciated what he said next.

"Hell, I don't care if he eats Sam Carson's bacon. If he can help us win, get him."

Coach Cross turned to me.

"Do you know what we're talking about?"

"I think so." Big Chuck said, "Tell us." I thought a minute, then said, "Helping the team." That seemed to satisfy both of them. Big Chuck leaned back in his huge swivel chair.

"Goddammit, I went up to Missouri the other day and saw a Charolais white as a redneck's belly chompin' grass with a couple of Black Angus. They didn't fight or rumble or hell, even much notice each other. Now why in hell can't humans get along like beef bulls?"

"You got me."

"What's the boy's name?"

"Moses."

"Hallelujah, 'cause this team needs savin'." He got up to go enjoy Sam Carson's surrender. "Go on, get it done, sooner the better."

"I've got to call Mrs. Morley," I said.

"Let Franklin do it."

Sure enough, when I got back that afternoon, Franklin looked like he'd been put through one of our grinders and turned into chopped beef.

"What happened?" I asked with fake innocence.

"Go to hell, " he said.

#

When we got in my car, Coach Cross noticed the tigertail

hanging from the rearview mirror. "Interesting."

"A gift from Mary Louise."

"Have you two set a date?"

"No sir. If you want to know the truth, I'd like to take it slower. Not rush into anything."

"That's not Mary Louise's way."

"No sir."

We drove through Levy and I saw Joe Wright working at the gas pumps, meaning it was a slow day in the garage. I was sure my Uncle Bob was holding court inside, regulating the civic problems of the day, and couldn't be disturbed by customers needing a fill up.

I wondered what Joe would think about our foray into his neighborhood.

We crossed over Main Street and headed due east. We passed Lindy's Barbecue, a small roadside joint with a woodfire grill in the back.

"Best barbecue in town," I said.

"Don't I know it. I live off their ribs."

The houses got smaller and more rundown, the streets more rutted and less spic and span, the lawns more patchy, and soon we were on Division Street.

"Ever been in this part of town?"

"Not really, no sir." The way led over railroad tracks--the line toward Memphis-- toward a weed-choked sandlot baseball field. A group of black players were playing a pickup game. Coach Cross led me over to a decrepit chickenwire edifice serving as a backstop.

"This is what I wanted you to see."

The players noticed our arrival but didn't leave off their game. We watched the action. The pitcher was warming up with tosses to the catcher.

"Pitcher's got a good arm," I said.

"He's taking it easy. You're not seeing his best stuff. Control? He can hit the hind end of a flea."

A batter stepped up to the plate and yelled out, "Don't give me that bazooka action now."

Coach said, "A lot of changes are taking place in our society, Tom. In the long run, they're for the best."

Mose delivered a pitch. The batter swung, hit a grounder to the second baseman who scooped up and tossed to first.

I thought Mose's fastball was good but nothing special. I did notice though that when he gave up a hit and the other team threatened to score, he turned it up a notch and got an out. That was a good sign. It meant he wasn't just a thrower but a thinking man's pitcher.

When the teams left the field with a lot of good-natured ribbing and joshing, we could see they were trying hard not to make us seem any more conspicuous than we already were. Only Mose came over. He shook hands with Coach.

"You're gettin' to be a regular customer."

"Y'all are the best show in town, next to watching Tom's team play. Mose Jones."

"Hi."

"How you doin'."

"How about chunking a few to Tom?"

"Sure thing, but...we don't got a catcher's mitt."

"I brought my glove," I assured him.

He looked a little dubious and I heard a few snickers from the players who had stayed around. "Let's see what kind of stuff he's got," Coach said.

I squatted behind home plate, which actually wasn't a plate at all but a wooden diamond-shaped plank buried in the dirt.

"Cut it myself," Mose said, maybe reading my thoughts. "Had to get the size just right."

Coach Cross stood to the side and a few of the other players watched.

"Show us your stuff," Coach said. Mose had just been lobbing warmups to me. One of the players said, "Give him that bazooka action, brother."

"That what you call a fastball?" I joked.

The player nodded yes. "Faster'n a speeding bullet."

"So he's Superman? I've caught a few fastballs in my time."

Coach Cross was looking on with an air of wry amusement. I

yelled out to Mose: "Bring it." The player said "Brother, your time's 'bout to change."

Mose wound up and his bazooka fastball came blistering in. I just had enough split-second to get my glove up, but the ball literally blasted it out of my hand and sent it flying behind me. The players whooped it up.

Mose said, "You all right?"

"I'll let you know when I can feel my hand."

Coach Cross looked happy and satisfied. "He'll make a hell of a relief pitcher."

Mose threw a few more and I hung on to the ball each time, but wished I'd had a catcher's mitt. They'd been fabricated for times like this and pitchers like Mose, and it was exciting to think he might join our team--no matter what we might encounter.

We walked with him to his home and while Coach talked with his mother Mrs. Jones, a very dignified and it seemed to me, lady of great fortitude, who wanted only the best for her son but had no illusions about the road he might be taking if she let him play with us.

Mose fired some balls at a target he'd painted on a hulking tool shed. He had a handful of tattered baseballs. "Bet I've thrown a million at that thing." I noticed that he hit it square about 80% of the time.

"I'll give you a game target." I picked up a stick to use for a bat and moved over to the target.

Coach Cross was sitting on the back porch of Mose's house and I heard him say "Fans'll be leery of him at first. Standoffish, some of them. If he pitches like I know he can, they'll come around."

"And the country towns? I know what they can be like. I'm afraid for him."

"Mrs. Jones, it's been years since Central High. We've buried a lot of prejudice since then."

"Not enough."

I stood beside the target as if it were home plate, waving the stick bat. "Let's see a heater." Mose fired a fastball smack into the target, whooshing it past me.

"Not too shabby. You got a curve?"

"Never needed one."

That would pose a problem at some point if he kept playing organized baseball. But at the speed he threw, I thought yeah, he might not need anything but his fastball. I went to pick up the baseball and throw it back.

Mrs. Jones was saying, "He was only four when his father died. I raised him myself. He's my last. The others have drifted off. They're good boys, but they've got wildness in 'em. They don't have the anchors we used to have.

"He plays on that sandlot from dawn to dark. I used to praise the Lord he made the sun go down, so I could have my boy back. I couldn't stop him if I wanted to. He's too much in love with baseball."

I took my stance beside the target, waving the stick bat. The ball wasn't going to go anywhere but I wanted to see if I could make contact with his very best fastball. "All right, gimme a bazooka. Your best stuff."

I rarely struck out and even with the fastest pitchers in our league I was able to make contact with the ball and send it somewhere.

Mose wound up and fired a bullet. I saw it coming and had time to swing, but by then the ball had banged into the woodshed target like a cannonshot. This was a different breed of fastball and for a brief second I felt sorry for opposing hitters who would have to face Mose, but the sentiment didn't last.

"Welcome to the team," I said.

7. OCCUPIED TERRITORY

The boys from Dogtown were all sleeping like babies—which they had been not long ago—one night in September when jeeps came rumbling down from Camp Robinson Road.

Bill Bowers was older than us and still awake that night, having just finished watching "Casablanca" for the first time on the Late Show.

"You know me, world class cynic," Bill recounted, "but I was about to cry some crocodile tears when Rick let her go off with her husband, even if the guy was the hero to end all Resistance heroes. Hell, he could even sing the Marseillaise without an accent. Then I hear this noise on Camp Robinson. You know how that road was then. They folded it up at dark to let the terrapins cross in peace.

"I look out the window and see these Army jeeps loaded with soldier boys in combat helmets and rifles with bayonets and I'm thinking, either I've fallen asleep and I'm dreaming how Rick joins the war with Captain Renault and here they are heading off to liberate Paris, or our President's decided to occupy Little Rock.

"Think about that. Here's Ike and the last time he's really at war he's in a schoolhouse in Reims France telling some German generals if they don't sign on the dotted line he'll let the Russians enter Berlin all by their lonesomes and how do you like them apples, boys? 'Heil Ike' or find yourself dreaming about Borscht, assuming you can unfreeze your tongue out there in the Siberian gulag.

"Now here he is President of the US of A, playing a lot of golf in Palm Springs and every now and then making a decision but not too often 'cause this is the fifties and not much is happening except Leave It to Beaver and some vinyl furniture rolling off assembly lines for the greater glory of bad vintage fashions.

"Except then some hick governor decides he ain't going to

obey the Supreme Court 'cause darn it, rumors are there just might be violence if these outstanding young black teenagers walk into a schoolroom. So he calls out the National Guard to guard against rumors.

"And note well ladies and gentlemen, the Guard aren't there to escort the black students inside. It's to keep them outside where the mobs can yell and spit on them, these tender housewives and their flattop progeny who've just come from a long night stealing hubcaps."

I had never heard Bill so wound up and motormouth angry. "Ike tries to negotiate with the hick governor, but when that doesn't work because said governor knows he can write his own election ticket now for years and years, until he gets tired of robbing the state till and finds himself a new young sexy wife who's going to take all the minding he can manage— which won't be enough by a long shot—Ike does what he does best, and sends in the real troops.

"101st Airborne Division, with helmets and bayonets and everything, and all of a sudden the flattops yell their insults from a safe distance. And records show not a one of these flattops ever challenges a soldier boy to duke it out. Spit on the ground, maybe. Yeah. That puts the fear in a couple worms and Goddam, we made a point didn't we Bubba?"

Bill popped a beer. His tirade had been brought on after an afternoon when he'd been covering a state assembly session and some one of the state's legislative finest had railed against "outside agitators."

"Yeah, right," Bill said, "that means anyone who thinks 100 years of segregation ought to end."

He'd invited me to take a ride. It was late summer after our first losing season and school hadn't started yet.

"Faubus brought it on," Bill said, referring to our hick governor by name. "Wasn't for him, we wouldn't be known around the world as mad dog racists chunking gobs of spit on 9 black kids."

Bill meant of course the 9 black students chosen by Mrs. Daisy Bates, head of the NAACP, to integrate Little Rock's

Central High School.

"The white kids would have bitched and moaned but ended up just treating them like the usual zitfaced goofball outsiders, of which yours truly is an alumnus. You know, misfits and losers in the eyes of those paragons in letter jackets with their snotty girl friends.

"When you call out the National Guard and say they're here to protect against violence, you're raising smoke and right quick you've got a fire. And fires get out of control.

"Not to mention that your fire has been outlawed by the Supreme Court."

In fact Bill had driven over to the scene of the crime, as it were. He parked at a curb not far from the school's main entrance. It was quiet now. Nobody around but us. "Like we're really going to see an eager student coming to start the school year a couple days early." He offered me a beer and I took a few sips even though I knew I was inviting trouble if the cops caught sight. But they were "off on a highspeed chase after donuts," Bill theorized.

They'd been ineffectual in those days of September, and the Governor controlled the National Guard, so Eisenhower used the power of the federal government and the Army to enforce the Constitution.

Bill said, "I went over here a couple of times to see what it was like. Here they'd come, these 9 students, arriving in an escort of federal troops while an assortment of hoods, scuzzballs and harpies shouted insults. I mean, it was all they could do to string together a subject and verb. I wouldn't let a single one of them sit on my sofa and if by some cruel twist of fate they did, I'd need some of that stuff your Dad used to use to wash the oil and grease off his concrete. Superior race my shriveled ass."

"Look," I said, "we've come a ways since then."

"You haven't noticed that Faubus keeps getting reelected? Almost twelve years now he's been governor."

We stared at the elegant stairsteps of the school entrance. It looked very peaceful. "Peaceful now," Bill said. "But only because Ike and Daisy Bates and the Arkansas Gazette and some other people stood up to Faubus. I didn't have the guts. I just stood and watched."

"Hey," I said "in those days you couldn't walk so good. Not even sure you could stand."

"Not an excuse. Recognizing injustice isn't enough. It's some. But not enough."

8. OPENING NIGHT

Everybody has his own ritual before a game, and Opening Day just magnifies the nerves that the ritual is meant to control. They always started kicking in for me late in the afternoon.

This year for our first game we were playing a team sponsored by Derks Construction. We liked to call them Jerks Construction, but they'd beaten us 6 times in a row and their catcher, Harvey Harris, gave us a lot of shit, me in particular.

After the last game last year where they whomped us in humiliating fashion, he'd said beating us "didn't take no more effort than a good fart."

Winners can say what they want, and you want to avoid humiliation, but Coach Cross always chewed us out royally for negative thinking.

"Nerves can be a good sign, because they mean you want to play your best. And that's what I want. Nothing less. Give it everything you've got."

Coach said his main preparation before a game was washing off the dirt, grime and grease he'd picked up that day at MoPac railroad, working on the rolling stock at the yard, one of the biggest if not biggest in the USA. He said it took a while and a load of Ajax, and sometimes it seemed a hopeless task.

"Like us?" I asked.

Cletus said he had to work extra, like a dog, to finish all his daily work at his father's lumberyard. That was the only way he could convince his father to let him go off and drive to Dogtown and play a frivolous game.

"Every time I drive off, he's watching me and I can see him thinking, 'This time's the last.' So the next day I work even harder."

Spencer used to arrive late for games, but he said this year he'd be working on an "innovative agricultural project" for Mr. Snookums, and could tell by the position of the sun what time he'd have to leave for the ballpark.

He said this year he meant to relax by "smoking a doobie."

"What's a doobie," I asked.

He said, "You'll know one day, in the course of time and tide."

Mose said he would spend an hour firing his tattered old baseballs at the target painted on the side of his backyard shed —bullet after bullet directly onto the target.

"I like to hear 'em hittin' the shed. Music to my ears, you know. Bang, bang, bang!" He added, "Mama's ears like it better when game time comes round."

Me, I liked to work on my bat. Each game I would unwrap the tape from the handle and then rewrap it, heft it, swing it once, twice for the feel and grip, balance it in my hands. The idea with tape is to make the grip firmer and easier.

Another reason: superstition. The day I stopped might be the day I couldn't get a hit to save my life. Don't mess with God or the Devil. That's baseball.

When I arrived the sun was setting. The field looked crisp, curried, the grass deep lush green, the lime boundaries firm and white as newfallen snow. The groundskeeper had done a good job, though later I learned that Coach Cross had come by early and given a few pointers.

I hung around, just walking a little to keep myself on an even keel. Little by little, then by a lot, spectators and players arrived. At game time the stands were packed. We had a concession stand calliope and it was jingling madly. I saw the press box had three reporters, up one from last year, and saw Bill Bowers scribbling on a note sheet.

Mose hadn't arrived yet and Coach Cross was talking to the coach of Derks Construction's team. They were league champs last year and looked to be tough again this year. Harvey Harris looked like he'd put on some bulk, which meant he'd be slower and easier to throw out at first base, assuming he didn't hit the ball a country mile where no one could catch it.

Coach Cross had told me he wanted to alert the Derks team to our new player and for me to do the same for our guys. He said he didn't want to throw Mose into the fire during the opening game when so many people and press were present, but you could never tell what fate might have in store. And anyway he said, "Let's give fate some guidance."

So I called the team together and broke the news.

"His name's Moses but he goes by Mose."

"Wow," Cletus said, "bet he had to think hard for that one."

"If you say so, Clete." He didn't appreciate that, but I wanted to cut that kind of talk off at the pass, right now if not sooner.

"He's a real nice guy. Let's give him a chance, okay. I think he can really help this team."

"What position does he play," Billy asked, "'cause first base is taken."

"Coach wants him in the bullpen."

"We ain't got no bullpen," Cletus objected.

"We do now. We need a stopper."

"Him and my ass." Cletus looked so upset he turned his back and moved away a few paces. I looked past him and saw Mose in the distance, walking up the long road toward the field.

Cletus saw him too.

Coach Cross came over and didn't waste a single second on niceties. He looked as serious as I'd ever seen him.

"Boys, you see those white lines out there?"

He meant the soft white chalk powder that's laid out from a small striper wheelbarrow very carefully before each game. At the plate a rectangle on each side marks the box where a batter is obliged to stand. It gets erased during the game when batters kick it every which way as they try to dig their spikes into the dirt and get a good solid stance.

Down the left and right field lines, stretching from the plate to the outfield fence, the lines mark the boundaries of the game. Any ball hit within is fair, outside is foul and not in play.

Sometimes a batted ball will land directly on the chalk line and kick up the dusty powder, which tells the umpire and everybody else that it's a fair ball and has to be fielded.

Coach continued, "I used to lay out those lines and who

knows, maybe one day when I'm retired and looking for some valuable work I can still do, I'll take it up again.

"It's a different world inside those lines. Inside those white lines 4 balls is a walk and 3 strikes you're out. You've got rules and everybody has to respect them, bar none. Not like the real world outside where too many people don't play by the rules. Remember that.

"And remember this: those lines aren't white because they're meant for white people. You're going to hear some insults and some of them will be horrible and they won't all be directed at your new teammate. They'll be directed at you. But you've been insulted and laughed at before. In this game they give you lip all the time.

"Remember this. Somebody tears you down, they're going to have to take a bat and go up to that plate and show what kind of guts they got.

"That's life inside that diamond. Not how you look. Not what bullshit you spout. How you play."

We'd never heard Coach cuss before, and his words startled some.

We knew what he was saying, even though at times I thought Cletus was listening but not hearing.

About that time Mose joined us. It occurred to me he might have walked all the way here from his home. Several miles.

"Fellas, this is Mose Jones," Coach said. "He'll be playing with us."

"How y'all doin'?" Mose said.

I shook his hand and the other players followed suit. Cletus had disappeared. It was a good ten minutes before I saw him again, coming out of the bathroom located behind the concession stand.

"Must have been a big dump" I said to him when he got back to the dugout.

"Yeah, real big one. Had a lot of shit to get out."

He immediately grabbed his glove and went down the sideline for warmups with Spencer, our starting pitcher. He did not move over to shake hands with Mose or even look his way.

I went with Coach to home plate to witness the exchange of lineup cards. I could see in the stands some people were looking toward our dugout and buzzing with conversation.

Mr. Fredericks, an insurance salesman by day, got the season started with an announcement over the loudspeaker. Bubba used to say, "He doesn't need a loudspeaker. If you ask me, the speaker cuts him down. Bet he makes a ton of sales 'cause people want to spare their ears from permanent damage."

"Welcome ladies and gentlemen to the sixth season of the Intercity League. Tonight we feature teams from Derks Construction and the Dogtown Packers."

A roar went up from the stands. If we'd had a visiting team playing us or another hometown team, the roar would have been double for the home boys. But it was opening game and it was loud enough because the stands were packed.

At the dugout everybody was shifting around in various states of tension and excitement.

Mose was sitting at the end of the bench, looking anxious. Coach Cross leaned against the dugout fence near him.

"Butterflies?"

Mose nodded.

"Looks like a good crowd but…you never can tell."

"I'm ready."

Big Chuck Frankenheimer came barreling up, wearing a red cap two sizes too small for his head, its bill blazoning Frankenheimer Foods and a T-shirt Dogtown Packers.

"Howdy boys!"

"Howdy Mr. Frankenheimer etc." greeted him back.

"You gonna win me some games this year?"

"Yes sir, we sure are sir, etc."

"You better. I'm getting tired of explaining why I sponsor a bunch of drag-butts."

In passing he said to me, "Mary Louise can't make it. Said something about a party."

She'd sworn she'd be here.

"Damn," I said to no one in particular.

Big Chuck approached Coach Cross, put his arm around his

shoulder and lowered his voice, though I could still hear him less loud but very clear.

"How's the colored boy doing?"

"If the fans just let him play, he'll do just fine." Big Chuck nodded and turned to us.

"Good luck, boys. Play tough!"

He moved toward the stands to a chorus of seconds from all us players.

I was the leadoff hitter and had selected my bat. Spencer came up with his jacket on to keep his throwing arm warm and he entered the dugout, but Cletus stayed outside. He looked sullen, and angry.

"What's bugging you?"

He nodded toward Mose.

"Moonshine."

I tried diplomacy.

"Sooner or later it was going to happen."

"Tell that to my old man. What are we, a bunch of stinkin' guinea pigs ?"

"We owe him a chance."

But that was the wrong thing to say.

"I don't owe him jackshit."

The Derks players charged out onto the field and took their positions. After the crowd roar died down Mr. Fredericks announced that the national anthem tonight, contrary to the usual recorded version piped over the speaker, would be sung in person by "a local songbird."

We had no idea who that might be until Randy said, "Thank God, now I don't got to hear Francis Scott Key every night from the shower. I'm a patriot and all but Jesus…"

Sally Bright walked out onto the field and took a stance at home plate where a microphone had been set up on its stand. She wore a simple blue dress and for practically the first time I'd ever seen her, wore her hair down. I had imagined she wore it up for the simple reason it might cut down, if only a little, on the number of harassing, salivating admirers she encountered every day.

She electrified the crowd into silence just by standing there.

"Never knew she could sing," I said to Randy.

"Who says she can? Half what I hear is running water. Anyway she won't go nowhere. Ain't got no ambition."

Mr. Fredericks asked everyone to stand for the anthem. He started the background instrumental, turned down lower to accommodate Sally's voice, but he needn't have. When Sally started to sing, it was as if this local songbird was in fact an angel, descended from on high to grace us mortals for one shining moment.

"Ethereal" doesn't come close to describing what we heard. Besides the timbre and tone of her magnificent voice, Sally added what I felt was genuine emotion, as if it were the first and last time she would ever sing the anthem like this and would leave the land of the living afterward. Every single note came from her whole heart. Coach Cross who was at my side had abruptly turned and walked some distance away, and I wondered if he hadn't choked up with tears and didn't want to let us macho types see it.

Usually when the anthem ends, there's some perfunctory applause, a few patriotic yells and then we get down to the game ASAP. But when Sally hit the last "home of the brave" every brave person and then some in the crowd stood and applauded for what was probably just three or four minutes but seemed like fifty.

George nudged me.

"Look at Mr. Simmons."

Mr. Simmons, a diehard fan who'd lost both legs in the war, had asked two men in the crowd to lift him up out of his wheelchair.

They held him up under the shoulders and with his hands free, he was clapping wildly, giving Sally his very own personal standing ovation. When Sally finally made it back to the stands and the applause died down she noticed Mr. Simmons still upright and rushed over and gave him a warm, lasting hug. I could see she was crying.

Mr. Simmons' wife, rumor had it, had put up with his

infirmity for a while when he returned from the war, then started to play around and finally he preferred to divorce her and live alone, scraping by with his disability pension and VA aid. Whatever pleasure he still got out of life, baseball sure as hell was one of them. He came to every game he could.

George said, "Sally just made his year."

"Maybe the rest of his life, " I added. "They say he was one great soldier."

"Cost him."

"Batter up!"

The home plate ump meant me. I moved toward the plate.

The umpire was almost hidden behind the bulk of Derks' catcher Harvey Harris. We'd had a debate about each other's virtues way back to Little League.

"Well look here, it's Harvey Harris. The vice squad off duty, Harvey?" Harvey chuckled.

"Surprised to see you boys. Seeing as how last year we whipped you worse than a suck egg dog."

"Bet you know a lot about suck egg dogs, Harvey."

"I know one thing. We don't go recruitin' in no cottonfields."

"Good thing. Somebody might take you for a boll weevil."

The ump said kind of plaintively:

"Can we play ball now, fellas?"

The Derks pitcher, Jimmy Price, was good, nice fastball and crafty, with an effective curveball and changeup to keep batters guessing. But I'd faced him before and had an advantage--he was a lefty and I batted righthanded. Which meant his curveball would break right toward me, where I could hit it.

An elementary fact of baseball is that hitters have odds in their favor if the pitcher throws from a different side. Babe Ruth had been the greatest home run hitter of all time not least, I believed, because most all pitchers of his era had been righthanded.

The laws of physics could explain this aspect of the game but my high school physics class came and went without me being one single bit the wiser about the subject. Our teacher had resorted to grading on a curve for the class, and mine had been a circle. In the end, I think I got one of Randy's age passes.

Physics or not, I felt confident as I stepped up to the plate. Jimmy started with a fastball that caught the inside corner of the plate for a strike. I could have swung at it, but part of the job of a leadoff hitter is to make the pitcher work and throw more than one pitch. Do this enough, one batter after another, and by the 7th inning or so the pitcher would tire and be much easier to hit.

The next two fastballs missed the strike zone outside. Jimmy, I figured, remembered that I'd hit him well last year and he didn't want to give me an easy pitch to hit. So he was trying to be careful. And missing.

"Come on, Jimmy!" Harvey said politely. "This guy can't hit shit!"

For the next pitch, I guessed that Harvey, with his limited capacity for logical deduction, would think I'd be expecting another fastball—that Jimmy would want to avoid walking the first batter of the game—and therefore I'd be fooled by a curve.

Yep. The ball left Jimmy's hand, started out wide of the plate and began to curve to right over the middle of the strike zone, in a perfect place for me to hit it.

I was waiting. I swung and got the thick part of the bat handle squarely on the ball, sending it into right center field on a line.

For a moment or two as I ran toward first base I thought it would clear the fence for a home run, but no, it banged off it. The center fielder quickly grabbed the rebounding ball and fired it back to the infield but I easily made it in to second base for a double. Our dugout went wild and our fans in the stands as well. Big Chuck was on his feet, bellowing as only he could.

Mary Louise wasn't there, so I clapped for myself. Great way to start the game and season and I just knew everything would be different this year. We were going to win.

George followed with a single into left field and though Coach knew the play would be close, he waved me home.

I slid across the plate just before the throw and beat Harvey's tag. I was thrilled to hear "Safe!" and see the look on Harvey's face.

"More where that came from," I said to Harvey.

"Bullcrap on that."

But bullcrap or not, we got three more runs as the game went on. Spencer was pitching well and we held on to the lead till the 7th inning when he ran out of gas and Derks rallied.

Coach brought in Mickey to pitch. He got a couple of fast outs, but then Harvey Harris slammed one of his fastballs over the center field fence. It was a monster shot and got out of the park almost faster than you could blink.

In the dugout later Mickey said ruefully, "Any birds get hurt?" George said, "Not yet."

Usually when you hit a home run and trot around the bases, protocol says you can wave your arms and celebrate but not jaw at the pitcher or other opposing players.

Harvey was not one to respect protocol though, and he surely didn't know what the word meant. As he passed in front of me he said, "Sent that one to kingdom come. Don't bother lookin'."

Derks had momentum now and in the bottom of the ninth they loaded the bases with two outs. Any kind of hit would tie or win the game for them, whereas if we could get the out, we would win by a run.

Coach called time and came striding slowly toward the mound where Mickey was waiting for the inevitable. Cletus, as the catcher always does, joined and I came over from shortstop.

"He's struggling," Cletus said about Mickey, it being his job in like situations to tell the honest truth to his coach.

"We can see that," Coach said, and waved toward the sideline where Mose had been warming up. I had seen him, but Cletus had not. "You did fine. Take a rest," Coach said to Mickey.

He took the ball from Spencer and beckoned toward Mose as Mickey left the mound for the dugout.

"He going to pitch?" Cletus asked.

"We need an out."

"Folks ain't going to like it."

"If he gets us a strikeout, they'll like him just fine."

"I ain't catching him."

Coach Cross looked at him quizzically, like he'd just seen an alien.

"It's against my beliefs, sir."

This time Coach looked at him and it wasn't a sympathetic look. I had never seen him look so angry and Cletus hadn't either.

"Take off your gear and hit the pine. And don't take your time. You understand me, boy?"

Cletus knew enough not to jaw any more. He turned and stalked off before Mose could reach the mound.

Coach looked over at Larry at second base.

"Suit up," he said. Larry jogged toward the front of the dugout where Cletus was dropping his catching gear.

Coach waved toward the dugout for Bubba to come out and take Larry's place at second.

"Substitution," Coach explained to the home plate umpire who was starting to get impatient.

When Mose got to the mound Coach Cross said, "Don't show your best stuff warming up."

He looked over at the batter who was coming up. It was Harvey Harris.

I said, "He's a good hitter 'cause he has no thoughts to mess up his head "

Mose said, "I got an idea."

Coach nodded and handed him the ball.

"Block out everything but throwing strikes. Do your best, son." He looked at me. "Let's help him out." I nodded. Then as he walked off, he yelled to all of us: "Let's give him some chatter! "

Larry had put on the gear and walked over, squatted down behind the plate. He pounded his catcher's mitt and held it up to give his pitcher a target.

He looked uncomfortable. Even if he'd played some catcher in Little League and Babe Ruth league, it wasn't his natural position.

Coach Cross stayed standing in the dugout so he could watch the action better and shout orders. Cletus sat on the bench behind him and looked stunned by what had happened. And furious.

Mose started warming up. I could tell he wasn't firing his best fastball, as Coach had counseled him.

Harvey Harris was standing several paces away from the plate, watching the pitches. Like any good batter, he was studying the pitcher's speed and whether he had a good curveball and control—whether he was consistently finding the strike zone.

Most pitchers do their best in warmups and don't hold back —that's what warming up is all about—but the flip side is, the on-deck hitter gets a good read on his stuff and can prepare himself for what's coming.

One pitcher I used to watch on television did not do this, preferring to not bring his best heat. His warmups were just warm, and sometimes just lobs. This pitcher was the great Sandy Koufax. When warmups finished and batters stepped up to the plate, they found a big surprise waiting for them. Sandy wasn't lobbing any more.

Maybe Coach had taken a page out of Koufax's book, because Harvey did not look impressed by what he was seeing from Mose. The pitches weren't that fast and he did not see a curveball. He looked eager and confident to get up there and slam a hit that would win the ballgame.

As Harvey was cockily waving his bat, he seemed to remember our little conversation to start the game and he yelled out at me:

"I'm gonna send him back to the turnip patch."

Mose wound up and fired.

The pitch sailed way to the side and just missed Harvey. About as wild a pitch as a pitcher can throw—assuming he isn't trying to throw the ball exactly where it went. In this case, Mose was.

Harvey stumbled back, looking like a fumble-bum.

"Hey boy" he shouted at Mose, "The plate's thataway!"

"Got away from me," Mose replied calmly.

I could just hear Harvey mutter "bullshit," but he said it low this time—in the interest of a temporary peace, just long enough, so he thought, to get up to the plate and slam his gamewinning hit.

Larry put on his catcher's mask and crouched behind the plate. The umpire settled in behind him.

As Harvey rubbed some dirt on his hands and got ready to step up to the plate, I took a quick survey of the stands.

Bill Bowers sat in front of the pressbox. I could see he had his pen poised to record the event.

Big Chuck was seated near our dugout, in a special folding chair to contain his bulk. He had a cigar which it looked like he was chomping extra hard on. For once he wasn't laying down the law to the hangers-on standing beside him, who just a moment before had been mumbling whatever hangers-on mumble to a rich businessman who can change their income and maybe lives with some manna from heaven.

Coach Cross stared from the dugout and rubbed his stomach —his nerves were working on his ulcers.

The crowd remained quiet and in a way respectful, conscious of what they were seeing and maybe still surprised it was happening. No slurs were hurled Mose's way.

Even as tall as he was, I thought Mose looked small and alone on the mound as he faced the wall of grandstands, players and spectators.

Just him against them and expectations, high noon coming late this evening.

Harvey stepped in, waved his bat back and forth.

Larry hid the sign with his glove on knee, but everybody on our team knew what it would be—one finger for a fastball.

Mose wound up and fired a bazooka toward the plate. Harvey swung way late, missing the ball by a mile.

Harvey stepped out of the box, stunned, and asked the umpire: "Where was it?"

"Down the middle...I think."

Harvey stepped back in, more tentatively I thought. Mose delivered again. The ball blazed toward Larry's glove.

Same result.

Harvey stepped out again."I can't hit the sonovabitch if I can't see it."

He looked down at Larry.

"How you catching that thing?"

Larry answered, "Braille."

In the dugout Coach Cross and the subs were on their feet, sure we'd get a strikeout and win the game.

Cletus sat sullenly on the bench, saying nothing.

Coach Cross rooted Mose on."One more, Mose!"

The next pitch was high and inside, sending Harvey lurching back.

The next one came in even tighter, just missing Harvey's helmet.

One of his teammates yelled out, "Let it hit you, Harve. A walk is as good as a hit."

"Hell with that. I need this head."

I called time and jogged over to talk to Mose.

"Nervous?"

"Some I guess."

"Just bust it down the middle. This guy won't catch up to it till tomorrow."

Mose nodded and I jogged back to my position.

Sometimes devout players will make the sign of the cross before their at-bat, either hoping the Lord will protect them from injury or gift them with a basehit. I have seen many a major league player attributing his home run to the Lord.

Even though raised a Catholic, I never did this because I didn't want to blame the Lord when I made an out.

And in fact, since a batting average of .300 is considered tip-top, if the Lord base hits it and not the player, it means he fails 70% of the time. I thought the Lord played better than that.

Now I saw Harvey making the sign of the cross.

"Hey, Harvey, since when have you become a Catholic?"

"Since right now."

I turned to my fellow infielders and outfielders too: "Chatter!" I yelled.

When your pitcher is on the mound and going mano à mano with the hitter, even though he knows his fielders are there to help him by catching the ball, it helps before the pitch to yell out encouragement: collectively, chatter.

We all started in, with "One more, Mose," "You got him," "Come on Mose, come on man," and so forth.

Nary a poetic line in the bunch, but the pitcher, as George often said, "doesn't need iambic pentameter." He just needed to know we were behind him.

On the road, when the fan crowd is all against you, it's a way of countering them. The world is against you, but we're keeping spirits high come hell or high water.

Once last year we had fallen behind 12-0 and had about as much chance of rallying as a snowball that belts Lucifer in the back of the head, but Big Chuck wanted chatter and I harangued everybody to keep it up.

"We're gettin' slaughtered," Bobby protested.

"Look," I said, "even the little lambs when they're heading to the chopping block, they squeal right up to the last second. I've seen 'em. That's guts, man."

"That's supposed to be a pep talk?" He had a point, Bobby did, but since that time we were able to chatter even while Rome burned, and now we raised a storm.

Mose wound up and threw a fastball that I felt sure reached almost 100 mph. It was so fast Larry couldn't get his mitt square on the ball. As Harvey swung and missed the ball sailed and deflected off a corner of Larry's glove and went zipping toward the backstop.

In this situation the batter has struck out but provisionally. If he can make it to first base before the catcher can retrieve the ball and fire to first base, he is safe.

Harvey lumbered toward first and the runner on third base raced toward home. If he crossed the plate it didn't matter as long as Larry could retrieve the ball and fire to first before Harvey arrived.

The first rule for a catcher with a passed ball is to hurl off your mask so you can see better.

Since he hadn't played catcher very much, Larry didn't do this right away and he just spun in place, thinking the ball was at his feet.

We all screamed at him to chase it down behind him. Both Billy at first and Randy at third raced in from their positions to get the ball and Mose rushed toward home plate.

We'd all realized it was too late to get the out at first. Now home plate had to be protected.

All three arrived at the ball at the same time, but by then the runner at second had come all the way around and reached home plate while Mose stood there helplessly, watching the winning run score.

This kind of play happens about once every ten years, and it had just happened to us.

Bill Bowers told me later that he'd rarely seen a tableau— that was the word he used, "tableau" —like that.

"They looked like the Three Stooges standing there, and Moses was saying to himself, Lord, you really want me to lead these yokels to the Promised Land?"

The Derks players poured out of their dugout to congratulate each other on their win. Even Harvey, who had won the game by striking out.

We all went over and shook hands, the ritual after every game where sportsmanship is meant to take over for competition.

I shook hands with Harvey and heard some bullshit: "He ain't that tough. Just surprised me. I seen a lot better fastballs."

I said: "Yeah, and I just saw the Abominable Snowman."

"Who's that?"

The other Derks players to their credit shook hands with Mose, the Coach included.

We dragged back to our dugouts, losers of the opening game for the third time in three years.

Larry hurled his catcher's mitt against the dugout fence.

"I ain't no catcher."

Billy seconded him: "You sure as hell ain't."

Larry glared at him and squeezed his hand into a fist, but George got between them.

I threw my glove down and sat on the bench, discouraged with the same old same old. Cletus sidled over. He had left the dugout to go congratulate the winners but quickly left off and come back to take off his cleats and pack his gear.

"See, a pitcher and catcher got to be like this." He held up two crossed fingers. "Brothers."

I saw Coach Cross pat Mose on the back and say "We'll get 'em next time."

Cletus just shook his head at the sight. "I can't be his brother. Henry's got to understand that."

I didn't answer, just reflected for a minute, then got up and left the dugout.

Bill Bowers was waiting near the stands.

"Can't lose for losing."

"That's about right," I concurred.

"I'm running a separate story on your new teammate. Going to interview him tomorrow."

"He's nice, real patient and motivated."

"He'll have to be. Old Henry Cross sprung a big surprise." He paused a moment, not so usual with Bill who'd been called more than once "motormouth."

"About time. I'm counting on you, kid. Counting on you."

#

I drove Mose home. At first we didn't talk much, both of us still trying to absorb what had happened and how we could have lost the game. I didn't want to talk about Cletus.

"They won first place last year. And the year before. We were right there with them. Shoulda won."

"Some good players in this league. I want to play the best, you know. I want to be the best. Bob Gibson, he's my idol. If I could be half the pitcher he is, man..."

"Way you throw, with a lot of hard work and a little luck..."

118

"I ain't kidding myself though. It's gonna be rough. But I've got my dream, and if you want to see it happen bad enough..."

Neither of us could finish our sentences, which meant I thought that the future lay ahead and neither one of us knew what it would bring. We arrived at his house.

"You were gonna walk to the park every game?" His look said it all.

"I'll arrange it so I can get off work a little early and pick you up."

He didn't say anything but his look did, a mix of surprise and gratefulness. It didn't seem that big of a deal to me. Years later he told me it was a big deal. He held out his hand and we shook.

"We'll get 'em next time."

"Damn straight," I agreed.

9. PETIT JEAN

When we went on the road we carpooled, depending on who had a car in working condition or whose parents crossed their fingers, offered up prayers and turned theirs over to their son for the trip.

Cletus always left early, given the uncertain state of his vehicle. He always carried along spare quarts of oil that he called his "car medicine," and sometimes he had to overdose. It was best for the respiratory system not to trail behind him.

Big Chuck had usually driven me and a couple of other brave souls in the two years past, and that was always an adventure. He would lay back on the seat of his custom-made Buick, resembling nothing so much as a whale at the wheel, one arm on the steering and the other on the seat back, and give us a running discourse on at one time or another (1) baseball and how we needed to learn how to play it, (2) his competitors who would not remain long as competitors if he had anything to do with it, and (3) the breed and quality of whatever livestock grazing in the pastures we could view in passing from the highway.

He'd punctuate his spiels with "What say, hoss, huh?" But never wait for an answer. He would however usually turn and look you in the eye, which led us to freak out and wonder if he navigated by some radar. The car would swerve into the other lane and we hoped to God he'd come to the point before an impact. Sometimes we'd see the whites of the oncoming driver's eyes, but Big Chuck always managed to swerve back onto our side of the road and avoid a collision.

And not once did he seem to do it because another car was about to ram us to kingdom come. It just seemed like his normal way of steering.

It made for interesting rides and when our nerves didn't explode, it prepped them very well for the task of facing a speeding baseball.

George, who was the only one of us who knew any philosophers besides Yogi Berra, said that he thought of these trips when he read Nietzsche's phrase, "What doesn't kill us makes us stronger."

When we played Morrilton that year, Big Chuck said he wanted to treat Mary Louise and me to a weekend getaway. We would go up to the park in separate cars and spend all day Saturday and night in one of their stone cabins on the bluff overlooking Cedar Canyon, then I'd play in the game Sunday afternoon.

In fact he'd rented three cabins, one for each of us. "Appearances," was all he said to explain this arrangement.

"Prehistoric," in his daughter's view.

He asked me to ferry him up in my car because "I'll be more certain of arriving in one piece" than if Mary Louise was driving.

The next day I found out there was another reason, to wit, big bosses always have assistants to drive them around, and though he knew he was a big boss, tomorrow he wanted the world to know it.

Petit Jean is not so much a mountain as a forested plateau arising above the Arkansas River plain, but it is high enough to have its own cooler microclimate.

I spent most of Saturday hiking while Big Chuck worked the phones from his cabin and Mary Louise swam and sunbathed in the lodge pool. I had invited her but got the response, "In those woods, with all the bugs and this heat and humidity? Not this bimbo, darling."

I hiked the long Seven Pines circle trail through a lovely pristine forest, passing sponge rocks and a grotto and a couple of hollows where once bootleggers in the great American tradition of flouting the law had bypassed Prohibition with their homemade stills.

I once asked my uncle, who'd been in his twenties during that time and who I knew liked to have a glass every now and then, what Arkansas moonshine tasted like. Just my saying the word brought a slight grimace to his face, like he was still in pain.

"Rotgut, Tom," he said, "they invented the word to describe this kind of moonshine. You know, Al Capone used to come to Hot Springs for the hot baths, and they say somebody gave him a jug of the real article. He drank a pint and next day when he woke up he said 'Friends, this likker's so dangerous for the American people, they'll have to end Prohibition.' And darn if he wasn't right. Couple years later he lived in Alcatraz and folks been drinking weak stuff ever since."

When I got back I passed through the lodge to the swimming pool where Mary Louise hadn't budged, except to turn over every now and then for a full body tan.

A man and woman were lying on lounge chairs nearby and the man was directing conversation her way. He was explaining the virtues of zinc oxide which swathed his nose.

"I swear by it. It beats Coppertone any day. I mean, you wouldn't want to use it on your body but the nose is one of the most sensitive parts of the human anatomy. I don't know if you knew that."

I arrived before Mary Louise could answer this burning question. Mr. Zinc Oxide was with a woman who looked like she appreciated less and less her companion's helpful hints to a girl who could be said to outclass her in the sexy department. He turned to her as if by obligation when I arrived.

"Let's swim," she said, caressing his arm, but he pointed to his nose. Definitely the water would wash off the ZO.

I wanted to hike down to the falls. Mary Louise took one look at the heat and humidity visible all over me--my hair was almost dripping wet from sweat-- and said, "Don't even ask."

When I left Mr. ZO pretended not to notice, but I knew he'd resume his inane flirting even before I hit the trail just behind the lodge. Especially as his companion was doing laps.

The Cedar Falls trail leads down switchbacks to Cedar Creek, then follows it for about a mile and a half to the falls, which plunge into a wide pool which one can circumnavigate. I only encountered two fellow hikers in the blistering heat, and those who passed on this adventure like ML missed something because when I waded under the cascade, it was blissful and refreshing to let the water pour down on me. I could not have done it in winter, when the cascade bursts over the cliff above and literally booms down below, but now in June the flow was reduced just enough.

Afterward I lay around on the rocks until the sun fried me anew, then jumped back into the water for my shower bath. When the sun dipped under the forest at clifftop, just like that the temperature fell and the wind picked up, so I headed back.

Mary Louise was just picking up her towel and Coppertone.

Her admirer had stuck around all afternoon and now he was suffering the consequences. He'd wrapped a blanket around his sunfried legs and found a Petit Jean State Park cap from the gift shop, which did nothing to shield his face from the sun's rays and in one afternoon he'd become a redneck.

His nose however was still protected by the zinc oxide. Mary Louise said he'd reapplied it liberally throughout the afternoon, each time repeating his lecture about its virtues. His companion was nowhere to be seen.

That night we grilled some Frankenheimer steaks and sausage on the picnic terrace outside my cabin and amused ourselves. It was a natural progression from "Mr. ZO" to "Mr. Zoo," and my repeated references to Mr. Zoo sent Mary Louise into a fit of giggles. In between she managed to say, "She was his wife! They're here on their honeymoon!"

She said he'd kept ogling her whenever his new bride turned away and he thought she wasn't looking, so his neck got a workout, swiveling from one to the other so much he reminded her of a jack-in-the-box.

I said, "Mr. Zoo's in deep shit. He'll have to make it up to her more than once tonight."

"How crude."

"Boo-hoo for Mr. Zoo."

"She needs to put him in a cage." She went into another fit of giggles. She enjoyed her effect on men.

Big Chuck hadn't been listening much as he gave priority as always to grilling the meat just right. He mixed some cocktails but drank the lion's share as I had to save myself for the game tomorrow. He'd had to bring his own mixings, as we were in a dry county, which made the still I'd seen that day ironic.

"You can make a law in daytime," he said, "but the moon shines at night."

"Well then," Mary Louise said, "maybe I better drink this in the privacy of my own cabin. Can you escort me, Tom? I saw some raccoons hanging around. Maybe they're rabid."

"Not as much as Mr. Zoo."

She cackled again, and Big Chuck cautioned me, "Y'all have fun but don't forget we got a game tomorrow. Don't leave it all in the cabin."

#

The next morning I managed to get up early and head out to the lake where I rented a one-man kayak. I paddled out in the cool early-morning mist and enjoyed the freshness and silence. When I reached a beautiful garden of lily pads, large and green and perfectly formed, I slowed and took care not to disrupt the little Sargasso.

The mist lifted, and when I looked up I saw at bankside a range of pines and one very large and tall dead tree whose branches were occupied by perching hawks. Over a dozen by my count, which was done in haste as they seemed to be staring down at me like their next prey. I'd seen a Hitchcock film called The Birds a couple of years before and watched a couple of citizens pecked to death.

Not wanting to experience the same fate, which would have been worse because these hawks looked fierce and unwelcoming, I paddled quickly back to the dock and left the lake to them.

I joined Mary Louise and Big Chuck at the lodge as they were packing up. Mr Zoo and his wife were leaving too. He was putting their bags in the car trunk while she watched, though watched over might be more accurate. He didn't dare lift up his eyes at us and Mary Louise--just got in the car with his wife and drove off.

"That boy done got a talking to," Mary Louise said.

On our way back we stopped at Petit Jean's grave, a lovely spot at the edge of the plateau overlooking the river and plain, with eagles soaring overhead on the updrafts that constantly caress the bluff.

Local legend has it that give or take 2 centuries ago in Paris a French noble attached to an expedition to Louisiana territory in the New World had fallen in love with a beautiful girl named Adrienne Dumont. He loved her so much he refused to take her along with him to chart this wilderness territory that could harbor savage animals, Indians and unknown diseases.

She loved him so much she refused to be left behind. So she disguised herself as a young man and managed to get taken aboard ship as a crewman--small but apparently strong enough, nicknamed Petit Jean or Little John.

The expedition landed in New Orleans, headed up the Mississippi to the Arkansas, then past the small outpost called La Petite Roche, and arrived at a mountain plateau where local Indians lived and farmed.

Somehow Petit Jean managed to hide her true identity from everyone, including her lover.

"No way," Mary Louise affirmed. "He'd have had to be one stupid Frenchman not to recognize her."

Big Chuck interjected, "When you're settling the wilderness 24/24--"

"No man's ever that busy."

I had to concur with her there.

At any rate, whether the nobleman Charvet trysted with his lover on the sly or according to the legend did not discover her true identity until it was time to quit the mountain and head back to New Orleans, she became gravely ill.

The Indians adored Petit Jean and tried everything to help Charvet save her, but she died before the expedition could head back to New Orleans. She'd asked to be buried on the crest, on the clifftop under soaring hawks and eagles. It is said that her spirit hovers over the place.

"All I can say is, she bet on the wrong horse," Mary Louise said.

"Something's here though. I feel her presence." And I did. Maybe it was the wind ruffling the trees or the raptors overhead or whatever microclimate, I felt an intangible sentiment and wondered if love was like that, real but intangible and could only be recognized in, say, an act of sacrifice or willingness to go to the ends of the earth for your lover.

I didn't say any of this in front of Mary Louise and Big Chuck, though. A sense told me they would not understand it.

Mary Louise tossed a pine cone at a squirrel and then got in her car. She was headed back to town, skipping the game and the real reason Big Chuck had treated us: he wanted me to accompany him as his "assistant" for a closeup look at Winrock Farms.

#

Big Chuck had done some research and discovered that a Frenchman named the Marquis de Morès had attempted a short-lived cattle business in North Dakota in the 1880s. He'd come West after marrying the daughter of a wealthy New York banker and when the residents of the small cowboy town of Little Missouri gave him a cold shoulder, he just moved across the river and founded his own town. In true gallant Gallic fashion, he named it after his wife Medora.

The town grew, the Marquis built a large house on the hill and called it the Chateau de Morès, and for awhile it looked like he'd succeed in his bold operation. But weather, conflicts with the local cowboys and a testy relationship with a fellow young rancher named Theodore Roosevelt hindered him, and finally the behemoth Armour Corporation beat his prices, and him too. Medora's father pulled the plug on financing and de Morès went back to France, dreaming other dreams.

Big Chuck said he would claim to be the descendant of one of the Marquis' "love children," i.e. he loved his wife but what can you do, he was a French lover. This to explain, if pressed, why he--"Mr. LeBoeuf"--was planning on reopening the cattle business in North Dakota and hoped to pick up pointers from the Winrock experts.

I found the whole plan ridiculous, but felt there might be just enough verifiable history and Big Chuck panache to carry it off. Anyway he'd gotten an interview with Winrock's director of operations.

"That Yankee carpetbagger's running scared I'll put him out of business. If I give him my real name they'll shut up tighter'n Sadie's underwear."

We followed the signs that featured a big healthy-looking bull on the logo. "Santa Gertrudis," Big Chuck said matter-of-factly.

It was a huge place dominated by two looming silos among more than one stable-like ranch buildings. We could see pasture and stock, and somehow Big Chuck had managed to wangle a jeep tour from the man who was waiting for us, a Mr. Hurley, operations manager and, as his badge said, "Stock Engineer."

After the introductions, where Big Chuck without embarrassment called himself "Charles LeBoeuf, from Dakota. North, the southern part. "That's why I have a little accent."

"Your first time here in Arkansas?"

"This part. I love your state's natural beauty and agricultural possibilities."

"Well, that's what drew the Big Boss here. Plenty of grass and water and sunshine. I'm from New York originally too."

"And mosquitoes. A real scourge. Even the horse flies are bigger down here. The Big Boss ever get homesick? I mean, plenty of opportunities up north too."

"Not that I've seen, but most of the time I've got my eyes fixated on bulls, cows and calves."

"What you want in a stock engineer. That high-falutin' lingo for a foreman?"

The engineer or foreman ignored the dig, if he caught it, and said, "Come on, I'd like to show you around."

We piled into Mr. Hurley's jeep and he drove us out to the grazing land. I had been introduced as Mr. LeBoeuf's assistant, so I ended up in the back seat pretending to take notes. We jounced and bounced over the grassy hummocks and oysters left behind by the cattle and Mr. Hurley seemed not to care which was which, grass or dung.

At one point we slowed down and circled a small copse of trees. I'd seen several like it around the wide pasture, as well as small rivulets with some rainwater still left. Mr. Hurley yelled over the car motor that both had been planned and were man-made.

"A thirsty animal can't plump up no matter how much he feeds, and the trees give them relief. We believe in de-stressing our stock. A happy cow is a fatter cow."

Big Chuck said nothing, but afterward when he confided to me he came down hard: "Like these animals need a shrink. Hell, if they can't kick back and do nothing in Arkansas, they can't anywhere. There's a Yankee idea for you."

When Hurley came to a stop we put our boots on the ground so they could check out a couple of bulls first hand. Big Chuck was complimenting--"hell of a fine animal," and I could see he was impressed--when another jeep came rumbling toward us.

This was a brand spanking new one and the driver sported a Stetson about as big as the state of Texas. He was a big man, wearing cowboy boots and a shirt that even a fashion clueless person like myself could see had come off a very expensive rack, like Abercrombie & Fitch.

"Hi, Win Rockefeller."

No one had to tell us though who the Big Boss was, and I was surprised at how sincere Big Chuck sounded when he shook hands and introduced himself as Mr. LeBoeuf "from Dakota, the southern part of the North."

"That would be, North Dakota."

"Yes sir, exactly right."

Hurley mentioned something about a family history dating back to Medora, about which Big Chuck had tried to be as little forthcoming as possible. That was the whole idea about being an illegitimate offspring, to hush-hush inquiries. Rockefeller said, "My family knew a banker back in New York who lost a lot of money on the cattle business out there. Some crazy Frenchman. Of course that was a long time ago."

"Small world. Times change, you know. The grass gets greener if you know where to look for it. That's why you're here I imagine and that's why I'm here."

He might have gone on like this but thankfully Rockefeller moved the discussion to insider info. They discussed Herefords, Red Angus bulls, the Angus Field Day that was coming up real soon--"my assistant Thomas here will be going to learn all he can"--and finally lost me completely with a technical analysis about screwworms and Mexico's cooperation in eradicating same.

I noticed in the distance that one of the bulls had decided to go to work and had mounted a willing partner. He was doing his job so enthusiastically and loudly that our conversation came to a halt and we all watched the show.

Hurley said, "He's usually not that active."

"When the Big Boss is watching..." Big Chuck explained. He thanked them profusely for their time and attention and Rockefeller made a quip about LeBoeuf being a perfect name for a cattleman.

"Er...are you folks worried about Frankenheimer Foods? They've got a big share of the market, I've heard."

The Big Boss looked puzzled, and Hurley explained: "One of our competitors."

"THE competition, or so I've heard up in South Dakota."

"North, southern part," I came to Big Chuck's rescue.

Rockefeller said, "We respect all our competitors, but we can only control what we do." Rockefeller had run for governor against Orval Faubus and lost, but the latter had finally decided to leave off politics and virtually everyone expected the Big Boss would run again next year.

"The little people," Big Chuck said, "can't forget the little people. In business and politics."

"True words. Thanks for reminding me." As he said it he was already in his jeep and jouncing away. Hurley motioned and we hopped back into his jeep.

"Well, he's got my vote," Big Chuck said, and Hurley smiled at a job well done. On our way down from Petit Jean for the ballpark I asked Big Chuck if he'd been sincere about the vote.

"Hell, I'm a Democrat and he's an old carpetbagger. Knows his stock, though."

All during the game, which we lost, I could see him in the stand making notes, and after the game he didn't rail against our ineptitude, which he surely had a right to do because we didn't play well and it didn't look like we would in the near future, either.

"What were you writing about?" I asked.

"Ways to eliminate stress in Santa Gertrudis."

10. FORT SMITH

After several up and down games where we could have won but didn't because of errors, a concentration lapse or lack of team spirit—Coach said it was an intangible thing but that he and we would recognize it when we saw it, and he hadn't seen it yet—we were going nowhere fast.

Big Chuck had set up a full weekend of games against Fort Smith, a big town that always fielded solid teams, and as it was a weekend series and long drive to get there and back, he decided to foot the bill for a downtown hotel. It was old and historic and dated back to the days of Hanging Judge Isaac Parker, judge for Oklahoma Indian Territory.

I wondered if one of the rooms in the musty hallways had lodged from time to time the judge's trusty hangman, and what he thought about his job--watching someone writhing on the rope till death parted him from the land of the living, that is.

Randy opined, "Probably thought like anyone who's got a shit job. Let's get this done so I can get my money and a beer."

Big Chuck told me that at first, he'd thought this kind of competition on the road would get us ready for anything, and especially for the state championship which would be played this year in Belleville, home of the reigning champs.

But as that hope, the championship, fled faster and faster away with each disappointing loss, he saw Fort Smith as a bonding experience. Maybe two days together would do just that, bring us together. We'd have nothing to do and nothing to break our concentration on baseball, as we were underage and couldn't buy liquor and anyway, we'd be in a city hotel and he and Coach Cross would be just down the hallway.

He hadn't counted on the resourcefulness of the intrepid teenagers playing--or going through the motions of playing--for him at that point in time.

I drove Mose in my car along with Bobby who didn't want to ride with his older brother for obvious brother reasons. We got ahead of the pack and arrived first. I wondered why and found out later that Cletus' car had suffered what he called "that time of the month troubles."

In other words, he explained, sometimes his auto, or what passed for an auto, tended to act up. Cletus said that usually meant it needed some oil, and he carried multiple spare quarts, or just some tough love.

George who had given a ride to Coach Cross and Randy, stopped beside the highway where Cletus' car was marooned, its hood up under the patient attention and TLC of its owner. Sammy and Mickey were standing nearby, BS-ing and drinking cokes.

George stopped and asked if they needed help.

"Just a few prayers," Cletus said. He gestured and Mickey handed him the bat he was holding. Another gesture and Sammy got behind the steering wheel.

Cletus yelled, "Ok, one, two, THREE."

And with that Cletus took the bat and brought it down like a sledgehammer CRASH on the carburetor simultaneously with Sammy turning the ignition switch. George said the car grunted, sputtered and roared to life. Cletus slammed the hood down and rushed to take the driver's seat.

"Let's go before it changes its mind."

George drove back onto the road and in the rear view mirror saw Cletus following him. He said later that Cletus had confided that he wished that stubborn carburetor had been "Henry Cross' head. One's as hard as the other."

"Carburetors don't have heads," George corrected, ever the linguist. George said he'd got into a debate with Coach after the episode. "I'm surprised he's even making the trip."

"It's his decision when he wants to play, not mine," Coach responded.

"He can play outfield. He just doesn't want to catch Mose. What's wrong with that?"

"Plenty."

"I don't see it."

"George, a team's a team, not the Selective Service."

That ended the conversation, but not George's reflections. Sometimes, I would find, much as I respected his brainpower, he missed the forest for the trees. I told him that once and he said, "If you don't see the trees first you can't see the forest."

Whatever that meant.

#

Even though Arkansas had come a long way from 1957, Big Chuck had gotten on the phone and "bent some ears" at the hotel so Mose would be treated with all the civility he deserved. He and I roomed together, next to Coach's room. All the others were stretched down the hallway and we took up all the floor, but one room had to be rented one floor down, and as fate would have it, Mickey and Cletus got this one. It became the scene of the crime, as it were.

We fought hard Saturday afternoon but lost by a run when our bats went silent in the late innings. Coach said that was why we were here, to find that extra juice you need when playing in front of a hostile crowd on the road.

"We'll get 'em tomorrow," he said. "Let's get a good night's sleep and come out firing on all cylinders."

Coach rarely used cliché phrases like that, and could be it was a sign that all of us were about to hit rock bottom.

We were teenagers after all. Stock teenagers. And at the time we didn't deserve a more creative phrase, the kind of eloquence that is said after deeds merit and call for it. Big Chuck hadn't known that we'd have an outlier room on a different floor, or that as the night wore on it would draw almost everybody like moths to flame.

Almost, because Mose and I took a stroll around downtown, far from a crowd that would become madding. We didn't see much in the city streets that would interest us and like many downtowns at the time, folded up the sidewalks at 6 pm.

We crossed John Kennedy Boulevard and the conversation got onto the topic of the late, assassinated president. Like me and my family, Mose and his family and actually everyone he knew had spent the same agonizing four days of mourning and

133

funeral ceremony in front of the television those last days of November, 1963.

"My mama cried for four days, nonstop. Kept saying, 'We ain't got nobody to save us now. The Lord must have needed a right hand man.' "

I said, "I never saw so much hate back then, before Dallas. Couldn't understand it. He set up the Peace Corps, got us headed for the moon, faced down Big Business. I mean, when did you ever look forward to when a president gave a news conference?"

"I didn't pay much attention to all that. I kinda knew he was different but you know, had my thing to do. Then there's this one night, I'm watching TV and my show ain't on, it's a special speech by the president. Well, I was ticked off but then he started talking about civil rights. Mama said, 'You boys listen up.'

"He looked mad. Even disgusted I'd say. Talked about we'd ended slavery and here we were 100 years later living with segregation. Like everything had changed but nothing had changed and he said, it's time. This is going to stop. This government is going to make it stop. We're gonna integrate this country. My mama started crying and said, 'He better not come south. They'll kill him, sure as I'm standing here.' "

"He came to Texas," I said. "I was in school that day, on lunch break. The rain started pouring down, a real gullywasher. Come from Texas. Later I said to myself, if it had only kept pouring in Dallas. They wouldn't have opened the top on his limousine and he'd be alive today. That goddamn rain."

"You know what I'm proud of? Been a lot of killin' in this country. Gonna be a lot more. Every time there's a killin', people look at us. We're the usual suspects.

"But nobody ever blamed a black person for killing JFK. They know. No black person in this whole country would have ever laid a hand in anger on John Fitzgerald Kennedy. We owe him too much. I owe him. 'Cause of him, one day I'm playin' ball like always and I look up and see Mr. Henry Cross watching the game. Watching me."

"And here you are. How 'bout a coke?"

"Dr. Pepper."

"Come on."

We headed down a floor to the soda machine and crossed paths with Randy and Billy who were lugging sacks and a big carton full of beverages that I could see weren't Dr. Pepper.

"Guy at the liquor store thinks Randy's 21."

"I'm dumb but I'm old for my age," Randy said. And as they opened the door and went in to Cletus and Mickey's room, I heard raucous chatter inside.

"Oh shit," I said to no one and everyone.

#

Inside Cletus' room, George told me much later after all the "sound and fury signifying nothing," they'd all been playing cards, some poker, some In Between.

The doorway had been a constant turnstile of entrances and exits. At one time or another everyone but Mose and I stopped by.

Cletus groused on and off about being "exiled" to a separate floor and laid it to Coach Cross trying to teach him a lesson, but for everybody else the room provided a safe haven. The authority figures were one floor up, and out of sight and mind.

George said one of the most remarkable things about the night was how no one, nobody but nobody ever stopped the shenanigans or said "Hey, we've got a game tomorrow. Maybe it's time to get some shuteye."

"That's supposed to be your job. Where was oh captain, my captain?"

"Asleep, dreaming stupidly that the Dogtown Packers were adults."

Billy and Larry Bain, of all people, had split from the hotel. George said it happened like this. When he got to the room, Billy was haranguing Larry Bain. "You want to be a virgin all your life?"

"Who said I was?"

135

"Hey, I'll give you a demo. These chicks don't care somebody's watching. They've been dying to go out with studs like us."

"They don't got studs in Fort Smith?"

"We're from the big city. We're like celebrities, man. Come on, they're waiting downstairs."

Larry didn't look too eager, and Billy turned to George. "See? No cojones."

Larry's face turned red and George thought he might punch him right then and there. But he just said, "Bring 'em on."

"Whooee!"

Billy motioned for Larry to follow and they headed toward the stairs, not wanting to risk the elevator and run into Coach or Big Chuck.

"Fear not, gentle thrustmen," George yelled after them, "if ye use protection."

"Hell with that," Billy responded, "Don't make 'em big enough for me."

So George went inside and started to play cards with the others. All went politely and they threw in nickels and dimes and quarters to make the pot. Then Randy arrived with his six-packs of beer and after a few suds and then more suds, as time passed and the hours got wee, so did the brainstorms.

George remembered Cletus downing a can and crushing it angrily, tossing it into a trash basket already piled high and asking, "He won't even let me pinch hit?" George gave him the thumbs down sign.

"I'm getting the shit end of the bat."

"Henry's being a Nazi, that's all there is to it."

When he told me this I said, "You actually said that?"

"Heat of the moment, lad, heat of the moment."

"Yeah, it fried your brain."

George said the guy abusing the alcohol most was, of all people, Mickey Crutchley. The most logical of us all, a future lawyer because he was always showing us both sides of a question.

Coach Cross said whenever he'd be coaching the baseline

and wave Mickey on to take another base, he worried that he'd stop to debate the issue. Mickey was piling up the empty cans next to his cards—"against shark eyes," he said—and very quickly his eyes started to glaze.

George said that looking back, they all should have known Mickey's usual powers of analysis had been affected and the intellectual imprimatur he gave to the project they hatched came more from the beer than Mickey's head.

But at the time, "When he waved around his Pabst Blue Ribbon we thought we'd just won a prize for Idea of the Year."

#

While their teammates were hatching schemes, Larry "became a man," according to his definition of such.

He told me the tale a couple of days later when I ran into my cousin Betty and her new boy friend: none other than Larry. They'd started dating, she said buoyantly.

When she headed off to work Larry took me aside and told me he'd felt guilty about going out with Billy and the two local girls but the whole experience just made him appreciate Betty more. Plus initiated him in the art of lovemaking. He hoped I'd understand, and if I kept his secret, he'd tell me one.

"Why do I need to hear a secret?" I asked.

"'Cause it's a lollapalooza."

"Ok, shoot." He said that the two local girls had not been much for small talk when he and Billy found them sprawled out on the vintage leather sofas in the hotel lobby. They wore cutoff jeans and T-shirts and didn't need small talk to attract the male persuasion.

"Loaded for bear and guess what, we're the bears," Billy said to Larry on their way to a wooded spot the girls knew that overlooked the river. They went in two cars and all along the way Billy coached Larry about how to "satisfy a chick."

"Don't I just got to stick it in?"

"Spoken like a virgin dickhead. No man, you got to get 'em worked up." And he talked about various forms of preliminaries.

"You've got to pretend like you want to know her as a person."

Larry said he was surprised at first to hear any form of respect for women coming from Billy, but then again, it was fake, all part of his seduction tactics.

Brenda, a "va-voom blonde," gravitated immediately to Billy who rivaled her a lot more in physique than Larry, while he, Larry, had no choice but to hang out with Linda, who he said rather unkindly was the sort of girl who if you found yourself sitting next to, you might not notice someone was sitting next to you.

"But she gave me a different viewpoint right quick," he said. "I woulda bit my tongue except she was doing that."

They had all gathered in Billy's car to down the 2 bottles of Cold Duck Brenda had brought. "My first time drinking champagne," Larry said, and didn't quite understand when Brenda said "Yeah, it's the real French stuff" and they all laughed.

"It's real comfy back here," Linda said, and Billy explained he'd added the mohair blanket just for that reason, "to give comfort to my many friends." He added, "It's handwoven, if you know what I mean."

Larry didn't, and he thought the girls didn't either, but Billy laughed a lot at his own joke.

The Duck went down easily and Larry said he and Billy learned all they needed to know about Fort Smith, and the girls showed a passing interest in Dogtown.

"But it was like, just as soon as the last bubble of Cold Duck went down Brenda looked impatient and said 'Bet the river's real beautiful under that moon.'

"What moon?" Larry said, and got dirty looks from both Brenda and Billy, who jumped in "like a horny chigger."

"Love to see it," Billy said, "can you show me?" And "they were gone lickety-split, without a hiddy-ho," Larry said, with Billy taking another mohair blanket for comfort. Linda said, "Geez, took 'em long enough." Larry said he was going to engage Linda in conversation, "preliminary shit," but she got straight to the point.

"I like you, uh…"

"Larry."

"I live with my Dad and right now he's busy getting drunk, on his way to passing out like every night. I've been looking for love all my life. The night belongs to us, darling."

Larry said he fell to with a will, as the poets say. At any rate he described their lovemaking in terms that were almost poetic.

"She opened up a new world for me, and I knew I would never be the same. Anyway, who'd want to be the same after that?"

It had been awkward rolling around on the back seat of Billy's car. He started to go into what George would have called panegyrics to her introducing him to a new world etc. but just like that, she was back on top of him.

Larry said if anybody could judge sex by sheer gymnastics, they graded out to a "10". Linda said, "That was fun! You wanna be on top this time?"

Larry said he was puffing and gasping like "that old barn horse my uncle used to have. From stud to dud, that's how I felt." But he refused to let on that he needed a break.

He thought he found an out: "Out of rubbers. Too bad. Got to be careful, you know. Didn't you say you had a fiancé at Fort Chaffee?"

"That's what he calls himself. I'm waitin' for the ring, and if it's five and dime, he's gonna be all she wrote."

She reached over the front seat for her handbag. "No sweat, honey. A gal's got to come prepared."

She unwrapped a package she pulled from her purse and held up some equipment for his inspection. "Ain't they cute? I made 'em myself out of Saran wrap."

Larry said he would have rolled his eyes and groaned except he wasn't sure he had the energy.

"Oops, must have wrapped a greasy chicken in this one."

She tossed it out the window and handed him another of the home-made prophylactics, and shifted into position after Larry had armed himself. He said this one smacked of a baloney sandwich and he had enough brains left to admire her sense of economy. "She'll make old soldier boy a good wife if he's got enough horse sense to buy a decent ring."

Linda hit the saddle again. "Anyway, like I said to Brenda, I said, 'These old local boys burn out faster'n a bad match. A girl can't hardly get started.'"

Larry said if Linda had paid any attention she'd have seen far more agony than ecstasy on his face, but somebody suddenly banged on the car window.

It was Brenda, and she looked pissed.

"Let's go, honey. I need a cold shower quick." Larry gasped, "Where's Billy?"

"Looking for his bat. Take my word for it, he needs it."

From the darkness down the road they suddenly heard howls of rage, like a wild animal in pain, followed by a series of crashes.

Brenda yelled out, "Oh, now you've got some mustard!"

The yowling continued as Brenda tapped her fist on the window insistently. "Aw, we were just getting started," Linda complained.

"Try Casanova back there. Maybe you can raise his dipstick. Come on."

Linda grabbed her clothes and purse, gave Larry a last kiss and hurried out. "Shoot!" she said.

Brenda was still steamed. "Telling me he was a lover. Hah!"

Larry said he had just enough energy to absorb this information about Billy before he slowly turned on his side and more or less collapsed.

It was a while before he heard the front door open and the car start up and head off. Billy didn't say a word all the way back to the hotel. Just before heading off to their respective rooms he said, "She wasn't my type." And slammed the door behind him.

"There you go," Larry concluded after he'd told the whole story. "He's a sorry bastard and he don't deserve any consideration. Way he's been braggin' about his women. But man, he looked so hangdog. I mean, he was shakin' in his boots, scared I was gonna spill the beans. Kinda pathetic, ya know."

"Don't. He'll jump in the Arkansas River, and we'll lose a first baseman."

"Yeah. For the good of the team and all that."

"And third, if you spill the beans I'll spill some to Betty, and trust me, she's got a temper."

"No shit?"

"Her ex-boyfriend's still got red ears."

Larry said he'd promise not to let anybody in on our little secret, and he kept it, if only because "he saved me from trying those chicken wrap contraptions."

#

In Spencer's room the night waned and and so did good sense. George said he and Cletus got into an earnest drunken conversation.

"I'm going far just staying on the team. If my old man finds out..." Cletus shook his head like he was horrified at the thought.

Mickey Crutchley suddenly pounded his table in frustration. His pose and attitude suggested Bogie in "Casablanca."

"Fifty million teams in the world and I gotta play for these losers." George knew Mickey had just seen "Casablanca " and had been much affected. He pounded the table again.

"Losers!"

Cletus sympathized.

"See there? For the good of the team, we've got to do something."

Spencer, Randy et. al. were chattering drunkenly around Mickey. He suddenly turned to them and yelled:

"Stop that racket. You know what I want to hear. Sing it! Sing it for Mickey!"

They eyed him groggily, not understanding.

"Sing 'The Ballad of Big Chuck.'" This they understood. Sammy jumped up and shouted at the top of his lungs. "Let me hear you!"

And George said it was like a choir that had sung together for years suddenly synchronized without a conductor.

Everyone started singing together:
"He came from the hills of Arkansaw
Best durn butcher you ever saw
Pork and beef and poultry too
Big Chuck chops the meat for you."

They hoisted beer cans high for the chorus. The empties were stacked in a pyramid in the middle of the room. Spencer had a beer in one hand and a joint in the other. In b.g. Cletus and George were still in deep conversation. The song picked up again:
"Big Chuck, Big Chuck,
Big Chuck's got the meats for you,
Sausage and ham and bacon too,
Big Chuck's got the meats for you! (singing together)
Big Chuck, Big Chuck,
Big Chuck's got the meats for you!"

Cletus shook his head. Suddenly his eyes lit up with inspiration.

"I've got it!"

He pulled George over and started yelling in his ear. George said a lot got lost in the ensuing din, but he caught the gist. He said everybody was now so individually and collectively drunk they turned the song into a slapstick opera.
"Saw those prices way up there,
Said 'Whoa brother, that ain't fair.'
Took his knife and chopped prices down.
Big Chuck's got the best buys around."

Two unsavory looking wieners appeared in Spencer's hands. As the song proceeded he beat time with them in various ways: on beer cans, teammates' heads, his body and between his legs.

Sammy and Bobby started playing pitcher and batter with a succession of beer cans as they sang; with each hit beer sprayed through the air. Randy started dancing in his underwear in time to the music.

Two other players were mooning out the front door, singing while they worked. George said he knew they played for the team but at that hour and in his state, he couldn't quite identify them.

"Let me hear you!" he yelled.

"Big Chuck, Big Chuck,
Big Chuck's got the meats for you.
Big Chuck, Big Chuck,
Big Chuck's got the meats for you.
Big Chuck, Big Chuck,
Big Chuck's got the meats for you!"

They blasted the ending of the song with a surge of lung power at the precise moment when Mickey collapsed head first on the table where they'd been playing cards. A pile of beer cans and a pile of cards went flying all over, landing here and there. George said he didn't care and nobody else did either, and that whoever could notice was surprised when they looked out the hotel room window. Dawn was breaking.

No sleep tonight for these Dogtown boys.

#

The game started at one o'clock in the afternoon. When we ate breakfast at the hotel and checked out, I could see in my teammates' faces that the game would feel longer than their night. Larry was relatively alert, and Mose and I in tiptop shape after a restful sleep, but the others looked like zombies.

Sammy started the game at pitcher and got lit up like a firecracker. I got a couple of hits and Larry got three—"I'm energized like the bunny," he said, and at the time I didn't know what he meant.

At first base, Billy looked hangdog literally as well as figuratively, as a line drive went right over his head and he made no attempt to leap for it.

"You could have caught that ball," Coach said.

"Really?" and he wasn't being sarcastic.

The runs piled up as one would expect when a refreshed, alert team plays zombies, but as the game went on Coach thought he saw some animation returning. He put Mose in and he doused the fire. Now all we had to do was score some runs of our own.

"Let's go now. We're not out of this game yet. Show me some hustle!"

He got in Mickey's face when he said that, because Mickey looked pained and limpid. Mickey went up to the plate like he was visiting a dentist for a root canal and started swinging at every pitch, like he couldn't wait to get back to the restfulness of the bench, but on the third swing he somehow managed to make contact and bloop a hit down the right field line.

Mickey ran down the first base line like every step was misery. I was coaching at first and saw the ball roll all the way to the fence. I waved Mickey on to second base. "Go, go!"

Mickey turned and headed toward second almost reluctantly, and a heck of a lot slower than normal. As he neared the base I yelled: "Slide!"

Mickey dived into second with a headfirst slide, almost as if he viewed the base as a warm bed where he could sleep off what was ailing him. He just beat the shortstop's tag and the second base umpire screamed, "No, he's safe!"

He said to Mickey, "Good hustle, son."

"Aaarghh!" Mickey barfed the night's dissipation on the second base bag.

Both shortstop and umpire and I and everyone in attendance that memorable (for the wrong reasons) day just stared in shock at this unique event in our baseball lives, one I've never seen repeated before or since—and never want to see again.

George said on the ride back home coach Cross was mostly silent but did venture, "I've done about all I can with this team. It's up to them now."

George mistook this for a kind of "carte blanche" to go ahead with Cletus' strategy, even though as he said later, "It had been born in beer, and maybe had more suds than savvy."

11. BOYCOTT

Big Chuck as promised sent me to the annual Polled Hereford Day, two days of livestock and livestock lore. I heard as much as I ever wanted to hear about the business I was in and might well be in for the next 30 years. So I listened attentively even though much of the discourse went in one ear and out the other.

There were many facets, ranging from raising the animals, the proper amount of feed and pasture and so forth almost ad infinitum, it seemed, to processing, production and marketing. I realized that to really learn the trade would take much time and study.

As a boy, one of the year's highlights for me was the annual Little Rock Livestock Parade, where marching bands with pompom girls and mounted rhinestone cowboys and cars with VIPs and covered wagons and just about any showman or woman who could finagle a spot marched down Main Street.

It was such a big event you could get out of school if your parents asked, and mine did.

Then that night and all week you could go to the livestock fair and play the dart games or shooting gallery or my favorite, the toy cranes which you could manipulate in a glass-enclosed wonderland of trinkets and gadgets, hoping to catch something in the bucket. I never could, but every year hope sprang eternal. At the time I could have cared less about the livestock, the raison d'être of the show, penned up all around with their breeders ready to expound and make sales. Now I had to, and at the Hereford Day I gained new respect for the men and women involved in the trade.

#

I was strolling between two stalls as Hereford bulls on both sides stomped around, and for a second I thought they might be reacting to the footlong hot dog plate loaded with mustard, chili, chips and pickles on the side, in the hands of a man resembling Ichabod Crane—if Ichabod Crane wore a red bow tie.

I thought he might be planning to lunch with the bulls, but no such luck. He was zeroing in on me.

"I'll bet a dime to a donut that you're Tom. Boy, Mary just nailed your description."

"That or my name badge. You'd be Johnny Benson."

"Gosh, how did you know?"

"Your name badge," I fibbed.

"Usually I tell people, 'Just look for the scarecrow. It won't be a scarecrow though, it'll be me!'"

He laughed at his own joke, and even if you charitably gave it a 4 on a scale of 10, ten being a belly-whopper, you wouldn't chuckle away as long as Johnny did, especially as this was probably his 1,000th version. But Johnny loved it and added, "Clients love it when I say that. Breaks the ice, you know." Now that he'd broken the ice between us, I not-so-subtly asked how he'd discovered the bauxite pits where Mary Louise and I'd gone swimming.

"Oh my goodness, I'd never take Mary near one of those death traps. They're exceedingly dangerous. No, I showed Mary the plant. Did you know that during the war they were turning out 6 million tons a year? That's short tons, of course. The production process is so fascinating. Mr. Frankenheimer wanted me to look into pig aluminum. He thought we might be able to rig up a joint ad campaign."

"I took care of that."

"By golly you did. I don't mind saying Tom, it's brilliant, The Ballad of Big Chuck. I sing it in the shower. I told Mary, hold on to that man, he's going places." He said it with as much sincerity as he could muster, and he did it well, the mark of a crackerjack salesman, but I detected just a touch of plaintive jealousy in his voice, as if the scarecrow wished wistfully to become human so he'd have a chance with Mary Louise.

"You should hold on to her too, Tom. She's a top breed."

"Never thought of her in that way, but hey, I'm keeping you from your lunch."

"Oh, this. I already ate a toasted tuna sandwich with lettuce. This is for show, so the ranchers can see I'm a good ole boy. Part of my sales strategy. I carry it around everywhere and when the flies start buzzing around, I know it's time to trash it."

He went into another peal of laughter and I seized the moment to get the hell out of there, saying I had a "hush-hush meeting."

"You mean like, confidential?"

#

Later I wondered if part of Johnny's success wasn't based partly on the "gnat strategy, " i.e., you make a deal, any deal to get him to stop buzzing around.

I reproached myself for being uncharitable, but then I couldn't help amusing myself. I imagined Johnny overcoming his caution and going swimming at the quarry pit with the top breed, and I saw them in my mind's eye: his Mary on the bank polishing her nails a bright red while he bobbed in the water, explaining the complicated process of converting bauxite ore to aluminum and not realizing she wasn't listening to a single word he said.

On the side would be two footlong hot dogs that Johnny had brought for their picnic, with chips and pickles and a couple of mustard packets. I imagined Johnny as having overcome inhibitions and swimming in the nude, but unable to doff his bowtie, and it lent a nice red color to the waterline.

A very uncharitable fantasy, for sure.

#

Thus sidelined among the Herefords and Johnny Benson, I did not learn for awhile about the plan Cletus, George and Mickey had cooked up in Fort Smith. They went around to all the players like politicians and buttonholed them for support.

Most everybody agreed to take part.

After it was all over George told me they'd been surprised out of their minds when they went to Lake Pleasant where Billy worked as a lifeguard.

They'd hardly got the plan out of their mouths when Billy asked, "Is Larry Bain with you?"

George replied, "We haven't talked to him yet."

Cletus said, "I reckon he is. He hates catching."

"Yeah...well fellas, I'll give your plan some thought." George said Billy was strutting up and down in his swim trunks and Lifeguard T-shirt and didn't mind a bit showing off his bod in front of all the sunbathers and swimmers at the lake, which a couple of years ago had been converted to a swimming and picnic spot complete with tables, a water slide, floating buoys and a dock for desperate fishermen.

Just as he was saying a perfunctory goodbye two bikinied girls waved excitedly to him from the swimming area.

"Hi Billy!"

They were nubile and Cletus' eyes bugged out, but Billy just said "Get lost!"

George and Cletus were as shocked by this response as the girls. Billy answered their looks: "I've given up women. Too damned demanding."

#

Much later we were able to laugh about what happened when George went out to Mr. Snookums' farm to confab with Spencer. He had to go down a narrow dirt road between acres of cottonfields stretching away on both sides.

Spencer explained "I'm working with Mr. Snookums on my concept of microclimates. If he follows my ideas he'll up his yield thirty, maybe forty per cent."

"I thought your specialty was physics."

"My brain branches in many directions." Spencer pointed to a tree-bordered patch where a crop of plants was flourishing.

George said he didn't immediately recognize the type and Spencer "did not forth come," just said "Mr. Snookums lets me use a half-acre in exchange for my work."

Leisurely harvesting some of Spencer's plants was a young guy with shoulder-length hair and Christ beard, beads, "Peace" T-shirt, cut-off jeans and sandals. He was singing "Go Down, Moses" while he worked, but George said he found the work to be a very individualistic interpretation of labor.

"Go down Moses, way down in Egypt land,
Tell ole Pharaoh to let my people go."

"My friend Errol, visiting me from Frisco. You might say he's singing for his supper."

"He some kind of medicine man?"

"Yeah, weed medicine. Well, I've got qualms about your idea, but let's give it a shot." They shook on it, then George moved over with Spencer to the "weed" patch to join Errol.

"Did you check those soil samples?"

"Soil? Sample?" Errol replied.

"Dammit Errol, you've been nibbling the crop again."

"I dig the boll weevil, man."

"Omigod, there's Mr. Snookums."

"Ole Pharaoh!"

"Let me do the talking, okay?"

Mr. Snookums came up. He had a game sack slung over his shoulder and dangled two dead squirrels by the legs. He held a .22 rifle in the crook of his arm.

Mr. Snookums nodded at George and Spencer but seemed more fixated on Spencer's crop.

"How's them experiments coming, Spencer?"

"Real good, Mr. Snookums. I'll have the results in a couple days."

"Jiminy, them what-do-you-call-em plants…"

"Stoneweed."

"They're sproutin' like Paul Bunyan's pecker. If your science can do that for my cotton, I'll be one happy fella."

Spencer had been watching worriedly as Errol prowled around Snookums like a dog sniffing for a bone. Errol suddenly spotted the squirrels.

"Holy shit Spencer, look at this. Davy Crockett time."

"Errol—"

Errol turned to Mr. Snookums: "Beat that cannon into a plowshare, man. We're already blasting Asia back to the Stone Age. You want to do it to Arkansas, too?"

George said Mr. Snookums didn't know what to make of this strange apparition.

"I uh, just bagged some game for supper."

Errol reached into his waist pouch. "You want supper? Here, have some sprouts. They got vitamins and minerals and all that good shit."

Spencer was freaking out."Errol, will you please—"

"Those squirrels had lives, man. Families. Little baby squirrels. But did you think of that? Naw, you were too busy with this macho Daniel Boone shit. I mean if you've got to bang something, bang your old lady."

"Errol!!! Please, please…wait for me on the knoll, okay."

Errol ambled off toward the nearby knoll, still muttering. "This is heavy shit, man. I mean what would Walt Disney say?"

Snookums, George and Spencer watched him go, Snookums still in a kind of shock. George said he had all he could do to keep from bursting out laughing and almost doubled over trying to keep it in.

"Spencer…" Mr. Snookums said as Errol broke into another verse of "Go Down, Moses," "forget the crops, Spencer. There's the job for science."

#

I learned about the coup d'état afoot when my mother and I went to Larry's father's Protestant church for a Sunday service where my cousin Betty was singing as part of an inter-denominational choir.

They sang wonderfully, all manner of gospel songs the way they should be sung, I thought, and my mother approved even though she was and always had been a devout Catholic.

Reverend Bain gave a sermon where he attacked Vietnam War protestors as misguided, unpatriotic and traitors to the mothers who'd raised them. He cited a recent demonstration in Washington and kept repeating, "Where were their mothers?"

For a moment, incognizant of either the demonstration or very much about the war other than Bill Bowers' updates, I thought I'd missed Mother's Day. But no, Reverend Bain meant to sound a call to arms, of a kind that might yet influence the young people he said had lost their way. He made no mention of the fathers.

After the service we stopped to pay our respects to Reverend Bain who was standing on the steps socializing with his departing congregation.

I saw George and Cletus conversing with Larry over near the parking lot. The conversation looked animated and I wondered what they were talking about. And I figured I would soon find out. Larry turned away from them and came over our way. George and Cletus hung around, no doubt to talk to me.

My mother congratulated the Reverend Bain on his "passionate sermon."

I got the sense that Reverend Bain had to reflect a couple of seconds about the word passionate, but then concluded that my mother meant it in the sense which I knew it did, very involved and sincere.

"Miriam," he said, "I felt we'd heard enough from the Communists and hippie freaks. It was time to give the Lord's view of this war."

"Tom got the notice for his draft physical."

"So did Larry."

"I pray the Lord will end the fighting soon."

Larry had come up the steps, nodded at me and overheard this last bit of conversation. He added, "I'm betting it'll all be over in six months."

His father stared him down like he'd just confessed to being a Communist. "You'll do your duty to your country and your Creator. There'll be no slackers in my family. I apologize for my wayward son, Miriam. He has a way of forgetting his

151

responsibilities."

"All I said was—"

"Don't bandy words with me." He pointed toward an elderly woman. "Help Mrs. Williams to her car."

Larry clenched his fists, the picture of helpless frustration, but controlled his temper and headed toward Mrs. Williams.

Betty had been obliged to leave with her fellow choir members. I felt she might have softened Rev. Bain. I kind of thought Larry was used to this kind of dressing down, but that didn't mean they were any easier to take. And Larry wasn't the kind to take them easy.

My wonderful gentle mother said in her own gentle but unmistakable way, "I knew what he meant."

#

Before we left, George and Cletus buttonholed me and divulged their cockamamie plan.

"No way!" I said.

"It's for the good of the team," George countered.

"Bullshit. It's bullshit."

"I beg to differ. We followed established democratic principles."

"Jesus!" Cletus said, "Told you it wouldn't work. He don't give a damn what we say. Let's go."

He stalked off. George lingered.

"Look. You want to win, don't you? This is our last year. We'll never have this chance again for the rest of our lives. Think about that."

"I have. But I won't cross Henry. And Mose."

"It's clutch time. And you're choking. But you still have time to change and join your band of brothers."

"Why don't you take a hike before I forget you're my best friend." He got the message and gave it up. And took a hike, leaving me wondering where all the flowers had gone.

#

My mother and I drove over the bridge into Little Rock, to the VA cemetery where my father was buried.

It was an infernally hot day, with constant sun and no breeze and humidity, typical of an Arkansas summer. I used to wonder how my father could possibly spend 10 hours or more a day on the service station concrete where temps would climb even higher. He would come home dripping from sweat, open a cool beer and say simply, "Dog, it was hot."

After dinner he'd spend the evening in what cool there was on the front porch where he could chitchat with the neighbors. In those days before television zombied the American populace, people still had things to say to their neighbors and said them, and my father found relief in the jokes, repartee and general conversation. Plus he would have opened another beer or two.

He taught me how to hit, pitch and field almost as soon as I could walk. He would take a rubber ball and throw me pitch after pitch, always with a plan: starting with pitches down the middle, easy to hit to boost my confidence, then inside so I could learn how to turn on the ball and drive it into left field, then outside so I could guide it into right.

The guiding principle was, "Hit it where they ain't."

The second was just as important: how to flick your wrists when making contact with the ball. That is where the power comes from, not from how hard your arms flail. I developed wrist strength from hours and hours of real and practice swings and realized how brute size made less difference in propelling a baseball than common sense would have it.

When my father went to work I would spend hours and hours bouncing a rubber ball against our front porch steps and fielding grounders on the rebound, then working on my hitting by collecting the berries from our backyard chinaberry tree. When I had a sackful I'd toss them up and hit them toward the vacant lot conveniently located behind our house, playing imaginary games where I'd have to pound a homer to win the game.

Sometimes I did, sometimes I didn't. A chinaberry is significantly smaller than a baseball. At least I didn't have to worry about broken windows.

When I got older, my cousins and I played practice games in the vacant lot. Only a small one-room shack sat on the property, in a far corner, inhabited for a time off and on by an unemployed oldtimer who called himself "Bicycle Bill," based on his sole means of transport. We never learned his real name, and one day he just disappeared. Sometimes he would come out of his shack and watch, and he "right admired" this or that hit, always I thought a little baffled at how some young kid could do that.

"Our first fan," I said to my cousins. At the age of 10 we went to the tryouts for a Little League team and I got my first glimpse of Big Chuck Frankenheimer, who didn't pick me or us. Neither did anybody else.

My father came to the rescue. He talked to a customer at the service station who was sponsoring a new team in a new league at Burns Park. They were desperate for players.

And just like that, we got caps and uniforms and started playing organized baseball. As befit our status as last-minute fill-ins, we batted in the lowest spots of the batting order, but as the season went on and we got more confident, we played better and better and I went from last to first, the very important leadoff batter.

At 12, our last year in Little League, I became a pitcher and developed a curveball. In the playoffs involving all teams from the city, we almost beat the perennial champions, none other than the team coached by Big Chuck Frankenheimer.

I inherited my father's hand-eye coordination, but didn't measure up to his. If he had not grown up in a country house in the middle of deep woods with 11 brothers and sisters--one could say dirt poor except the dirt was richer--he might have been a professional baseball player.

Instead he wandered west to join one of my uncles picking produce in California's Imperial Valley. By nights he became a topnotch billiard player, and I like to think of him circling that pool table, often running it, chewing on a half-smoked cigar and waiting till he missed to return to a half-drunk beer. More often than not the beer would be warm by the time he got back to it. I doubt his luckless opponents ever took him for a hustler or objected too much when he whipped them. He liked to say, "I can get along with anybody."

When he came back from the war he said goodbye to his vagabond days, married my mother and settled down to supporting a family by working 6 days a week, 50 weeks a year, with two weeks vacation that often involved painting or fixing up the house. In the early years we'd go to livestock shows, downtown parades, drive-in theater, and weekends back to the country where most of the family still lived.

After I started playing baseball, watching the games became his chief city pleasure. I wanted desperately to play well, to win and show him how well he had trained me.

#

I parked the car and we walked to my father's tombstone. My mother put flowers on it and even though we wanted to stand vigil there for a while, it was so hot we took refuge under a nearby tree that provided a little shade relief.

My mother with her usual intuition had realized something was going on with me and the team but I tried consistently to shield her from my problems. Out of the blue she said: "Sometimes I think we didn't prepare you right for the world."

"How's that?"

"We never really fought in front of you. Sure, we'd have our little disagreements, but not an out-and-out quarrel. We were so lucky, what are the odds anybody can ever do the same. Nobody I know. You'll have to learn to live with disappointment."

"You both showed me how it could be, a happy marriage. If that ever happens to me, I'll be twice lucky."

My father had passed away during one of the VA's periodic funding cutbacks and did not have an upright tombstone.

155

Instead it lay on top of the earth, among many others, so his section of the cemetery resembled a grass lawn with paving stones. It took maintenance to keep the stones free of mud and weedgrass and naturally, the VA had not considered this drawback. We'd been very unhappy at the time, but as we waited there in the shade a gray squirrel hopped over the stones on his way to a nearby tree and perched for a moment next to my father's.

This probably happened often, and it would have pleased Dad greatly. "I half expect him to pull out his .12 Gauge," I said to Mom. "If anything can wake him up, it'd be that."

He gave proof all his life that you can take the boy out of the country but not the country out of the boy. He liked nothing so much as to go squirrel hunting in the winters, and when my cousins and I got to be teenagers, old enough to fire a shotgun without shooting off our foot he'd take us along. We'd get up in the freezing cold of a winter morning, learning once again that Arkansas had a real winter, pile into his truck and begin the 3-hour drive to my Uncle Wiley's farm where he'd greet us, gab a bit, then grab his .22 rifle and his hunting dog Penny, and we'd head out into the deep woods. Frost would still be on the ground and among the trees where the sun hadn't got very far up in the sky, it was even colder.

We'd tramp through leaves and brush and slosh through sloughs, hoping the moccasins were as frozen as us, waiting for Penny to tree a squirrel. When she did, we'd haul off running till we reached her.

When we spotted a squirrel high up in the branches, it was every boy and his shotgun for himself. My father had turned over his gun to me, preferring to let us do the shooting while he watched and enjoyed the pleasure of being back in the deep woods where he'd grown up.

And shoot we did. I remember once my two cousins and I blasted a treetop so much it resembled a flattop haircut. Uncle Wiley remarked drily, "Raining buckshot" as the pellets fell down leaves and branches, posing a nuisance to the various creepy crawlers down below. That squirrel lived to laugh at the city boys another day.

If we got lucky or had better aim we'd bring down one or more and call it a day around 2 in the afternoon. Sometimes we'd debate over a sandwich lunch who'd hit the squirrel in mid-leap from one high branch to the other, it not being easy to distinguish in that OK Corral burst of firing.

My Uncle Wiley carried his .22 for a reason I never quite grasped, because he never used it. I am sure he did not want to embarrass us by bringing down a squirrel with a single pellet. Maybe it was just to reassure Penny that if we passed the whole day without hitting a squirrel, he'd bring one down so the dog wouldn't feel like she'd done all that treeing in vain.

In the afternoon when the sun had finally taken the edge off winter we'd pile back into the truck and head home, usually sleeping most of the way after stopping at a local grocery for sodas and candy or fried apple pies. My favorite was a Barq's cream soda or sometimes a ginger ale.

When weeks or months later we'd dine on our kill--for we never went hunting purely for sport--the meat tasted good, but we had to be careful to spit out the buckshot pellets that would be lodged in the flesh. On those evenings I could almost read my father's mind as he roamed back to that winter day.

He could grease a car blindfolded and do many other things very well, and he did like his Budweiser, but what he loved most was being out in those woods, where in my Uncle Bob's words, "He could walk where he wanted and spit his tobacco and pee on a tree, out there where he belonged."

The best thing I heard at my father's funeral was from my Uncle Bob: "He was just a good old boy."

157

BOOK 2

THE ROAD TO BELLEVILLE

12. BATTLING THE CHAMPS

It was the Fourth of July. Red, white and blue bunting was everywhere. In the stands all around the Belleville ballpark an occas ional firecracker exploded or sparklers flashed.

The mayor used the holiday occasion to fete the crowd with not-so-subtle political oratory.

"Fellow citizens of Belleville, in these chaotic times of strife and dissent you need a mayor who can keep on protecting our precious freedoms. You need a man—"

A man in the crowd yelled out: "Who you got in mind, Marty?"

"Figure it out, Ted."

That brought laughter from the stands.

"You need a man--me--whose record in office has been as sterling as the pride of Belleville, the Belleville Pioneers!"

The crowd erupted in cheers. Some of the Pioneer players clustered around their dugout doffed their caps to acknowledge the applause.

Coach Cross was huddling with the Belleville coach and other town dignitaries. I was sitting with Mose on our bench watching the festivities and in particular the Pioneer players.

"They've won three state championships in the last five years and looks like they'll do it again." I pointed to a tall tough-looking Pioneer player who looked like he thought the crowd's applause was all for him, the way he was strutting like a cock of the walk. "That's Jim Bunch. Good hitter, real good pitcher. He's their star stud and he knows it."

We were the only two on the bench.

Randy was flirting with a girl in the stands, maybe because he hadn't yet figured out what to do. She didn't seem that interested and looked our way a few times, at me I thought, then down the sideline. All the boycotters were there, waiting for Coach Cross. Mose followed my gaze.

"Guess it's showdown time."

"Yeah. You know..."

"Don't sweat. I can handle it."

"You a saint or just act like one?"

"I got my faith. We shall overcome." He said it with such determination and force I didn't know at first what to say in return. But then I found some words and was proud then and for the rest of my life that I did.

"We shall."

I decided what the hell, I'd take the bull by the horns and try a last time to knock some sense into their hard heads. I went down and started haranguing them, on the lines of it wasn't too late to reconsider.

George didn't want to argue. "Listen, we've chewed this over, it's all about hanging together. It's just a lineup change."

Cletus said, "When he pitches, I'll sit. I'm sacrificing for the good of the team."

"Band of brothers, that's it," George concluded.

"George, I finally read that goddamn Shakespeare play and you know what? You've forgetting something. Yeah, old Henry and his brothers won when they were outnumbered ten to one but you know why? 'Cause their enemy forgot about all for one and one for all. It was some guys from Paris take the front lines, no you guys from Normandy do it, and that bullshit went on and on till they turned tail and ran like rabbits back to Paris and Normandy."

Actually I didn't know if any of this was true and worried that George might flat out laugh at my analogy, but he seemed impressed.

"Losers," I said. "That's what you are. I've been thinking it would change but now I know everything they say about us is true. We're a bunch of losers."

By this time I was so angry I had to turn and walk away or else get into a fight. George told me later they'd all been impressed by what I'd said and turned to him, knowing he was my friend and an intellectual and had thought all this through-- in theory.

George said that despite his pride and satisfaction in my

160

having read Shakespeare, he said to them well, they'd come this far and why not give it a shot. Maybe Coach would agree. They had a 50-50 chance, right?

When I got back to the dugout Coach Cross was waiting. He looked over at the boycotters.

"You two know what that's all about?"

"Yes sir," I admitted.

"Care to tell me?"

I said, "You might say they've got a burr up their butts."

"Well, let's go see if we can get it out." He headed down toward them.

Mose said, "I'll hold the fort."

So I walked alone, trailing Coach Cross. When I got down to within earshot they'd already laid out their beef. They'd been practicing and it came out quick.

Coach said, "Let me see if I understand you boys. If I don't play Cletus, you won't play. Is that it?" George answered for the others: "Yes sir. It's kind of like a friendly ultimatum. But a democratically chosen ultimatum."

Cletus added, "It's the will of the majority."

"And you think because you've got a majority you can make the rules, like in a democracy."

"Yes sir; what our country's built on."

"Well, you can take your friendly ultimatum and stick it up your democratic asses."

They were all stunned. I was too. After a moment Cletus said: "Sir?"

"Even a democracy needs a leader. Because sometimes the majority doesn't know what's right. Sometimes the majority needs to be kicked into doing what's best for it. Now I don't know who came up with this harebrained idea and I don't care, and if you show up in the next ten minutes ready to play I'll pretend I never heard it. If not I'll forfeit the whole season on the spot. You can spend the rest of the summer jerking off. Come to think of it, that's likely a better sport for you all."

He turned his back on them and stalked away. At the moment I said to myself, now George knows what "high

161

dudgeon" looks like. He loved to quote that phrase he'd read often in novels.

I would have said it looked like pure rage.

Cletus managed to mumble, "I reckon that's a no."

But nobody smiled or reacted or seemed capable of responding. They just sort of dispersed, like windblown leaves.

I turned and walked off the sideline. Our season was over and I wanted to cool down before heading back, grabbing my gear and driving home. Most of all I didn't want to talk to my teammates.

"You play infield?"

I looked away from the field and saw it was the girl Randy had been flirting with. She was tall and darkhaired and not a classic knockout like Mary Louise but I found her wildly attractive.

For a moment I couldn't find any words, even though it was a simple question, and dimly thought she might take it for rudeness or being unfriendly or not interested, but she read me well and helped me out--when I was much older, I realized that was what real lovers do, or those meant to be real lovers.

"I'd say, second base or shortstop. Your glove. It's got a small pocket, so the ball won't get stuck when you turn a double play."

"You know the game."

"I play softball for our girls team. Third base."

"Hot corner. Careful. We wouldn't want to see you bruised up." I thought I might be blabbering, but she smiled. She looked over at the boycotters milling about, disordered and doubtful.

"Something wrong with your team?"

"You could say that." I poured out the story.

"Don't know if I did the right thing," I finished.

"You did the right thing."

Suddenly we noticed Cletus had come up to us and he wasn't interested in introductions.

"Look at that piece of shit." He was pointing ruefully at his car, parked not far from us.

"A sane man would have turned it into a chicken coop. Not me. I've put enough blood and sweat in it to win World War II. Got to keep it running 'cause I got to get to the park. That's how bad I want to play. For this team. Fuck democracy."

He headed toward the dugout to speak to Coach Cross. And just like that, the boycott was history.

"Looks like we've got a game after all. Good luck, shortstop."

"Tom." She turned to head toward the stands.

"Hey!"

She turned back.

"Did your folks give you a name?"

"My mother is a little mystic. She loved the word aura but that's no kind of name, so she added an 'L'. Figure it out, Tom the shortstop."

#

We played inspired baseball. The dugout was alive with excitement from the first pitch.

Maybe it was the relief that came from knowing we were a united team again, maybe it was the chewing out from Coach that every lackadaisical team needs from time to time, maybe it was the one missing element—our experienced catcher behind the plate again—that can make all the difference in the delicate construction and function of a group.

Or maybe we'd just had enough of losing and decided to try something different.

Nobody expected us to win this game, and that could have been a factor too. We had nothing to lose—having lost about everything the past two years. We fielded, we hit, we scrapped like a team that thought it had a chance—and we did. We pushed across two runs in a way only a team playing together can do—with a walk, sacrifice, timely base hit.

And then in the 7th inning when Sammy doubled to start the inning, we played like Coach always wanted us to. Instead of swinging for the fences against Belleville's pitcher, a player who had a good chance to reach the major leagues one day—Randy waited for an outside pitch and pushed it to the right side of the infield. He hadn't been able to get a good swing and made an out, but it enabled Sammy to advance to third.

Then with one out Cletus came up and battled as if he needed redemption. The pitcher was throwing smoke, and Cletus too could have gone down swinging for the fences. But he too punched the ball to the right side of the infield. He was thrown out easily, but the second baseman—even though he was playing in close—had to go to his right to field the ball and couldn't make a throw.

Sammy scored.

Jim Bunch was irate. Hardly anything gets a team more steamed up than when the batter barely makes contact with the ball and dribbles it to the infield—and still a run scores.

"Who do these guys think they are?" he yelled out to his teammates.

We held the lead till the bottom of the eighth inning when with one out, the Pioneers got two men on base.

Coach Cross came to the mound and took the ball from Sammy. Mose trotted in. Cletus stood with him, in his catching gear. Coach Cross gave the baseball to Mose.

"Shut 'em down, son." He walked off, leaving Mose and Cletus on the mound. I jogged over. "Five outs and we win, guys."

Cletus looked hard at Mose. "One's a fastball, two's a curve, three's a changeup and hit my glove. Remember that and we'll get along just fine."

"Yeah?" Mose said, more sharply than I'd ever heard from him. "And when I shake you off? You gonna take orders from a black man?"

Cletus thought a moment. The moment of truth, really. I could see the umpire getting impatient. "No," he said. "But I will from my pitcher."

He turned back toward the plate.

"Hey," Mose said. And then when Cletus paused. "Welcome to the team."

I smiled, satisfied, returned to my position. I pounded my glove, my shortstop's glove. From time to time I had been glancing toward the stands. Laura sat there throughout the game and clapped for the Pioneers, but I'd made a great stop in the fifth inning of a line shot. I had dived to my left, gloved the ball just before it hit the outfield, and got up and fired to first just in time to nail the runner—Jim Bunch.

He'd flung his batting helmet in frustration and I'd run to our dugout under a hail of plaudits from my teammates. And then I heard a girl shout out from the stands: "Great play!" I looked her way, a little worried that the home town fans might not appreciate that, but she just smiled my way.

It gave me a funny feeling.

Mose wound up and fired a bullet past a swinging Pioneer batsman. As Cletus hurled the ball back he yelled: "Good pitch!"

We got the two outs without anybody scoring and everybody came in to the dugout whooping and hollering. I slapped Mose and Cletus both on the back as they entered the dugout.

"We're gonna take these guys!"

In the top of the ninth inning Mose led off with a walk. Though he didn't bat often and still had a ways to go to become a good hitter, he was getting better and he could run.

The next batter, Larry Bain, tried unsuccessfully to bunt him over and was forced to swing away. He sent a hard grounder to the shortstop.

Mose was fast and he got to second about the same time as the second basemen, who from my vantage point in the dugout seemed surprised and, I thought, stumbled. Mose slid and knocked him for a loop, and as he collapsed he screamed in pain.

We could all see blood staining through his uniform from his leg which had been gashed by Mose's spikes.

Mose looked stunned and helpless as the second baseman writhed in pain.

The Pioneer players and Coach Cross ran over and clustered in a circle around the second baseman. The fans unleashed a cascade of boos.

Coach said to Mose, "It wasn't your fault. These things happen."

Out on the field I could see Jim Bunch glaring at Mose and knew he thought it was his fault. I heard him say to his teammates, "That bastard came in spikes high."

The second baseman got up limping, was helped off the field to a chorus of applause, and we joined in.

In the bottom of the ninth Mose went out to pitch and weathered a storm of boos and catcalls, then just plain invective as he worked his way through two batters for two outs. One more and we would have an upset win.

The next batter though blooped a single into center field over my outstretched glove.

Jim Bunch came up, and I learned the truth of the expression "staring daggers." Cletus ran out to the mound and I joined them. Cletus said, "This guy likes to hit fastballs and he'll think we're gonna get cute. But let's go right at the sumbitch."

I said, "If he hits it, we'll catch it."

"Promise?" Mose asked.

"Promise."

So Cletus called for fastball after fastball. Bunch missed the first, two went wide of the plate, and the third he fouled off.

I worried that Bunch was beginning to focus in on and adjust for the speed of Mose's fastball. The next pitch he sent deep into centerfield. I said to myself, "Well, nice try while it lasted," but George raced back and leaped high at the fence. He caught the ball that had been destined to be a home run and turned it into the last out.

We all went nuts and George had trouble getting back to the dugout, we were mobbing him so much. Coach had a huge smile on his face and slammed George on the back, and so did Mose. All was forgiven, and nobody in the park could have been happier than George except maybe me.

As for Jim Bunch, when he saw George had converted his gamewinning homer into an out he had flung his batting helmet a country mile and walked off the field doing extreme violence to the English language and, from what I heard, inventing a few new cuss words.

As I was walking by the stands I ran into Laura. She looked like she was waiting for someone, and as the conversation went on, I started to think the someone was me.

"Congratulations."

"We played together--for once."

"Keep playing like that and you'll be back next month for the state tournament."

"I'd like that."

"How's the injury?"

"Doctor says he's gashed up. Lot of bandages but he's walking around ok. He'll be fine."

She preoccupied me and at first I didn't notice that Mose had headed toward the parking lot with Coach Cross. He said Coach wanted to give him a little pep talk about not taking the taunts too seriously, but Mose said "What taunts?" and that pretty much ended the conversation.

Coach headed off in the car with George and Bobby.

Mose said he'd thought about getting a victory snow cone but just then the concession window slammed shut. He saw me in conversation with Laura and thought the last thing I'd want was him butting in, so he just idled away for a few minutes.

That's when Jim Bunch got in his face. He'd commandeered a few other Pioneer players for backup.

"You cut Johnny real bad."

"I didn't mean to. I came in hard but clean."

"You're a liar."

"Don't call me that."

"Liar."

Cletus, Sammy and Randy were walking toward the parking lot together. They came to an abrupt halt when they saw the Pioneer players surrounding Mose.

Cletus asked, "What's going on?" and Bunch answered, "Private quarrel. You on his side?"

Sammy and Randy waited for Cletus, who looked like he couldn't decide at first. Mose said later that was the only thing he did that gave him credit. But finally he said, "On the field, " put his head down and walked away. Mose gritted his teeth. "All right, you mothers. I ain't runnin'. You lookin' for a fight, show me what you got."

Mose said Bunch hesitated when he said that, maybe surprised at Mose's bravado.

"What's the matter," Mose said, "not enough crackers to back you up?" He told me he knew that would set him off, but he'd had enough. "If I was gonna' keep turnin' the other cheek, I figured it was gonna get hit one day anyway. And I might as well give unto others what they were gonna give unto me."

Bunch waded in swinging and Mose belted him flush on the jaw, sending him to the ground. The other Pioneer players charged in. Mose was overwhelmed.

Sammy and Randy didn't react right away.

"Shouldn't we do something?" Randy wondered to Sammy.

The commotion of the fight got my attention. I was still with Laura.

"Shit."

I ran over as quick as I could. Mose had gone down under a jumble of bodies and Jim Bunch piled on top, punching through the pile at his face.

When I arrived I harked back to my football days and went flying in a blitzkrieg body block, knocking Bunch off Mose and with enough force to scatter the pile. We couldn't get up though. There were too many of them and we began a big tagteam wrestling match, with not enough room to throw good punches.

The odds were against us and we couldn't have held out long, but reinforcements arrived.

I managed to see Larry Bain ask "What's happening?" and get a shove backward from one of the Pioneer players who'd managed to get up.

"Buzz off," he said.

Wrong move. Larry pummeled the Pioneer player's jaw.

"You buzz off."

He waded into the melee and that was all Sammy and Randy

needed to finally join the brawl. Spencer was having a smoke before heading out with Billy Aycock when Cletus passed them without saying hello. He made a gesture with his shoulder that kind of said, look over there. They did and saw what was happening and took off running.

When Spencer arrived and saw Mose and me struggling to free ourselves from three Pioneer players, he calmly put the lighted end of his joint on their necks. As they howled in pain they were distracted enough for us to come up fighting.

Larry was battling two Pioneer players. When Billy joined, he and Larry pretty quickly made short work of them

As I got up I saw a bear named Bunch looming in front of me. "Come on. Just you and me," he said. I swung and he blocked it, but I ducked his punch and was able to land a good one before we started pounding each other. We could have gone on but a police siren brought everybody to attention.

We looked toward the road and saw two Belleville police cars coming our way. They passed another car heading in the opposite direction—Cletus'.

"Shit," Bunch said, panting. "I ain't getting busted on the 4th of July. You mothers take your sorry asses back to Dogshitville." He gave a signal to his minions and they zipped away to lick their wounds.

We thought skedaddling was a good idea but the cops were between us and the road. Then I saw Laura waving and pointing. "The lake! " she shouted. So we took selves and wounds and hurried toward the lake, out of the cops' way.

I saw her head over to greet them as they drove up and just had a confident feeling she'd find a way to explain away our little skirmish. She told me later she'd cited Rio Grande, the John Wayne film where his son engages in a "soldiers' fight," ergo a private affair. "I know those officers," she said. "They love John Wayne."

"So do I." That wasn't all I meant. By that point I had all but crossed the Rio Grande into foreign territory.

13. LAURA

Belleville's lake had been carved out of red clay and rock in the basin below just about the only elevated landscape around, a hillock covered with pine trees that dominated the surrounding flatlands. It reminded me a little bit of the pond and terrai;n near Pinnacle Mountain outside Little Rock, though on a less grand scale.

The pine trees went all around the shore, and that's where we took refuge to patch ourselves up as best we could but mostly hash over the fight. I felt sorry for George, who would have loved this band of brothers moment.

Laura was ministering to me and I gladly let her. She swabbed a cut over my eye with a damp cloth and washed various scrapes with lake water, which she said "will probably give you typhus or gangrene, take your pick."

We were at the edge of the forest, in view of the ballpark. In the hollow below the lights of the town twinkled.

"Somebody had long fingernails."

"Hometown folks are supposed to back their team."

"Not when they're wrong. I gave Jim a piece of my mind."

"How did he take it?"

"He said it hurt worse than the punch he took from 'that Dogshit shortstop.' Was he talking about you?"

She swabbed a little higher on my forehead. Truth be told, I wanted to look at her in the little bit of firelight that reached us where we sat a ways from the others.

Spencer and Billy had planned to hang around for the fireworks in Belleville tonight and had brought marshmallows and hot dogs, a few beers and a few coat hangers to use for roasting. Now they were sharing their provisions with all of us and had made a good fire in a pit they'd dug and rimmed with rocks.

Spencer was holding two bottles of beer against his eyes.

"They say beer beats cold steak any day." He held the bottles away, revealing two bruised, black-rimmed eyes. "Well?"

Mose said, "You need a cold steak."

Spencer shook his head and pulled out one of his cigarettes. "I'll try an herbal remedy."

Randy was applying a wet washrag to Sammy's bloody nose. "You better be glad Dracula don't play for this team."

Billy was unrolling his right sock while Larry watched. "Damn, I knew that guy bit me," Billy said.

"You shouldn't have kept stepping on his head."

When Spencer finished his smoke he stood up, hoisting his beer.

"A toast. To the Dogtown Packers. They came, they saw, they kicked butt."

Everybody seconded the sentiment with a hearty round of seconding cheers. Spencer sat down beside Randy, who was staring at him in awe.

"Jesus A. Christ.. How about you and me rigging up a brain transfusion. I'll go to Harvard too, 'stead of them rice paddies."

"Stanford. I'm thinking Stanford now."

"Where's that?"

"California." Spencer thought a moment. "You do know California?"

"Hey, I ain't dumb. It's out West." He paused a moment. "Somewhere."

Mose was laughing and joking and sipping beer just like the rest and I thought, he's one of us at last. Not that that could be considered a step up. But as doubt flicked across my mind, Sammy and Randy sidled over to Mose.

Sammy said, "Say uh, for what it's worth, we're sorry."

Randy added, "Yeah, for standing there with our thumbs up our butts."

"Hey, better late than never," Mose assured them. "Y'all rode to the rescue."

"Yeah, all except…"

"He's a different story." Mose had turned serious. Billy chimed in, "Hell, let's kick him off the team."

"NO," Mose said, and by the tone of his voice, he meant it.

"We're past that."

After we'd chowed down on the dogs and confirmed to ourselves that we'd whipped them boys so bad they went home crying to their mamas and likely wouldn't show their faces in public another month and similar fish story bullshit, we began to break up and head for home.

I took Mose aside and asked him if he minded riding home with Billy. "I'd like to hang around a while."

Mose said "No problem. For me, that is." Mose had met Mary Louise and like everybody, been impressed. "They talk about knockouts. She really is," he said. She'd been polite and told me later, "He speaks really well."

"He's not Stepin Fetchit," I said.

"Who knew?"

So Mose knew very well I was walking on the wild side, but he saw Laura waiting for me and said something curious:

"I feel things, you know. You know what they say, 'Don't do anything I wouldn't do.' Well, in this case, 'Do something I wouldn't do.'"

"We're just going to watch the fireworks."

"Set some off while you're at it."

George gave me grief a couple days later when I told him about my adventure.

"Lord, what fools these mortals be."

"Look, it was just a boat ride."

"That's what they said on the Titanic."

Laura led me down to a dock where a johnboat was tethered. "We'll have a great view."

"You're on."

I paddled us out toward the middle of the lake and then we just drifted. The moon hadn't yet risen and the whole sky blazed with stars. The evening was still warm, with a slight breeze from time to time that I could just see ruffling her hair. I felt an attraction like a strong magnetic force. Physical, but more than that. I could have resisted, but no part of me wanted to, and any sentiment of betrayal or doubt went sailing away in the wind and I let it. I preferred looking at and listening to her.

"They'll be starting any minute now. Don't expect a spectacle like at the Eiffel Tower. Belleville's a small town."

"You've been to Paris?"

"Dream #1." It turned out she was studying French at their high school--

"Here, in Belleville?"

"Our teacher has family back in France and learned it growing up. Arkansas used to be French territory, you know. That's why we've got names like Belle Fourche."

I challenged her with laissez--faire and she not only knew what it meant but pronounced it well--insofar as I knew, anyway. I told her the legend of Petit Jean and she seemed sincerely moved by the story.

"Would you follow your man across the ocean?" I asked.

"If I loved him, even to the moon. And hope he had a rose waiting for me. That's not too much to ask, is it?"

"On the moon it might be, but if he managed to find one up there, I'd say he was worth the trip."

"Well, a love song might do. If he sang it with heart."

I was afraid she might ask me to sing one now and once she heard me sing, that would be that, so I somehow segued into anecdotes about my composing and orchestrating The Ballad of Big Chuck.

"We heard it on the radio! Today!"

"Up here in Belleville? Well how about that. The power of the media."

"Well, you might say the DJ was making fun of it. I liked it though. I thought it was funny. Once you hear it a couple of times you can't forget it."

"Yeah, it's like a barnacle."

She started singing it and motioned for me to join it, so I did, reluctantly at first, but then we both got into it and chorused it together, louder and louder. We didn't think anyone would object, out there in the middle of the lake, but just as we were winding up, a flock of ducks took flight right over us. It looked like nothing so much as fleeing desperately to escape the jingle, and Laura and I had the same thought and burst into hysterical laughter that must have gone on for five minutes.

It was hard to recover. I laughed so hard I had tears in my eyes.

#

The fireworks began. They went on for about 20 minutes and certainly were not like any show in Paris might be, but bursting above the lake created kind of stereoscopic reflections that made for a double spectacle.

"Twice the thrill," Laura said.

It was almost as if we were seeing reality through the eye and simultaneously an artist's impressionistic rendering of it. Together with the occasional flash of sparks from expended charges landing in the water with hisses and a burst of flame, it was all wonderful to see, there on the quiet lake with her.

When the show ended, we were left in the dark as our eyes adjusted. I heard her say softly, "I can tell what you're thinking, Tom."

She sidled to the middle seat of the boat and I joined her. We began kissing. It had been a long day and I'd been knocked around and perhaps I was dreaming, out on the still water with the moon coming up.

When George got through lecturing me he made fun of me, saying "Well, at least there's only so much you can do in a boat."

"Sometimes it's how you feel, not how far you go."

"Hey, don't start sounding mature."

"Besides, she said her father had a big truck with a big shotgun inside and after 11 he got ready to use it."

"That I understand."

I drove her home. She lived in a cozy two-level house and had all the upper level to herself, with a window she said that looked out on a mulberry tree and persimmon tree and lawn that sloped to a small creek.

"I don't suppose we could slip upstairs without your father hearing and cocking his shotgun."

"Not so fast, cowboy. I hardly know you." She kissed me good night as she was getting out of the car.

"Maybe I'll see you again."

I said, "It would help to have a phone number."

"Check your glove, shortstop."

She went to the door and entered the house. When she turned on the light I caught a glimpse of the interior and thought it looked cozy and warm as I imagined it might be--a nice place to live.

The moon had risen to full height and gave me a lot of light to see the scrap of paper she'd somehow managed to slip inside my glove with the 7 vital numbers.

14. STUTTGART

On the Saturday in late July when we visited Stuttgart to play an afternoon game, Coach had well advised, "Bring some spare water."

Stuttgart lies on the flat Mississippi Delta plain and coming in, the road didn't get any higher than a speed bump. At noon it was 100° F and counting. The town is fertile rice country and home to the world's largest rice cooperative and what with the water needed for the rice evaporating and the sun baking down, we learned a little bit of what life in an oven would be like.

Between innings a line would form at our dugout in front of the water jug and if we went three and out real quick, you'd have to wait another half-inning to drink and no one wanted that.

That was later, though. When we arrived the Stuttgart team was nowhere to be seen. Coach phoned a contact number provided by Big Chuck, who had scheduled the game, but no answer.

A couple of senior citizens wandered in to watch the game, or else rest in the shade under the grandstand roof. They told Coach everyone was at a big wedding. "Our best hitter and a local gal, Miss Rice Paddy she was." They said it was bound to be a big shebang and if the preacher got emotional and went on, no telling...

We took refuge under the grandstand roof with the oldtimers. In the distance we heard a chorus of quacks, like a flock of ducks passing by.

"Duck calling competition," Sammy said. "I thought about entering but we had this game." I could tell from the look on his face that he was regretting his priorities.

After about an hour of of broiling we saw a guy hustling on foot across the outfield, almost running. He was dressed in a suit and tie which he was ripping off even as he hustled forward.

"The rest of 'em's coming," he said, and pretty soon they all straggled in, along with some spectators who'd been guests.

As soon as they had nine players and a home plate umpire, we got going. Later we learned the ump had been the preacher. Even so, he proved to be a good ump and not biased for the home team.

Coach said he didn't want to make a stink about the delay: "Love makes a good excuse for all kinds of twists and turns in life."

We got off to a big lead and coasted in the game, and our bats were on fire like the temperature. That was good, except that the more runs we scored, the longer we had to stay out on the field in the infernal heat which didn't show any sign of diminishing until roughly next Christmas.

Before coming up to hit, we had to grab gobs of dirt and coat our hands so we could grip the bat surely. I heard the ump mutter, "Lord Lord" as he pulled off his mask and wiped his brow, but the Lord didn't give us a break.

The duck calls in the distance continued all afternoon, and at one point when a Stuttgart batter lined a ball to right field Sammy didn't even move. We had to scream at him to snap out of his trance and give chase.

Coach Cross plopped him down on the bench and put Bubba in the lineup in his place. Coach told him, "You can listen better from here."

Along about the 8th inning none other than the newlyweds showed up. The bride still wore her gown. They accepted the congratulations of everybody in the stands.

The umpire called time and came over to see Coach. They conferred a moment and I saw Coach smile and nod yes. We were out on the field, on defense, wondering what was going on. Their Coach in the third base box said to me and Randy, "Thanks a lot, fellas. He's our best hitter and got horsehide in the blood."

So here came the groom up to the plate, swinging a bat, still in his Sunday go-to-meeting shirt and pants. And dress shoes.

Spencer had pitched a gem of a game, baffling their hitters

with all kinds of different speeds and junk pitches, but suddenly he seemed to have nothing but fastballs. Except they didn't go very fast and went right down the middle of the plate.

The groom got a good pitch and laced it over my head into the gap. Even in dress shoes he had no trouble making it to second base with a double. The crowd went berserk, especially his bride who blew him a thousand kisses. A pinch runner came jogging out.

"Better get cleaned up," I said to the groom.

"She don't love me dirty, she don't love me."

I had the ball which George had thrown in from the outfield. I gave it to him. "Souvenir. Treat her right."

"Thanks, man. Appreciate it. And I will." As he loped back to the stands the crowd went berserk again. His bride was waiting and they went off into the sunset.

When we got the last out and swam in sweat back to the dugout, Coach said they were heading off to Hot Springs for their honeymoon.

"Don't know why," Spencer said, "they got sweat baths right here."

"And ducks," Sammy added.

15. MARGARET

Coach Cross was giving an interview to Bill Bowers.

"Don't ask me why a team suddenly jells. One day you notice they save their fight for the field. Win or lose, they're on each other's side. It's a fine thing to see."

And it was. We started winning and ran off a streak of ten games in a row, moving into first place in our division. Our only loss was a heartbreaker to the team from Sheridan. We should have won, but they had enough luck that day to last for a season, and we went down by one run. Earlier in the year we'd lost by 7 runs to this same Sheridan team, so if General Electric could be believed, we were making progress.

Where before we had always found a way to lose, now we did everything right, and in some cases, more than right. We turned double plays, we got hits when we needed them, our pitchers turned into world-beaters, and most of all as Coach said, whatever we did we did as a team.

Larry let Billy know that he'd said nothing about what happened that night in Fort Smith—"Not everyone's as big an asshole as you, Aycock, " he put it delicately, and it was like they'd suddenly become best friends. Their right side of the infield became almost like a wall, stopping balls from getting through, because they were able to coordinate their defense like they hadn't ever done before. They were talking to each other.

Mose didn't call Cletus a chicken shit like some of us wanted him to do after the brawl with Belleville, and Cletus-- even though he no doubt would have done the same thing again, walk away--worked with Mose when he pitched like they'd been doing it for years. When Mose struck out a batter, we noticed that Cletus would scream and sometimes raise his arm high in the air. It became an intimidating factor against opposing batters.

Bill Bowers said to me with his usual ironic smile, "Don't tell that turkey he's giving a Black Power salute."

"What's Black Power?"

"Geez, every time I talk to you I feel like donating money to combat illiteracy."

I knew we'd truly banded together one night on the road. Generally we'd been met with respect and not too many jeers from opposing fans, but in this one town a less than upright citizen boomed out insults from Pitch One, mostly at Mose. He never resorted to racist lingo, but you didn't need a translator to understand what he was saying.

A lot of fans looked uncomfortable but apparently said nothing--free speech and all that--and the man, who was in his '40s, walked the thin line between acceptable and going too far.

Along about the 6th inning he expanded his repertoire and started in on Cletus, wondering how he could catch that guy. "Must be as thick in the head as your backside," he yelled out. I worried that our hardwon team harmony would collapse once Cletus took the guy's words to heart and started thinking he'd come down on the side of the devil.

But we got lucky. When we came in to the dugout in the bottom of the 6th Larry suddenly bolted for the bathroom. I didn't think anything of it at the time, but suddenly the next inning, it was like the vocal fan lost his voice. At any rate he "clammed up like an oyster," Randy said, "or a clam I guess."

Not a peep.

In the ninth inning he left and went home early. I saw him get up and leave, and if ever you could say a man had his tail between his legs, he was it.

After the game Larry told us why the guy had decided to become a gentleman. Larry had spotted him heading to the bathroom and joined him "in mid-pee."

He said, "I let him know his comments were not appreciated."

"That's it?" Randy asked. "You gave him a talking to?"

"Mostly. I told him if he kept up like that, he'd be in some deep shit. Good place to show him what I meant, you know?"

He wouldn't go into any more detail than that.

#

Bill Bowers had been dutifully recording Coach's comments in his notebook and I looked forward to reading something positive about us for once.

"I hear Belleville has recruited a couple more pitchers," Bill said.

"Let's win the city championship first. Then we'll worry about the state."

Bill nodded and moved away. We were standing around in street clothes, ready to head out to Hot Springs for a game. Coach had let us know in advance that he couldn't come with us and had turned over the reins to me as captain. He'd made out the lineup cards and everything.

"Well men, I won't be going with you to Hot Springs this weekend. Got some personal business to attend to."

George joked, "You'll miss the orgies, Coach."

"Earlier in the season I'd have worried about that, " Coach said with a smile."Now I know—"

"Henry!"

Coach Cross whirled and was as surprised as we were to see a frail looking woman with haunted eyes. She had sneaked up on us like a wraith.

"Margaret..." Coach said. "I was just on my way home, darling." We had never met Coach's wife, who looked pale and nervous but preened somewhat for us.

"The flowers, Henry, they need water. They're dying."

He took her hands reassuringly in his. "We'll take care of them right away, honey."

"Now?"

"Now." She noticed us as if for the first time. "What handsome young men! Are they married, Henry?"

"Not yet, dear."

She looked at my shoes "I love loafers, don't you? They're so comfortable and snug, like a baby's hand."

"Yes m'am." Coach said, "Boys, I want you to meet my wife Margaret. She's visiting me this weekend, and we hope a lot

181

longer."

We gave a hearty chorus of "howdy m'ams" and hellos.

'I know you're all fine, fine young men. Do you always try to be the very best players you can be?"

I answered quickly for all of us, "Yes m'am, we sure do." She smiled even though her eyes had drifted to another thought during my answer.

"Have you told them about Babe Ruth, Henry?"

"I clean forgot. Boys, Margaret once saw Babe Ruth himself play."

"Saw him play? He hit a home run for me, that's what he did. I was just a little girl and my father took me to New York. 'Let's see the Yankees play,' he said, 'let's see the great Bambino.' And we went and I saw him and he waved to me. It had to be me. Who else could it have been, Henry?"

Once again he patted her hand to reassure.

"And I wished and wished for him to hit a home run and he did! The crowd cheered and cheered for the great Bambino as he tippy-toed around the bases. That's how he ran, tippy-toe."

She mimicked him running with her fingers.

"He answered my prayer. He was the greatest player of all time. But now he's gone."

Her lips quivered, she looked distraught. We shifted uncomfortably. "The flowers, Henry!"

"We're going now, dear."

He hurried her off, nodding goodbye to us who were trying to come to terms with this apparition.

She resembled very much my Aunt Roberta, whom my parents would speak about in low anxious voices each time we planned to visit. "She's doing better," I would overhear, and the visit would seem to be a window of opportunity that might not come around again very soon.

It was never stated what ensued when my aunt was not doing better, but there were whispers about institutions, and always concern for my uncle's psychological health.

When we did visit she would regale us, and especially me, with stories about the bird population in the woods out back.

She was an avid birdwatcher.

She didn't appreciate it much when I told her of my pastime of propping up a wooden crate with a stick and stringing a rope line from stick to our backyard barn, after having spilled crumbs underneath the box to attract birds.

When they took the bait, I'd pull and the crate would fall and trap them inside. I had nailed a mesh screen over the box top so I could watch them flutter around inside. I told my Aunt Roberta that I wouldn't carry this on much longer because after several blackbirds and starlings, I'd reached the summit and caught a redbird cardinal. It was so exciting watching this beautiful bird up close.

I had thought she might like my interest in the birds, but in her eyes I could read horror, and I hastily added that I'd let them all go, even the starlings who my cousins swore robbed eggs from nests of other birds and told me to wring their necks.

"All of them?" my aunt asked.

"Every single one."

"Even the starlings?"

"Yes m'am, for sure. I never caught a robin or mockingbird, they were too smart I guess."

"Tom, if you see a scarlet tanager"--she paused, opening up her thick catalogue of ornithology illustrations--and there was a color photo of the tanager, which she pronounced "tanger."

"You must never catch a scarlet tanager. I've seen some, and Tom, it was the most beautiful experience of my life. They're bright red, and see the coal-black wings. Their colors light up the world around them. If you see one, just consider yourself blessed. It will be a very special day in your life. You have to hug those special days close to your heart, Tom. Because so many days aren't."

She'd had a special day when the war ended and she accompanied my mother to downtown Little Rock for a celebration, along with many other women who'd worked for the war effort and still tended the hearth during those long years. Our newspaper had captured a shot of my mother dancing with a GI and graced--that's the word--the front page with the GI waving his cap and my mother spinning and laughing with joy and my Aunt Roberta on the sidewalk watching, smiling radiantly and innocently.

She'd had no concerns then about "doing better" and the future may have seemed like the long wide and unhurried flow of the Arkansas River. It was not, but she still had the birds and if nothing else, one reason to rise each morning and hope to catch sight of a beautiful scarlet tanager.

#

George said, "I wondered why we never met Coach's wife."

I looked at everyone and said forcefully, "Let's go win him a ball game."

16. LOOKING FOR LOVE

The week we had won enough games to take over first place in our league standings, I drove up to Belleville to see Laura. We'd spoken on the phone a couple of times, conversations that lasted a while but were always awkward for her because her parents moved in and out of the vicinity.

"He plays shortstop," I heard her say once when one or both of them seemed to be hovering around the phone, and I felt sure they were concerned about the potential hurt that could be wreaked on their daughter's heart by some city boy, not to mention whatever Bellevillian she'd been seeing--a subject we danced around, just as I avoided mentioning the skeleton in the closet I was not anxious to let out. All in good time, assuming the good time came, and I would know more about that after seeing her again.

She was playing in a softball game with her girls team, and they were already warming up on the sideline when I arrived at the park. She came over and said, "Don't make too much fun of us."

"I'm here to pick up pointers."

"Don't pick up anyone else."

I went over and took a seat in the stands. I had hoped that my nemesis Jim Bunch wouldn't be there, off gigging frogs or stealing hubcaps or standing in front of his mirror asking who was the biggest stud in the land, but no such luck. He was in the stands making the rounds of admirers. When he spotted me he asked politely, "What the hell are you doing here?"

"Watching the game. I heard it was a free country."

"With exceptions. Communists and outside agitators ain't welcome."

"You're pretty agitated right now. Maybe you ought to eat a snow cone and calm down."

"Say goodbye. That'll calm me down right quick."

Laura's team took the field to cheers and clapping and Laura took her position at third base. Bunch followed my gaze and put 2 and 2 together, which surprised me as I didn't think he could count up to 4.

"Laura's got this habit of taking in stray dogs. You know, mutts no one would give a second look."

"She told me one of them's named after you. That right, Jim?"

"Shit, I'd invite you out back but last time didn't teach you no lesson. Just be wasting my time. Tomorrow I'll take her and get her head examined. That'll be the last we see of you."

"Until the state tournament."

"Yeah, you and the Harlem Globetrotters."

He moved away and spent the next few innings bullshitting with some spectators and a couple of Belleville players I recognized. Bunch had alerted them to me because they looked my way--more curious than anything, I thought.

Being Laura's guest must have helped keep the peace, or else Bunch's attentions to the team's scrappy, fiery catcher who appeared to be his girl friend. She was about half his size but based on what I saw of how she led the team, and shouted out position commands, twice his intelligence.

Laura was a hell of a player. She had a very strong arm and fired throws to first base like, I dare say, a man. She batted third and had a lot of power. In the first inning she smoked a line drive to left that the other team's shortstop didn't look too eager to get in front of.

In the 7th inning with the game on the line she slammed a long drive that just missed clearing the fence. It banged off the wall and caromed toward center.

Laura rounded second base and headed to third for a triple, but her coach waved her home. This astonished everybody. Inside the park home runs in softball, as in hardball, are extremely rare.

She hurried toward the plate and slid--the throw had her beat, but the catcher fumbled the ball and she scored for the home run. Everybody in the park knew they'd seen something special, something they could pass a long time without seeing again, and pandemonium broke loose. I was on my feet cheering like everyone else. Jim Bunch even looked like he'd forgotten a mangy dog was in the stands.

Laura was mobbed by her teammates and it took a while for the umpire to get them to leave off celebrating and get back to finishing the game. As she headed back to the dugout she turned and tipped her hat toward the fans--and to me, I hoped.

Her team won thanks to the homer, and again it took a while for her to get away from the clamor and postgame celebrating. She came over with her gear after most of the spectators and other players had left.

"Can I have your autograph?" I asked.

"I always accommodate my fans." We went to the local hangout restaurant and had a nightcap of root beer floats. From time to time friends and teammates would come up and congratulate her and she'd introduce me. Curiosity became the order of the evening.

"You're my mystery man."

"Call me your groupie."

"What's that?"

"An adoring fan who follows a star like a puppy dog."

"I've already got one of those and it doesn't feel so right."

That was the closest we got to discussing our involvements as at that moment Jim Bunch came in with his girl friend and ordered some food to go. She came over to our table while he waited at the counter stewing.

"I'd like to join you," his girl friend said to us, "but he doesn't want to hang out with the enemy"--to me, "He calls you the enemy."

"His name's Tom."

"Hi."

"Jodie."

"I like the way you call a game."

"Thanks," then to Laura, "he doesn't seem so bad."

"Tell Jimmy we'll promise to play nice."

Bunch was really glowering at us now, and her too. He had the food and was waiting.

"Guess I better go. Get his mind on other stuff."

She went over and they walked out together.

"She's nice," I said. "Maybe she can civilize him."

"When you get to know him he's not half bad. Trouble is, he's not half good."

They kicked us out at 10 and we drove to an out of the way lane near her nice cozy house and talked and got to know each other in other ways too. I knew I was getting myself in trouble, the best kind of life-changing trouble, but that it would come at a cost. I was ready to pay, even if it meant saying goodbye to a rich and cushy future for a more uncertain one. Where I was wasn't where I was at, but I hoped it soon would be. When we said goodbye before I began the long drive home, I said, "Time for that autograph. From the star of the game."

"I've already given you a few. Here's one for the road."

And she gave me a long, lingering kiss.

17. FIRST PLACE

We clinched the league title against Derks Construction, the same team that beat us on opening day. It was very satisfying.

Even though Harvey Harris got a couple of hits, Mose struck him out swinging in the 8th inning and made him look helpless. Cletus held on to the ball this time. Harvey pounded the dirt so hard with his bat I was glad that no poor moles were living down there.

He shook hands with us in the spirit of good sportsmanship but he said to me, "You suckers don't fill up your gas tanks. You won't go no farther than Little Rock"--meaning the regional playoffs.

That went a tad too far, so we all got together and chipped in a few cents and sent him a package of lollipops with a note: "Consolation Prize--because we know you suck."

I wasn't sure Harvey could read, but apparently yes, and write too, because he sent back a picture that Bill Bowers had taken of a group of us hoisting the league championship trophy. It was a red mess of dried juice and pocked with seeds, and we understood Harvey had used it for a target as he gobbled down a watermelon. "Thinking of you," he wrote, though I thought he came close to misspelling "of."

We went to Little Rock and played before big crowds and won the regional tournament. We did it with efficiency and the kind of team play we'd learned, though there was a 2-1 nailbiter game that went down to the last pitch, when Mose gave up a couple of hits and had to get the last batter out or lose the game.

Coach Cross said afterward, "Sweated that one out. I must have lost five pounds."

Big Chuck was just absolutely delighted that we'd beaten a Little Rock team to win it all. "Those uppity snobs thought they could just throw their gloves out there and beat us. I told 'em, next time throw out some players. I'm giving a big bash tomorrow night fellas, everything on me, and while we're eatin' the best meat in the South they'll be eating crow."

That gave us an idea. We hadn't forgotten that Harvey Harris said we couldn't win the regional. Sammy took his BB gun and downed one of the pesky crows that had been tormenting his vegetable garden. We actually grilled it and ladled on some barbecue sauce. It looked disgusting. We sent it to Harvey with a note saying to serve this with mashed potatoes and turnip greens and a glass of wood alcohol.

We thought he'd be really steamed and report us to the SPCA, but he sent back a note saying he'd eaten our "vittles" and had his best supper in a long time. I didn't believe him, but George said you couldn't put anything past Harvey. "He's a Neanderthal, and didn't they eat anything that walked or flew?"

Big Chuck rented a pavilion at Burns Park for our bash. He'd ordered all kinds of fixins' and determined that this would be the feast to end all feasts, to be outdone only "when we win the state championship."

We couldn't have just any watermelons. We had to have the best in the world, watermelons from Hope down in the southwest.

Barq's had furnished cartons and cartons of sodas in all their variety and they were cooled in buckets of ice we tried to keep in the shade of the pavilion, which meant some jam-ups as everyone tried to get to a cream soda or root beer and the like.

Before the food we had a trophy ceremony. Bob Habiner, the Legion baseball commissioner, awarded the trophy to Coach Cross and Big Chuck while we stood around cheering and applauding. Bill Bowers was there, duly taking notes and directing the newspaper's photographer, and as many parents and friends who chose to attend.

Mr. Habiner gave a little preliminary speech to the crowd: "It wasn't easy to beat that Little Rock team. It wasn't easy to beat all those teams the Dogtown Packers whipped this summer. But Henry--you did it. Congratulations."

He handed Coach the trophy to a wave of applause and cheers. We shouted and cheered as he hoisted it high for all to see.

It was a truly sweet compensation for all the setbacks and disappointments we'd had to surmount.

Habiner concluded: "Next week they're going to have the state championship trophy. Belleville, here we come!"

This brought down the house. We were playing about as well as we could play, and even though Coach Cross kept emphasizing that we had some weaknesses—"got a thin bench," he'd say often—we'd already beaten Belleville once. That meant we could do it again.

Habiner turned the mike over to my friend Bill, who'd come up from Hope with the watermelons and said he just wanted "to say a few words to the good people here" about the quality of the watermelons and how happy he was to be able to organize the delivery.

He went into a riff about Hope and hope and what we hoped to do in the state championship, and also about the importance of supporting local farmers and producers. Big Chuck was beaming and told me, "My ears haven't heard music like that since The Ballad of Big Chuck."

Randy asked me, "Who's Mr. Slick?"

"His name's Bill. I met him at Boys State. He was elected president."

"Shoot, I wouldn't vote for him for dogcatcher."

"He's a natural born politician."

"Mr. Slick? Shoot, he won't go nowhere, and you can quote me on that."

When Bill finished he started working the crowd, shaking hands right and left.

Everybody laid into the chips and dip and hors d'oeuvres laid out on a dozen tables, and we players took turns at the grill helping the cooks from Lindy's with the barbecue. Big Chuck was right about the meat—it was great.

For a while the idea had circulated to have the Huggins Quartet sing, but having gospel resonate while people were pigging out and otherwise prioritizing the pleasures of the flesh didn't seem appropriate.

I called Country Joe Slade and after a brief negotiation where he pretended he'd have to cancel multiple better paying gigs, he agreed to play and brought along some backup musicians who turned out to be outstanding. Two were black and young, and you couldn't help but think about the future they might have after Country Joe hung up his guitar.

In any case, we all felt lucky to have the group with us and they played on and on into the afternoon, even after Country Joe took a break that stretched on and on as he chowed down, happily signing autographs in between spareribs.

Bill Bowers called me over for a photo with Mr. Habiner. He was congratulating Big Chuck and Coach Cross.

"You showed everybody you could integrate and still win."

"Credit the kids," Coach said. "They did it all."

The photographer snapped a photo, then Bill called over Spencer, Sammy, Mickey and Mose, our pitchers. He gave them all baseballs.

"Hold them out toward the camera, fellas. And don't act like they're hot taters." They did and it turned out to be a great picture.

"I'm going to call this 'the Golden Soupbones,'" Bill said.

And then of course Bill couldn't pass up a photo of Sally Bright in her Dogtown Packers T-shirt that I guess she'd stenciled herself. Bill said he was doing a favor for us. After the male readership spent a few hours staring at the picture, he said, they might, just might, notice the Dogtown Packers lettering and become fans of the team.

"It's not like you have any reservoir of success," he said. George as usual mooned around her and asked an inevitable question: "You coming up to Belleville to watch us, Sally?"

"I wouldn't miss it for the world."

I was kind of surprised at that, because Randy said she'd got a gig singing for a Little Rock nightclub and was doing a lot of modeling, but she'd always been a fan.

Mrs. Jones, Mose's mother, had come to the celebration at Mose's urging, and Coach Cross and Big Chuck saw to it that she got everything she needed. When it came time to eat, they sat next to her. Sally joined them as well.

"Thanks for all you've done," I heard Mrs. Jones say to Coach.

"The kind of person Mose is, he'd be accepted anywhere."

Big Chuck asked, "Mrs. Jones. I sponsor this bunch of hooligans, and what I want to know is: you got any more at home like Mose?"

"No. But we've got some neighbor boys play pretty good."

"Glory be, Henry!"

Larry had come with my cousin Betty and her friend, but he and Billy hung out together. The way they were huddling and nodding heads, I rather thought they might be discussing a mutual pact not to reveal their escapade in Fort Smith. Billy was saying, "I'm telling you, women are just a pain in the ass. They're not worth the trouble."

"They've got some uses."

"Hey, I don't need sex. I've got a good TV." He wouldn't give it up. "They're queen bees. They drain the life right out of you."

"This is Cindy, Betty's friend."

Billy gave her a perfunctory "Hi," but kept carrying on. "It's like a great man once said: 'Women—shit.'"

"Cindy feels the same way about guys." She nodded. "They're jerks," she said matter of factly, like it was very much fact.

Larry said when their eyes met, it was like an electric bolt passed. They spent the rest of the day together, sunbathing on the grass. When I passed by at one point I heard Billy saying, "Women screw you over every time."

"Men are worse."

He was solicitously arranging a blanket for her to lie on.

"Here, sit on this."

"Thanks. I usually don't accept favors from men."

"I usually don't give them."

Alcohol had been strictly forbidden at the bash, though no one searched anybody's car, and sometimes the vehicles seemed occupied for no reason.

Spencer was sitting on the passenger side of Randy's car with the door open and when I went over to BS with them, I noticed Randy was inspecting one of Spencer's cigarettes. He'd unwrapped it and was eyeing its contents.

"Shit, just looks like a bunch of grass to me."

Spencer said, "It is."

"Big fucking deal!"

"When the time is right, I'll introduce you to its pleasures. Some people in San Francisco plant their yards with it. They've got happy lawnmowers."

#

Mary Louise was late, and I wondered if she would show up at all. Even her father couldn't account for her whereabouts this time. I had noticed a public phone in one of the pavilions nearby, and I slipped discreetly away and used it to call Laura. The sounds of the celebration just barely reached here, but she said she could hear them and was happy for us.

"I knew you'd win. I just had a feeling."

"Tell Jim Bunch to get ready, 'cause we're coming back."

"He won't be happy."

"Will you?"

"What do you think?"

"See you next week."

"Next week."

It was a mundane conversation, though she'd said "next week" in a kind of soft seductive way that sent a thrill through me. I thought I'd save what I felt and wanted to say for when I saw her in person. Plus I thought I needed some time to sort through the mess that my personal life would become if I quit Mary Louise.

As fate would have it, she had chosen the moment I'd left to arrive, and was waiting with arms folded, frowning, tapping her foot impatiently.

"It's about time. Who do you think you are, me?"

"Where were you?"

"Let's talk about the present. The season's over, you're a winner like I always knew you were and Daddy couldn't be happier with your theme song. And our relationship is really progressing."

"Yeah, I turned on a couple of extra lights."

"What?"

"Nothing. Private joke."

"Hah hah. I've been thinking it's time to take the next step. I mean, we've been going together for four months and we're intimate and all."

"You mean like, get engaged?"

"I mean like, build a future. I don't have to spell it out, do I? I mean, girls aren't supposed to pop the question. The guy's got to have some testosterone."

Even though I was caught off guard, I knew I couldn't let this pitch go by or I'd strike out and end up on the bench, arranging the bats and picking up splinters in my butt while others played the game for me.

"I don't think we should rush into anything. We've got time."

She didn't answer right away, very unusual for Mary Louise. Just stared at me.

"Who is she?"

"Er, who?"

"You never dump someone without having someone else. Everybody knows that. I've done it myself. Once or twice. Never mind, I don't want to know. Well you listen to me Tom Hargadine, you can have your little flings, I can't fend off every stray tramp who throws herself at you. But if you jilt me I'll kill myself."

"Will you just listen-- "

Big Chuck interrupted us, thankfully. He had Bill Bowers and the photographer in tow.

"Y'all do your sparking later. Bill wants some photos of us and the trophy."

"Like you're the queen of the ball," Bill said to Mary Louise, "except I'll call it Queen of the Ballplayers."

"Gladly."

She stormed away, glad of the chance to make a fiery exit. As if this wasn't problem enough, George and Cletus buttonholed me.

"He can't play in the tournament," George said.

"What's the problem?"

Cletus said, "My work's been piling up all summer. Before, I could make it up in August but this time we're still playing."

"Can't your father hire another hand?"

"He could but he won't. He's a hard man." He just shook his head and moved away, morose and disappointed and so was I but what was there to do? I saw more than one hope vanishing, no matter that Bill's watermelons were still circulating.

The noise and bustle built up while Mary Louise hopped atop a picnic table beside the championship trophy and the crowd gathered around. The photographer began to snap photos of her and the trophy. The crowd applauded.

I heard a fly buzzing in my ear and didn't react at first, but it kept pestering until I realized it was in fact, Johnny Benson, and I couldn't ignore him any longer.

"You've got two trophies up there, Tom. What a lucky man you are." He was gaping like a fish with his mouth caught on a hook, which I guess he was in a sense. For a fleeting moment I thought about matchmaking. "You know, she really likes you."

"You really think so? Wow." He pondered this epic possibility for a moment. "She does say I calm her down. She yawns a lot when we're together." He hastily added, "At business functions I mean."

The country music band broke into a spirited rendition of "The Ballad of Big Chuck," with Country Joe voicing the lyrics like he'd been doing it for years. I watched Mary Louise adopt various striking poses as the noise, music and hullabaloo intensified. She saw me looking and tossed her hair defiantly. It added to her sex appeal which didn't need much adding. Johnny Benson whistled with admiration and gaped even wider. "Some photo, yessir, some photo."

I wasn't in it, and it occurred to me with a jolt that that was just fine.

18. UNCLE SAM WANTS US

When I got my notice for the draft physical, Bill Bowers just gave one of those cynical chuckles he specialized in whenever something reinforced his notion that most mortals made fools look smart.

"You do know there's a war going on, don't you."

"Sure. I read the newspapers."

"Yeah, and tomorrow I'm going to run a marathon in two hours."

"The headlines and your sports columns." Southeast Asia seemed very, very far away from my concerns, which mainly were Mary Louise, work problems and how to win our next game.

"In a way I don't blame you. First, you're a hillbilly and the last battle your folks fought was with the Hatfields against the McCoys. Second, you're not sweating 'cause you're going to college and whatever this war's about it should be over in four years, right?"

"I guess."

"Third, if you do happen to read past the headline it'll say in the latest battle our boys killed about a thousand Viet Cong and suffered one casualty, a private who sprained his finger pulling the trigger. And of course then you won't bother to wonder why every other day the President announces we need another 50,000 troops."

"Maybe they just can't count."

"Yeah, right. Hey, one of these days if Mary Louise lets you come up for air, educate yourself a little bit. And when you take your physical, see if you can't find a list of Uncle Sam's next invitees. If my name's on it, get ready to shake hands with Ho Chi Minh."

The day after this conversation I tried to remedy my ignorance of contemporary events and read the first page carefully. Bill had hit the nail on the head, as the President was calling for more troops. But the number had gone up to 75,000.

I was more struck by an article which read, "Science Seeks Pill to Make Man Less Palatable to Bugs."

I was disappointed they weren't looking for a pill to make us unpalatable, not just less, but Arkansas had a tropical climate and so much the better if science could make us even a little bit less tasty to ticks and chiggers.

#

George and I were still groggy from the championship party the night before, or shall we say, the yesterday that continued into today. I hadn't slept and neither had he.

"Don't worry," he said, "we can sleepwalk through this," before banging into the curb where he parked the car, not far from the recruitment center. "A free medical exam, courtesy of Uncle Sam."

It was a stately brick building built around the time of World War I, and maybe expressly for it. Alas, this great country had gotten involved in enough wars since then to keep the building in business and "young horseflesh like us coming to meet our Uncle," George joked. I wasn't in a joking mood, even if I did plan to attend college.

"Look," he assured me, "by the end of the next four years we'll see a return to isolationism. The farthest you'll have to go to keep the peace is New Orleans, and who wouldn't want to keep the peace there?"

We walked up the hard concrete steps and entered the grim cold interior. On the walls hung various official recruiting posters and Uncle Sam pointing and assuring that he wanted us. The place seemed to me not far removed in ambiance from a hospital, or asylum.

A harpy whose desk plate read "Henrietta Madloch" greeted us by barking: "Names?"

She rifled through various lists, found us and checked off our names. I had a catch in my throat when I pronounced my name and imagined seeing it on a similar list of casualties.

"In there," Mrs. Madloch growled.

As we moved away George said in my ear, "Grenade victim —no God would have allowed that face to leave the warehouse."

I stupidly thought she might make matters easier and turned back to her: "Say uh, what's this going to be like?"

She smiled ever so slightly, a harpy smile, and we discovered she had very good ears. "It wasn't a grenade. It was a bazooka. In Vietnam. Happy trails, boys."

We entered a large exam room. A couple of dozen of America's youth were lined up in two rows. They were stripped down to their underpants. I saw Larry and Randy among the group.

"Get those damn clothes off!"

That was meant for us and came from a whitecoated intern, one of three regarding us like some of Big Chuck's beef heading for slaughter, except not so respectful of their meat quality. The intern staring contemptuously at us wore a crewcut that had been greased flat until it resembled a small plane landing . The word "scuzzball" came to my mind.

One of the two army doctors—"Massa" read his name tag— looked at us with some amusement. "Maybe these gentlemen can't tell time," he smiled, and the two dozen American youths smiled with him. If you need to butter somebody up, a time when you needed an exemption from combat was a good one.

His colleague Doctor Heinz scowled. He looked like he did it often. Where Massa was dark-haired and probably with some Hispanic heritage, Heinz looked to have Nazi roots. Both had flashlights in hand.

He came over to us, George and me, and looked down at our underwear like we hadn't followed the dress code and he'd send us to the Army just for that.

"You understand English?"

"Yes sir," we both said in unison.

"Bend over and show us where the sun doesn't shine." I hesitated, stupidly not sure what he meant.

The Scuzzy Intern cackled. "Your ass!" His mates cackled too.

Doctor Massa announced: "You gentlemen better mind your manners and keep the gas inside because my colleague is going to check your other equipment. If I yell, he might squash your jelly beans."

This time the laughter from the group had a nervous edge.

Massa began moving down the row, checking for hernias. He looked like whatever he saw disgusted him, and I thought the odds were at least one of us would have a problem. But apparently none did.

Or maybe he was turning a proverbial blind eye. George said to me later, "You really think the Viet Cong won't shoot at a hernia?"

Meanwhile Dr. Heinz was checking for ruptures. He reminded me of a Las Vegas dice player, except the latter treated their wares more gently.

At first I thought the Army had moved a tank into the room, but no, it turned out to be Harvey Harris. Maybe he thought he could sweet talk the good doctor. He said to Heinz, "Them's the family jewels, Doc"—smiling broadly. Heinz said, "If this is all you got, you'd better go back to Woolworth's."

Heinz wrenched his balls and left Harvey gasping and about ready to lose his breakfast. He limped around after that.

The Scuzzy Intern had been eying us impatiently. He said to his colleagues, "We got till five o'clock to get these fuckers outta here."

George and I were bent over waiting our turn.

"Can you believe these scumbags? Oof!"

He fell victim to Heinz's inspection.

When we got herded into the next room we found the interns waiting for us, handing out vials for our urine samples.

Some guys had come in from another exam room and Spencer was among them. He winked at us and looked even more spaced out than usual.

Randy said, "I wish they'd give an IQ test. I'd be outta here in a second."

"No," George said, "the Army loves people with your lack of capacity."

The Scuzzy Intern shouted:

"Pee in the bottle! If you can't pee in the bottle, move on!"

Most everybody suffered from the basic performance anxiety all men have when peeing in public, but I managed with no problem. Last night's beers helped. Harvey was next to me, almost growling in anger as he tried to coax out a sample. I didn't look down to check him out and make matters worse, which the Scuzzy Intern did by conspicuously directing a stare at him and shouting again: "If you can't pee in the bottle, move on!"

Harvey kept trying though. As I placed my sample on a shelf with all the others, I could hear his huge growls in the background. The Scuzzy Intern was getting ready for another sadistic shout his way when Spencer handed him his sample directly.

"You'll like this one." The Scuzzy Intern was momentarily speechless, wondering what he meant.

Both doctors were waiting with syringes as we filed into the next room for blood tests. They did the job quickly and efficiently, as you would expect. George and I got pricked one after the other and moved on.

Harvey came up behind me. From the way he was smiling I figured he'd finally succeeded with his urine challenge. "Gave you all the pee you want and then some, Doc," he confirmed to Dr. Heinz. He looked at me proudly.

"We'll give you a medal," Heinz growled, and poked his arm with some force, I thought. When he pulled out the syringe, Harvey didn't move.

"Move on!" Heinz said brusquely.

Instead Harvey's eyes rolled backward and he fainted dead away, falling flat on the concrete floor. It was like a thunderclap hit the lab room. Heinz was unperturbed and just moved to the side so the following persons wouldn't have to step over Harvey.

"Next!" he yelled.

George and I stared at Harvey lying there and even though he seemed to be coming out of his faint, it didn't seem fair to just ignore him.

"You want us to help him up?" I said to Heinz.

"If you love him that much, darlings," Heinz riposted. He was busy taking blood from one after another, like on an assembly line, and kept his back turned.

George and I helped Harvey to his feet. It was like lifting a large boulder that amazingly enough, had a rudimentary power of speech.

"Where am I at?" he asked.

"Where you are," I answered rather unhelpfully. He didn't get the joke.

"I'm gonna whup that guy's ass," he said, meaning Heinz.

"Sounds like you're feeling better," George said.

For the eye exam we had to get in line and face the Scuzzy Intern.

He was seated at a desk and the exam consisted of flipping various slides of a chart with a number printed amid colored camouflage.

"Like a Rousseau jungle," George said. Neither Spencer nor I understood the reference, but it was easy to see the numbers as the slides were flipped one after the other, and waiting in line as we were, it would have been a simple matter to just memorize them. But who wanted to succeed?

Apparently a guy who was in line just in front of us. As he sat down he stared intently and seriously at the first slide. I reckoned he was a country boy and had been raised to be honest, truthful and dutybound.

The Scuzzy Intern flipped one of the chart leaves to reveal a 6 among a lot of foliage.

"What number do you see?"

The country boy waited a moment before answering. He was staring hard and wanted to give the right answer but: "I don't know, sir."

The Scuzzy intern said "Jesus!" and angrily flipped to another leaf. "Can you see that?"

The country boy squinted hard: "No sir, I surely can't."

"Jesus! That?"

"No sir. I sure am sorry, sir." He obviously needed eyeglasses in the worst way, but maybe couldn't afford them. I said to myself, the US Army isn't about to take anybody who's half-blind.

The Scuzzy Intern glared at him.

"Can you see me?"

"Yes sir, I can see you!" He sounded relieved and proud. "There's this little blur but—"

"Fine! Move on." He quickly scribbled approval on the country youth's eye exam and the latter got one step closer to joining the Army.

Spencer took a seat in front of the color chart.

"See that number?"

"Wow!" He bent down to look at the sprawl of colors. "Far out!" His eyes glazed in wonder and delight. "It's the universe, man. Tune in and turn on."

The Scuzzy Intern stared at him like he'd just seen an alien. Which I guess he had.

Tom and George and I passed the eye exam in short order, then a perfunctory hearing exam and when we finished, we found ourselves with Larry and Spencer.

Larry nodded toward two offices where we could see Massa and Heinz arranging their desks.

"Final interview," Larry said. "Where the die's cast. They stamp you 1-A or else give you a deferment. Don't get Dr. Heinz. You could be a quadriplegic and he'd classify you 1-A. Get in line for Dr. Massa."

So we all did. We got to talking about the championship tournament and Belleville and didn't notice at first that everyone who'd been in the exam had lined up behind us. Harvey—looking a little pale—had come up behind Spencer.

Only one person hadn't gotten the word and stood outside Dr. Heinz's office--the country boy with poor eyesight. "Ole Zeke's gonna have a surprise," Harvey said. "That shit he's got on his shoes got into his brains." Our own line outside Dr.

Massa's office stretched back into the corridor.

Massa and Heinz came out of their offices and looked at the two lines. Without comment or expression, they then turned and crossed paths and went into the offices opposite to where they'd been.

En route, Massa patted the country boy on the shoulder and led him inside. As he headed inside, Heinz looked delighted at the long line of victims waiting for his 1A stamp.

Behind us I could see everybody looking longingly at the now completely vacant spaces in front of Dr. Massa's office. George said, "A classic case of bait and switch."

The sound of laughter drew our attention. The interns were cackling with delight at our mistake. The Scuzzy Intern said: "You boys take a wrong turn?"

He completely ignored our angry reaction and just turned to his mates, also ignoring the fact we could hear very clearly what he said: "Dumbest bunch of peckerheads we've had yet."

Larry left the line.

"Er, Lar—" I started to say, but he'd already marched up to the Scuzzy Intern, grabbed him and whirled him around.

"I've had enough of your shit. We're not peckerwoods. We're human beings." Then he just hauled off and slugged the Scuzzy Intern, who fell backward and crashed into a desk.

Everyone--interns, all us recruits standing there in our shorts, Heinz and Massa who came to the door of their offices--stared agape at what had happened. No one spoke for long seconds.

"Bet they don't see that every day," George said.

As if that were a signal, the other interns charged Larry. Others were arriving and they all started pummeling and grappling with him.

Well, if that's the way it was going to be…it's not like we hadn't prepared for something like this, up in Belleville. "Let's go," I said.

George and Randy and I went to the rescue. We pulled two of the interns off Larry, thinking they might desist and break off the fight. But they raised their fists. George and I punched them backward.

It became a general melee. All our peers yelled encouragement, even when a couple of uniformed soldiers, pretty big guys, ran in and started swinging away.

I noticed that Heinz had taken cover in his office and apparently locked the door, because Harvey had recovered some vim and was banging on the door, trying to get in and whup his ass.

The country boy had remained in Massa's office, watching as the melee became larger. He was shuffling papers around and at a certain point, I noticed him stamp one with what looked like an official seal.

Spencer told us later that he had total confidence in our ability to win the fight and instead plopped himself down in front of the multi-colored eye chart. He was just flipping cards and staring at them in ecstasy.

Larry put the coup de grace on the Scuzzy Intern with a punch that sent him tumbling backward into the exam room where we'd given urine samples.

I heard a big crash and simultaneously saw the country boy walking blithely out the door with a document in his hand—I was confident it had been stamped 4-F—and at the other exit door a piercing whistle that reverberated throughout all the exam rooms. It brought us all to attention.

A captain had entered the room with a squad of burly M.P.'s. At sight of these powerful reinforcements, the fight ended. All us recruits got quiet.

The captain turned to one of the MPs. "Go rescue that courageous doctor."

He meant Heinz, who was timidly peeking out from behind his desk where he had taken cover. Harvey was just about to rip the door off its hinges and when the MPs tried to corral him, he just flailed his arms and they went tumbling backward. The two soldier boys had to come over and help subdue the one pissed-off gorilla.

While this was going on the captain surveyed the chaos we'd caused. A table had been overturned, medical dossiers tossed willy-nilly everywhere, the eye chart ripped in half, a couple of army personnel on the floor and groggy. I didn't see Dr. Massa. We figured he'd hightailed it out of there and called the MPs.

The Scuzzy Intern was out cold and lying in a pool of liquid. It could have been water or it could have been something else. It did have a yellow tinge.

Oddly, the captain seemed kind of proud.

"Congratulations, " he said. "You boys are gonna make damn fine A1 good soldiers. Or should I say, 1A."

And he smiled a yard wide.

19. LUMBERYARD

Cletus was so occupied with his work he didn't see us drive up and park our cars outside the lumberyard, which stood on the edge of a woodland and I wondered if it belonged to the family also.

He was planing a block of wood, right in the middle of and almost surrounded by piles of shavings, chips, and high stacks of lumber.

Cletus inspected the wood carefully, put it back on the plane...and looked up to see me in some well-worn work clothes.

"With a little help from your friends, you can get this work done in no time. Where do we start?"

I'd come with about half a dozen of the guys and Cletus commenced a big smile on the order of, answer to my prayers, but it disappeared abruptly when he saw Mose in the group.

"Christ almighty. What are you doing here?"

"Helping the team."

"He's done some carpentering," I said.

Cletus turned like he was expecting the guillotine. I saw a man I imagined was his father standing outside the lumberyard office beckoning him over.

"Christ almighty. Uh, start cutting them 2-by-4s in foot blocks."

He moved away. George and I and the rest looked with some trepidation at the skyscraping stack of 2-by-4s. "One word," George said. "Sisyphus."

I went over toward the office where Cletus joined his father, a tall fierce man. Cletus looked rather like a condemned man. I thought I could help explain things if need be, but right away I saw Mr. Judson didn't want explanations.

"Who's that?"

"Uh—"

"You ain't tellin' me he's associatin' with your team. You

ain't tellin' me they've gone that crazy down there." Judson clenched his son's shirt fiercely. "Workin' with 'em is one thing. Associatin' is another."

"He's a sawmill hand, pa. I think he worked some for Huggins. They'll work for nothin' to help me out."

"We really need Cletus," I jumped in. Oh shit, I thought. If Mose didn't know which end of a saw cut, we were dead.

Cletus turned and gave me a look like we're in for it now. We went over and we rejoined our teammates. They were busy sawing, planing and stacking the cut 2-by-4's. I could see Cletus' father standing in the office doorway, watching us like a hawk. In fact, he resembled a hawk I thought, like one of those raptors I'd seen at Petit Jean.

Cletus said to Mose, "My old man thinks you're a field hand."

"What?"

Judson spied them talking and headed over. Cletus started to panic. "My old man's meaner than the KKK. If he finds out you're on the team I'll never play again."

Mose didn't budge.

"For Christ sake, do it for the team."

"Maybe we can say..." But I trailed off. What could we say? Judson approached. Cletus was sweating bullets. "Please!"

Mose said loudly and seriously to him, "Is you uh, is you want this lumber over here, boss fella?"

Cletus was rendered speechless by Mose's field hand routine, but his father pointed to a stack of lumber. "Over here, son."

"Yes suh!"

He went over and placed the wood neatly on the stack, shuffling in his best Stepin' Fetchit manner and warbling, "Jesus loves me, this I know, 'Cause my Bible tells me so."

He started to plane a 2-by-4. He did it well, and all the while he kept up his gospel song.

Judson watched him so carefully he didn't notice how odd it was that we'd all stopped working in order to stare at Mose, newly converted and ready to help the massa. "Good worker,"

Judson said and headed back to his office.

Mose came over with some wood. "I done built me a woodshed for my mama and I like them tools you got, suh. They ain't rusted and all like my mama's. Is you done be happy now?" Cletus all but collapsed as the tension drained out of him like air from a balloon. He managed a nod. "Praise de Lawd!" Mose said.

He launched into more verses from "Jesus Loves Me." As we all got down to work, it was all we could do not to join in and start resembling the Huggins Quartet. We settled for low humming.

At one point later I heard Cletus explaining to his father how Mose had gotten into the habit of singing while working for Huggins Lumberyard. He didn't miss a trick in his explanation and now that I'd met his father, I could understand why, and also how he'd been shaped in his beliefs.

He'd come far just to get to associatin', and perhaps that was the most we could ever expect.

20. KNOCKED UP & KNOCKED DOWN

We had a week before the state tournament started. I worked at the office and we had a couple of practices, Coach Cross talking strategy and preparation and how important it was to think winning. He knew we could win and we knew it too. We just had to believe it. Cletus was on board and the team was set.

After the party Mary Louise was surrounded by admirers and I was able to duck another fraught encounter. She just said to me, "You're on probation, buster." I hadn't seen her for a few days and I figured she was punishing me. As it turned out, she had turned my case over to a parole officer.

One morning as I left the house I saw a huge black Cadillac parked at the curb. The tinted glass, running motor and smoking exhaust made it seem like a Mafia kingpin's car.

I approached it warily. Just as I reached it, I flinched as the front passenger door suddenly swung open.

Big Chuck was at the wheel, chomping on a big cigar. He beckoned for me to get inside.

I thought he might be wanting to discuss the upcoming game or whatever, but for a while he most uncharacteristically said nothing. He was drinking a concoction from a hog-shaped mug. It did not look like coffee. He drove with even less attention than usual, which meant that while he wove the Cadillac through the city streets, no stray human or animal was safe.

Finally he said, "Have one of them cigars. I bootlegged a bunch out of Havana." He had a bunch on the luxurious dash and they sure beat the brands my father used to smoke for style. They were wrapped in elegant and colorful designs like heraldic shields I thought, which made you think if you partook, you might enter a special kind of royalty. But—

"I don't smoke, sir." He knew that, so why he offered escaped my understanding. He seemed strange.

"First time for everything. A man learns that."

"Yes sir," I said, even though I didn't know what the hell he was aiming at.

"Want some of this Arkansas cognac? I brew it myself from wood alcohol and persimmon juice." He had a bottle stashed between the front seats. It did not have an elegant design or any design for that matter, but it looked pretty lethal. I declined.

Big Chuck abruptly swerved the car to the roadside and slammed it to a brake-jamming halt. His forced geniality turned to blazing fury.

"Goddamit boy, you better take something!"

"Sir?"

"I got one question. Do you or do you not intend to marry my daughter?"

"Well…" I took a deep breath. "Not…yet."

Chuck's brow clouded like a volcano, and I could see he was going to erupt, but I'd had enough.

"Goddamn it!"

He looked shocked.

"Don't pull this hooraw shit on me! Sir."

Big Chuck chomped hard on his cigar, steamed but stayed silent. "Sure, Mary Louise and I have gone together a while. But that doesn't mean we're right for each other. Understand?"

Big Chuck puffed hard, pondered…shrugged. "Well, I reckon she'll just have to get the abortion."

Now it was my turn to be shocked.

"You didn't know? Well, isn't that just like my little girl, not wanting to pressure you. She's a saint in some ways."

"Impossible."

"Not according to Doctor Jacobs. Got the report right there." I hadn't noticed an official looking paper under the cigar box on the dashboard.

"We took precautions."

"Hell, a strong young buck like you going fullbore, those little plastic contraptions just can't hold up. How do you think Mary Louise got borned?" Then I remembered that night at the quarry pits.

"First time, eh. Bingo. Shows you're some stud. We're gonna have a herd runnin' around the house, may have to add a new wing. That is, if you're ready to do the right thing."

I pondered, still stunned. Big Chuck puffed.

"When I think of some fly-by-night sawbones taking a rusty razor blade to my little girl…well, it's got to be done."

"After we win the championship."

Big Chuck raised his eyebrows quizzically.

"The wedding," I explained.

"Aw, that's good news."

He started the car and roared it back onto the road. I was drained of all thought, emotion and reaction.

"Go on, have a cigar. Do you good."

"I'd prefer the cognac."

#

I decided to take the morning off and Big Chuck was as sympathetic as he could be given the situation.

"Come by the house and swim. Mary Louise is working on her tan and y'all can play around all you want."

But I begged off with an excuse that I had to see Coach Cross to discuss the lineup.

The Missouri Pacific trainyards are gigantic and it took me some time to track down Coach. Even though my grandfather on Mom's side had worked there, I'd never visited.

I found Coach Cross heaving a half dozen side cars onto a track. It looked like strenuous work and he was all alone doing it. His face and work clothes were smudged black and he strained against the winch. When it was done as I walked up, he almost staggered as he left off and came over to greet me. He was panting from the exertion.

"Tough job?"

"About usual."

I whistled with surprise and respect and he smiled and said, "You do what you're paid for. Maybe when I retire I'll have a rose garden. What brings you around?" I pointed at a boxcar on a nearby track.

"One of those just hit me."

We strolled through the rail yards and I told him everything. He was easy to talk to and confide in. We moved through a welter of steam and smoke from chuffing engines, clanking hammers and drills and toiling workers.

"You didn't need a shotgun to your head," he said.

"I accept my responsibility. I just wish... ."

"The price wasn't so high. I know how you feel."

We'd reached the edge of the rail yards. The rails in front of us stretched like black ribbons toward the horizon, many of them crisscrossing in a pattern that I was sure made sense to the people running the railyard, but not me. Appropriate, I thought.

"I bet you're looking at these rails and thinking boy, wouldn't it be great if I could just hop a freight and ride out of here."

I didn't know he was a mind reader.

"I almost did it myself. Margaret had just taken sick, the doctors said there wasn't much hope, and I figured, why don't I just get away. Leave everything behind. I could always be a train ride ahead of my troubles. But I didn't."

"Why not?"

"I looked closer at those rails. They don't run forever, you know. And they're all linked together. Sooner or later if you ride long enough, they'll bring you right back to where you've come from. Back to what you've run from."

I took this in.

"And being your basic lazy cuss, I figured what's the point." A whistle blew. He'd told me he could take a break because it was pause time. That meant back to work.

I looked at him and he saw I understood. "We'd better get back," I said. "We'd better," he agreed.

He put his arm around me, and we walked back toward the yards where we'd come from.

21. STATE TOURNAMENT

The state Legion baseball tournament is a big event. If you win, you go to a regional tournament of surrounding states and if you win that, you go to the national championship which this year was being held in South Dakota.

We weren't thinking about that because standing in our way were the Belleville Pioneers, the two-time defending champs, and 6 other good, hungry teams like us.

It was a single elimination tournament. One loss and you're out. Win three consecutive games and you'd get a championship, with all attendant pride and bragging rights and the chance to move onto a bigger stage.

We'd learned how to play together and what was not exactly the same thing, how to win—something not at all as evident as it sounds. Winners expect to win, but they know how to do whatever it takes to do it.

"It's something you can see," Coach said, in the little things you do like moving a runner over on a groundout. "But it's also intangible, something you got inside. You take that with you in life, you'll know you got what it takes to win even if you go into a slump. And that's something to count on in the worst of times."

We also had a difference-maker in Mose. Unlike the other teams, with the exception of Belleville which had a deep roster of experienced, talented pitchers—that was one of their strengths—we had a relief pitcher who could come in during the late innings and shut down the opposing batters. It gave us a confidence.

What we didn't know though was how we'd perform under the pressure of the spotlight, and here the spotlight was the brightest we'd ever seen.

We arrived and saw banners and bunting everywhere announcing the tournament. A portable wooden dais had been brought and set up near the concession stand for the opening and closing ceremonies.

The press box already was bustling with reporters from around the state, discussing with local organizers how to arrange seating and priorities. Bill Bowers had traveled up with us, and he spoke unkindly about the local Belleville sports reporter, Chet Williams.

"He's a flack."

"What's a flack?" I asked, risking another reproof.

"Someone who's paid to provide good publicity. The day you catch him saying something negative about the homeboys, that's the day you know somebody else has lined his pockets."

"You'd never do that."

"Are you nuts? Sure I would. Give me a million and I'll write anything. I'll say Genghis Khan was a good guy, just let his scimitar get away from him. I can always say later it was a printing error."

All the hoopla and attention, knowing we'd be playing before a big crowd and the whole state would know if we'd met the challenge, created huge pressure before we even stepped out onto the field—where the pressure would hit us like a blow to the gut.

"It's called choking," Coach said to us when we'd just driven up to Belleville and he decided we should all go together and take a look at the field. He didn't want us to arrive cold the next day and maybe get intimidated by the banners and whatnot.

"Choking comes from fear. There ain't a man who's ever lived who didn't feel some fear at one time or another. The trick is to deal with it, not let it paralyze you to the point where you can't perform. Another word for it is panic.

"That's why we've played so many games this summer and practiced so hard. I wanted you to get so used to hitting and fielding it's almost like breathing. You do it by reflex and don't think about the bad things that can happen."

Randy piped up and said, "That's a good life lesson, Coach."

"Right you are, Randy. Right you are."

"I ain't dumb," Randy said to us.

Coach looked around at the field.

"Take a good look around. Tomorrow when you hit this field, come ready to play. And win."

This wasn't anything he hadn't said before, and often. But he was right to say it now. Playing for such big stakes made a difference.

#

I had decided to break the news to Laura as soon as we arrived in Belleville, and she met me at the park just after the others headed to our motel.

I had been strolling around, alone, watching storm clouds building up in the sky. The groundskeepers always look out for thunderstorms in August, and they'd laid a heavy tarp over the infield.

The first drops—big ones—were starting to fall when she came walking up. I knew now she didn't live that far away from the park, but still I hadn't expected her to be on foot. It was an aching feeling seeing her walking alone toward me, in the shifting light and dark of the rumbling thunderclouds.

Just as I blurted out what had changed in my life, the rain started to fall. We took refuge under the bleachers, not a particularly effective shelter, but neither of us cared. We watched it rain and felt the rain inside us, too.

"It will blow over," she said. "Anyway it's been so hot it'd have to be a gullywasher to rain out the game. "

A huge thunderclap shook the earth. "That's like us. Strong and intense while it lasts, but gone before you know it."

"They call it doing the right thing. They don't say who it's right for."

"You have to, Tom. You have to. Anyway as soon as the tournament's over I'm going to forget you. You'll do the same. Out of sight and out of mind. Pretty soon I won't even remember your name."

I hoped she was just saying that to make me feel better. But I wasn't sure.

"I might be up here again some day. Work and stuff. Maybe we can—"

"Let's don't do that to your family." The thunder moved off to the east and the downpour turned to sprinkles. She'd been right, as usual.

"Listen to me now. Are you listening? You're the shortstop, the most important position on the infield. If you don't play well, your team loses. When you get out on the field, I want you to forget all about me and us and everything but playing good."

"It's going to be hard. You're —"

"No! I'll be in the stands, just another spectator. Promise me!"

"I promise."

"Okay. Good."

And then she said quietly: "I don't want to see you play bad." In that moment of goodbye I felt again the odd feeling I didn't fully understand until years later.

#

We played the first game in the tournament, which added to the pressure.

Mayor Marty Bascomb gave an opening game speech from the dais at home plate, with platitudes about sportsmanship and so forth, but naturally he mentioned in every other sentence the hometown Pioneers, which brought raucous cheers.

If we were fortunate enough to play the Pioneers in the championship game, we would have the extra disadvantage of a rabid local crowd boosting their favorites.

I hoped that their comments would not be racial and figured the hard cases would hold back, given the public stakes. But one never knew. And then there were the other Pioneer players we'd tussled with the last time up here.

In any event Mose didn't look stressed at all.

"Sometimes the man you fight becomes your friend," he said to me.

"Yeah," I said, "but I don't see myself grabbing a burger with Jim Bunch anytime soon."

Bunch was strutting about as usual, seeing and being seen. When the speeches finished and everyone had absorbed the politicians' insights—Bill Bowers said he'd "put his brain on coma" during them—we got down to what we'd come for.

Playing baseball.

Our opponent was an excellent team from Paragould, and it was close all the way.

Coach Cross started Sammy, and he was hoping to get as many innings as he could out of him. That was one of our weaknesses as a team—thin pitching depth. Spencer was our best pitcher at that point in time, but Coach made the decision to save him for the next game, or the game after.

The risk obviously would be no game at all. We'd lose and go home. But Sammy pitched the game of his life. Being a hunter and laid back by nature (and the duck hunting in the Belleville area apparently being not so good), he didn't seem to feel an ounce of pressure. And that's what we needed.

Nobody did much of anything until the fourth inning, when George drew a leadoff walk. Coach decided to "make things happen" and gave George, our fastest runner, the steal sign.

The Paragould pitcher may have guessed, as he sent at least five attempted pickoff throws to first. George always managed to get back in time.

Sooner or later though the pitcher has got to throw to the batter, and when he finally did it, George raced to second. He barely beat the throw. Billy, our batter, popped out weakly to the second baseman for the first out and George could not advance.

We'd been having a lot of trouble with the Paragould pitcher. He was throwing very well, and it was tough to get a hit off him.

On the first pitch to the next batter, Sammy, George took off running and stole third base, just ahead of the tag. It's difficult to do that, because the catcher has a short throw to third. The element of surprise helps, and George surprised everyone, including his Coach who said as George was dusting him off, "Where'd you get that idea?"

"You said to make things happen, Coach."

"So I did. Call me a genius." Sammy flied out to right field, not a well-hit ball but far enough for George to tag up and score easily for our first run.

We held the lead until the 7th inning, when Sammy faltered and Paragould pushed across a run on a double and 2-out single. Tie game.

In the top of the eight I'm proud to say I led off with a single, and after a sacrifice to second, scored on George's single.

So we went into the ninth inning with a one-run lead. Paragould was the home team, and they had the last at-bats. Coach brought in Mose. He walked the first batter, just about the worst thing you can do, and the next batter doubled off the wall in left field. We got the ball back in time to prevent a score, but this left runners on second and third base with no outs.

If one crossed the plate, tie game. Two, we lose. Coach came out to the mound to talk. Even though Mose had said he wasn't feeling any pressure, maybe he was.

"How you feeling?" Coach asked?

"Okay. Guess I got us in the soup though."

Cletus said, "It was my fault. I screwed up. Called for a changeup."

Coach said, "We could walk this guy and set up a force out all around. But that doesn't give you a margin for error."

Mose said, "I'd like to go right at him."

"Okay, do it." He patted him on the back for encouragement and headed back to the dugout.

That's the way it is. Your coach can boost morale, but then it's still you on the mound, facing a demon named the batter.

"We're gonna play in," I told Mose. "We're behind you."

"Okay."

That meant we on the infield would move in several steps, almost to the infield grass. It would make it easier for a hit ball to get through and end the game, but it also meant if we caught the grounder before it got through, the runner at third would not have time to score.

Or if he tried, we'd have an easy throw to home to get him out. Mose noticed that Cletus was still looking fit to be tied.

"Shake it off."

"Don't give me no damn sympathy!"

"OK. Get your head out of your ass!"

Cletus pounded his glove. "All right! Let's get this guy!"

We moved in. Mose reached back and found some extra smoke in his fastball and the first two pitches flew right by the batter, who swung helplessly.

"Contact, Freddie, contact!" his coach yelled out.

It was one of the marks of a smart team and coach. Freddie moved his hands higher on the bat handle. It cut down on his power but it meant he had just a short stroke and much better chance of making contact with the ball.

On Mose's next pitch, he did. But luckily for us, and thanks to Mose's smoke, he sent a weak grounder toward Larry at second. He looked the runner back to third, and fired to first. One out.

The second batter was their best hitter, at cleanup. He worked Mose hard, fouling off several pitches and taking the count to three balls and two strikes. It seemed like a month he'd been up at bat and each pitch drew out the tension—not to mention the intervals in between.

I looked toward our dugout and noticed everybody sweating bullets. In the stands the spectators looked drained—and the game wasn't even over yet.

I saw Laura watching, chin on her hands like she was having trouble breathing. It looked like she was making an effort not to look out toward me, but maybe that was my imagination. Anyway I remembered what she'd told me.

Finally the cleanup hitter made contact and sent a rocket toward me. I caught it, looked the runner back and fired to first, yelling "Yeah!" as the ball flew for the second out.

Now we just needed one more. We moved back on the

infield, but even though we were still just one hit away from losing, Mose had been so charged up by those two outs we'd gotten when it seemed like there was no way we could not lose, not to mention Cletus shouting encouragement like a maniac, he found an extra cylinder and blew three strikes right by the batter.

Win #1.

#

Our next game was against Sheridan, which had beaten us twice during the season in games we thought we could have won. They had a right to be confident when we took the field. They started the same pitcher who had beaten us once before, and they were the home team, so like Paragould, if they went into the bottom of the ninth and scored enough runs, they would win and we'd have no chance to come back.

Not to worry. By the time the ninth inning rolled around, they had only one thing in mind—get out of here and back home before the Packers score any more runs and humiliate us any further.

It was one of those games where you start out hitting and don't stop, and nothing the opposing team can do makes much difference. You just have to sit back and take a shellacking, watch your opponents run around the bases and try not to get a crick in your neck.

I drew a leadoff walk, moved around on a hit and another walk, then Sammy hit a grand slam home run. 4-0 before Sheridan even came to bat. In the next few innings we scored ten more runs and by the 7th, we had such a comfortable 16-1 lead that coach brought me in to pitch. He wanted to save our pitchers for the championship. I hadn't done it since Little League and they whacked me for three runs, but I got through the rest of the game with my pride intact and most of all, we won in a laugher.

Not for Sheridan, of course. A few of their players were in tears as we shook hands at the end of the game. For us it was a sort of retribution, release of frustration over those two losses during the season. For them it was a buttkicking they wouldn't forget any time soon.

I had thought that Laura might pass by and make some crack about my pitching, but I didn't see her anywhere around. Maybe she thought it was for the best. Maybe it was.

Everybody on our team had been hyped to the maximum.

"Whoo, kick ass!" Billy yelled.

"Bring on the Pioneers. If they've got the guts." From the stands where he'd been watching, Jim Bunch stood up and yelled over: "Enjoy it while you can, mothers. Your day comes tomorrow!"

They had won their two games without being tested. Our guys responded in kind, and Randy was incensed: "Hey hoss!" he yelled.

He dropped his trousers and mooned Bunch, who in the general uproar that followed had to be held back by his teammates.

I said to George, "That's an image they won't soon forget." And he yelled out to the Pioneers, once again showing the brains and literary talent of which I had very little, "Once more unto the britches, my friends!"

And he mooned them too.

#

Big Chuck came up to Belleville to watch our game against Sheridan, and he relished each and every run. "They say, 'Don't pile it on.' Well why not. You pile enough bricks, one day you got a skyscraper."

He'd driven up with Mary Louise in her car, and he said, "Now I know what the Indy 500 must be like. Look hard at my throat, you'll see my heart."

Mary Louise didn't stay to see the game but chose to lounge around the Holiday Inn pool and do some shopping in downtown. She was already thinking maternity clothes and "didn't want to wear a sack."

Coach Cross let me forego eating with the team and we had a separate table at the Holiday Inn restaurant. I could hear the repartee of the guys even while carrying on conversation with my future father-in-law and wife, which made for some schizophrenia.

But I figured I was getting used to it, what with my affair with Laura, such as it was.

Mary Louise had not been impressed by Belleville. "You've heard of one horse towns. This is a no-horse town. Maybe women up here wear tow sacks when they're pregnant. Can you imagine me looking like a sack of potatoes?"

"We'll get you something beautiful, honey," her father said, "even if we got to go to St. Louis."

She turned to me.

"If you love me like my Daddy, I'll be so happy." Big Chuck beamed. Even if he liked to talk discipline with her, he was 300 pounds of putty in her hands.

The waiters brought what seemed like a whole coop of fried chickens to the neighboring tables where my teammates sat, and they were pigging out while recapping the glories of our big win.

Coach Cross tried pretty vainly to keep their minds on the next game.

"How long is the game tomorrow?" Mary Louise asked me.

"No way to tell. As long as it takes I guess."

"Well geez Mary Louise, don't take all day."

Big Chuck just shook his head and said to me, "If you teach her a little bit every day maybe she'll start to understand the game. Take as many years as you want."

"That's just it, Daddy. A game. Why do men get so worked up over a game? After tomorrow you can start becoming a man," she said to me, adding as an afterthought. "And you can forget about the daily baseball lessons."

"If we win tomorrow, I'll have to become a man later. We'll be heading to Oklahoma City for the southern regionals."

"And once we win that, South Dakota for the nationals," Big Chuck added.

Mary Louise said, "South Dakota? Isn't that where Tonto was born? Do they even have cities there?"

When we'd finished I told them I was going to hang out with the guys, who showed no sign of being sleepy.

"Coach left early and I've got to make sure these guys don't take advantage."

Big Chuck said, "If they don't take tomorrow seriously, let me know and I'll throw 'em in a pen with some Razorback hogs. That'll get their adrenaline going."

"What about mine?" Mary Louise said. "I'll be in that hotel room all alone."

"You bring your nail polish?" I asked. "We talked about this team rooms thing."

"Yeah, but I didn't think you were actually serious."

But I was. They left together, father and daughter. The conversation had depressed me for reasons I couldn't exactly put my finger on, so I sat down at the big table where the guys had clustered to eat dessert and assembly line cokes and Dr. Peppers.

A TV on the wall was showing the news of the day. Everybody had stopped talking for a moment to watch footage of police quelling a mass demonstration on a college campus whose name I didn't catch. They were using hoses and nightsticks to subdue the protesters.

Randy commented, "I thought you went to college to study. I am dumb. Hey," turning to Spencer, "what are you gonna be studying at Stanford?"

"Physics and dope."

"No college for me. I couldn't even pass orientation."

"Get a job as a programmer. All you have to do is feed a bunch of cards into a computer. Haven't you gotten mail from one of these companies?"

"Yeah, every day."

Cletus opined, "Hell, there ain't no future in them computer contraptions."

Bubba quipped, "Right. Isn't that what they said about automobiles?"

And then Mose quickly corrected, "No, just his automobile."

We all laughed, recognizing this as a sally for Cletus who riposted: "I recognize the humor in that remark. If not the intelligence."

Now the news was announcing the passage of a landmark civil rights bill pushed through by Lyndon Johnson, guaranteeing the right to vote for minorities. I'd thought only Mose and I had noticed, but Mickey said, "Now politicians will have to change their tune. They don't know it yet, but they will. The law's the law."

"Rockefeller might actually become governor," I said. "A meat packer."

Cletus added, "If he does I'm moving to Tennessee." And then to Mose, "Bet that would make you happy."

"I'll help you pack your two shirts."

They had developed this kind of back and forth and it was a hell of a lot better than what came before. But Cletus always made sure he was seated at the opposite end of the table when the team ate together.

We went on like this for a while, not saying anything about the game tomorrow and I thought that was a good thing. Give the nerves a rest. My own were still stressed though and I got up to leave.

"Don't stay up late and don't forget to say your prayers, " George helpfully advised.

Billy said, "Lord, please help us tomorrow to kick some ass."

Like a chorus everybody chimed, "Amen."

I left to the satisfying sound of all their laughter. It occurred to me that a moment like this would never come again in our lives and we should savor every second.

#

Coach had said when he left that he needed to get some sleep, implying he didn't want to be disturbed. But he'd been so easy to talk to and I felt I needed to talk.

He'd taken a room on a higher floor, to get away from the

constant pressure, I guessed. I'd noticed him holding his stomach more than once over the last two days, like his ulcer was giving him real problems. But he didn't let on that he might be in pain.

When I got to his room I knocked. There was no answer and I noticed the door was ajar. I hoped nothing was wrong.

I eased it open.

"Coach?"

Inside I could hear water running from the shower. That was why he hadn't answered.

I was standing there, wondering if I ought to go on in or just wait till he got out of the shower. Then I noticed movement in the bedroom.

Sally Bright came into view through the bedroom doorway. She was wrapped in a white bath towel and her hair was wet. She was combing it with a hairbrush but stopped when she caught sight of me. We stared at each other, both at a loss for what to say or do. The sound of the shower continued from the bathroom.

Sally just stood there, wordlessly and with great dignity. I edged back, pulling the door shut hard and fast, and headed back to my own room for the night.

22. CHAMPIONSHIP

We knew this day and game were special if only because of the number of major league scouts who were in attendance: three. One was a whitehaired gentleman there to represent the St. Louis Cardinals. We'd seen him at the game yesterday, taking copious notes.

I didn't think he would be interested in me, because I didn't have the height and bulk to be the kind of major leaguer he was looking for. Billy Aycock maybe, though he wasn't having a great series. I said hello to the scout, who introduced himself to us as Mr. Charles, and he wished us good luck in the game. He said he wouldn't put any money on the game because he figured it would be close and "go down to the wire."

That made me a bit more nervous than I already was, but I remembered what Coach had said about choking and put on a confident front. As I headed away he said, "I know you can hit a curveball." That wouldn't get me a contract, but it was nice to see he'd noticed and thought that.

Bill Bowers came over and said he hoped against hope we'd win because he'd got sick to his stomach reading Chet Williams' "puff pieces—that's what you call an article that reads like whipped cream. I don't see how the Pioneer boys can even walk with all that stuff on 'em."

I saw Chet up in the press box, already all business. "He's waiting for the coronation," Bill said. "Probably already got the piece written." He looked over toward our dugout and my teammates milling around, getting ready for warmups.

"You see the news yesterday?" and then without waiting for an answer. "Big civil rights bill passed. Going to change America."

"We're doing our part right here," I said.

"Damn right you are." And he whipped out his notebook and made a note. "Win or lose, I'm quoting you on that. For posterity."

"Like posterity will really care about the Dogtown Packers."

"Maybe they won't. But you will." He saw the Mayor arriving with various bigwigs in tow.

"Oh-oh, gladhander alert. Got to put my brain back into storage." We shook hands and I walked over to the stands to exchange greetings with our fans.

Some parents had driven up, people we didn't always see. Mose's mother hadn't been able to come and he was sad about that, and my Mom didn't come either. She had an irrational superstition that when she was present, we lost. And vice versa. In short, she didn't want to jinx us.

I was surprised to see Mr. Snookums. He waved at me and yelled, "I left my peas and corn for you boys. Don't let me down."

I was very happy Mr. Snookums had seen fit to make this effort and sacrifice.

Mary Louise arrived with Big Chuck and he put down a big cushion for her to sit on. The night before he'd cracked that she should wear something very sexy and sit near the Pioneer dugout—"to distract them. Mind games, we call it."

I didn't agree, and neither did she. "I'm not a prize Angus," she said.

"Yeah but if any of them boys got close they'd put a blue ribbon round your neck in five seconds flat." Finally she sat nearer our side of the field, but she was wearing shorts short enough to distract even from a distance.

Mr. Simmons had been driven up to Belleville and he was in the stands in the same place as was his custom. I went over to say hello.

"Everybody back home is rooting for you, Tom, win or lose."

"We don't plan to lose, Mr. Simmons."

"That's the spirit. But you know, the best laid plans of mice and men…" He shook his head, but had a sort of wry smile. It was hard not to think he was thinking about his infirmity, and how he'd probably never once thought he'd end up in a wheelchair. Maybe he read my thoughts.

"We never think about the daisies we'll be pushing up some

day, but we will. In the meantime, give everything you've got to living hard and well. And kick their damn butts!"

Sally had come over and she heard this.

"Now don't you fill his head with too much philosophy. He's got to fixate on a baseball."

"You singing today?"

"No sir."

"Now that is a shame. That's cause for kicking their butts right there."

"Like you say Mr. Simmons, we'll give it our best," I said. Sally looked straight at me and said "We could all use some happiness. Helps us get through the days."

"Amen," Mr. Simmons added, without knowing exactly what she was referring to. But I did.

I added, "Yeah, and like I heard somebody say, the best of us need it the most." This was for Sally. She smiled.

Mr. Simmons added, "Whoever said that needs a medal. I'll give him one of mine."

Sally said to him, "You've got so many, they weigh you down."

I shook hands with Mr. Simmons and gave Sally a hug and headed toward our dugout.

#

The Powers That Be had decided to reserve the dais for the closing trophy ceremony and so Mayor Bascomb was just milling around at home plate, readying to make some announcements and get the game rolling.

On the sideline Spencer was warming up with an intensity I had hardly seen before. A guy I now recognized, despite Bill Bowers' low opinion of my knowledge of current affairs, as a hippie type, came to the fence beside him. It could only be Errol.

"Hey man." He proffered Spencer a neatly rolled joint. "For strikeout action." Cletus yelled over, "Hey, none of that shit."

Spencer looked genuinely moved. "Gee man, thanks, but

I've got to go cold turkey today." He handed it back to Errol who said, "Heavy, man. I mean, heavy."

In the dugout everyone was dealing with their pregame butterflies in different fashion, adjusting caps and gloves, retying their shoes, knocking mud from cleats, shifting around in various states of tension. Sammy was sitting beside Mickey, who was sifting fistfuls of dirt from hand to hand.

"Look at 'em. They're so scared they're shaking."

His own voice was none too steady.

"Yeah, sweatin' blood."

Mickey's own hands and arms were wet with sweat despite the dirt he was constantly pouring on them.

Big Chuck came barging over to the dugout and started exhorting: "Put it to 'em, boys. Lay a lickin' on 'em. Get brutal, kick their butts and stomp on 'em. A humiliation whuppin', that's what I want, humiliation WHUPPIN'!"

He was gesticulating so animatedly, his hand bumped into a big man wearing a huge Stetson who'd come up behind him: Winthrop Rockefeller. He was accompanied by Mrs. Daisy Bates, very elegant in a bright blue dress and stylish white hat, which made Big Chuck even more embarrassed.

They shook hands with the discombobulated Chuck.

"Nice to see you again, Mr. LeBoeuf."

"Hi, I'm Daisy Bates."

"Er—er—" Tongue-tied for once in his stentorian life, Big Chuck motioned toward us. "My boys."

The dignitaries moved over and began shaking hands with us.

"Hi, Win Rockefeller." When he shook my hand he smiled broadly, probably recalling me as "Mr. LeBoeuf's" assistant. To Cletus he remarked his catcher's gear and said: "The tools of ignorance. We're trying to stamp those out."

When he'd passed by Cletus said to me, "That's what he calls a joke."

"At least he knows some baseball," I countered. Cletus snorted. "Yeah, probably a Yankee fan, which don't give him no credit at all in my book."

Daisy Bates had been a signal figure during the Central High School integration fight and created a great deal of enmity in traditional and out-and-out racist quarters and remained an activist and controversial figure. The fact she was here was a sign of the changing times in Arkansas.

"Daisy Bates." Cletus shook hands with her though he looked uncomfortable.

To Mose, Rockefeller said, pointedly I thought, "Good luck."

"Thank you sir." To Mrs. Bates Mose said, "Real privilege to meet you." She squeezed his arm, like she wanted to transfuse what she said next into his fiber: "Play hard, all the time. That way you'll never lose."

Coach Cross shook their hands vigorously. "Thank you for coming."

The Belleville announcer either hadn't noticed their arrival or was asleep at the switch, or maybe just as likely, chose to wait until the distinguished visitors crossed over to the Belleville dugout.

"Please give a rousing Belleville welcome to our distinguished visitors, Mr. Winthrop Rockefeller and Mrs. Daisy Bates."

Rockefeller waved his Stetson high and Mrs Bates waved to acknowledge the applause, which was polite but not raucous. The mayor shook hands with them both.

Big Chuck opined, "Old carpetbagger's running for governor, that's for sure." Randy opined in turn, "A Republican governor in Arkansas? Ain't never gonna happen."

While they were pressing the flesh I looked up and down the packed stands but did not catch sight of Laura. Mary Louise spotted me looking and waved to me. I felt like a two-timer but kept looking around anyway, and finally saw Laura among the people who were setting up folding chairs along the Pioneer sideline. She was with an older couple who I imagined were her parents. She was talking animatedly with them and didn't look my way.

I gritted my teeth, literally, and turned to the task at hand. I accompanied Coach Cross to home plate to exchange lineup cards. Naturally the Pioneer captain was Jim Bunch.

The umpire told us it had been decided to do a coin flip to determine the home team. He said to Bunch, "Since you're defending champs, I'm sure you'll defer and let him call the toss."

"If he knows the vocabulary." The ump and two coaches smiled at what they thought was a pleasantry, but I knew it wasn't.

"Wow, a five-syllable word from you."

"Gentlemen," the ump reprimanded politely. He tossed the coin and while it was in the air I called "Heads."

We looked down and heads it was.

"You're the home team," the ump said. "Your lucky day."

"I hope so."

"Dream on," Bunch said.

"Gentlemen! Shake hands and may the best team win."

We shook. I guessed Bunch would shake as hard as he could to intimidate and was ready with a grip as firm as I could make it. We had a short staredown contest which Coach Cross cut short, having had enough of these mind games I suppose: "Let's play ball."

At the dugout he gave us one of this shortest pep talks of the year: "I'm proud of how you've come together, win or lose, I'm proud of you. But I'd prefer you win. Let's hit it! "

We hit the field to cheers from our contingent of fans. Belleville hadn't gone to any special pains to invite a singer for the national anthem, and a recorded instrumental band version was piped over the loudspeaker. While it was playing I thought of Sally and how if she had been singing, the hills would have come alive with the sound of music even if there weren't any hills. I wondered what would happen to her and Coach Cross.

I looked toward the stands and saw Errol had taken a place beside Mr. Snookums, "old Pharaoh." Mr. Snookums was looking around, a little frantically I thought, but there was no room to move. The stands were packed. Well, I thought, baseball can bring people together.

Down the sideline I saw Laura had placed her hand on her

heart and her lips were moving—she was singing along softly to the National Anthem. When the music ended a wave of applause swept all around, then diminished to a silent wave of tension and anticipation.

We were between the white lines and it was time to play.

THE GAME

Being the home team gave us an advantage. We knew that if we went into the ninth inning tied, we'd have the bottom of the ninth to push over the winning run and Belleville would not have another chance.

On the other hand, the Pioneers had a slew of supporters in the stands who cheered them on like crazy and Chet Williams had whipped up the fan fervor with his puff pieces in the local paper.

The first Pioneer batter stepped to the plate amid an exuberant wave of chatter from the crowd and his teammates. He didn't try to make Spencer work and take a pitch or two. He swung away on the first pitch and hit a line drive toward left field.

I had noticed from our first game that this batter liked to pull the ball and I shaded over toward third base.

This made all the difference. I was able to get a jump on the ball, leap to my right and glove it. I tumbled to the dirt but came up holding the ball high.

Out number one.

In the stands the Packer contingent were euphoric. I saw Errol exuberantly slapping Mr. Snookums on the back. "Big D stands for defense!" he yelled. I could see Mr. Snookums happy about the out, but probably wondering about his seat mate.

Mayor Bascomb shook his head. He was perched on a special chair near the Pioneer dugout, and I could read from his expression that he was thinking it might be a long day for his favorite team.

Inning after inning, it stayed tight. Each team played great defense and the pitchers had no lack of adrenaline to put extra smoke in their fastballs.

Spencer was at his crafty best, and it seemed every time a hitter was salivating expecting a fastball, he'd spin off a curve that tied the poor sucker into knots.

It was the kind of game where if you were watching on TV and had no stake in the players or score, you'd call it boring. But if you lived and died for your team or had someone you loved playing, each inning—each pitch—had suspense, and it only heightened as time went on.

In the sixth with one out Cletus broke his bat when it made contact with the ball and both bat shaft and ball went blooping toward the shortstop. The bat dropped on the infield grass but luckily for us, the ball dropped just over the shortstop's head and into left field for a single.

I came up next and managed to push a ball just past the right of pitcher—if he'd been lefthanded he'd have gloved it easily —and out of reach of the leaping shortstop who bellyflopped just in front of Cletus who chugged right past him and made it to third.

George came up next and he hit a grounder to shortstop. It was hit just hard enough that if the second baseman caught the force out toss from the shortstop and swiveled quickly enough, the throw to first would mean a double play and no run would score.

It was the same second baseman who'd been injured by Mose, and whether he was gunshy or not, my job was to barrel in with a slide and try to disrupt the throw to first.

I didn't—completely—but his equilibrium was shaken just enough that George, fast as he was, beat the throw.

Cletus scored and we led 1-0.

In the top of the eighth the Pioneers rallied. Jim Bunch lined a leadoff double and a sacrifice sent him to third. Then a sacrifice fly scored him. Textbook baseball and a tie score, 1-1.

The next two batters lined singles. Runners at first and third, two outs. Coach Cross called time and came out to the mound. I joined him and Cletus, to whom Coach Cross just said "Well?" Cletus told it like it was: "He ain't got shit left."

Spencer said, "I need some ozone, coach."

"All right." He beckoned to where Mose was warming up.

Coach said to Spencer, "Take it slow and let 'em get a good look at a pitcher who did a hell of a job." Spencer was a little taken aback and moved by this tribute. He did take it slow, walking off the mound toward the dugout to appreciative applause from the Pioneer fans and a standing O from ours.

He yelled at Mose who was arriving at the mound, "Go get 'em!"

Coach said to Mose, "I'll second that." He patted him on the back and headed back toward the dugout.

Mose looked at Cletus, then at the batter standing waiting in the ondeck circle. Cletus said, "This guy's good but I've been settin' him up." He meant he had purposely called for certain pitches in previous at bats and now that the crunch time had come, he would spring a surprise on him. "You trust me?"

"About as far as I can throw you, and that ain't far." Cletus and I both smiled. If he could joke like this, he didn't have nerves.

"Do it anyway."

"I'll second that," I said, and headed back to my position.

After his warmup pitches Mose got set for the first pitch. Cletus set a target on the inside corner and his fastball hit just where Cletus' glove was. A called strike one.

Cletus moved the target to the outside corner and Mose missed twice with blistering fastballs. The next one hit the corner and the batter got his bat on the ball. It went screaming toward right field--but foul.

"Let's go now!" Cletus yelled out to his pitcher. He signaled for the next pitch with three fingers. That meant a changeup. Cletus hoped the batter would set up for another outside fastball and swing even earlier, which meant the slow pitch might fool him completely.

On the other hand, if he wasn't fooled, a slow pitch was just that, a balloon floating begging to be hit over the fence.

"Oh shit," I said to myself.

Cletus set up on the outside corner again and that's where the pitch was. Completely fooled, the batter swung before the pitch arrived, way too early. He almost stumbled over, he looked so foolish. Third strike, third out.

We yelled like banshees and came running in to the dugout. In the stands I could see the Pioneer fans looking worried and deflated. The Mayor was shaking his head, wondering I imagined how they were going to win if they couldn't hit Mose. The game was still tied but we felt the momentum and we were home team.

In the bottom of the eighth Mose came up first. He'd been getting better and better at hitting and he was able to work the count against the pitcher, making him throw lots of pitches. Time and time again, if you can do this, you will eventually get a good pitch to hit.

Mose did and lined a single to left field. The fielder bobbled the ball and it went to his side.

Bubba yelled at Mose to "Go! Go!" toward second. Mose did, as the left fielder retrieved the ball and fired toward the second basemen.

It seemed to me afterward very obvious that Mose had on his mind what had happened previously. It was the same second baseman, and you could see his bandaged left leg. As the throw came in, Mose had to slide.

He beat the throw, but slid awkwardly and his leg twisted under him. He screamed, rolling in the dirt, clutching at his knee.

The ump called time and Coach came running out. He and the Pioneer players huddled around. We could hear Mose's groans of pain. Coach gestured toward us and George and I went jogging out. Mose was grimacing in pain. "Take him by the shoulders," Coach said. We bent down together and lifted Mose up by the shoulders. The Ozark coach had come out and joined us.

"Doc Philbin lives a couple blocks over. We'll call him." Coach Cross nodded appreciatively.

The Pioneer second baseman said, "Hang in there, man." We helped Mose off the field. Billy was standing outside the dugout, looking bitterly at the Pioneer players.

"You guys are even now."

We laid Mose down on a blanket that Sally Bright had got out of her car as soon as she saw what happened. "Lay him down on this, it's soft." Coach Cross thanked her with a look and I knew a lot lay behind it.

Cletus was there, looking worried. "You gonna be able to pitch?"

"If I don't have to stand up," Mose answered, grimacing in a lot of pain.

While this was going on the Pioneers brought in Jim Bunch to pitch. They had taken a page from our book and saved their fastest, most intimidating pitcher for the late innings.

Bunch made short work of us, striking out the first two batters so our pinch runner Sammy couldn't advance, then getting a pop out for the third out. Sammy came in to pitch. He wasn't used to relief, but we had no other choice.

The first two batters in quick succession lined hits. The Pioneer fans were cheering like mad, and our contingent gone mum except for Errol who I heard yelling out a series of random chatter that sometimes made no sense in baseball terms, but stoned-out encouragement was better than nothing at all.

Mr Simmons yelled, "Hold 'em, boys!"

Jim Bunch came up. He was a jerk but a very good hitter and he lined the first pitch over my head. In football I had noticed that it was much more a game where individual effort made the difference. If you were playing pass defense you might get fooled and someone catch a pass over your head, but if you learned and played smart and got in the right position, that would not happen very often again.

Here, in baseball, Bunch's hit could not have been caught no matter how much effort I made. I did not stand ten feet tall and couldn't grow to be. I could only watch, count on my teammate to field it, and hope that if we played hard and well, fate would be kinder next time.

Life, I would learn, is very much like that. No man can

control it, and you can never completely make your own fate. Brutus may have learned that the fault lay in us, but the stars had their say and we had to make do with their capriciousness.

Now, with Jim Bunch on second base and no outs and two runs in, we could either have let fate take another trip round the bases or suck it up.

The latter.

Sammy bowed his neck and got a strikeout, and then George made an incredible catch at the wall. Bunch went to third with two outs, but on a sharp grounder I roamed way to my right, speared it just as it hit the outfield grass, and made just about the best throw of my life to first base to get the runner.

Everybody slapped my hand as I came in to the dugout. We were two runs down but it could have been so much worse. "Fuck fate!" I shouted.

Score: 3-1 in favor of the Belleville Pioneers. We had the bottom of the inning and three outs to make a rally or go home losers.

When Sammy came off the field he hurled his glove down angrily. "I fucked up."

"You did the best you could, " I said.

I went over to Mose, who was sitting on the grass beside the dugout, a towel wrapped around his injured knee. "How's it feeling?"

"Get some runs and it'll feel just fine." He yelled over to the others: "Let's get 'em back now, you can do it! "

Coach Cross eyed his dispirited group.

"Mose hasn't given up. Have you?"

We all exchanged looks. George said: "Hell no."

When the game is on the line, you go with your best, Coach had said to us a hundred times. But now that the game and championship were on the line, we had the bottom of the order coming up to bat—the weakest hitters in the lineup.

In swift succession Mickey and Larry were thrown out at first. For a minute I thought Larry was going to attack the first base umpire for calling him out, even though he didn't come close to being safe. He just wanted to vent his anger. But he held off—barely.

Bunch preened around the pitcher's mound like a cock of the walk.

The Pioneer fans' clamor was deafening. They all got to their feet, ready to charge the field after the last out. Even the mayor got to his feet. "One more!"

All our fans were downcast but kept shouting for us to rally, except for Mary Louise who I saw was blithely sipping a coke.

She said something to her father and I thought I read on her lips, "Is it over yet?" Big Chuck looked fit to be tied.

I clapped Randy, our next and maybe last hitter, on the back. "Let's go. We're not dead till we're dead."

"That's supposed to cheer me up?" He smiled. The thing about Randy, I said to myself, was that even though he wasn't nearly as dumb as people said he was, he didn't trouble his mind thinking about failure. Or success either for that matter. His job now was to get a hit.

And he did. Bunch fired a fastball and he swung late but managed to get his bat on it, sending it over the first baseman's head and down the right field line. He rumbled to second base for a double.

That quieted the Pioneer fans some and so did the next pitch which hit Cletus in the side. He got a free pass to first base. He told me later he knew he'd be overmatched against Bunch and had crowded the plate. "You might even say I leaned over the plate," he said, "but the ump didn't see it."

Bunch did. "That sucker didn't try to get out of the way," he yelled at the ump, who fired back, "You threw a wild pitch, son."

And just like that we had the tying runs on first base and I was coming up to bat.

In the space of two pitches, the game had changed. Baseball is like that. The Pioneer fans had suddenly been deflated, ours charged up. Our dugout was in an uproar.

The game of baseball depends on good hitting and pitching, but close games where the matchup is equal or almost often depend on decisions and split second plays. A couple of seconds can make the difference between winning and losing, and strategy can buy those couple of seconds.

Coach Cross now had a decision to make. Cletus was on first base, representing the tying run. He was very slow afoot. Probably he could beat a snail or tortoise, even though the latter has been known to win a race over a hare, but he would undoubtedly win by a lesser margin than anybody would expect.

So logically Coach should replace him with a pinch runner. Bobby couldn't run as fast as his brother George, but he was lightning compared to Cletus.

But if the strategy worked and we tied the game, that meant our catcher, Cletus, would be lost for the rest of the game. We might have to play many long extra innings with the same handicap we'd overcome earlier in the season.

If on the other hand we managed to score three runs in the inning and not two, we would win and nobody would care.

Coach said, "This is it, now or never. If we don't score two runs we go home and wait till next year. 365 days of grinding our gums on what could have been."

He sent in Bobby to pinch run. "Pick 'em up and lay 'em down, bro!" George yelled. "All you got to do is run!"

But Bobby couldn't advance or do much of anything if the next batter didn't get a hit. And that batter was me.

At the mound Jim Bunch was kicking the dirt, especially because he'd let a pitch get away from him and beaned Cletus. Their manager called time out and went to the mound. This was good strategy. It was a way of trying to calm his pitcher and he took care to give me a long look, a staredown as it were.

A tactic that can rattle a batter a lot. With my senses at top acuity, I could overhear their conversation, which they didn't try to muffle.

"Just one more, dammit," their coach said to Bunch.

"Dammit, I'm trying. These peckerwoods don't know when to quit."

They all looked toward the ondeck circle where I stood.

Bunch said, "This guy's been hitting us like a drum. Want

me to pitch around him?"

He meant to try to avoid the center of the plate, aiming at the corners where it was difficult to hit the ball very well. That was an advantage, and if the ball was off the plate and the batter "fished" for it, he'd likely either miss it or dub it somewhere it could easily be caught. The obvious disadvantage was if you missed the plate four times, you would walk the batter and in this case, put the winning run on base. In any event the coach vetoed the idea in terms even Jim Bunch could understand: "No, I want you to do your job and get him out."

He stalked off. For an instant I thought Bunch looked a little worried, but that could have been wishful thinking.

While they were talking on the mound I had taken a look around. There they all were, the fans packing the stands, now all on their feet, on edge:

The pressbox, where I saw Bill Bowers and Chet Williams, who looked worried and just that moment crumbled up a sheet of paper—I hoped it was an arrogant article he'd written in advance about the Pioneers coasting to victory.

Big Chuck wracked speechless by the tension, chomping hard on one of his Cuban cigars. Mary Louise was trying to get his ear, with no success. I wondered if she knew what was happening.

Coach Cross shouting encouragement from the third base coaching box.

Mose shouting for me to get a hit, on his feet even though with his injured knee it should be the last thing to do.

My teammates, nervous, nailbiting, some with heads buried in their hands, afraid to look.

No matter how much support you've got from fans and cheers and prayers even, ultimately you have to go up to the plate and hit a pitch knowing everything is on your shoulders.

Like Coach once said, "Every at bat is a challenge, but when the game is on the line, it's kind of like your high noon. It's you facing four gunfighters all alone. You can't count on anyone to help you, maybe even the woman you love." I looked down the sideline on the Pioneer side but Laura was no longer there. I made a last scan of the surroundings and saw her then, behind the backstop screen, leaning against it.

She wouldn't ever have shown herself rooting against the home team in this kind of game. But she'd come over to our side of the field, and stationed herself behind home plate. I told myself, maybe wishfully, that she couldn't stand beside me, but she's standing behind me.

I rubbed some dirt on my sweaty palms.

Stepped into the batter's box.

Waved my bat back and forth, waiting for the first pitch.

Bunch's best pitch was his fastball, but he had a good curve too. I had a hunch that he and his catcher might think I'd be expecting a fastball, and ergo they'd start off with a curve, thinking it would surprise me and they'd be ahead in the count and could get an advantage, and besides get me confused about what was coming next.

Bunch wound up and delivered the pitch.

He was righthanded, and the ball started out coming right toward me…then curved sharply over the plate. It was higher than Bunch wanted, and as I was expecting it, I got a good look and was able to lash the ball over the shortstop's head, far into the gap in left field.

As their left and center fielders gave frantic chase, I raced toward first and then second. Randy scored easily from second.

All eyes turned toward Bobby, running for his life and our team around second and toward third. Coach Cross waved him home, something I would have done myself. It was now or never, win or lose. If Bobby scored, we'd tie the game and have a chance to win if our next batter got a hit.

Baseball can be a game of bounces. In the top of the inning, the Pioneers had scored when Bunch's ball hit to the same area of the field had gone to the outfield wall. But it had scuttled through the grass.

My hit took one hop and bounced off the wall, so the center fielder gloved it quickly and fired the ball toward the shortstop, the relay man.

So instead of Bobby scoring easily, the play at home was

going to be close.

As I rounded second base, I saw that the shortstop had the ball already and I slowed my pace. I was hoping to block the shortstop's relay throw or at least divert him enough so that Bobby could score. I could see that he had reached only halfway down the line.

The shortstop double pumped, costing him a couple of precious seconds, then stepped to the right and fired. The ball sailed just over my head.

I could have reached up and grabbed it, but that would have been interference and I would have made an automatic out and then, game over.

So I just watched it go past, seeing every stitch on the horsehide, as if I were seeing it in slow motion.

But the ball wasn't traveling slow. Having to compensate for me being in the line of fire, the shortstop had sent it high and the catcher had to jump to catch it. Jim Bunch was standing behind him as backup, but by the time he'd caught it, Bobby would have scored.

The catcher came down with the ball.

Bobby slid toward home.

I had a good view from where I stood, maybe the best in the house.

The catcher made the tag as dust flew.

One split second before Bobby's foot touched home plate.

The umpire waited for what seemed like an eternity to everybody else in the park, before almost leaping up. If the ump's hands stay low and make a fan or paddle motion, the runner is safe. Otherwise he raises his arm, thumb up. It's the opposite of what terrified gladiators in the Roman arena who knew thumbs down meant death, but alas, in the modern world of baseball it means an out, a sort of game death.

And that's what the ump said in a tone that merited the word "stentorian."

"HE'S OUT!!! "

The Pioneer players charged the mound and went down together in a heap while their fans in the stands erupted. I could see the mayor clapping everybody on the back exultantly.

Sally Bright was crying and had her face buried in her hands, Mr. Simmons was just shaking his head sadly.

Big Chuck Frankenheimer must have hurled away his Packer cap in disgust and was just glaring at the field. I saw Mary Louise mouth the words, "What happened?"

Finally Bobby got up and shuffled toward the dugout. He was crying, devastated that his one moment in the sun had turned to defeat. George went over to him and put his arm around him for consolation. Sometimes big brothers act like big brothers.

I joined them, patting Bobby on the back, and we walked to the dugout together.

Coach Cross looked at his players. We were seated on the bench or standing in attitudes of dejection. In the background the victors' celebration continued and the concession stand had fired up a victory song it was sending out over the loudspeakers.

Coach Cross said, "You played your hearts out, even when you looked whipped. That's not the mark of a loser. Now let's behave like champions and go over and congratulate our opponents."

I exchanged looks with George. "Let's go."

We led a parade out of the dugout and across the playing field toward the Pioneers.

We all mingled at the pitcher's mound, players and coaches alike, with handshaking and the ritual "good game."

It was harder to say that this time than it had ever been after a loss, knowing we had missed a chance at the championship and this would be our last game together.

The frazzled mayor shook hands with Coach Cross. "We got all the breaks today."

The Pioneer coach clapped Coach Cross on the back. "A hell of a team, Henry."

The Pioneer players I thought seemed as much relieved as exultant. I shook hands with their shortstop.

"Great relay throw."

"Aw, it was luck."

I found myself face to face with Jim Bunch. After a slight moment's hesitation, we shook hands.

"Way to pitch," I told him.

"Hell, I didn't fool you none." Big Chuck had been cutting a wide swath through the group, congratulating his players and their opponents alike. He shook hands with Bunch and said, "Son, you are prime beef."

He moved on. Bunch looked over at Mose. "How's he doin'?" I thought a second and then said, "You'll have to ask him." To his credit, jerk though he was, Bunch went over. I trailed after.

I noticed that Cletus had not joined in the group congratulations and had stayed near Mose, stewing over something. I wondered what.

Bunch looked down at Mose and said, "Good game, fella." Mose didn't hesitate: "Same to you." They might even have shaken hands but an avuncular gray-haired man arrived, no doubt the local doctor because he said, "Ah, here we are. Let's take a look at that, young man."

He bent down over Mose and began to inspect his injured knee. Bunch turned and went back to his teammates who were gathering for a team picture.

Cletus said, "Good game my ass. If you hadn't got hurt, they wouldn't have had a chance."

"They'd have hit me, too."

"No way. You'da blown them sumbitches away." Mose and I both looked at Cletus, surprised by what seemed to be genuine respect.

Mary Louise grabbed me and gave me a big kiss and hug. "Tough luck, honey."

"Did you see my hit?"

"No, some rube chick was standing at the fence and blocking my view. Talk about lack of courtesy. I was going to give her a piece of my mind but then you know what happened."

"Did you see where she went?"

"Back home to L'il Abner I guess. Who cares?"

I did, but whenever I could scan the crowd I saw only people I knew and people I didn't but not the one who counted most.

"Now we can get busy planning the wedding. Omigosh, there's Johnny Benson."

Him indeed, recognizable as always, lurking around the stands. "In all the excitement I didn't even see him. Don't tell me he came all the way up here to see the game. Now that's what I call a fan."

"Go thank him for his support. I guarantee he'll appreciate the gesture, coming from you."

"There you are again with your silly jealousy." But she scooted off to do it, and a few minutes later I saw her laughing and chatting animatedly and Johnny nodding like a Jack In The Box at every word.

I went over near the stands to see if I could spot Laura. Spencer was standing there with Errol and Mr. Snookums, who seemed like great buddies.

"My good buddy Jim is throwing a party," Errol said.

"All the food and drink you boys want. It's on me," Mr. Snookums said. Spencer said "God bless you, Mr. Snookums. Maybe we can just add a little stoneweed to the provisions."

Finally I saw Laura among the big crowd surrounding the Pioneer players. She was talking to Jim Bunch and smiling. Well, I thought, I chose my camp. It's only natural that she should choose hers. Most likely she had huddled at the backstop, blocking Mary Louise's view, because she wanted to watch Bunch's pitches blow past and strike me out.

Everybody was crowding around home plate for the team picture and Bill Bowers' photographer was getting them lined up for the best shot.

I went back to help Mose. The doctor was finishing his examination of Mose's knee.

"We'll need to take X-rays."

Mose protested, "I want to be in the picture. Come on, Doc."

"Well, be careful. I'll bring my car over." He turned to Cletus. "Don't let him come down on that knee."

"Say what?"

Before Cletus could protest, I moved away toward home plate.

"Hey!" Cletus yelled after me.

"Hurry it up, guys." I yelled back. There was a method to my madness. I hoped I would not have to help.

Mose struggled to his feet by grabbing the fence. He tottered there. Cletus made no move to help.

"Gimme your bat." Mose said. Cletus did so. He looked in a kind of befuddlement. Mose used the bat as a crutch, began hobbling toward us at home plate. Cletus watched him, torn by indecision as Mose struggled to make progress.

George came over to me and said, "Hey, let's give him a hand." I put a hand on his arm to hold him back. "Hold on."

Mose was wielding the bat like a stick of silly putty and looking very helpless.

"Jesus," Cletus said. He came over and put his arm under Mose's. "I ain't gettin' my bat busted on accounta your sorry ass."

He helped Mose toward home plate. One by one we all left off what we were doing and saying and watched this procession.

I heard Mose say, "Don't sweat, I won't tell your old man."

"Hell, he wants to hire you temporary." Not until they got near did I come over and help.

We all received Mose and Cletus into the group with shouts, smiles and pats on the back. I jumped to the front and led the cheers.

"Let's hear it for the Dogtown Packers, together at last! Hip hip—"

"Hooray!" The photographer prepared to shoot.

"Hip hip—"

"Hooray!"

Coach Cross had joined in and was cheering with all of us. He had a wide smile and I realized it was the first time I'd seen him smile like that. Even Bill Bowers was smiling. I could see Bunch and Laura and the Mayor and spectators look over at us with astonishment.

Our fans had clustered together like theirs, and they were all there: Sally Bright, Mr. Simmons, Errol and Mr. Snookums, Mary Louise wondering what was going on, Big Chuck looking proud...

"Somebody tell those guys they lost!" Bunch said.

"One more time for the Dogtown Packers!" And this time our cheer went straight up toward the sky.

"HIP HIP HOORAY!!!

The photographer snapped the picture and captured the moment in time.

23. OLD BALLPLAYERS

The Pioneer team I was watching played just like the one we faced years ago, with solid hitting and pitching and impeccable fundamentals, gaining a victory that according to the announcer meant another trip to the state playoffs.

Déja vu all over again, as Yogi Berra once is said to have said. I was hoping for another kind. Among the stands of rooters were several parents, couples and also single mothers. I stared, wondering if I could recognize Laura. She would be of an age now to have a son on the team.

Mine had been like his mother and never gave a damn about baseball. He'd never been much of a team player and resisted attempts by me and his grandfather to interest himself in the sport. He loved cars, repairing them, going fast in them, and more than once crashing them. Any lecture on the value of discipline ran ashoal in the person of his mother.

As a last resort, we dispatched him to military school. Even his mother had had enough of latenight calls from the police. I imagined Charley as a future stock car driver, barnstorming and boozing, a massive disappointment to his parents just as we had been to him.

When the failure wasn't overt with disagreements and scenes and absences, it was four seasons of subsurface discontent. We did our best to love him and in fact did, but we had never loved each other, and this night when the past came back I realized that clearly and without denial.

So I scanned the stands, wondering if Laura was there, how she looked and how her life had been.

I noticed a woman who was not a natural blonde who resembled her, or so I thought. She had a cigarette in one hand and a beer in another, and she definitely had it in for the Belleville coach, criticizing his every move even though they were winning. His wife, I thought. She cussed every now and then and I doubted Laura would do that, but many things can change over the years.

Another woman I felt could be her. She sat proudly beside her husband on the sideline in a padded folding chair, like his. He nursed more than one cigar, and hardly could follow the game because one citizen after another came by to shake hands and engage him in a conversation that always seemed serious. I imagined him as the mayor, successor to Marty Bascomb, or a fat cat businessman. Fortunately or not, he hadn't been invited to my afternoon's sales pitch.

I ambled around and more than once passed in eyesight of the two women, thinking if one of them were Laura, she might recognize me. A stupid move, but humiliation was spared. Neither gave me a first look, much less second.

When the game ended everyone except me filed out of the stands and field toward the parking lot. I lingered. The car lights and motors gradually faded away and finally I headed back to my own vehicle. Some dust was still settling in the glare of the field's beacon lights.

A darkness fell over the land and I knew the groundskeeper had finished inspecting field and concession stand and locked what needed to be locked. If he was like Coach Cross he took one long look before hitting the OFF switch.

"I always feel a little sad afterward," he told me once. "Don't know why really."

But I think he did.

I'd worked at Frankenheimer Foods for many years to support our family, though Mary Louise reminded me over and over that she didn't need to be supported.

One day I'd had enough reminders of my lackey status and resigned so I could start my own enterprise. I went from one kind of sales and merchandise to another, each one no more successful than the previous. They took me on the road all over the state, and I spent many a night in motel rooms calling a home phone where no one answered. Mary Louise, who never let any grass grown under feet anyway even during our son's first years, couldn't stand being alone and would call up a friend and go out.

At first it was a girl friend, then she moved on to one of my friends and saw no reason why she couldn't have drinks with him, like on a date.

Then the dates became more vaguely described. Johnny Benson skedaddled off to Missouri after our marriage for a dairy products company. He'd assured Big Chuck that "my heart will always belong to beef and pork," though I thought it might belong elsewhere. Charley grew up long and lanky and taller than me, but Mary Louise would cut off any insinuation before it left my or anybody's lips. "Get your filthy mind out of the filthy gutter," she would say, and having a filthy mind, I thought back to Bill Bowers explaining a non-denial denial.

But I never pursued it. I didn't want to know. That made calling it quits easier, because I could justifiably say to myself it wasn't over our son, or in any slightest way his fault.

The fault lay in his parents' stars, and their own decisions.

#

It was late and a long drive home, and I'd seen more than I wanted of swinging and missing.

I drove out of the parking lot and passed quickly down Belleville's main street, passing the local Dairy Queen where a lot of the players had adjourned after the game with their girl friends. The restaurant where I'd gone with Laura had gone dark an hour ago, but I liked that it had remained in business.

Once out of the downtown speed zone I hit the gas and put the headlights on bright, as the full moon was late tonight in rising.

Farmland lay on both sides and in a minute I'd pass the lake and then follow the highway cleaving through forest. I figured the chances of me encountering traffic were little or nil, and pushed the pedal further down.

Wrong. Somebody turned onto the highway behind me and his lights got bigger and bigger, meaning he was gaining on me.

That could only mean one thing, so I slowed and let him turn his flashers on, which State Policemen like to do. Or maybe it's in their operations manual. It was probably the same trooper I'd seen watching the game, and I hadn't taken into account that he'd still be around, probably on his way home. Might as well show a big city boy that he couldn't come here and flout our local speed limits. I knew better than to give lip to a State Policeman, especially in rural areas where you might end up in the local hoosegow, bunking with a drunk or much much worse. So I resolved to be polite and got my license out, ready to hear and abide his lecture on speeding. He took his time getting out of his car and as he swaggered up, it occurred to me he no doubt didn't appreciate me delaying his beer and midnight snack. Reason to be extra polite.

"80 in a 50-mile zone. Where's the fire, hoss?"

I said without looking up: "Sorry, officer. In a hurry to get home."

"Must have a lady waiting. Women'll get you in trouble every time. I always say, you can't live with 'em and you can't shoot 'em."

I'd held my driver's license out, again without looking up, hoping he'd give me a citation and I could get this over with quick and get on the road again, but most state police officers didn't chew the fat like that. I looked up at him and recognized him at about the time he looked from my license to me.

"Well I'll be damned," I said.

"Keep driving that fast and you will be," Jim Bunch said. He held out his hand and we shook.

"What brings you up here?"

"Sales meeting. Or supposed to be."

"People up here got hard heads. Hell you ought to know that from when we butted heads."

I smiled and was a little surprised I did. He'd put on some weight and had a gut but he was the same, hard head and all. Maybe just a little less the cocky asshole.

We bullshitted a while about old times. He'd gone to Vietnam and said he'd liked being in the Army but "the peaceniks won and we had to get out. Still get to carry a gun though. Joys of being a po-lice officer."

He said their coach had retired but came out every now and then for the softball games that he and a lot of the old team played in an adults league.

"I play too," I said. "Got to keep the groove."

"Hell, I play for the beer. Win or lose we tie one on. My old lady don't look like much no more but she can cook. We got three crumbsnatchers now."

"Me, one."

"You marry that blonde with the short shorts?" I nodded. "She was something to look at."

"Still is. Should have stopped with the looking. Couldn't live with her and couldn't shoot her. And vice versa."

"Funny how things work out. Or don't." He thought a minute. "You remember Laura?"

The expression on my face gave him the answer.

"She's still a looker. Still treats everybody right. Married this peckerwood from Jonesboro. He played ball if you could call it that. I must have struck him out 20 times. Hell, I coulda just thrown my glove out there and he'd have whiffed.

"She said to me 'Jimmy, you can't extrapolate from baseball to life.'

"The hell you can't, I said, even if I didn't know what extrapolate meant. Why it took her so long to divorce his ass escapes me. I may be dumb but I can spot a loser any day of the week. Hey, I'm gonna have to write you up."

"Well, I deserve it."

He pulled out his pad and while he wrote up the citation I told myself, I'll find her even if I have to go door to door in Jonesboro or wherever she is. Maybe she wouldn't remember me and maybe even if she did, so much water had flowed under the bridge I'd drown. Maybe I'd just be chasing a memory, like some old duffer who still talked about the home run he hit to win a game nobody but him even recalled, and sure as hell didn't care about.

And yeah, we'd lost the championship. Maybe that was my destiny, to go through life a loser and when Laura laughed in my face, that'd be one more signpost on my road to nowhere.

But for what it was worth--probably nothing--Jim Bunch hadn't lumped me in with the peckerwood from Jonesboro.

Yet. He handed me the citation. "We'll see if you deserve it."

He hadn't filled out the citation. On the name and address lines he'd written Laura and her married name, together with an address in Jonesboro and phone number.

"Give her a call. Tell her it's community service you got to do, 'stead of paying a fine. That way she'll have to listen to you. Maybe you'll strike out, maybe you'll get past first base."

It took me a minute to react and he waited patiently. I didn't think he had that in him. "Thanks, Jim. Thanks a lot."

"Hell, us old ballplayers got to stick together." He turned to go back to his car.

"I'm goin' off duty now. Watch those curves around Stonebridge."

I watched him get in his car and started up my truck, eased it onto the road. Before I turned, I waved and he waved back. I didn't speed. Now I had a reason to get back home in one piece.

#

The radio had been playing softly and I hadn't noticed it before, but now I did and turned to the Golden Oldies channel. It was playing "Turn Turn Turn" by the Byrds.

I passed the lake on the left and saw moonlight reflected on its still waters, as it had done years before. Then the road entered a thick pine forest and stretched long and straight, with enough moonlight that I hardly needed the headlights.

I didn't know if my life had turned too, but I knew that whatever else lay ahead, whatever else I had been or might be in the uncertain future, I was an old ballplayer and I was going to speak soon to someone who might appreciate that.

BOOK 3

THE ROADS AFTER

24. LOVE

After my divorce from Mary Louise I'd rented an apartment up on Scenic Hill, where developers had supplanted some of the old homes with the idea that young up-and-comers would be willing to pay an inflated rent for the status of being up there.

You could say I was a downcomer the way I floundered with my sales ventures and debts, but I liked it up there looking out over Burns Park, and the complex had a swimming pool that was about a dozen times less Olympic than Big Chuck's, or even our former married home in the posher district of Sherwood, but it would do and kept Charley somewhat occupied when he came over and managed to get through his obligatory visit to his old man. Mary Louise had only entered once, her nose turned up the whole time, to drop off the golf clubs I hadn't managed to fit into the rental truck I hired for the move.

From my small terrace I could look out over the park and sometimes see a strolling deer, think in tranquility or make phone calls, and up on the hill the breeze blew cooler than down below or inside. So that was where I made the call to Laura.

I'd hesitated for a while and even written up a kind of script with possible repartee from me and possible responses from her, but threw it out when it occurred to me I might be jinxing myself, preparing golden verses that the audience might not want to hear. The conversation, assuming there was one and not the killer phrase "get lost," could turn sour in a flash.

I had avoided building castles in the air, but refused to deny myself hope. I had to see if I deserved it, like Jim Bunch said. He'd thrown down the gauntlet and like that day in Belleville long ago when I'd met Laura and fought with him, I picked it up.

So one Sunday afternoon near 5 o'clock, when I thought

most people would be thinking about preparing dinner or relaxing in the waning heat of this hot sunlit summer day, I picked up the phone and dialed the number Bunch had given me.

The voice that answered was deeper than I'd remembered, but then again years had passed and mine had aged and mellowed as well, so quickly, after I'd asked if I was speaking to Laura, nervously bumbled into the usual "I don't know if you remember me--" blather, gnashing my teeth that I had thrown out the golden verses, when she cut me off: "It's Tom the shortstop."

"Yeah. Yeah. I still play, for a softball team."

"A little bird--no, check that, a big loud bird told me you might be calling."

I had something else to thank Jim Bunch for. Talking about him let us laugh and break the ice.

"He always says becoming a cop was the only thing that kept him out of jail. Probably right."

"Did he end up marrying Jodie?"

"Wow, you remember good. What if I told you my hair is red?"

"I'd say you got tired of dark black and colored it." I hoped she hadn't, but then again, I knew I was taking a big risk--and she would too if she cared at all--in chasing what could be just a memory. A lot of years had passed.

She said Bunch did marry Jodie and liked to brag that he had her "well-trained." If he was splayed out on his sofa watching a big game and finished his beer, all he had to do was extend his arm with the empty mug and she'd grab it right away and take care of the refill.

"But whenever she calls him 'James,' I notice he hops to it right away, beer or no beer."

"That's a lot of years to be together in today's world," I said. "I can't say the same."

"That makes us both losers, Tom."

"All I know is, as a condition of not paying a fine I have to do community service. You know, like help the restaurant business in Jonesboro." She laughed.

So with that scary moment of asking for a date out of the way, we made plans to meet in Jonesboro on a Saturday evening, fairly early because I'd have to make the drive back. I didn't expect an invitation to stay over and didn't get one.

She ended the conversation with, softly, "It was nice to hear from you again, Tom. I hope you're not disappointed. Don't expect too much."

That was brutally honest and very direct. I was fearing the same but would have never been able to say it so forthrightly.

"Red hair. That's all I'm expecting."

But it wasn't. It remained as dark as I remembered, but shorter.

"It's summer and I still play softball, you know. I got tired of tying it up into a ponytail."

I had driven up to meet her at a restaurant she knew in Jonesboro, neither too chic nor shabby, where the cooks were ranged around a metal grill and you chose what you wanted them to cook at a buffet, then unloaded the plate for them to "do their magic."

"We're hicks up here, but innovative hicks," she said. I'd arrived early on purpose, and was nursing an iced tea when she walked in, wearing a one-piece dress and no jewelry except a green jade necklace that stood out in its beauty and simplicity, and in a flash I thought, like her.

"It's vintage, like us," she said.

Even though I'd told myself not to be superficial and beauty had only been one of her attributes, Laura was even more striking than before I thought, and in better athletic form. She'd only been a teenager when I met her, and now was very much in the prime of life.

"I'm a step slower," I said, "maybe two. Or three."

"You think I'm not? I still play softball too, but now I have to hit a double to get a single."

"I don't believe it, sorry."

"After a glass of this, you might believe anything." She put a bottle of French wine on the table. "I never drink hard liquor or beer but I know some French, remember? Corkage fee is only three dollars. Do you drink wine?"

"From time to time. Blue Nun and Boone's Farm, stuff like that."

"Right...well, welcome to another world." She'd looked at me with genuine pity, and looking back, I understood why. Probably homo sapiens regarded the Neanderthals in the same fashion, but luckily for me she did not call for my extinction, but pulled out a corkscrew and opened it like a professional wine steward.

"I go to Memphis and stock up at a store there. I'm still keeping up my French."

"Been to Paris yet?"

"My ex didn't like to travel north of the Mason-Dixon." We then got into an expurgated history of our failed marriages.

"I've been thinking there should be a marriage school," I said. "A place where people go and make all their mistakes and hopefully, learn how to deal with them."

"You could say we've already been and got our diplomas. Try the wine."

I did, and a whole new world opened up.

"Well," was all I could say. And then, "Well."

"A Bordeaux. Not the best, but ok."

"This is what you call ok?"

She was employed as a social worker but said she devoted a lot of spare time to ecology issues. "You mean, the environment?"

"Yes. We've got to protect it. Starting around here with the lake. You remember the lake?" Smiling coyly.

"I remember there was a lot of fireworks," smiling coyly.

We got to the end of the dinner and the last of the wine, and both had loosened me up. I told her that no matter what happened now, I regretted all the years that had passed. So much water under the bridge.

Before she could respond a man who'd just come in to the restaurant with a teenage girl in tow came up to our table. He didn't bother with hellos.

"Can she stay with you tonight?"

"The storm's getting really bad, Mom, they're talking about twisters," the girl said, and he added, "Your house's built better and I've got to get up real early tomorrow."

Laura gestured toward me and said, "This is my friend Tom."

"Evening," I said. He gave a cursory nod and she likewise, a bit sullen out of deference to her father. "I'm Marie-Laure."

"Nice French name."

"My Mom's idea."

He said, "Her friends make fun of it."

I knew this kind of crack from my own divorce school and had learned in certain ways how to handle it. It was meant for Laura but Marie-Laure lay in the line of fire as well. And of course, so did I. So I said,

"Not her best friends, I'll bet."

Marie-Laure looked at me with some surprise and some appreciation, I thought. Her mother had a slight smile on her face as well. The ex-hubby did not, but had no comeback. As Jim Bunch said, he struck out a lot.

"Would you like to have dessert with us, honey?"

"Um, I'm really not that hungry." In fact she had spotted some of her friends at a nearby table and looked like she wanted nothing more than to join them. Laura said, "Go ahead, we've got time."

"Nice meeting you," I smiled. She moved over toward her friends' table.

The ex said, "Maybe we're upsetting some plans."

I had known him for two minutes and already thought he was an asshole.

"If you're going to get up so early, Fred, better head home and get your shuteye."

"Yeah. Night."

"Night."

He said it to her, ignoring me. He turned and headed out. We'd heard the thunder for a while and now it was really booming, getting closer.

"He's deathly afraid of tornadoes. I'm happy he thought of

her for once. He was really a stickler for family togetherness, eating at table and all that. It didn't help."

"Close doesn't depend on distance."

She looked at me for a long moment. "If we'd gotten together back then, you might have been the one walking through that door. We were really young, Tom."

"Yeah."

"If you lose something you like and by some chance you get it back, you appreciate it more."

"And try not to lose it again."

A thunderclap broke right over our heads and shook the windows of the restaurant. Even Marie-Laure and her friends stopped their chatter for a moment to listen as the thunder rolled over. I remembered the last storm we'd been in and didn't want this one to lead us to the same fate.

"I respect tornadoes and know what they can do, but I'm not afraid of them. I'd like to escort you both home."

"You're most welcome."

#

I'd checked around and it seemed to me that any company that seemed to be making profits and invested some of them in sponsoring a baseball team had something going for it.

Randy knew somebody at Wal-Mart and got me a job interview and most likely the job too, because his computer company had done a lot of work for them.

I moved up fairly quickly. At first the job took me around the state, and when I came up to the northeast Laura and I spent as much time as possible together. But I could see a manager's job on the horizon if I got lucky, and that could be a long way away from Jonesboro.

Decision-making time approached. I'd made mine but didn't know about her. What I did know was that I wasn't going to fete her with a bottle of Boone's Farm or Cold Duck. This girl was class. I couldn't speak French except for "vin rouge" which I'd learned by doing, but I determined to do something

262

along gallant lines or bust.

She'd told me more than once, "Diamonds aren't this girl's best friend." At first she said it in relation to the jade necklace, to show beauty came in many colors, but later on I thought she was making a point.

Yes, I was making money now and had managed to scrabble out of debt, but she knew very well I couldn't buy out Cartier's. Or Tiffany's. Or Bijoux Jewelers in Little Rock.

"Well," I said, "what if a diamond just lay at your feet. Would you pick it up?"

"If it wasn't stolen."

"Ok, let's go to Crater of Diamonds Park. People find diamonds there all the time. I'll find you a big beautiful one. Like you deserve."

"You think you're that lucky?"

"I found you, didn't I?" So one weekend we made the long drive west to the State Park. A park staffer rented us mining tools and I went to work prospecting in the dirt terrain discovery area.

"It just rained so our chances are better. Good conditions when the earth turns up like this.'"

"So far all I see is mud. It's hard work. I respect more now those people at Sutter's Camp and Yukon territory. Let me help."

"No. Just work on your tan and give me some water now and then. Plus moral support."

"Don't I always?"

"Every week somebody here kicks over a dirt clod like this and there's a one thousand, five thousand, twenty-five thousand dollar stone. You get it cut and polished and it only cost you the 3-buck entrance fee. God Bless America."

"Four bucks."

"I'm going to find something. I guarantee it."

In fact I was absolutely sure because I already had it in my pocket, courtesy of Bijoux Jewelers who'd sent me back into debt. But she was worth it. It just had to find its way from pocket to ground at the appropriate time.

I dug and scrabbled and sweated bullets all morning, then we sat down to a picnic lunch.

"You know--" she began.

"Yeah, I know. But I believe in the stars."

"Yeah, but they're up in the sky, not down here."

I went back to work. At one point Laura left me to "take a spin," and when she came back she was carrying a Stetson. "For my prospector." She claimed I was the cutest diamond-digger in the field, which numbered then about 25 other determined sunfried souls, but she may have been biased. In late afternoon she asked if she could try and started turning over the earth with the spare spade. For a while we worked together.

"Hard work. You really have to earn your diamond." I let her do her thing for a while then announced "Hey, I found something."

"Really?" She hurried over and peered down where I was pointing.

"Oh my God, you really have."

"Pick it up, it's all yours."

"How lucky. It's already polished and somebody put a band on it."

"See if it fits." It did, because I had carefully measured one of her rings so the jewelers could get it just right.

"You are a rascal. I don't know whether to laugh or cry. I think I'm going to do both."

But first she gave me a long hug and kiss. Then a few others. It was now or never. I kneeled down in the dirt.

"Would you marry me?" She thought about it a brief moment, then started to cry.

"Go pick up my shovel."

Didn't expect that. "That's your answer?"

"Partly."

I said to myself, I will never understand women. When I bent down to get the shovel I saw a bright white object amid the dirt. "It's a quartz crystal," I said.

"No honey, it's like you--a diamond in the rough. And the

answer is yes."

It wasn't the largest diamond ever found at the park but it wasn't the smallest either. We had it cut and polished and inlaid for a beautiful necklace that Laura wore along with the ring on our wedding day.

Our friends said that in diamond hunting as well as other ways, we made a good team.

#

We got married in a little chapel in Belleville that had a view of the lake where we'd started our life together. The ceremony blended faiths and music and vows, which besides the time-honored one to love and cherish we'd added a couple more personal to reflect our separation and reuniting.

Even some of the hard hearts among the congregation found it moving. I know I did. Randy, Spencer and Mickey came up from Dogtown. Cletus sent his regrets, stating he had a court date to finalize his divorce from his second wife and given the acrimony from her "trying to take me to the cleaners," he might "rain on our parade" and didn't want that. At that time I had lost touch with Mose.

I invited Bobby who was living in Dallas and he said he wanted to come up but he made various excuses why he couldn't, and finally I understood that really, he just could not stand to return to the scene of his biggest public failure.

Bobby had married, had two children and stayed with the same insurance company all his working life. He once told me, "When it comes time to mark my tombstone, they won't find anything to say. But I like that."

He said he and George went to Greers Ferry Lake one weekend and George rented a motorboat that he loved to max out. Bobby thought more than once they'd capsize on a wild turn or ground on a shoal or even run into a tree at shoreline.

"He pushed the possible, you know. Or maybe you didn't. You kind of kept him on an even keel. He didn't like limits and if he'd stayed around, he'd have wanted to cross every single one of 'em. I wasn't like that. Hell, that's why I sell insurance. I hate risk."

He said after a day of this George needed to take a break from risk and turned the wheel over to him, and when he got the boat rolling, kept prodding him to go faster. Bobby did, enough to keep his brother off his back, but didn't take any chances until they went past a swimming beach packed with bathers.

George yelled, "Give 'em something to remember us by, bro'. Surf's up, folks!" He reached over and hit the gas and it took Bobby a moment to regain control of the wheel. In their wake he saw big waves roll toward the beach area and rock air mattresses and swimmers.

"I saw those people looking at me, real pissed off, and I didn't like it. George said, 'You just don't like to make waves, bro,' and that's just about right. I mean, moving to Dallas was a big deal for me. Hard on my nerves, you know. But I had to make it work for my family. Had to do it and now I can say I'm used to it. Sure hope we don't move again, though."

#

No one had ever come close to being as close a friend as George, and I had a lot of drinking and golfing buddies, and I was still close to the guys on the team who'd made the trip to the wedding. Bill Bowers lived in New York and just couldn't get away.

Finally I asked Jim Bunch, of all people, to be my best man. The only person more surprised than him was me, but he said yes, why not, "You need to have a winner on your team."

Laura said I was right, that when Jim stopped me on the highway that night, he didn't have to be civil, much less volunteer her phone number. The fact he did gave hope for us all, and we needed to keep him at least partly civilized.

We'd gone over to his and Jodie's home for dinner a couple of times and he was right, she was a very good cook. Afterward Jim would always turn on the TV while we chatted and was sure to belch or fart at least once during the evening, and apologizing never once crossed his mind.

At first he wanted to wear his state trooper's uniform for the ceremony, but Laura convinced him that if he did, people would think I was a felon out on temporary parole for the wedding. They'd be looking at our wrists to see if I was handcuffed.

So he ended up wearing a suit and tie that Jodie had to tie for him, and did all the right things during the ceremony, which he should have because we'd rehearsed it enough. I thought sure he would fumble the ring and we'd see it go clattering down on the chapel floor, but he actually got out some stats from his ballplaying days with his fielding percentage, and I had to admit they were pretty good.

He told me Laura looked like the prettiest bride he'd ever seen, "even as old as she is," but admitted he might be biased given she was his cousin. I said I was biased too, but I agreed.

#

We were saving up money for Paris but weren't about to miss out on a honeymoon after the wedding, so we took a page from the book of the Stuttgart couple and many others and spent several days in Hot Springs. We stayed at the stately Arlington Hotel and tried to find the suite where Al Capone had stayed, but not being rich and successful gangsters, we settled for a room with mineral water piped in and luxuriated in it and the hotel spa and pool. Laura treated herself to a full massage and managed to survive the rubdown given by Alcinda, an ex-Marine who swore that when she "worked those muscles of yours, they'll stay worked for a while," and my new wife testified to the truth of that fact.

The racing season at Oaklawn was winding down but I managed to see a couple of races without winning anything, but kept my shirt, and that was the goal.

On one of our daily hikes we climbed above the city to the north and came across a "sacred tree." A hippie girl who was meditating there told us the tree was decorated with necklaces and bracelets and all manner of mementoes because the tree stood at a vortex of planet energy.

We both seemed to feel something, but I said to Laura maybe it was our own energy shooting into the vortex rather than vice versa. "Should we share or keep it to ourselves?"

"Both." She wasn't about to leave behind her diamond necklace on the tree, sacred or not--"it will keep us together, *n'est-ce pas*?"--so I collected some pine branches and oak leaves and sprigs of honeysuckle and fashioned a wreath. It was late spring but the honeysuckle blessed the air pungently.

I strung the wreath as high up on a branch as I could, where it was conspicuous among the other silver and metal ornaments. The tree overlooked a bluff and valley in the opposite direction from Hot Springs, and up there on the promontory, may indeed have had a direct path to the sacred.

At least we hoped so. A breeze kicked up and the wreath swayed in the wind.

"That is so cool," the hippie girl said.

"You can say it comes from the heart," I added.

#

We moved around a lot the first couple of years because Wal-Mart was expanding faster than I think anybody in the company ever predicted. But their dreams were coming true and we hoped ours would too. We had a wonderful girl and named her Michelle, because this time Laura wanted a name that worked in English as well as French.

One day my boss called me in and said the firm was opening up a Superstore and he wondered if I wanted to take on all that responsibility. "Is it harder than being captain of a baseball team?"

"Beats me. Was it hard?" I said I felt my background might help me meet the challenge.

"You haven't heard the kicker yet. Our latest boondocks emplacement."

One of the secrets of Wal-Mart's success was implantation in rural communities where we would attract business from all the outlying farms and isolated homes in the middle of nowhere. So I braced for Nowheresville.

My boss mentioned the name and said, "This is the place. Better make sure you and your wife can handle it."

He made it sound like the North Pole, or a no man's land war zone, but when he said the name I understood his hesitation. He said, "You won't be playing baseball this time. Softball maybe. They might have teams there."

When I announced the possibility to Laura she said, "Well, it can't be that bad of a place to raise kids. You grew up there."

So we moved to Dogtown and got a house up in Sherwood not far from the golf course. When Michelle got older my mother babysat on nights when we played softball. We formed the left side of the infield and though spectators often buzzed at how good the third baseman was, quite rightly, I did manage one season to go 40 for 50, an achievement even for slo-pitch softball. Laura made some calculations.

"You're hitting .800. Amazing. Now to get up to .900, You'll need to go 50 for 50. On the other hand, if you go into a slump and go 0 for 50, you'll still be hitting .400. And that's darn good."

With growing older her vocabulary had expanded to words like "darnn," and sometimes "golly darn," which our daughter picked up on when she began speaking. They were most often used about things or mischief I'd done, not Michelle.

One time and one time only, because we weren't invited to the same parties, we ran into Mary Louise and her new husband at an event.

Johnny Benson had joined a Missouri fertilizer firm, and he'd done well selling various kinds of "soil enrichment compounds" for farm, home and garden, but his heart "lay back home," and I knew exactly where it lay, because he wheeled and dealed and got a branch of the fertilizer firm set up not far from where he'd cut his teeth in sales, i.e., also not far from Mary Louise.

"She needed some landscape work done because frankly, their property out back had gone to waste. Even a self-respecting worm wouldn't want to roam around there. I recommended a combination of--"

Where anybody else would be bored to death, Mary Louise operated at such a high-watt pace he brought her back to normal, or at least functioning electric current less liable to overheat and explode. Like he once said, he calmed her down. So somewhere between hanging around a lot to till and oversee the garden growing, he became part of the new landscape.

I told him I was happy for them.

"I made a promise to her Tom, I said, 'I'm going to keep you in clover.' And I will, Tom."

"Well, you've definitely gotten into your new field of work. As it were." I didn't realize I'd made a pun, but Johnny got it and cackled with laughter for about a minute.

"You said it, yes sir, you said it. Have you heard about UC Davis? They've got a course on soil enrichment--"

"Excuse me, need another drink."

"It's full, Tom. You forgot to drink it."

"Yeah well, guess I was too absorbed in the conversation."

That led to a spiel on soil absorption of nutrients, and I realized that virtually everything one said could lead to a topic in Johnny's new line of work--"We'd be nothing without agriculture," he assured me, "the hunters and gatherers realized that and they were so right"--so I guzzled the drink as fast as I politely could, then left him in mid-methane.

I only spoke to Mary Louise in passing, as she was surrounded by the usual gaggle of admirers who knew she was married but hoped to get lucky anyway. She wore her standard summer outfit of non-outfit, so did not lack for attention.

"Haven't I seen her somewhere before?" meaning Laura.

"Only from the back. A long time ago."

"I know it's catty, but she's not the kind of person I'd remember."

"I know. but I did." I rejoined Laura. She had a cocktail in her hand.

"Since when do you drink hard liquor?"

"I don't know, I was talking to Mr. Benson and suddenly I felt like I needed a strong drink."

"He does that to people. That's why he's such a successful salesman. If you can't get away for a stiff drink, you sign off on whatever he's peddling as fast as possible. But he's a nice guy really."

Laura did her best not to say anything too severe about Mary Louise, as with everyone, but offered an observation: "I know it's catty, but if the Barbie doll I had when I was a kid grew up to be a big girl I think she'd look like her. Not so baked and sundried, though." Luckily we all got out of there without anyone getting hurt.

#

After I'd saved up enough money so that we wouldn't have to live on the streets like one of Victor Hugo's street urchins, I invited Laura on a trip to Paris. We found a beautiful little hotel with a garden near the Latin Quarter that only became available via a last-minute cancellation.

"Monsieur is very lucky," the manager told me.

"He means I was pretty dopey not to have booked in advance," I told my delighted wife, who adored having breakfast in the garden with croissants and brioches and the excellent coffee.

"We're in Paris with luck on our side."

We took a Bateau Mouche on the Seine in bright sunlight and warm temperatures--"Monsieur is VERY lucky," the manager said about the weather--and joined a multitude of other tourists in Montmartre. Laura loved the view from the top of the hill and Sacre Coeur cathedral, and so did I after I caught my breath from the walk up.

We crossed the only cabaret left in Paris, the Lapin Agile, and decided to spend an evening there. "That means, agile rabbit, right?"

"Your French is getting better!" We drank the concoction

they offered and sat on wooden benches that may have dated back to the days of Toulouse Lautrec--we liked to think so anyway--and listened to a parade of musicians and comics who if only from the reactions of the other patrons who understood French, must have been pretty funny.

Laura of course understood much more of the jokes than I did. "You could call it earthy humor for the most part. And pretty funny."

After that first concoction ran out I ordered other concoctions, and as the evening wore on I noticed a man sitting near us who was small, wore glasses and I swear resembled Toulouse Lautrec.

I said to Laura, "Say something to him in French. I swear he's a dead ringer for Lautrec. He's come back to life."

Laura admitted he did resemble the famous painter but did not believe in reincarnation. Finally though she agreed and in between acts posed a question to him in French.

He answered back in English, a guy from Brooklyn with a strong accent who said so many people over the years had made the Lautrec comparison he'd decided to come to Paris, enjoy the City of Light and why not, act the part. "I don't wear glasses but when I put them on and looked in the mirror I felt like picking up a paintbrush. I feel the vibes here," he said.

And so did we. We passed a wonderful soirée.

We went to Versailles and I found the chateau itself gaudy and pretentious. "That was the idea, Tom. Impress the citizens and make them proud of the glory of la France."

"Well, la France went broke and cut off their heads so frankly, they had a hard time seeing the glory."

"Mon Dieu."

We both liked the Petit Trianon though, with its many erotic paintings that Laura said made it clear it was Marie Antoinette's love nest.

"Some nest," I said.

"We've got a Petit Trianon"--in an accent which to my ears was superb.

"We do? Where?"

"Wherever our bedroom is." I loved her for that.

In Montmartre at the Place du Tertre I had badgered one of the artists in the square to paint Laura's portrait and slipped him a chunk of extra money. "I will paint you something to remember," he promised. And he did. The painting now hangs in our Petit Trianon bedroom at home.

We saw Napoleon's tomb and at the Eiffel Tower I felt so happy and refreshed at being alive and in Paris that I climbed the steps to the top rather than take the elevator. I arrived still happy but less refreshed, and not a bit regretful. "It's a way of honoring the workers who built this thing," I said. "They came up here risking their lives to build this monument."

That went double for Notre Dame, undamaged then, which had to be an obligatory stop. "The work, the labor, the artistic style that went into this. Incredible," I said.

"Honey, I think you're becoming more cultured by the minute."

Maybe, but I didn't tell her I'd run into Harvey Harris, my favorite foil from the old days, just before coming to France. When I told him we were traveling to Paris, he thought I meant Paris, Arkansas and wondered what there was to see there. When I corrected him he asked, "Is that where they have that Eiffel Tower?"

At one of the cheap souvenir shops I found a postcard with one of the cathedral's gargoyles and sent it to Harvey with a note that it reminded me of him.

On our last night I splurged more or less a year's salary and took Laura to dine at the city's famous Tour d'Argent restaurant. From our table overlooking the river we were able to watch the boats passing and city lights blooming all around as night fell.

When the darkness was well advanced, we saw the Eiffel Tower light up in a blaze of a thousand sparklers that went up and down the frame until finally settling on a multicolored illumination like a Christmas Tree.

"Every night it's Christmas," Laura said.

"Next time we'll come on Bastille Day and we can compare

the fireworks with Belleville's."

"They'll be bigger and better but not so memorable."

The waiter Jean was quite young and spoke good English. We asked him to help us with the wine selection and he was very happy to oblige. It turned out he'd just come up from what he called France *profonde*. "It doesn't mean profound," Laura said. "It's kind of like backwoods."

He wanted to learn how to be a sommelier and starting as a waiter at Tour d'Argent with its world-renowned wine cellar had been like a dream come true, even though he'd had to leave his family and friends.

He loved the fact we'd come from Arkansas and from time to time during the meal we exchanged pleasantries. Laura made him laugh out loud when she told him how Arkansas locals pronounced the name of the Anguille River, where catfish lived in abundance.

"Here," Jean said, "our chef would make a su-paire recipe for this catfish. It would be a *régale*, uh, delightful dish."

In his naiveté he probably thought we would serve it battered and fried.

Laura pointed to the *carte de vins*. "An excellent choice, really and truly, Madame. Not so expensive but very good, Madame has the very good taste."

I could have sworn he looked at me questioningly, wondering how she could have slipped up there, but Laura said no, his look meant you've found a gem here. Probably the reality lay in between.

In any event both wine and food were a *régale*, delicious, and we could not have been happier. As we were finishing with a traditional coffee--I'd gotten used to the small cup servings and now thought them *normale*--Jean came over with his boss the Maitre D', a very elegant man in a tuxedo.

"Well," the boss said in good though accented English, "couple from Arkansas, you have enjoyed our humble restaurant?"

We assured him we did, even though he knew it from our frequent compliments to Jean during the meal.

"Jean wishes to show you our *cave*, the wine cellar." "

Laura said, "The famous cellar with thousands of great bottles?"

"Just so," the manager said with great pride.

"I would be so very pleased," Jean said. So we found ourselves in the famous cellar where one vintage after another, many costing a small fortune, lay in perfect tranquillity, aging to a perfection ordinary wines could never attain.

Jean said that during the war, they had actually built a wall to resemble the original medieval one and hidden the best bottles behind it from the Nazi officers. They were served with wines artfully counterfeited with grand cru labels but in fact, *vin* very very *ordinaire*. They never caught on to the fact they were drinking swill instead of a wine costing thousands of francs.

"The real piss" Jean said, pronouncing it "pees." "After the war, it all went in the toilet. No French could drink it."

When Jean said goodbye to us at the elevator, I asked him for his opinion and pronounced "laissez faire." I said, "My friend pronounced it like that. Was it good?"

"Impeccable, monsieur. Tell your friend this."

"He would have been happy."

"Ah...these separations, they are very hard."

There was a catch in his voice and Laura understood immediately. "She will join you here, Jean. I am sure of it."

"Merci, Madame."

And then like a gallant Frenchman, he took her hand and gratefully kissed it.

#

The night I'd had dinner with Laura in Jonesboro, she and her daughter and I had driven to their home under a dark violent sky riven by lightning bolts, the loudest thunder I had ever heard and a wall of torrential rain.

We'd arrived just before the worst hit, and Laura said it was out of the question for me to attempt a drive home in these conditions.

"We have plenty of room." She looked at her daughter, who rolled her eyes.

"It's all right Mom, I know about the bees and birds."

Her mother was speechless.

"We're just good friends," I said.

"Yeah, right."

Laura and I both laughed, but out of the mouths of babes...I did not spend the night on the couch. At one point in the night we lay in bed listening to the rain and thunder, talking softly about what had just happened, which at times had seemed as intense as the storm.

"I've been saving all my love for you, darling," Laura said.

I had been married before and I'd dated very much after the divorce, and I wasn't so very far from middle age, but that night for the first time, because it hit me viscerally like those lightning bolts coursing through the night sky, I felt what love was.

25. GEORGE

With his topnotch grades, recommendations, sports and extracurricular activities, not to mention IQ, George had had his pick of colleges and chose Princeton.

In early September, after the disappointment of the championship game loss and the searing summer heat had both begun to fade a little, we played golf together with Bill Bowers. For some reason, maybe to change the subject from the previous hole which all three of us had bogeyed, the talk turned to our futures.

Bill said he had newspaper ink in his blood and if he went anywhere in the years to come, it'd be to a bigger paper in another state. Not the New York Times, he joked, because he'd now decided to focus on sports and he couldn't see himself covering Ivy League games nobody but Ivy Leaguers cared about when, say, Alabama was playing USC.

Au contraire, George said. "That's French for on the contrary. F. Scott Fitzgerald was listening to a Princeton game on the radio when he keeled over from a heart attack. The excitement of the game killed him."

"That's probably the last exciting game they've played," Bill countered.

They knew I had decided to stay close to home at the local college--going to be a young father and all--the all being Mary Louise and Big Chuck who'd mapped out my future promotions in the company without bothering to ask if I'd sign off on them. Despite what I'd once said, ham hocks loomed on my horizon as far as I could see.

George had said, "Sorry, you're no Horatio at the bridge, just one man. It took a lot of men to storm the Bastille and the Bastille was a piece of cake compared to the Frankenheimer family."

George's next four years at university seemed mapped out, so for Bill and me, end of discussion. Bill stepped up to the tee on #4, the most difficult on the course.

"Aren't you guys going to ask me when I'm leaving for Princeton?"

"What a burning question," Bill muttered as he lined up his tee shot.

"Ok," I said, "when are you leaving for Princeton?"

"Not going."

Bill sliced his shot directly into the bayou.

"That one's on you. I'm taking a mulligan."

"What the hell do you mean, not going?" I asked.

He was my best friend but had not let me in on his change of mind. It took the rest of the round for him to explain and at the end all our scores had gone into the bayou. He went off into his "band of brothers" spiel about the troops who'd covered themselves with glory on St. Crispin's Day and forever after and deep into old age would meet and share memories of the miracle they'd wrought with their teamwork and mutual valor.

"It gives worth to all your life, something like that. Not sitting in a library poring over poetry."

"Or writing it," I said, "like Shakespeare. Poring over his play. Easy for him to count coup on St. Crispin's Day."

Bill interjected, "Gimme a pen. I'm gonna write an article: 'Idiot seeks brotherhood in rice paddy.' "

"Listen," I added, "you've already got your band of brothers. They're called the Dogtown Packers. 50 years from now we can meet and bullshit about our games till we're blue in our wasted faces."

"The British were fighting for their country," Bill said. "Our fearless leaders say we're fighting so Vietnam and Cambodia and all those other countries that make good restaurants don't start to fall Communist. One after the other, the domino theory. Think about that. We're fighting for dominoes."

"Look, I'll spend a year helping my country, then I'll come back and go to college and serve in other ways. Hey, a combat medal will look good on my resume."

"Or your coffin," I added. I was afraid for him. He'd grown up the eldest son, so gifted in every way that perhaps he needed to live dangerously. He had the kind of looks that would only make him more distinguished as the years went by. His problem so far in life had been not finding any genuine peers, someone on his level or who cared to be. He tolerated dopes like me but he looked for more.

"Princeton will still be there when I come back." He'd already enlisted and been assigned. "The scuzzballs at the Recruiting Center shook my hand."

"Hell of an honor that is," I said. "How much Ajax did you need?"

"I'll shake it when you come back home," Bill said. "I'll be waiting here at Burns to tee it up. Don't let me down. Come back."

#

George became a sergeant and led a platoon and from his letters I could almost follow the progress of the war. He fought in the thick and stayed much longer than a year. He'd been particularly upset by the Tet Offensive. He said they'd beaten back the Cong, him and his band of brothers, and he raged against the government publicity machine that had given the public false optimism.

But after years of inflated body counts and the government declaring imminent victory, the mere fact of a huge offensive hit Americans hard, and support for the war drained away day by day.

I never dared to ask George in one of my letters if he still believed in what he was doing.

He got a couple of medals for bravery in action, then got his walking papers. The Army figured he'd done enough, and George said to himself, "Time to follow in Fitzgerald's footsteps and go to Princeton. Fucking ironic, isn't it?"

He'd actually been heading back to post, in a section of land the Viet Cong had ceded weeks ago, when he stepped on a mine that blew off both his legs.

"I'd led a charmed life till then. Must have really pissed off the Wicked Witch of the West."

He spent six months at a military hospital getting patched up enough to sit in a wheelchair, then got sent back home to the VA hospital at Fort Roots on Scenic Hill.

I visited him often. He exercised his arms and upper body constantly and above the waist had never been in better shape.

"Mr. Simmons would be proud of me," he said.

His recuperation was going well. Princeton was waiting for him in September and he'd arranged living quarters with wheelchair access and transport to and from campus.

"By September I'll be a man again."

I didn't like this kind of talk. "That's bullshit. Listen, you're going off to one of the world's great universities and when you finish, find a job with the elite. You'll BE the elite. Fifth Avenue New York, cocktail parties with the movers and shakers. I'll be here peddling whatever I'm peddling, depending on the meat stocks. All I'll be moving and shaking is my ass."

That seemed to get his attention, or at least get his attention off self-pity.

"Hey, let me show you my hiking trail."

He wheeled over and out the door of his ward where he had an individual room with lots of comforts. He waved toward the nurse who barely acknowledged it. George said he could take care of himself pretty well now and the personnel trusted him.

"I'm the fastest wheeler on the ward." His arms formed by years of swinging a bat together with exercising had turned him into what he called "the champeen speedburner." I had to pick up my pace as we moved down a paved footpath to a fenced barrier. There was a gate there and George lifted the latch to open it and we moved onto a walkway that paralleled the crest of Fort Roots Hill. We had a superb view of the river and beyond, the Little Rock downtown skyline.

"Hey, do you remember that game we played here in Little League?"

I did. It had been against an outstanding Little Rock team, maybe their best, and we'd come from behind in the ninth inning to win.

"Remember that triple I hit to lead off the ninth?"

"Yeah. A low liner down the third base line."

"No way that should have been a triple. I turned on the speed, man. And it wasn't like their left fielder didn't have a good arm. His throw came in right on a line."

"You set the stage. We loaded the bases, right?"

"Right. Wasn't any way they could stop us then, except for a miracle and God must have been busy that night. Going from second to third, that made all the difference. That was the fastest I ever ran."

I changed the subject by pointing at one of the benches set up on the bluff for patients and personnel and visitors to sit and admire the view.

"Hey, take a look." Sponsors had their names engraved on the bench back, and this one had been furnished and paid for by none other than Frankenheimer Foods.

"Well," George said, "buying good will is better than none at all."

"I wonder why he never sponsored another team. It's not like he didn't have any spare change."

"Hey, you've only got one heart to break. Come on, I want to show you something."

He started down the short grassy slope to the cliff edge. Down below, a sheer drop of over 500 feet, we could see a johnboat tied up to the riverbank.

The great river flowed past and I was surprised at the speed of its current which we could see even from here.

"You got a brake on that thing?" I asked.

"Yeah, the nurses get freaked. But it's the only place where I can see the bluffs."

I followed where he pointed to some sheer rockface cliffs a ways downstream. They were yellow and brown and composed of the hard crystal-like stone you can find frequently in Arkansas, but not often so high or impressive. Down below we could see a jumble of rock and boulders that erosion and storms had sent tumbling down.

"Try to imagine," George said."You're Jean-Baptiste Benard de la Harpe and the governor of New Orleans sends you exploring up the Mississippi and then west on the Arkansas. Your men are battling the current all the way and you're sympathetic but hell, they signed up for the mission and you, you're busy recording what you see in your journal. A lot of science and figures and judgement calls like, should we stop and pick through this forest or keep paddling and fight the river and skeeters? I mean, you've got wild animals everywhere and you can't speak the Indians' lingo and trees, trees everywhere. That was 300 years ago and we still haven't made much headway clearing them. This land is so tropical it beats the tropics sometimes.

"And the $10,000 question: is this part of the New World worth enough you can write to the King and say, 'let's keep investing in it.'"

George was on a roll and I let him roll without interrupting. He'd been thinking about many things, it was clear. When you recuperate from a life-damaging injury, you either do that or don't think at all.

"So here's De La Harpe, floating into the unknown like he is, and he sees Pinnacle Mountain on the left that's shaped like a *gateau*. I'm sure you don't know that means cake in English."

"You'd given me a couple of months I could have figured it out."

"Right, sure. So I'm thinking he arrives here at sunset. One of those days when the golden hour is really golden, maybe a cloud or two, and it's just after a rain so the light glows like God's personal sunshine. And it hits those cliffs. And De La Harpe can't believe what's he's seeing. He thinks, if this isn't heaven, it's what heaven must look like. So he rows over to the *rive gauche* and sets up a camp. He can't stay, he's got to push on, but he leaves a few men there in a camp. A little settlement. Just so he can stop on the way back and take another look at heaven."

"You really think it happened that way? I mean, maybe he just had to stop somewhere and that *rive gauche* was as good as any."

"Come on. You really think he stopped because there was a *petite roche* on the bank? A little frigging stone? No, he was captivated by the big roches. He was no laissez faire guy, De La Harpe, he was a poet, he had soul. You can tell it from his name.

"Go over to his boulevard at sunset, in September like now when the light's sharp after a good rain.. Get out of your car and take a look. You're going to see a show you won't forget."

I did go over to the Little Rock side where the boulevard named after De La Harpe stretches for miles in parallel to the river bank. I had to wait a year, for another September sunset that promised to be spectacular, after an afternoon of late summer showers when the sky had cleared. The light was low and sharp and, as George said, golden.

That evening I remembered his wide radiant smile of joy when he talked about De La Harpe and the cliffs, so unusual in those days when he was struggling to cope with not having the legs that once let him stretch a sure double into a gamechanging triple.

He'd been finishing up his therapy and arrangements and in only a few days would head off to Princeton.

It must have been a sunset like this. The nurses said he took off wheeling toward his favorite viewpoint and they'd been stunned at how fast he was going. They'd never seen a man in a wheelchair move like that. They couldn't catch up, even on the run. Because it looked like he didn't intend to stop.

And he didn't. They said he had worked up so much speed when he went over the cliff it seemed like several seconds before gravity took over. Enough time for him to twist the wheelchair around in midair.

They couldn't understand why he did that. They said he'd given in to despair.

But looking across the river, I saw what he saw. The light hit those cliffs like God's own personal sunshine, brighter than the pearly gates, and I knew he'd been smiling and yelling out loud saying, "Heaven, here comes a speed burner."

26. BILL BOWERS

After a stop at the St. Louis Post Dispatch, Bill moved on to become a sportswriter for the New York Times.

"It's crazy," he told me once on one of his trips back home to see friends, "rejuvenate my Arkansas accent," educate me about what was going on in the world and beat my ass at golf.

"Here I am a handicapped guy covering world class athletes who can run like cheetahs and jump over the moon. Hell, when we're in the same room it's a wonder I can find some air to breathe. They hog the space, you know."

"You mean to tell me you're handicapped? And sometimes you beat my ass at golf? I don't believe it. I can tell you this buddy, if I catch you parking in the handicapped zone I'm calling the cops. You try to con them, I'll show 'em your scorecard."

He was touched by my tough love. "Geez, your new wife is turning you into a viable human being."

Bill's columns and game reports always have verve and spirit and just a touch of humorous cynicism, and he's become well known for viewing sports as not the be-all and end-all but something vital nonetheless. He knew what it meant to be able to run and jump and would never take it for granted or dismiss it as child's play.

"They say it's the glory of youth," he once told me in a very rare moment of direct sincerity, "but it's the glory of any age. If I could dance on my coffin before settling in, I would and be a whole lot less unhappy about it."

As for the Times, the country's greatest newspaper, he said "I owe everything to you and the Dogtown Packers."

"How's that?"

"First, you guys had so many highs and lows I covered every register. Nothing ever surprised me after those years. I mean come on, who's ever seen a guy in his wedding suit come up to bat and slam a gift double? A story by the way nobody north of

284

the Mason-Dixon believes really happened. They think it's my weird southern humor."

At first Bill had been assigned to the "shall we say, minor sports. Now I have to say I enjoyed the lacrosse matches but you know how it is here, as a sport it ranks just above tiddlywinks. Everything started to change one day, thanks to that 4-ball golf tournament we played in. You remember?"

"I've blocked it out."

Bill and I were playing pretty well at the time and a 4-ball is set up to utilise a team's complementary skills. For example, I was much longer off the tee than Bill and if I hit a great drive, he didn't even have to hit. For the next shot whoever had been hitting his irons better would go first, and if it wasn't good enough the other would take a crack at it. In essence it is a "best ball" tournament.

Bill was a much better putter than I was. "Got no nerves. After what I've been through, who gives a damn if a little white ball doesn't go in the hole?"

Being eager to win and it has to be said, less than honest, in the qualifying round we gave it less than our best. As the tournament was divided up into flights according to qualifying skills, we figured we'd be in with players less skilled than us and therefore would have a good chance of beating their tails and winning the flight.

The practice is called sandbagging.

"Well, we won't sandbag too much," Bill suggested. "Just enough to be with a bunch of losers." We salved our consciences by telling ourselves, one or two other teams might be doing the same thing.

As it turned out, all the other teams were doing the same thing, so we ended up being placed in a flight where everyone had the same skill level.

Bill said, "We're golf's answer to the Peter Principle."

"What's the Peter Principle?"

"Tee off and while we're playing I'll try to explain it to you. Luckily we've got 18 holes." Peter Principle or not, after the first two rounds we had tried to play our best but fumbled a lot of shots and remained in fourth place. On the 11th hole, a sharp dogleg left over a marshy creek, Bill had got so frustrated he teed up a ball and sent it straight toward the water just for practice.

"Let's help the gods of ineptitude. See? They didn't have to lift a finger. Maybe they'll laugh and give us a break, go have a beer or something."

Instead, they sent us Homer and Jethro. "Those weren't their real names, right? Homer and Jethro?" Bill asked.

"I've blocked it out."

We had bought new golf shoes for the tournament, plus sunglasses and stylish visors. "For the photo after we win first place," Bill assured me. So this day I wore a bright white T-shirt I'd mail-ordered from Abercrombie & Fitch in New York —Hemingway's favorite store, Bill said, and "don't ask me who Hemingway was." It ended up the day with egg all over it.

When Homer and Jethro stepped up on the first tee, we thought they'd mistaken the course for a plowfield.

"You fellas here to play?" Bill asked.

"If you can call it that," Homer chuckled. They both chuckled a lot but attacked the course, indeed, like a plowfield, like they knew where every worm lurked and only had to choose the right club. We noticed that each time they cut a fairway divot with an iron they replaced it impeccably with just the right amount of dirt and grass so you could hardly tell the earth had been upturned.

"Respect the earth and it'll respect you," Jethro said.

At first we found it hard to respect them because where we wore the latest fashion shorts and I my Abercrombie & Fitch T-shirt, they wore coveralls and calico shirts and Homer had a straw hat that reminded me of the scarecrow character in Wizard of Oz.

And their golf clubs had wooden shafts, of a kind not seen since the very early days of the sport.

"Adam used them when he played in the Garden of Eden," Bill said, "but no one has since."

"I'll bet you anything they made 'em themselves. Just cut a

hickory tree and whittled them down."

"At first we talked a load of shit," Bill said when we reminisced. "Like: 'Shouldn't we take them aside and say they're missing the churning? And the cows. Cows can get lonely, you know.'"

"Let's ask them for some buttermilk." On the first tee it was all we could do to hit our balls, we tried so hard to stifle laughter.

"We're no spring chickens, boys, but we'll try to keep up," Homer said.

"Would you happen to have some chickens back home?" Bill asked, trying to do it innocently.

"My brother here's the man with the chickens." He turned to his brother. "That rooster went wild this morning."

"Well, you should have got up and hit some practice shots."

"We're in third place, boys. Real fortunate." That was higher than us, and we found out why as we began to play and they analyzed each shot--

"What do you think, Homer. 7-iron?"

"Yep, slap it with an ole 7 and just let that sucker roll right up there, Jethro."

This was said about a shot where 100 times out of a hundred Bill and I would use a pitching wedge to loft the ball up and down onto the green. You did not want to let the ball roll and risk it hitting a tuft of grass or rock and caroming way off course. Made no sense.

But Jethro would literally hitch up his overalls, take his wooden-shaft 7-iron and do just that. Avoiding tufts, rocks and any other stray recalcitrant hazard. "Respect the earth and it'll respect you," Jethro explained.

None of their shots looked very pretty but somehow they consistently reached the holes in fewer strokes than ours.

As we started the back nine Bill and I needed desperate measures.

"Let's talk like them," I suggested to Bill.

"Accents and all?"

"Especially the accents."

But that didn't help either. On the 17th hole we found ourselves searching around in the woods while the brothers allowed how there was some good feedin' for the squirrels in there.

"Big fat suckers. Y'all missed it, a big ole hawk just dipped down and took one home to his kids."

Jethro added as Bill and I straggled out, having of course found no balls but a couple of chiggers: "I thought y'all was gonna stay in there."

"Thought about it," I admitted.

When we added up the scores we confirmed that they'd beat our tails and arrived in second place for the tournament. We would have been placed in the "also-ran" category except our names somehow got fudged.

"BB," Homer said to Bill when he handed back the scorecard, "you sign with your initials?"

"Yeah, an old habit I have. Saves time, you know."

I signed and Jethro noted, "You too?"

"That's why we're partners," I said, "on the same wavelength."

We detected a trace of pity in their looks as Homer and Jethro shook hands and said goodbye. "Well fellas, we've got to change into our Sunday-go-to-meetin' clothes for the prizewinners picture. It's been a pleasure playing with you today."

"Same here," I lied for me and Bill.

"Look," Bill said acidly as they headed toward their, naturally, beatup truck and we slunk over to our cars for the slink home, "they practice in their pastures with all the humps, weedgrass and Rocky Mountain oysters, and then they get out here on a course like Burns Park and it's easy pickins."

"You can stop talking like them now."

"Look, that's why Jethro got so much height on his short irons. He's out there staring a bull in the face and if he doesn't get it up over the horns right quick he'll hit him right in the snout."

"All I can say is, from now on I'm respecting the earth."

Bill almost forgot that he'd arranged to have a "victory beer" with a colleague over in Little Rock. They sat on a terrace beside the river directly across from the golf course clubhouse and Bill said, "I swear I heard people laughing. It echoed all across the water and I can damn well guarantee you they weren't laughing at Homer and Jethro, now they were duded up in their Sunday go-to-meetin' clothes."

"You're paranoid. Probably just some ducks."

"No, I heard the ducks. They were laughing, too."

#

Many years later during a slow day in the New York Times newsroom Bill said he decided to regale his colleagues with the story.

"I changed your name to protect your reputation." Nobody laughed, not once, and Bill told a story well. When he asked why, they said in effect, doesn't everybody in Arkansas dress and talk like Homer and Jethro?

This grated on Bill, and since he'd been writing good stuff about lacrosse and tiddlywinks and a day came where he'd have to spend all day in the press room, he decided to go to work dressed like H and J.

"A costume store in the Bronx that worked with stage and screen. Had everything." He caused a sensation. Colleagues from all floors and departments dropped by during the day to stop and stare, "like I was a native aborigine. Which in their minds I was."

Late in the day the Top Man himself came by. People said they hadn't seen him with the groundlings since the Watergate days. He asked Bill his name and even said he'd read a couple of his articles, especially one on a game involving his Ivy League school. "You made it sound exciting," he said.

This happened to coincide with one of their reporters' foray to Alabama to interview the legendary Bear Bryant, known for his brilliant coaching mind and downhome humor. The Bear told a few jokes and dispensed his wisdom for a good hour. The reporter was a New York native "and I couldn't understand a damn word." He knew the jokes were funny because everyone in the room was roaring, and he had to fake it as best he could.

Luckily he'd taken along a tape recorder. His editor asked Bill, "You're from Arkansas, right? Like Bryant?"

So Bill did a transcription, and then they asked him to do up the article. An era was aborning where teams from the south, and Alabama especially, were competing every year for the national championship, and Bill became the go-to guy for the Big Games. He even appeared on television.

"All of which goes to show," Bill likes to repeat, "in today's world, better to be a hick than remain anonymous."

"Or a shitty golfer," I added. He thought a minute.

"Given how I owe so much to Homer and Jethro, why don't we invite them for a rematch?"

"Hell no. They'll beat our tails again."

27. SPENCER

Spencer went West to Stanford, not admittedly for its excellent academic reputation but because he wanted to "explore the many facets of dope" and the school was only a hoot and holler away from the Haight in San Francisco where Errol had rented a pad.

Spencer said he showed up just enough in class to pass, and spent most of his time sampling the trendy and diverse pastimes of the Haight.

He said he learned more about free sex than free love, because for the latter, you had to stick together for a while with your lover and he didn't. He'd been much impressed by Bob Dylan's song "Like a Rolling Stone" and when he wasn't pitching a game for us, he'd hum it in the dugout to the point where we'd threaten him with a Louisville Slugger on his noggin to get him to stop.

Once in Frisco, he became a rolling stone for real.

"I was happy," Spencer said, "insofar as I remember. After a while I kept a record of my couplings, for posterity, if I had posterity, and by force of numbers it looked like I would."

He came on to Janis Joplin when he met her at a club but she turned him down, and he convinced himself it was because he told her he hailed from "her neighbor state, Arkansas."

"Being from Houston and all, she looked down her nose at us. Even when it was filled with coke."

Spencer said it all started to sour for him when Errol O.D.'d. He'd passed from pot and coke to LSD and tripped more and more often, then started mixing in other "mind-fuck" substances. Eventually "he had no mind left to fuck" and he lived in a state of perpetual hallucination.

"When you go that far, you need a guide who's sober enough, so you don't mistake a rooftop for a stair step, but who can guide a junkie like Errol had become 24/24? The cops found him by the wharf, with enough shit in his blood to kill a dozen horses."

That straightened up Spencer right quick, and then just as the '60s ended, "Manson killed everything."

The era, he meant. Everyone now looked twice at long hairs and wondered if helter-skelter lurked inside. Woodstock came and went, then really went.

"Looking back, I heard a swan song." He read his list of couplings and realized there were three Lucys "and for the life of me, I couldn't keep straight which was which. Then they found out about each other and 'for the life of me' became a meaningful concept."

He drifted down to Los Angeles and like most all devotees of San Francisco, looked down on the city, ridiculing it as a "superficial sunbaked skillet of fried brains," even as he commenced to spend days and days lounging on the beach.

"I took up surfing," and managed to work just enough at odd jobs to support a beach bum lifestyle. He had girl friends--but one rule, no more Lucys--and still gathered no moss.

He told a story and swore it was true, how one day he was lying on the beach in Santa Monica because the coast road to Malibu had been closed to traffic. One of the periodic wildfires that hit California after summer months of zero rain (he wrote me once, "If you visit in summer, don't bother to pack an umbrella") had struck the posh beach homes. Columns of black smoke were rising into the unclouded sky.

In the winter it did rain, he said, sometimes torrents, and the deluge was wont to send a clifftop house sliding down from the heights above in a sea of mud.

Spencer had seen one once, plopped right down in the middle of the PCH, mud and all, virtually intact. The house hadn't been destroyed in any way, just displaced.

"They closed off traffic a whole day while they got a moving truck to come out, and let me tell you, nothing pisses off LA people more than preventing them from hauling ass in their vehicles. I saw the owner telling his story to a cop and some flunky insurance guy and he literally had trouble being heard with all the jammed-up cars honking like crazy. I managed to hear the cop tell him, 'Sir, I'd advise you to gather your personal effects.'

"Now you've got to see that to believe it. The cop goes over to the roadblock to explain to these knucklehead motorists that there's a goddamn house blocking the road and until they can find a big strong guy to lift it off, all they've got to do to reach their destination is fly over. Yeah, just put your stick shift in the fly gear.

"And meanwhile we see a guy wading through mud in LA, which is a desert, in the middle of a highway, to his house to get his personal effects. I mean, where do you start? With your Lakers cap?"

Anyway, on this particular afternoon another kind of calamity had struck LA's beach communities and Spencer was lying there on the sand watching the smoke and working.

"Working?" I asked.

"Yeah, in LA when you sunbathe they call it 'working on my tan.'"

The thought crossed his mind that the poor guy whose home he'd seen slip sliding away in the winter might have given up on hillsides and relocated to a beachfront home, and what if now it was going up in flames?

A couple of surf bums next to him suddenly stirred from their habitual torpor when they spotted a friend of theirs up on the coast highway.

"Hey Jimmy, what are you doing here? We heard your house was on fire."

Jimmy yelled back, "Yeah, I think it burned down or something. Hey, how's the surf?"

Spencer said he realized then he was en route to becoming Jimmy, a veg, "a big wad of algae. I was becoming a double cliché--a burned-out hippie and an LA clam. But since I'd already moved so far toward clamhood, I didn't do anything to change my situation. I was working fulltime on my tan and that took energy, man. Plus the surf was just fine."

Then fate stepped in, in the form of Mr. Snookums. When he passed away Spencer learned in a letter from the lawyer who'd drafted his will that he'd left him a half-share of the farm. The other half went to Gilbert, the only son, with a stipulation that if Gilbert did not want to work the farm, Spencer had first right of purchase.

Spencer said Mr. Snookums knew his son very well. He confided once that when Gilbert came out of the womb, his mother slapped his fanny for real. He was a pain to deal with from birth. Spencer said the term "n'er do well" was invented for Gilbert, a true-blue couch potato.

Spencer went back and checked out his half of the farmland. He'd razed his pot plants many years before.

"I plowed 'em up and made a big picnic around a bonfire. For a week everybody walked around in a happy cloud."

Arkansas' finest still regarded pot smokers as heinous offenders second only to serial killers, so he did not reconstitute his "very own Dogpatch." He planted vegetables-- lots of them--and corn. The Amish farmers who were his neighbors grew just about the best-tasting corn in the south, and he learned a lot from them. They did not use pesticides or any other form of chemical enrichments.

"The concept of pesticides is to eliminate pests, but they're a part of life, and like George used to say when he got into his philosophy BS, you can't know good if you don't know bad. Plus, I had been a pest on the body politic for a long time. My father used to say, 'DDT was invented for kids like you, Spencer.'"

He paused a long moment when he told me that, reflecting. "Maybe that's why I tried so hard for so long to escape. My old man was no picnic. I sent him a couple bushels of corn from my first crop. That was the least I could do, and that's what I wanted--to do the least for him I could."

He'd had several poor harvests but he stuck it out and started to make profits.

Then one day Gilbert got up off his couch and decided he wanted to move to the city where less effort was required to shop for beer, chips and pre-cooked pot pies. Spencer looked up Sammy and got an advantageous bank loan.

Spencer said, "I'll never be rich, but I'll always be organic."

I'm ashamed to say I made fun of him at first when I contrasted Spencer's flawed fruits and vegetables to the perfect, waxed-shiny offerings we found in the supermarket produce section, but Laura educated me in the virtues and agriculture of organic farming. Every year now we order a truckload of Spencer's harvest and stock it all in the freezer. He offered a discount for old time's sake but we refused.

"We'll pay more to eat well and be glad about it," Laura told him.

Spencer said when he looks back on those years of vagabonding and counter culture, he couldn't say if had been a true golden age or only seemed it at the time.

"You know, the Zeitgeist. I do know something was in the air. You just have to look at the music. Every week we heard a new classic. Maybe this kind of big aura settled over the earth and we moved under it like guests at the swingingest party there ever was. It had its bad sides but it was like, you looked up in the sky and really did see diamonds."

Then he paused before concluding: "I know I saw a few Lucys."

28. LARRY AND PREACHER BILL

Larry and my cousin Betty got married in a ceremony at his father's church, where I felt his sermon, though heartfelt at times, sounded more like the less-than-hopeful sendoff of a parole officer to a repeat offender. Larry and Betty did their best to put on a happy face during the ceremony and reception--"We got through it," Betty told my mother, and seemed relieved that the chains were off. Less than a year later they moved to Amarillo where Larry got a job in construction.

For a long time the family lost touch with them, but stories would filter back about trouble with the law. Larry had never knocked the chip off his shoulder, and away from his father's iron hand and without a group to channel his energy and frequent rages, Betty said "He fell into the wrong company and went to the wrong places. I didn't get invited and that was fine with me, but that's when the big trouble began."

He and his cronies had apparently robbed more than one bank before they picked the wrong one in the wrong town and led a high speed chase that careened across a good portion of the Staked Plain before their car got diverted into a coulee and even then Larry, who was driving, managed to outmaneuver a couple of cop cars.

They say he coldcocked two officers and it took another 4 to bring him down. He was carrying a gun but didn't use it.

Betty stuck with him till he got out of prison, but she said he still had "too many demons inside" and it didn't work out. She divorced him and moved back to Arkansas, and thinks that the high wild Panhandle didn't do them any favors but at least Larry might find himself one day in those canyons and coulees and run out of folks to fight. Or else pick one fight too many.

Betty said he never laid a violent hand on her, and whenever they went out she knew that if anybody talked shit or came on to her, he'd get straightened out right quick or end up on the floor. Usually both.

"I have no regrets," she said. "If he ever changes his ways and gets back in touch, I'll listen."

She paused and added, "But I'll never set foot in that church again," meaning of course Larry's father's. Word is he still preaches fire and brimstone against the evils all men are prey to, but especially the young, and has never forgiven his son for not meeting his expectations.

#

Spencer confided to me once that the only time in his life he regretted our Packers camaraderie was when Billy Aycock visited him in Los Angeles and ended up crashing for months.

He'd lost touch with Billy and truth be told, we all had. He'd been signed to a free agent contract substantial enough to pretty much buy out the men's department at Pfeiffer's, and that was where I ran into him, the last I saw of him for years.

"You think I always slob around in cutoffs and a T-shirt?" he said. "Man, I like looking good."

He flashed off the field for sure, but on the field he washed out after two years. His father, who we'd see sometimes at games, always being ignored by his son in favor of whatever girl Billy'd invited, said unkindly, "You've got to have a brain too, you know."

Which I took to mean, despite his natural talent and strength, Billy couldn't figure out pro pitching.

He'd got married to Cindy, despite their professed aversion to the opposite sex, but very quickly they discovered an aversion to each other, not to mention that Billy had gone to work for the railroad to support himself and his wife after blowing all his baseball bonus and he hated every minute. "Grease and dirt ain't my thing, man."

After a lot of debt and scenes they divorced and Billy found himself footloose and fancy free, with alimony to pay--or not pay, as it turned out.

So he was drifting when Spencer, back home to visit his mother, ran into him and "in an excess of nostalgia and pot fellowship," invited him to a change of scenery at his Venice Beach pad.

Billy came out, slept on the sofa and got into the scene in a big way. Beach, hanging out, hitting on teenage girls headed in, out and around the surf, and evenings, scrounging around singles bars. Even Spencer, after his long history of free love, had enough finally of maneuvering around Billy and his "squeeze du jour," and this moment of fed-up-ness coincided with both Billy's running out of whatever pennies he still had and his being invited by a lady of a certain age and wealth to move in with him at her house in the Hollywood Hills.

"For a while he had it good," Spencer said. "Even if he had to be at her beck and call, like a doctor with a pager, she had enough girl friends and lunches and functions where it wouldn't do to show off her young stud, so he'd pad around the pool in shorts and shades and watch the po' folks down below on Hollywood Boulevard. 'Worker ants,' he called them.

"Then I don't know what happened, 'cause I was moving out and leaving the scene, and some way or other he fell in with the Jesus freaks. And not just any freaks."

He meant a couple who'd become well-known in southern California, Matthew Mark Hammond and his wife Mary Magdelene Hammond. "Everyone knew those weren't their real names, but hell it's the land of fake monickers. Try to find a birth certificate for Cary Grant or John Wayne. They said they'd been born again and started marketing their ministry, and that's the *mot juste*--marketing. It became a big business. Every lost soul around stumbled into their clutches--and in SoCal that's a whole big bunch, man. They used to drive around in a big bus they'd painted with psychedelic colors. If you'd been smoking you could trip out just staring at it."

Spencer said they held revival meetings that gave "holy rollers" new meaning. Billy became a disciple and bought in to what Billy said very sincerely was a genuine faith.

Spencer lost touch, even when the Hammonds pulled up stakes and moved their "Christ in Revival" ministry to a small town in southeast Arkansas, near where Mary Magdelene

Hammond had been born.

Rumor had it, Spencer said, that they were dodging the IRS and a few consequences of sins of the flesh, and backwoods Arkansas provided a safer haven.

Spencer heard that Billy had moved with them, but didn't look him up. "He got to the point where he couldn't say hello without preaching."

#

Many years after, when I was peddling my wares of the moment, I passed through a part of southern Alabama that still hadn't quite made its way out of the Great Depression, though I was damn careful not to say anything like that to a potential customer, such as there were in those parts.

Billboards lined the roads about as frequently as trees, because they brought some cash to the counties, and on one I saw a pasted flyer announcing a revival meeting the next day for the "Church of Revival Gospel," featuring "Preacher Bill."

Time and tide had done some work on his features, but I thought for sure I recognized someone I'd once known named Billy Aycock.

I went to the meeting. It was held in one of those long aluminum and tin fabricated buildings with concrete floors that had replaced oldtime tents. All the folding chairs were taken, and I had to join the standing room only "witnesses."

A combo/country band that reminded me of the Huggins Quartet opened the meeting and played throughout, especially during the times when the crowd was asked to contribute money "to keep our ministry alive" and particularly, finance the new church which it was hoped would be the "best advertisement for the Lord's mission in southern Alabama."

The preacher came out to thunderous applause, jubilation music and shouts from throughout the congregation.

I recognized Billy--older but still movie actor handsome. A very attractive woman dressed in all white had walked out discreetly behind him and took up a strategic (as I thought) position at a corner of the stage and I assumed correctly she was his wife and partner in the ministry.

Preacher Bill had a sort of rhinestone cowboy dress jacket with colorful curlicue designs reminiscent, I thought, of Elvis Presley but also the Marlboro Man, and I remembered that Matthew Mark Hammond at one point had had a line of flashy clothing. Spencer had called it "dressing loud for the Lord."

Preacher Bill may have taken a cue from his mentors, but tonight he wanted to talk about the shiny boots he was wearing. He segued from them--which he said were for sale at the church boutique--to their "lace bootstraps," and their virtues. No matter how low you sank in life, you could always "grab ahold and pull yourself right up there and see the horizon and way above the stars in the sky, that big vault in the universe where heaven waits for those who believe in Jesus. He's given a lifeline, friends, but you've got to grab it. You've got to grab those bootstraps."

He went from there into a long and increasingly passionate speech about failure and how you could never have real success without it. He cited Jesus himself, and this surprised me and I imagine a lot of people there present who had never thought of Jesus in those terms, as a failure, but then when Preacher Bill launched into his peroration about how Jesus had risen from the depths of death, the ultimate failure, and triumphed by living again for all eternity beside his heavenly father, just as all would do who believed in him and had sincere faith, every man and woman rose to their feet and roared with joy, as if he'd brought them eternal salvation right then and there. Emotion rolled across the room like a giant wave of hope and joy, and one couldn't help but roll along with it.

Afterward the sick and infirm came up for a laying on hands healing ceremony. One man who walked with a cane shouted that he felt washed of sin and become "a new soul for the Lord" and conspicuously walked away without limping. The crowd exploded in a frenzy and it was some time before I could wade through and get to Billy.

He recognized me and invited me to lunch the next day at

the town diner. His wife looked at me suspiciously when I explained I was a "friend from the old days." Her husband added a hasty coda about the baseball team, but she hardly changed expression.

Not surprisingly, he came alone to our lunch at the town's principal Mom and Pop diner. He was dressed casually but I noticed still wore the same boots under his jeans. I told him I'd been very impressed with his sermon.

"It's more like a message of faith and hope I just pass along from above. I just translate the exhortations of the biggest Coach there is for all those faith-hungry sinners."

He ordered a chicken fried sandwich, some of the homemade fries and washed it all down with a couple of Dr. Peppers, which had always been his favorite drink. He smiled. "Lot of things have changed, but some don't."

He asked if I'd seen Larry Bain and I told him last I heard, he was doing prison time in Texas. He said, "I met him at a young and wayward time in my life. Now I'd know how to counsel him. Knock some sense into his head instead of out."

From time to time a follower, or would-be, came over to our table to pay respects. Preacher Bill was always polite and ended with, "God bless you."

He talked regretfully about the Hammonds. "Matthew Mark is a great man but when Mary Magdalene went to the green pastures, he went looking for love where he shouldn't."

He looked hard at me.

"Yeah, I've changed, been born again through and through. The Lord got a rope and Lily Lynn tied me down with it. Now when my eye wanders, the rest of me can't follow." He ordered some pecan pie to go with a coffee.

"God made the carnal so the spiritual could exist. One comes with the other in His unfathomable creation, and we sinners have got to accept that.

"I was living in that Sodom and Gomorrah called Hollywood with this lady, rich as Croesus. Sure, she was 30 years older than me but what with surgery and her life style and bank account, she kept herself up.

"And one day she just up and threw me out. I asked her, why? Just yesterday you said you thought you loved me. She just said, 'A new moon's rising'. Now go figure that out."

He paused and reflected. "They've got a wax museum in Hollywood and I dropped in one day. Some of the figures reminded me of her, all polished up and shiny and not a breath of life in her. But that was later. I appreciated our days together, empty as they were. They led me to Jesus.

"I didn't have much more than a dime to my name and let me tell you, when you fall down from the Hollywood Hills to Hollywood Boulevard, you fall a lot farther than from Scenic Hill. I found an old apartment on Argyle you could rent by the week. It had a Murphy bed that folded down from the wall and furniture that dated back to the heyday '20s and '30s. Little lamps in the hallways.

"That first night I was lying in bed taking stock and wondering what to do and where to go when I heard these sounds coming from the kitchen. Hiss, hiss, hiss, like some kind of nasty snake. You remember those little footlong baseball bats they used to give to the kids at the Livestock Fairgrounds? Crazy thing but I'd taken it with me, like a souvenir.

"I picked it up and snuck into the kitchen real quietlike.

"What did I see but dozens and dozens of cockroaches running all across the floor and counters. When you've got so many bug feet moving like that, it makes the hissing sound I heard.

"I felt the wrath of God in me and started beating them to death with that little bat. I beat those counters into a killing field, just one roach cadaver after another, then I got down on my knees and beat the floor.

"But they kept coming. When I'd killed everything in sight, I swept them up and went back to bed. But a few minutes later, hiss hiss. Back again. Like everything I'd done was for nothing.

"I knew I'd have to live with them for a week, and maybe that was as it should be. They're God's creatures too, I said.

302

Here on this earth for some purpose.

"When I was hanging my two shirts in the closet I came across a letter stuffed back up on the shelf. Written but never sent. I folded it open. It was from a woman to her mother back home, and honest. She poured out her heart to the person who'd carried her into this world, trying to make sense of her life. She'd married a man and they'd moved to LA with their new baby.

"She said he sometimes beat her bad but didn't hurt their baby, and he couldn't find a job and their money was running out and what they did have they were starting to spend on drugs but not to worry, Mama, they'd get through these trials.

"She started to reassure her mother that things would get better and not to worry but then the letter ended.

"I wondered what had happened to this woman and her baby and the profligate, misguided husband. In those days you'd walk down Hollywood Boulevard and near gag on the incense and hash odors from all the freak shops, when you weren't bumping into a drug dealer or strung-out hippie or bum just living right there on the sidewalk.

"Were they just like me, from a good home back in the heartland, drifted up on these godless shores like so much rotting wood?

"That's when I fell in with Matthew Mark and Mary Magdelene. Call 'em a sect if you will, but they took in these lost souls and tried to help them. Did anybody else dirty their hands with these children of the Lord?

"Mary Magdelene was from Arkansas like me, and I took that as a sign. I stayed with them for two years and could have become an elder, but I saw the abuses starting to happen and when they decided to move to Arkansas, I thought they didn't need me any more.

"And anyway, I'd found my own mission.

"You know what, I've memorized the entire Bible. Ask me for a verse. How about Galatians?"

I had to admit I hadn't read the Bible through and through.

"Do it, Tom. It will change your life. And could be your life needs changing. Come out this afternoon. We're raising the roof on our new church. Meet the fellowship."

He insisted on paying for the lunch. "The Lord's business is doing well."

We went outside and I saw his jeep. It had been painted all over with gaudy, richly decorated colors, and the Church of Revival Gospel name had been drawn in curls and filigree worthy of the Middle Age illustrated manuscripts.

"We have artists in the flock. There's still time to be saved, Tom. You know where to find me now."

Before we could say goodbye two teenage girls in too short shorts came up and in their own giggling but direct and straightforward way, asked him if they could help with the construction work this afternoon even if they didn't belong to his church.

"The Lord would welcome you, and so would I and the congregation," he said.

They almost jumped for joy and headed off, giggling excitedly.

"In the old days I would have demeaned those two young ladies by calling them jailbait, but I've changed, Tom. I've come down square on the spiritual side of life. Oh, I know temptation is out there. We just saw it, like the Devil was saying, here's your old pal and don't you want to fall into the old ways? Live it up again, just like you used to? Change women like you do your shirts?

"I fight the Devil every day, and I'm winning."

He got in his jeep, waved goodbye and roared off, waving en route to the two girls who were sashaying around the main street and collecting admirers. I wondered how long he and fidelity could coexist. He had said himself how tight the emotional bonds become when you're together doing some intensive mission work. Bonds form, emotions lock in and can carry you away. You're fighting for a cause and you become a person different from what you are in the hither and yon of daily life. Drugs can do that, he said. Make life exciting even as they destroy.

"Know what I mean?" he said."Like when we were fighting for the championship. We got so close."

It was the only time he mentioned our baseball past. After all was said and done, I thought, if the spiritual did grow out of the carnal, his brethren were in good hands.

29. MOSE

Every major league scout who'd watched our games in the championship tournament had been drooling over Mose and his fastball. I heard one of them say, "There's a kid in Texas named Ryan who can throw absolute lights out. Best arm I've ever seen. But this kid is right there with him."

They fell all over themselves bidding up a signing bonus and with it he was able to buy his Mom and family a new house. "I'm in high cotton," he told me with deserved pride.

I told him, "Don't try to come back too fast and hop around like Pegleg Pete. Don't blow this chance."

And he didn't rush it. He gave his leg time to heal from the torn ACL and the Dodgers waited patiently. He dreamed of the day he'd worked through their minor league system and could walk out onto the field in LA. But first, "I'm gonna get off that bus and go straight to the beach and dip my toes in that water. If I look hard enough, maybe I can see Hawaii."

Scouts had said he didn't need a great curveball, just enough of one to keep hitters honest. I worked with him some when I could, showing him how to spin it over thumb and forefinger and snap the wrist hard.

For some reason he couldn't get much spin and the curve never did break much, but finally it was respectable and along with a changeup here and there, I saw his path to the major leagues lining up directly ahead.

I saw him off on the Greyhound that was taking him to the Dodgers' minor league affiliate in Tennessee. He had a smile a yard wide.

"Don't break a leg," I said and he laughed. He told me many years later when we'd reunited after losing touch that when he arrived and started firing the fastball, really firing it in games and not warming up with me like we'd done, he noticed something disturbing. The speed was there, but not THE speed.

At 90 mph you've got a good fastball. At 100 mph you join

the rarefied elite who strike so much fear in batters they make up excuses not to play on the day you're scheduled to pitch--"Got an inflamed nostril, coach."

Mose gave it his all, but he couldn't get back to what he'd been. He figured something had been lost in his leg, the force and propulsion to push off the pitcher's rubber and give that final thrust of velocity.

He got hit, and his ERA never got much below 3.00. For a relief pitcher brought in to put out fires, that was fatal. "They started saying, 'Here comes the arsonist.' I knew I was done. After a while all I did was sit in the bullpen and watch. Like I was the Invisible Man."

The team cut him and he caught on with a semipro team that played in backwater towns across the south. He heard all kinds of shit from the local rednecks and had all he could do not to get into big trouble. As the civil rights movement brought legal equality to the country after 200 years of slavery and segregation, Mose lived in a time warp where nothing had changed and he took it all because "it was so hard to let a dream die. So hard."

When he did he buried the hurt in dope and drink, then moved on to harder stuff. By then he'd drifted to St. Louis and stopped communicating with his family--"Low as I was going, I couldn't let them know." He moved from one flophouse to another, then spent time on the street. He stole, then held up a couple of convenience stores to fuel his habit. He said to himself, "I ain't a complete nobody, 'cause I didn't get caught. That's something. That's my future. Being a criminal."

But one day he overindulged. "And that took some real doin' at that point in my history." He was using whatever he could inject in his body to forget himself and failure, and then he managed to forget time.

One day he woke up in Florida, with no recollection of how he'd got there or how long it had been. "I said to myself, that's what dying's like. A big nothing. Except I came back."

But he got picked up by the local cops on a loitering charge. He didn't have a cent, so they threw him in jail. A big jail, with some hard cases.

"There was this one guy, real mean-looking white guy. And I mean big. I could see he was aiming to corner me in the shower. All he had to do was pick the right time, 'cause we went in shifts, see. So I made like I wanted to clean up the premises and you know the guards, they're happy to have you do all the work."

"They're like company executives. Lot of managers, too. We've got a few."

Sammy said that. Mose was telling him and me and Randy the story over pizzas and beer at a Dogtown restaurant I liked to go to.

"I got me this bucket with a mop and when he came in the shower room I jumped him. Beat his head with the bucket and when he was down, I stuck the mop handle down his throat. I said to him, 'You got one minute to decide if you're gonna die or leave me be.' Well, I'm no killer so you know what happened."

I thought whatever was left of Sammy's hair was standing on end. "Another round?" he wondered.

When they released him he hitched back home and his Mom took him back in. She'd almost given up hope of ever seeing him again and didn't pose many questions. "See, somewhere along those long lonesome roads back home I laid my fastball to rest."

By then he'd lost touch with just about everybody but he still had my number. I talked to Randy who knew just about everybody but we couldn't figure out at first how to get around his past.

Even Sammy hesitated--"An ex-con? In a bank"-- but Randy and I worked on him. We went out for pizzas and strategized.

"Listen," Sammy said to Mose, "it's like when Coach Cross recruited you. We're giving you a chance and we know you can deliver. But it's not like they're gonna help much. You've got to prove yourself, like every second of every day."

Sammy himself had a manager's post, on the cushiest cushion imaginable, at a local Arkansas bank that was making money like gangbusters and looked like it had nowhere to go but up. When we asked him what he did at the bank, he said, "Occasionally I make a decision."

But he couldn't remember one to cite as example.

"You've got to get past the application form," Sammy said. "They'll love how you're a former professional baseball player. They may even use it in their advertising. But if they do, get them to pay out the ass."

"Well, it was only a couple of years."

"Fudge that to 5 or 6. Tell them you were making the rounds trying out. Who was that semi-pro team affiliated with?"

"Nobody. They were independent."

"They were in Georgia?"

"Yeah."

"Hell, they'd have given an arm and a leg to link up with the Braves. Fudge that with 'an offshoot of the Atlanta Braves' or some shit like that."

"I'm doing a lot of fudging."

"It's called high finance, fudging other people's money so you can make a lot of your own. Now look closely at this question. 'Have you ever committed a crime?' Answer yes."

"I'll be done for."

"It says 'a' crime, right? Not every crime. So put "Loitering." If they ask you why, it's easy. Dumb-ass Florida cops figured a black guy from Arkansas had nothing better to do than hang around their precious real estate. State pride, that's what's gonna get you hired."

Whether it was that or Sammy calling in favors, Mose got hired and worked his way up steadily in the bank hierarchy. He ingratiated himself with colleagues and customers and brought in a lot of new business. He'd taken his training very seriously and become really, really good at what he was doing.

"Sometimes I even make a decision." He said he'd learned a lot from that year he spent with us on the Packers, not least of which was how to deal with and maneuver past the aspersions and outright insults and hidden prejudice, though sometimes not all that hidden.

"Mostly they're surprised I can count and add up numbers," Mose said that night when we'd teamed up on his employment history and future.

"Speaking of that, here's the check," Sammy said.

"Don't mind if I do," Mose said after the guffaws died down. "When we were playing, you know, I couldn't walk in here alone. Now I can. Now I only get the evil eye when I walk in with you guys."

Sammy had changed into jeans after work, and Randy and I never blew anybody away with our sartorial elegance, so as usual Mose dressed and looked more distinguished than any of us, who especially after the beer, resembled more or less what the cat dragged in.

30. TIME

In the days, months and even years after that championship game, Big Chuck would be chowing down on his 3rd or 4th helping of spareribs and suddenly CRACK—he'd literally bite into the bone like an angry canine and gnaw on it, canine-like, for a long moment while everybody else at table waited for him to cease and desist.

Then he'd get a faraway distant look in his eyes and we knew he was traveling back into the past. Sometimes he'd just come right out and growl, "Like to stop time."

By which everyone knew he meant, not time in general or the course of US or world history, but that moment when the throw from the Pioneer outfield cut down Bobby at the plate and cost us the state championship.

Usually we just let the fantasy pass and Marvella would serve him another helping to bring him back to the present via his appetite, but one time when our son was almost four years old she'd had enough: "And what then, Chuck? You can't do anything when time stops because you'll be stopped too. And little Charley can't grow up. And then when time starts again Bobby will still get thrown out."

"No. Nothing stays the same, ever. The universe will keep working because time's relative, don't you understand Einstein? It'll reset. And when time starts again, we'll have a change. That's what I'm countin' on. That throw comes in, but it sails and goes wide, Billy slides and by God, he's safe!"

I never had the heart to tell him that we would still have needed to score another run as Bobby's would have only tied the game.

But probably he'd have had an answer. Like, we had the momentum and the universe would have flowed with it. Momentum, always an intangible but very real element in a baseball game. As hard to stop as it is to start.

#

Time in the real world did not stop, and one day after our divorce Mary Louise joined her parents for a Sunday afternoon barbecue. Our son was brinking adolescence and already, in the manner of today's teenagers, contradicting everything adults said, when not ignoring it completely. His grandfather grilled, and afterward they pigged out.

Big Chuck had finally thrown in the cleaver and sold his business to a Yankee conglomerate, and there was talk about Winrock and a merger. Invariably after a feast like Sunday's, Big Chuck would look around at the feasters and ask, almost pleadingly, if "they'd eat good." Everyone would assure him yes, knowing full well that he'd then ask if this corporate meat was as good as his had been.

He would then bask in a chorus of "no's" and comments about the quality of Frankenheimer Foods which would no doubt never be seen or tasted again.

"It was a golden age," Big Chuck would conclude. By then his ritual was to take a quick nap, and this day he watched his grandson gambol in the pool, then headed into the den's air conditioning and his handcrafted, oversize rocking chair, of dark-polished oak and a "Big C" carved on a silver plate on the chairback.

In two seconds he fell asleep and never woke up, and Mary Louise said what everybody felt, nobody could have planned a better leavetaking.

"He always said he wanted to head to the Promised Land on a full stomach, and he did. He'd even had an extra helping of the apple pie."

She wasn't being funny when she added that, and I didn't laugh. My only thought was, whatever walls there are in the Promised Land, they'd be shaking when he arrived and boomed out his displeasure that an outsize character like him who'd roared his way through life left it with nary a whisper. I could almost hear him using this as leverage with the Biggest Boss: "We need a baseball team up here. You be the sponsor and I'll coach and this time we'll win it all, and if we don't, we got plenty of seasons to play with. What say Hoss, huh?"

#

Orval Faubus finally stepped down from office after 12 years as governor.

As Big Chuck predicted, that "old carpetbagger" Winthrop Rockefeller promptly ran for governor a second time against a former state Supreme Court justice who "did not campaign in the colored community," and the carpetbagger won, becoming the first Republican governor in the state since Reconstruction.

Rockefeller made many progressive moves and appointments despite often being stymied by legislators.

After Rockefeller stepped down Faubus attempted a comeback and seemed well on his way when his opponent just barely scraped into a runoff. But said opponent, a young lawyer named Dale Bumpers, beat him handily and went on to become a popular governor, then US senator for many successful years. Faubus tried again to become governor, three different times, finally being soundly beaten by a handsome young dynamic incumbent governor, my friend Bill. By this time he had become a true dinosaur, and never seemed to understand that dinosaurs make unwelcome guests, much less governors.

Faubus had divorced his longtime wife and remarried a much younger woman. Rumors abounded about how he had become rich from 12 years of his hand in the till, but some years later they were separated and Faubus was working as a teller in his hometown bank.

It was at this time that Mose, who'd been promoted to regional loan officer at his own bank, found himself having a business meeting where Faubus was said to be working.

"Sure enough, he was there at the teller window, taking checks and everything. Strange thing, he didn't seem too good at small talk. Maybe he'd burnt out."

Mose said after his meeting and before lunch, he went up to Faubus' window to withdraw a couple of hundred dollars.

313

"I told him, 'I'd like five ones, a fiver, another five ones, a tener, three ones, a fiver, four ones, then two ones, and so on like that till I got to 200. It's real important to get them in that order,' I said."

Mose said Faubus looked at him like he was wondering, "Is this some crazy coon or is he just messing with me?

"He had to be professional though 'cause he'd seen me with his boss, and he said, 'I'm sorry sir, I lost you at the third fiver. Could I ask you to repeat? '"

Mose said this was a pretty mean tactic, because he figured this black guy would never be able to repeat in the same order.

"But I did," Mose said. "I'd prepared. He jotted down everything. 'Did I go too fast?' I asked. He said with this fake smile--I mean hey, he'd had twelve years of fake smiles so he was good at it--'No, I think I got it. '

"Did I mention that after the sixth fiver I'd like 2 in silver dollars, #1 and #3, and after the eight set, 2, 4 and 5? 'No, I don't think you did, but it's no problem.'

"So he laid the bills and coins out one after the other in the right order. I complimented him.

"He said, 'It's clear you received a good education.' I said, 'Yes sir, I went to a white high school.'

"By then he knew I was messing with him. He just smiled and said, 'I expect you know who I am.'

"Now that was Faubus at his best, or worst if you will. He was inviting me to say something like 'Yeah, you're Teller #3, like it says on your little window.' So then he could hate me and tell all his buds so they could hate me too.

"So I just said, 'Yes I do, sir.' That took him down a notch and since he didn't know what to say, he reached down and pulled out a book. 'The Faubus Years.' He said, 'It's already autographed. Take it with my compliments.'

"I've still got the book. I mean look, Moby Dick sat around for a long time before people recognized it for the classic that it is. Anyway it was another trap. He was expecting me to look at it like it was Mein Kampf or whatever. But I said, 'That's real nice of you. Books are expensive these days.'

"But he wasn't about to fall into that trap either. He just gave me a fake smile and said, 'Now don't spend all those 200 dollars in one place. That's a lot of money.' Meaning of course, a lot for ME, even though I'd outdressed him by a country mile.

"I said, "Well actually, I might. I'm taking your boss out to lunch.' "

#

Time didn't stop for Levy either. While the city itself expanded northward, with big 2-story mansions and residential streets and fast food joints and the Wal-Mart superstore I eventually came to manage, Levy saw its crossroads co-opted by the Interstate Highway 40 connecting central Arkansas to Oklahoma and Tennessee and points south toward Texas.

As the hills bordering it on both sides could not be razed, and after all why should they--who would want an interstate highway to pass right through?--engineers went OVER. So tall concrete buttresses support the interstate and cars that roar nonstop over Levy. Noise and exhaust rain down 24/24.

Some businesses had to go, and Uncle Bob's service station was the first, as it lay smack dab in the middle of Eminent Domain.

Now where once my father and Joe Wright fixed cars while Uncle Bob and his cronies tried to fix city, state and world problems by goodhearted laughter and chewing enough fat to make Big Chuck proud, in a little hamlet named after a Jewish merchant, you find nothing but dust, debris and concrete.

If you get down on your hands and knees and look carefully though, you will find a small plaque in a low concrete wall that names this area a square after my Uncle Bob. No one ever comes to this "square" and nothing much ever happens among the pillared no man's land, but at least this little plaque commemorates the mixed-race men and women who trod this space during some eventful times, and that is something.

BOOK 4

31. REUNION

Laura and I settled in well in Dogtown. I had never really left, but it was different with the new family. Our daughter grew up and did the usual teenage rebellion when the time came, but as Laura said, "It didn't match the carnage of the Civil War."

She had intensified her study of French after our sojourn in Paris and got a job teaching it at the high school. She loved Burns Park and volunteered to plan and blaze the hiking trails that now are one of the park's features. We often go there after work to unwind in a legitimate forest that is only a few minutes from the suburb where we live. Keeping the park's wild places means we often see deer and possums and many other wild animals, not excluding frequent skunks who get all the respect in the world from us.

Sammy Hobbs, still a confirmed hunter, told us he'd love to hunt the deer in the park but in the meantime was glad they had a refuge. "It's like a reserve, you know."

I said, "Half of them probably went there to escape you."

"That's about half right."

Laura added, "When the apocalypse comes and we need meat to survive, you can hunt them. But not before."

Sammy was the first to arrive at our reunion party. He had expanded greatly, as he preferred to put it, but one could still recognize in this overweight whitehaired gent the loosey-goosey right fielder of old.

"If you hit a ball right at me I might catch it," he said. "A foot to the right or left, no way."

"Well," I said, "being immobile helps in a duck blind."

"Yeah, but these days I spend half the time asleep. Them deer are starting to catch on and just pass during my siestas."

He said he was never so happy as when he bagged a deer and drove to Camp Robinson Road, which had turned into a business strip chock-full of markets, banks and fast food joints.

"I roll up to the meat market"--it had opened years ago and Big Chuck would have been proud to see it--"and they take the deer right inside--I don't got to lift a finger except take my money. Then I drive 10 feet over to Chucky Cheese and get some grub to go. Then I drive 10 feet back the other way to the liquor store's drive-in window. I order me some refreshments and head home. Don't even have to turn off the motor."

"Here in this suite you've got to walk over to the fridge."

"Hell, I can do that." And he did, stocking up on chili dogs and our local handcrafted beer.

#

When I was a kid my father would take me to watch the baseball games at Travelers Field, Little Rock's minor league park. We would cross over the river and drive West and it was always exciting to enter the big park which seemed immense and stately to me, our very own version of Yankee Stadium.

But over the years attendance fell and for one reason or another, most of which we never figured out on our side of the river, the City lost interest in the historic old stadium. When the new century came upon us, the City made the decision to raze the site and turn it into that most useful of modern conveniences, a parking lot.

I willingly and happily joined a group of our finest civic-minded citizens to raise a bond fund, and it even got the support of aldermen like Harvey Harris. Money was voted and a stadium built on our side of the river and just like that, minor league baseball flourished again.

Dogtown had a big, beautiful minor league baseball park. Various companies bought the right to suites overlooking the field and mine was no exception, so at my own expense I thought nothing could be so cool as to reunite the Boys from Dogtown and do our own very special housewarming party for the new park.

Spencer came solo. He had never married. "My address book got so full I couldn't add anybody else," he said, alluding to his adventures in the free love era. "Or maybe I just got real attached to my crops. They need a lot of TLC, you know."

Cletus came with his third wife, and Randy with his first and only. Sammy had come alone, as did Mickey Crutchley. Mose arrived with his wife Bethena, and they were by far the best dressed. "Thank God you came to give this bunch a little class," I said to agreement from everybody, even grudging from Cletus.

Between provisions and refreshments and occasionally watching the ongoing Travelers game, which we could do either by stepping outside the suite and taking a seat in the stands, or God Bless America, on the closed circuit TV in our air-conditioned suite, we kicked over old times and updated those present and missing.

#

Spencer said Preacher Bill had fallen out with his wife for various rumored reasons, mostly having to do with infidelity on the part of one or the other or both, and it turned out she had financed his ministry and when she divorced him, he was left with debts he couldn't cover. He sold the church building and everything else that could fetch a price, but still managed to make an earthly living with a regional TV show that aired once a week on a Sunday morning, so early Spencer said, "You'd be watching and hear the cock crow."

The last time he visited Preacher Bill he was living with an astonishingly attractive and very young girl who bossed him around a great deal, Spencer thought, but Preacher Bill seemed to overflow with gratitude at her presence. Spencer said Bill remarked a bit ruefully that she was the kind who stopped traffic, but that was good for him because then he could spread the gospel to the stalled drivers.

I told everybody that Preacher Bill had notified me that he couldn't make it but he'd sent a "message of faith" and asked me to read aloud. I did. It went:

"Two thousand years ago today, Saul set out on the road to

Damascus and on this very day two years ago Sammy posted on the Internet a picture of the wild Razorback boar he killed on a hunt."

"That's true," Sammy interjected, "Real wild vicious sucker."

"Pigs were animals possessed of demons our Lord and savior Jesus Christ cast out of sinners and then the pigs fled and jumped from the cliffs into the sea. I have a Razorback hog hat on my mantlepiece and on this day in the millennial year of 2000 I put it there on the same date years before Sammy posted his picture. Saul became Paul and spread Jesus' teachings throughout the known world. My middle name is Paul. The Lord hunts for all of us and aims true. Open your hearts to his arrows."

We were silent for several moments, trying to absorb and understand Preacher Bill's words. Finally Spencer said, "Gift of tongues. He found it somewhere."

"Amen," Cletus added.

"God bless," Randy concluded.

#

Coach Cross had passed away some years before, sooner than any of us expected, though everybody knew he'd been torn up inside with ulcers for a long long time.

He'd gone over to Burns Park after our season and stayed there for the rest of his life, coaching some Little League teams and working the grounds. He'd spent most days there in summer, preparing the turf, then managing during the games, then closing up field and concessions afterward.

He worked very hard and the fields--very quickly after he arrived the park had built new ones for softball and Legion teams--always looked immaculate. It seemed to me he liked that best, laying out those white lines he'd told us created a separate, more orderly world, living with madness as he had throughout his married life.

When he died, the city fathers named the park fields for him. Apparently he had only one request for his funeral ceremony, that Sally sing. She came down from Missouri and though her voice broke and she struggled not to break down in tears, she raised some glorious songs to high heaven for Henry Cross.

Randy said Sally married "a bigass exec from Budweiser." They lived in a mansion outside of St. Louis beside a lake--his lake--and it was so big Sally called it their "Loire Chateau."

Randy pronounced it like "lure, you know, like bait. I caught a couple of crappie in that lake." He said her husband was a straightlaced serious guy who taught his kids to respect the company so much it was "like the alphabet stopped at 'B.'"

"I kid you not, he said, "you sit down to breakfast at this big shiny table, and I mean big, and it looks like it's been spitshined every five minutes. You ring a little cowbell and the help come running with whatever your sleepy heart desires."

Randy said at breakfast you had a choice of coffee, tea, milk or juice--and Bud.

"I'm serious. Leonard--yeah, she married a guy named Leonard--said it was tops to get your urinary system going. Like I really need that."

Anyway Randy said Sally seemed happy enough and she came down to visit a lot, because her hubby was a Type A Grade A workaholic.

When Coach Cross was alive he said they'd meet for lunch. Even now he said, when someone mentioned his name, she'd get misty-eyed. Even in front of her husband, like it was something she couldn't contain or control and didn't want to try.

"Seems to me like she had some kind of crush on him," Randy said."

"Seems like," I agreed.

"His wife's still kicking," Sammy told us, meaning Margaret. "Coach never divorced her. You wonder why. I heard she got loonier and loonier."

"I don't know," I said, "maybe he remembered how she'd been and didn't want to betray her."

It wasn't like me to get philosophical like that. I wasn't George. But I remembered too how Coach Cross had been. He wouldn't have wanted Sally to spend her life as a mistress. He would have wanted her to have kids and live in a chateau. That was the kind of man he was.

#

Bubba Beasley sent us a message from Zurich in Switzerland, where he traveled often for "financial and investment opportunities."

Most of us hadn't seen much of Bubba in the years since, as he had become a very busy man and was now going under his natural monicker of "Barry M. Beasley." For a while he had worked at Stephens Inc., the Little Rock financial firm that had gotten very important in every Wall Street term imaginable, involved in financing political campaigns of Arkansas' favorite son but mostly, making tons of money.

Then Bubba—or Barry—had formed his own company and I said to the guys, "You know what old Satchel Paige used to say, 'Never look back, somebody might be gaining on you?' Hey, Bubba never had to look back because nobody was gaining on him. That boy couldn't field a grounder but I figure he never fumbled a financial statement in his life."

So there was the answer I said as to why the Bubba of those days sometimes let his mind wander away from minor things like whether our runner was getting picked off base. His brain was already making interest rate calculations.

"I do remember now once we were playing golf and he said something about a 'hedge fund.' I thought what the hell, that's space cadet Bubba, talking about hedges on a golf course where that's the last thing you'd find. Hell, I thought he was talking about the rough. That's where his ball usually landed. To him it looks like a hedge."

Mickey said, "You dope, if you'd listened to him instead of worrying about your 9-iron you'd be rolling in high cotton these days. Like him. Probably why you haven't been invited to his house. He'd start talking about junk bonds and you'd think he was talking about a yard sale."

Mickey said he'd been invited once to Barry's house and it was about as long and wide as a golf course and the thought crossed his mind that a golf cart might be parked somewhere. For sure, you'd get a lot of exercise walking from one end to another.

Barry traveled a lot internationally after making bundles on domestic investments and he always brought back or had shipped back items of furniture or art he'd purchased.

A lot of rooms had a theme, so for example everything he'd found in China was arranged in a "China Room."

"You'd walk in and swear it was like the Forbidden City, " Mickey said. "Then you'd go into the next room and you'd be in ancient Egypt. He had a bust of a woman that was nicked up a lot and the nose broken off. He swore it was Cleopatra and he'd bought it on the black market, just ahead of a New York museum rep who was one royally pissed off Yankee. I saw a couple of necklaces reminded me of King Tut's tomb and when I asked him about them he clammed up. 'Flea market stuff, ' he said, 'not worth all that much.' Yeah, right, and I've got some swampland in Cairo to sell you."

Mickey said it was like strolling through a world museum. Outside, the swimming pool was Olympic-sized and looked out over a lawn with fountains, like a miniature, Arkansas version of Versailles' backyard.

"You're shitting me," I said.

"No shit. If King Louis had had a wood barbecue, he'd have recognized the place."

He said though that Barry hadn't lost his Arkansas roots. He loved to eat wild boar that featured on many menus in Zurich, during the autumn wild game season, but he couldn't abide the local sauces. So he would always take along a bottle of Lindy's barbecue sauce to spread over his boar. At first the local restaurateurs looked askance at this practice, but he dropped enough hedge funds on the meal that they quickly did a "*volte face*" —a term Barry said he'd learned in Paris.

Plus he'd let them sample a bite of his barbecue boar and he could tell from the look on their faces that they were impressed, even though they wouldn't admit it and grumbled something like "it's rustic, but interesting."

"I'm rustic and proud of it," Barry said to Mickey.

He proved it by sending us all a very nice note from Zurich, regretting he couldn't be with us for our gathering.

At the end he included a list of companies he'd recommend for investment. "You can't go wrong with these," he wrote: "Call it your retirement stash."

"His clients pay a thousand bucks for advice like this. To give it for free to peons like us... He's still a Dogtown boy at heart," I said.

#

Mickey Crutchley became a lawyer and I wondered from time to time if his being one of the ringleaders of the team boycott hadn't stayed with him. He was the only one who'd come up to me afterward and said he felt ashamed. I told him to forget it, a bump on the road, but he came to be known as a man for defending the oppressed in every size, shape and fashion.

No doubt he could have made a bundle by moving to a bigger city like Memphis or Dallas because he had a gift for pleading. In front of a jury he gave off sincerity like an aura and people sensed, here is an honest man. He won many more cases than he lost, but since he took so many hopeless or near hopeless causes no other lawyer would touch, he never had the big paydays that would put him on Easy Street—assuming he'd want to live on Easy Street, which I doubted.

But he made a decent living and he'd married happily and lived in a comfortable house on the West side of Little Rock, where new spacious homes had spread out from the Heights—meaning, the well-to-do. In this respect he wasn't completely egalitarian, but he once told me, "Nobody wants a lawyer who lives in a dump, even those who do live in a dump."

He said he'd studied law at the University in Fayetteville and graduated with honors and the day he'd packed his bags to leave academe and go out into the wide world, he was walking out of the classroom building where he'd had so many classes and who should he see entering but a new teacher who'd just been hired.

Mickey said his first thought was, this guy isn't much older than me.

And his second thought was, I've seen him before. He held out his hand and said, "Well, if it isn't the Man from Hope."

He said Bill thought about that for a moment and he could see he'd liked the phrase.

"Damn," Cletus said, "you made Mr. Slick's political career. Weren't for you and your slogan he'd have stayed in his ivory tower."

Mickey told us he'd been involved in the infamous trial over the teaching of evolution. Not the first one, which got set in motion just after our season ended. Mickey was studying at Hendrix College when a Little Rock high school teacher went to court on behalf of other teachers in the state to challenge its law against teaching the theory of evolution.

The Supreme Court ruled in her favor and for the continuing separation of church and state, but some years later the state legislature pushed through a bill requiring schools in parallel to teach creationism.

It was an end around the Supreme Court decision. Yes, evolution could be taught, but the two theories had to be taught side by side. It had made big news all across the nation, a latter-day Scopes trial.

Mickey said he hadn't done the pleading and outfront work, but rather the groundwork in law and precedent that led to the judge's ruling against the law, on the grounds that it violated separation of church and state by obliging the instruction of a religious belief.

"Now I'm a religious man, but I think you can have faith and still believe in the science of evolution. Plus I couldn't stand having our city held up for ridicule. Fifty years after the Monkey trial and here we were again.

"And speaking of that, you all remember Harvey Harris?"

"Harvey? I've run into him a few times," I said. "He still resembles a tank with nothing in the turret. He's had a lot of kids. Once I asked him how many he was up to and I swear, he couldn't remember. He said 'seven' but he didn't look too sure."

Sammy said he'd seen him at the country club, downing cocktails after a hard morning on the course. "He fits into a golf cart but he has to squeeze. Think about that. He's got a three-level home and told me he'd had an elevator built to avoid walking up stairs."

"Why are you wasting our valuable time talking about Harvey?" I asked Mickey.

"Because it was Harvey who got in somebody's ear and pushed for the creationism bill. You know he's an alderman."

"The shame of the city," I said.

"He was the power behind the throne, if you can call it that. And was he ever pissed when we won in court. I ran into him at the Dixie Pig. All his kids were running around raising hell. His wife had given up and was standing outside smoking a cigarette. He didn't lift a finger to control his marauding army. Just sat there and gave me a shit-eating grin. I got my takeout and was heading to my car when he said, 'Hey hoss, remember that home run I hit off you in the opening game?' "

"What about it?"

"It just landed in China."

"Now that stumped me. We'd talked about putting him on the stand but couldn't. On the one hand, he was an argument against creationism because who could believe an intelligent God would create someone like Harvey? On the other hand, he was an argument against evolution because who could listen to him and think we'd outpaced the apes? But now I had to revise argument B. If he could make a remotely clever comeback like that, it meant we had evolved."

"You're being a lawyer," I said. "Don't give Harvey that much credit. He really did believe it just landed."

Despite his avowed patriotism and avowed desire to help the US military win the war in Vietnam--"LBJ says we gotta bring the coonskin back home for the wall and I've shot a lot of coons in my time"--Harvey got a deferment for four years. He went to a local university, majoring in Physical Education.

He got out just as Richard Nixon instituted the draft lottery, and Harvey's birth date was picked at #364. He could still have enlisted, but said, "You can't fight destiny. I guarantee you though, if it comes time for #364 to go fight, I'll be ready."

Instead he got some financing somewhere and opened up a used car lot. For a while he made a decent living, to all appearances. It was located just off the interstate out toward Jacksonville, and so readily visible it made for free advertising.

Then he started offering promotions, like a free shotgun for the purchase of a car, and started doing very well. He told me once, "I personally raised the level of home defense in this state. God bless the Second Amendment."

Spencer swore he hadn't talked to Harvey since our memorable draft physical, and even if he had, he wouldn't have mentioned sales techniques used in LA, but somehow or the other Harvey started emulating them and sponsored a series of TV ads where he'd be introduced as "Harvey Harris and his dog Zeke."

After a jingle that for sure hadn't been created by a gifted composer, Harvey would stroll through the lot, sales pitching various cars.

Spencer, who of course had spent time hanging around the fringes of Hollywood, used to say, "He was among the 2 or 3 worst actors in the history of audiovisual arts. He spoke his lines like he was a first grade reader."

"Which he might be," I said uncharitably.

But just for that reason, the awfulness, the ad spots became a hit. People watched them to laugh. After a time Harvey replaced Zeke with a cat, thinking this was the funniest joke in the world. "See, I'm saying here's me and my dog, but it's really a cat." None of us ever knew if he realized people were laughing at him and not with him, but in any case he himself laughed all the way to the bank, because he'd made himself known and became a celebrity.

"Say what you want," he told me once when I ran into him at Wal-Mart, "but you started this with that shitty Ballad of Big Chuck, and thank you very much. I'm making a shitload of money."

After the cat he moved on to a possum and raccoon and so forth, and people kept watching to see what animal would be featured next, but it all came crashing down when he chose an alligator.

The gator, which would not respond well to the director's commands during shooting--"It was a mean sucker," Harvey said ruefully--got loose and attacked the cameraman. They were able to pry loose its jaws, but the luckless cameraman lost a toe and promptly sued.

"They settled out of court," Mickey said. "Had to. Harvey said to this guy something like, 'Come on man, it's just a fucking little toe. Hell, that ain't the appendage your old lady cares about.' That crack cost him a lot of money."

But fame is fame, no matter whether deserved, and Harvey lives high on the hog.

#

Randy had married his most gracious and intellectual wife Libby, a math teacher at the University of Arkansas at Little Rock, and she'd done her best to bring him up to an acceptable level of educational awareness.

"I married up," Randy said, "way up. Like space station up."

She regaled us with some anecdotes. She said when they'd first traveled to Europe, Randy had looked all around London with wonder and she asked him what impressed him the most. "The cars. They're all foreign." She passed another day at the British Museum ("It's free," she tried to persuade her husband) but he'd have none of it and preferred to have a couple beers at a pub.

"I figured I could trust him out on his own. I mean, he sort of spoke the same language." But as Randy walked the streets to join her he felt a huge need to answer nature's call and knocked on the door of what he assumed was a public restroom. A well-dressed woman answered the door, which Randy thought was odd, and he used more elegant language than his habit, informing her that he needed to "come in and urinate."

She looked shocked and slammed the door in his face. When a still puzzled Randy related what had happened to Libby, she had to explain that the sign outside the flat, "TO LET," did not mean that somebody broke off the "I ".

"And the fun didn't end there," Libby continued. She said they'd spent a day in Paris and dined at a super resturant and when Randy adjourned to the men's room, he saw a graphic of a man in top hat and elegant vest on the restroom door. He turned away and hurried through the rest of the meal, "denying me the pleasure of dessert," as she put it. "Turns out, he thought there was a dress code for the toilet!"

Randy grumbled, "I know some French. If they'd wrote "Home" like they usually do I'd have been okay." He had gone to work right after age passing high school as a computer programmer and said "It's not as easy as you think putting those cards through them slots. We're talking hand-eye coordination and then some."

He'd worked his way up to more and more slots and made computers a lifetime's work. He fell into repair work on the machines and had become an expert. He said he knew them inside and out and sideways. "They ain't as smart as you think. I can shut those suckers down with one twist of a little bitty screwdriver."

All the same, he told us, "I'm waiting for artificial intelligence. When it gets up to speed, I'll be right there, first in line. You boys won't recognize me and even if you do, you won't understand a damn word I say. I'll make Spencer sound like a Bozo."

"Won't have far to go there," Spencer replied. "I've killed off most of my brain cells. Running on auxiliary power now."

#

With age and gravity Cletus had come more and more to resemble a stump. He reminded me of Toad of Toad Hall, and if for fun he ever got his old mitt and catching gear out of mothballs for a serious practice game, he'd hardly need to squat. He and the ground had gotten close.

He still had a good head of hair and though streaked with gray, you could say handsome. Women seemed to think so. He'd gone through two wives already and "each one cost me a lumberyard." On a trip to Vegas he met his third, a cocktail waitress who'd been serving him 99-cent margaritas.

"On the tenth I fell in love and on the 20th I got her to say yes."

Cletus inherited his late father's lumberyard and employed the standardization practices pioneered by food chains like McDonald's and KFC, and had branches throughout the state (minus the two granted in alimony). He was worth a chunk of money and arrived in a brand new Mercedes.

"Change every year. When the sumbitch runs out of oil, it's gone. But I still got my old Chevy. Put it up on blocks and in a barn, like a museum you know? Sometimes I go in there and just meditate. That old car taught me a lot, you know. When things don't go smooth and you need some fixing up, most times you can do it and keep going. You can get through life real good with an attitude like that."

"And some 40-weight oil," I added.

"Yeah, that's right. That's right." Cletus' wife Tamara, who hadn't been born when the Boys from Dogtown battled for the championship, had the kind of spectacular figure common to a Vegas cocktail waitress, the kind that rendered men speechless without the aid of several margaritas. Hence no one made conversation with her at first until Laura, who I told Cletus, feared nothing and no one and was so charitable she'd pulled me out of the ditch and stayed with me "to perform routine maintenance," broke the ice and got her involved.

"She's really sweet," Laura told me later. "Not a cliché at all."

"Who said she was?"

"Only every man in the room, with their eyeballs."

Mose had come dressed in a spiffy dress coat and designer pants, in contrast to Cletus' shorts and Razorback T-shirt. Bethena was the most elegant person in our group and they'd been married for years, winning the prize for marital stability in our group.

Cletus eyed Mose up and down and said, "Either you stole that from Dillard's or you're working. Or your welfare check came in."

They hadn't seen each other in years but picked up immediately on the raillery of old.

"Bank. Chief regional loan officer."

"What happened, they run out of pet rocks to promote?"

"You might not understand. It's called competence. You got any people of color working for you?"

"If I didn't we wouldn't get a board sawed. We're like Nairobi west. I even broke down and named one of 'em manager. He asked me how long his trial period was gonna last. I said, 'till the day you retire.'"

"Maybe we'll give you a loan. That way we can monitor your labor practices."

Mose turned to his wife.

"This is the racist I was telling you about."

She said, "He doesn't look so terrible in person."

Cletus said, "I got news for you buddy. Well, the first thing ain't news 'cause you know as well as I do: you are definitely not as smart as you think you are. Second, every time I go visit my Daddy's grave the ground's all messed up with him turning over and over."

Mose looked at his wife, puzzled: "You figure that out?"

Bethena answered, "I think I did, actually."

Tamara smiled and said, "After the 6th or 7th margarita he started talking about 'black individuals' and I said, 'I've got a little secret for you, baby.'"

Cletus said to Mose, "She's real light-skinned, which you probably didn't notice. Thank God you had a smart catcher."

"After the fifteenth margarita he said he'd turned color blind and proposed. I didn't say yes and I didn't say no because I had to go look for a wheelbarrow to take him to his room. It took him two days to sober up. I was having a coffee, getting ready to go to work, and he came over with this big bunch of flowers and said 'Honey, I'm gonna take you away from all this--all you got to do is say yes.' I figured well, this isn't margaritas talking but still..."

"Margaritas'll do that to you. Mess up your head and vision, permanent-like."

Mose said to Tamara, "You looked around at that beautiful casino and said to yourself, 'He's taking me away from all this to a lumberyard!'"

By this time all of us had gathered around to listen in on the conversation. Everybody was curious, and maybe even Cletus hadn't thought much about why she'd consented to leave the bright lights for a stumpy ex-catcher.

"Well, he did say to me, you know Vegas--if it doesn't work out you can fly back and get unhitched in five minutes. I told him that's what I call negative persuasion, and he can stop that right quick 'cause it don't work on me."

She took a sip of her drink which she'd mixed herself from the limited choice we had in the suite, and somehow it had been made to look elegant. She looked pointedly at her husband, who looked sheepish at being reminded of this reproof.

"I looked at the flowers and I saw he'd taken the time to really choose the prettiest ones, prettiest I'd ever seen. And I said to myself, if he loves giving beautiful flowers, maybe he's got some love in his heart to give to me. Anyway, black individuals aren't too smart, are they honey?"

"I don't say that shit no more. Except to Moses here."

Mose looked genuinely surprised. "Lord Lord, the world really has changed. Still," looking at Tamara, "you got your work cut out for you."

Cletus said, "You want the world to change, just serve it a lot of margaritas."

#

We'd all been so absorbed in this conversation and news, not to mention all the other reminiscing and hot dogs and drinks we'd hardly noticed the game. Our hometown team Arkansas Travelers were fighting from behind into the seventh inning when they rallied. They got their two tying runs on base and then their cleanup hitter came to the plate.

The visiting team brought in a relief pitcher. Warming up, he was hitting 98 on the radar gun that had been installed at the scoreboard.

"You used to throw like that," Cletus said to Mose, "'fore you got old."

"If I'd thrown like that I'd be out there signing autographs right now. Instead of wasting my time trying to educate you."

"You shouldn't of shook me off. Every time you shook me off, guy got a hit."

The banter might have gone on like that but the cleanup hitter stepped in and despite the speed and speed gun, he got around on a fastball and slammed a hit to the wall in left center.

Their Coach waved both runners home and the first scored easily. As the second runner sped toward home plate, the left fielder fired a relay throw to the shortstop, who flung it on a bullet toward the catcher.

We all watched and it was almost like slow motion, a replay of the same throw that had broken our hearts all those years ago. The ball reached the catcher about the same time as the runner slid headfirst to the plate and the catcher swiped the tag.

The umpire, right on top of the play, waited a suspenseful second, or two, or three, then finally made a swordlike thrust with his arm and screamed "OUT!!!"

We couldn't believe it.

Spencer said "Déja vu all over again," and pulled out a joint to accompany his beer. He looked like he needed both. We'd all been stunned and deflated.

Nobody said anything more for what seemed like quite a few minutes.

Then I said, "Must be karma. Get the Dogtown boys together and watch somebody get thrown out at home."

"Good thing after all Bobby didn't make it tonight," Sammy added. "He'd be shitting bricks."

"Why are you all so upset," Mose's wife asked. "The game isn't over yet. We can still win."

"Yeah," Mose said. "We're thinking about a game where we didn't."

I figured now was as good a time as any and pulled out a big manila envelope and opened it. I knew what was in it but hadn't looked at it yet, preferring to do it with all the guys.

"I've got a present for everybody, courtesy of Bill Bowers."

Bill had made a dozen laminated copies of the photo his newspaper had taken at home plate that night in Belleville.

I passed them all around. In truth I'd never seen the picture, because Bill's newspaper had chosen to run his story but not it.

"It figures," Sammy said. "We lost, didn't we."

Laura said, immediately and rather forcefully, "I just want to say, I was at the game that night and I didn't see any losers out there."

This got respect.

Randy said to me, "You know what I said about marrying up? You married over the moon."

"I forgot I was ever young," Spencer said a bit ruefully.

"You can tell I've et a few Chucky Cheeses since then," Sammy said.

Randy started pointing out and identifying the people for his wife. "That's Coach Cross, a great man I got to tell you. Big Chuck Frankenheimer, tryin' to look like his heart ain't broke. And that's your future husband."

"You look so cute in your uniform. No wonder I married you."

"So you had a reason. I been trying to figure out one for the last twenty-five years."

Tamara said to Cletus, "There's that old bat."

"The one you like to broke," Cletus said to Mose.

"Would you believe he's got it hung up in our hallway? I

know he's attached to it and all that, but I'm scared it's going to fall down someday and hurt someone."

"Don't worry," Mose said, "it's light. It never had any hits in it."

That got a big laugh from everybody, and Cletus said, "I recognize the humor of that remark, if not the intelligence."

Mose's wife Bethena, whose name we had all said in one fashion or another all evening, was as lovely as she was--"It's from a Scott Joplin song," she said--interjected: "I just want to say, you all look great. For your ages I mean." We all mumbled thanks in various ways for the qualified compliment.

"At our ages we'll take any compliment we can get," Mickey said.

Tamara said, "When I met Cletus he told me he was 52. Now I knew that was creative accounting."

Bethena said, "See, I was right. The Travelers came back."

She was the only one who'd noticed. Down on the field the players were shaking hands and heading for the dugouts. Apparently the Travelers had rallied in the ninth inning and pulled out a win.

Their game was over, but not one of us rushed to get away. It was a warm lovely evening. Across the way, beyond the outfield fence we could see the Little Rock skyline, but on this side of the river we had the baseball stadium and baseball played every summer.

I held up my glass of wine. "Ladies and gentlemen, a toast." I waited till they'd done likewise—"With the possible exception of Willie Mays and Mickey Mantle and maybe a couple of others, to the best centerfielder in heaven, George Bentley the Third."

"Hear hear, " they chimed in.

Randy said, "Geez, some outfield." Cletus raised his glass. "I got a toast. To the man who would've led us to the Promised Land, 'cept he couldn't slide for shit."

We toasted Mose, with smiles all around. Mose raised his glass. "To a hell of a catcher"—pausing for effect—"who was so happy none of our pitchers had more than three pitches

335

'cause he couldn't count past that."

After the laughter and toast Cletus riposted, "Must've taken you a week to remember all that."

Mickey held up his drink: "To our captain. Even if we didn't always follow it, he showed us the way."

"Hear, hear." Laura kissed me and I told her later, that was the most I'd ever been moved, with one exception. "What was the exception?" I just looked at her and smiled.

Laura said, "I have a toast. To all the Dogtown boys. Now and forever." This time nobody said Hear, hear. We just raised our glasses to the sentiment. Moved.

We'd fielded memories like hardhit grounders, of bat and ball and myopic umps and country towns where weddings came second to base hits, hot summer suns broiling us like ribs on a grill, long highways past Arkansas fields, humid mosquito nights and tower lights that barely shone, meaning you'd sometimes have to find a fly ball with ears and ESP, knotholed splintered grandstands where the love of your life in the full bloom of youth like yours might be waiting and watching, close scores that kept your head constantly in the game between those white lines where rules were rules and the world made some sense, and you knew you should hold the best moments of winning and camaraderie tight in your leather glove because they'd never come again.

We didn't know when if ever we'd meet again like this, all together. We were approaching the ninth inning and then the eternal postgame, which Spencer said he liked to think of as "one long head trip." Everybody knew we'd all gone through some trials, and losses a lot tougher than the one in Belleville, and we'd likely have more. But we knew we'd be there for each other, as Coach said and hoped that one summer long ago when we were young, until the very last one of us rounded the bases and crossed home plate and where we were would be where we were at.

Martin Copeland is a screenwriter, playwright and author of RIVER OF DOUBT and LA LOVE STORIES.

EPILOGUE - THE LONG POSTGAME by Laura

Even when he hit 70 and up, Tom the shortstop stayed in shape, slim and trim, which I attributed to my cooking and the natural ingredients I used pretty near 100%.

For years we used the organic produce from Spencer's farm, until that sad day when the Grim Reaper came calling. We'd gone out there on our weekly produce run and it was us who found him lying on his back in the middle of a weed patch, face up toward the sky like he was taking a last look, which it was.

It took some searching.

Spencer said he'd given up pot ages ago, but Tom found a little stub next to his hand and for sure, we knew Spencer didn't smoke those "cancer sticks" he was always railing about. I thought he had a little smile on his face, like he'd caught a glimpse of Kingdom Come, but Tom reminded me how Spencer had always joked about the film True Grit where the character Mattie Ross asks John Wayne to "lie beside me" when he passes on. Otherwise, she argues, he'll end up "in some neglected patch of weeds."

And Spencer would laugh and say, "My weed patch sure as hell won't be neglected."

And it wasn't. We found the telltale patch in a far corner behind the corn rows that you'd miss so easy if you didn't know what you were looking for.

Tom couldn't quite bring himself to believe Spencer was gone, but he still kind of managed to smile and say, "Once a hippie, always a hippie."

Over the years one by one the Dogtown boys went to their heavenly reward. Some we lost contact with completely, even if most of them had a presence on social media. Preacher Bill advertised for a long time, offering "salvation" on a cash or credit basis, but gradually his site seemed to get less and less traffic and fewer updates. Eventually the updates stopped altogether, or at least up until another posting, and Tom said, "That's how we get current these days on death or infirmity."

The wonderful Bill Bowers passed away in his sleep, about fifty years after his doctors had given him no more than a decade to live. He played golf till the last, even when Tom said you could throw the ball farther than his tee shots.

Barry "Bubba" Beasley purchased a villa in Italy and lost touch with us, even on social media. Mickey Crutchley passed away after some awful kidney problems. We visited him in the hospital quite often, or whenever he managed to rally from the painkillers they stoked him with. He managed to stay sharp and witty until the end, despite all, and even serenaded us once with "The Ballad of Big Chuck." Tom was touched and could hardly believe it, after all the years. "How can you ever forget such lyric genius?" Mickey chuckled. That turned out to be one of the last of his good evenings.

Sammy Hobbs died of a heart attack, kind of inevitable with a blood pressure off the charts like his had become, and Randy also succumbed to cardiac arrest. Despite his protestations and all the evidence one way or another that his "upstairs rooms ain't got nothing inside"—his words, of course—he had lived very well, progressed in his career and amassed quite a lot of wealth. "Better to be lucky than intelligent," he said once. Tom used to say that Randy never got any predictions right about politics, society or even where the wind might blow in the afternoon, and you wouldn't want to trust his opinions about anything, but when it came to making decisions about his life and work, he revealed himself infallible. "There he was both lucky and intelligent."

Just about the strangest thing I ever saw happened when Harvey Harris died. We would run into him from time to time and each time Tom would call it "another root canal experience." No matter how far up in years they got, the insults would blast back and forth like a barrage of artillery. One day at KFC when Harvey's third wife was ordering takeout that looked like it'd fill the back of their truck (Harvey said he'd lost count when Tom asked how many kids he had now)—I interrupted them and said "What are you two going to do when one of you heads to the Promised Land and doesn't have his favorite whipping boy?"

That gave them a moment's pause.

Harvey finally said, "I'll just find some suck-egg dog. Kick it around. Same difference."

And Tom: "I've got to admit there'll be a gap. It's not everyday you find a person with a minus IQ."

And off they went again. But somewhere in that barrage they managed to agree for the first time in their lives that whoever went first, the other would speak at his funeral. But not a eulogy. Insults. Like nothing had changed and life went on. I told Tom this was crazy, but Tom said, "It's normal, if we had to wait for someone to say something flattering about Harvey, the ceremony would never end. Or begin, I guess."

Anyway as fate would have it, Mr. Harris passed away first, in the elevator he used to access the upper floors of his home. He had long since renounced stairways, given how he had filled out over the years. He collapsed from a stroke and fell against the control buttons, hitting the emergency stop. It took a whole squad of firemen to climb up, open the doors and wedge him out.

His family said he'd insisted on Tom doing his "asshole best" at the funeral, and Tom said to the congregation "that was Harvey," and told the story about him eating crow after the Dogtown Boys had beat them for the championship. Literally eating. The mourners laughed and it paved the way for the rest of Tom's putdowns, which weren't all that putdowney, to be honest. Like suggesting we name a Rose City Junkyard in Harvey's name. Real softball stuff, you might say.

But that was my Tom. In 40 years + of marriage I couldn't find a mean bone in his body. We had our arguments, but they never got past the "spirited debate" stage. I considered myself one lucky woman.

My darling shortstop and companion left us on a warm May evening, just before the youth baseball season was scheduled to start. Tom had said over and over that he didn't want much fuss and tears at his wake and funeral, and wanted rather a ceremony where our remaining friends could just get together and share some memories and a good time. The one song he wanted to hear was Elvis Presley's "If I Can Dream," which he thought was one of the greatest single song performances he'd ever seen, not to mention the words and sentiment which Tom said he'd "like to hear in my grave."

So we managed to track down Randy's sister Sally from up in Missouri, and she came down expressly to sing Elvis' masterpiece for Tom, just as she'd done for Henry Cross' funeral. She said she hadn't sung in public for years and years, but we were all amazed how she still had the voice to match the angels in heaven. The tears flowed like a river.

Tom would have enjoyed his own funeral. His friends from work were there, plus practically all our friends from over the years. Mary Louise came alone, Johnny Benson having passed on to a sales job in heaven, or wherever they appreciated fine soil nutrients. Her most recent plastic surgery had been a success, if one could judge by the admirers who flocked around to console her for the loss of a husband she'd divorced forty years ago. The various kids and grandkids were there of course, and some of them asked me about the two Dogtown oldtimers who managed to make it to the ceremony. Cletus and Mose were still kicking, in the life sense, but also literally as they continued their repartee like they hadn't missed a note even after 60 years. Tom would have enjoyed remembering how he'd brought them to an understanding that took root and lasted.

Cletus had found a white shirt somewhere off some Goodwill store rack and a new pair of jeans that hung over his girth, plus a Native American belt with a huge turquoise buckle.

Whereas Mose, as we know was usual for him, was dressed to the nines and above, a fashion example if there ever was one. Cletus growled, "They forget to tell you them zoot suits went out like a hundred years ago?"

Mose just shook his head and said, "Coming from someone who thinks cuff links are what you put on criminals."

They went on like that until somebody arrived who kind of

tied their tongues—my cousin Jimmy Bunch. To say he'd put on weight since they last saw him, all those years ago when he'd been a hitter and pitcher in tiptop shape, like a Greek god except one who hadn't listened a second to his teachers in school, would be understating about 300 pounds +. In Wal Marts now he zips around in those electric shopping carts like he thinks he's a Formula One race driver.

He and Tom had become friends by our marriage of course, but Tom never forgot how Jim had given him my phone number instead of the traffic ticket he deserved. If Jimmy said it once he said it a thousand times that Tom deserved the citation more than me, and all thousand times we chuckled, to humor him. "Anyway, he was right," my gallant lover would say.

So there he was, 400 pound Jim Bunch rolling up in the go-kart contraption he'd had specially built for himself alone.

He looked at Mose, who was speechless, and broke the ice with "I'm the guy who kicked your ass back in the day."

Ever a man who radiated dignity and class, Mose said, "Thanks for coming. Glad to see you."

Whereas Cletus said, "Good thing you don't got to slide. Might leave a crater."

"Boys, you've heard about living off the fat of the land. I AM the fat of the land."

They left off the banter when the ceremony began, which was moving without being sad really, except for me. Tom had made me promise so many times not to show grief at his funeral, and didn't want any sad songs, and I respected his wish—mostly. I figured I'd let it all out when everybody had gone and I had to go back home alone to our dog and two cats and an empty porch rocker.

But in fact, I did have company.

After the eulogies, which came from our daughter and Tom's best Wal-Mart colleagues and Mose, who choked up more than once when he talked about the man who'd befriended him at a tough but momentous time in our nation's racial history. Even Cletus looked moved, knowing how he had been then and how he was now, with his lovely wife Belinda in attendance.

Later we all adjourned to Burns Park, the same pavilion where we'd spent so many wonderful picnics and special events. If you could say a good time was had by all at a funeral, you could say that. Like Tom wanted. I think he would have been particularly happy to see the Boys from Dogtown still as ornery as ever, and wonder of wonders, ribbing each other and Jim Bunch, who told Cletus and Mose, "Come to my funeral, I've got two plots already bought, one ain't big enough for a stud like me."

I know I was glad to see them and everyone else who helped me get through the day and some days afterward.

When everyone had gone home finally and got on with their lives, I moved around the empty house, cleaning and organizing and arranging our posessions that now were mine and mine only to catalogue as it were. I knew this kind of reconstruction, in more ways than one, came to everyone who outlived their partner. But all day I found it harder and harder to think I'd just lost my teammate. For sure, I couldn't bring myself to look back through this book and remember how we'd met, lost contact and then come together again after going off on unhappy detours. All the sweet memories afterward.

As the years went by and we waned with them, Tom and I spent less and less time scotched to the television or our cellphones watching some film or other entertainment. A lot seemed like, been there, seen that.

Toward what proved to be his last months, Tom liked to spend spring and summer evenings on our back porch. His father and mother did that when he was growing up, back then before TV when they had most all the neighbors to gossip with. That was before AC too, and everybody came out to cool off in the evening.

Nowadays of course that habit has gone the way of the wind. But we found it so restful to sit out back on the porch and just watch the stars and listen to the brook. The yard sloped down to it, which made it not much of a yard to linger in unless you enjoyed balancing on angles, but from the comforts of our porch the cooler earth rose up and brought some freshness after the usual Arkansas summer scorcher.

Tom had never gotten truly sick. He liked to say, in his youth he'd contracted just about every current disease a kid could, except the horrible polio, and had developed some kind of immunity. He had numerous little problems and the flu would knock him out for a week or so, but never cancer or Parkinson's or one of the terrible maladies that took our friends and relatives when their days ended.

He wondered out loud once, "So what's going to get me?" Besides the sentiment and reminder how we'd all be one day where we were at, like his coach Henry Cross used to say, I remember that moment with crystal clarity because suddenly he sat up—literally, like they say in books, in the gloaming.

"Fireflies," he said, "lightning bugs. They're back!"

And they were, swirling around in the gathering darkness on our lawn. It had been ages since we'd seen them in North Little Rock.

They continued their little dance, glowing on and off like sentinels, or else like Tom said, "An SOS for the planet." He was thrilled, and I was too, if only to see him so happy. "Saw so many as a kid," he said, "way back when. If they're back, it's got to be a good sign."

And he was watching them that evening when his heart stopped. I hardly noticed it at first, I was so entranced by the show in front of us. I'm a faithful believer, and I like to think he passed from one light to an eternal one, just like that so it was hardly a transition.

I hesitated about going back to the porch. I hadn't done so since he died. But when night fell on the day of his funeral and I was all alone and done just about everything I could think of to pass the time, I remembered that Tom always said when you've got a problem, meet it head on. He didn't always follow that dictum, but he tried, and anyway, I loved him even when he failed, like when the Dogtown Boys lost the state championship by a split second.

I poured myself a stiff drink, went out on the porch and sat in the rocking chair Tom had bought for me, a vintage one from his

344

beloved Aunt Bess. Still the drink wasn't stiff enough, and I felt myself fading into the darkness, and I didn't want to go off in darkness, but into light like Tom did. And lo and behold, here they came, a parade of the fireflies we'd been seeing and now counted as our friends. They swirled and floated and lit up the night, and I remembered how Tom described in his book how he'd seen them that night in Belleville when he revisited the past and decided to go back to the ballpark where we'd first met, watched the game, then drove home too fast and got stopped for speeding by a State Policeman who turned out to be Jim Bunch. Who gave him my phone number because thickheaded as Jimmy was and is, he'd seen the sparks flying between us years ago and thought we'd "make a good left side of an infield."

I first saw Tom on the sidelines, under baseball stadium lights, and felt something thrill inside me. Through ups and downs and that first long separation, I guess you could say we kept a little light burning. So I blessed the fireflies and hoped they would keep coming around every night until I suited up and joined Tom again.

www.ingramcontent.com/pod-product-compliance
Lightning Source LLC
Chambersburg PA
CBHW070754280626
47162CB00016B/386